HANNAH ROBSON

by

Brenda McBryde

Magna Large Print Books
Long Preston, North Yorkshire,
England.

British Library Cataloguing in Publication Data.

McBryde, Brenda
    Hannah Robson.

    A catalogue record for this book is
    available from the British Library

    ISBN 0-7505-1088-9

First published in Great Britain by Hodder & Stoughton,
1991

Copyright © 1991 by Brenda McBryde

Published in Large Print 1997 by arrangement with Hodder
& Stoughton Limited.

Magna Large Print is an imprint of
Library Magna Books Ltd.
Printed and bound in Great Britain by
T.J. International Ltd., Cornwall, PL28 8RW.

HANNAH ROBSON

Hannah was 12 when her mother died in agonising childbirth and she determines to support herself and never be at the mercy of a man. After years of thankless toil on her father's Northumbrian farm she sets out alone into the world. Although she encounters kindness and friendship, trouble dogs her footsteps. In the bustling port of Newcastle, her courage and intelligence are rewarded, but it is only the pain of near-loss that will free her heart to love.

TO PAT

1

Hannah Robson wiped the window pane with the corner of her sleeve and peered into the kitchen. The Widow Dodds, it seemed to her, was taking over the whole place with her huge behind, her swinging skirts and steaming kettles, while she and Sarah had been bundled unceremoniously outside and the door shut fast against them.

Her little sister tugged impatiently at her skirt. 'Lift me up!'

Hannah pushed away the pestering hand. 'There's nowt to see.' A myopic hen pecking at her bare feet was sent squawking into the air. 'Nowt but that auld body bustling aboot.'

The tranquillity of a summer morning hung over the Burnfoot homestead. Flies and bees hummed cosily amongst the gilliflowers and lavender bushes in Mary Robson's garden. The domed sky, like a shell held to the ear, vibrated with larksong and the distant bleating of sheep, but the woman lying within the house, tossing her head distractedly on her damp pillow, denied the outside world. In the capsule of her travail there was no day, no night, no lark singing, no white-faced children at the window. Her only measure of time was the diminishing respite between the contractions of her womb, inexorable, beyond her will, driving her deeper into the agony of giving birth to a child who was too big for her body, a child she did not want.

'Push, hinny,' exhorted the midwife. 'Push for the love of Jesus. 'Tis almost there.'

Twelve-year-old Hannah in the yard outside was acutely aware of crisis. A great deal was expected of her in this unbelievable situation which seemed to be outside her mother's control. The da was up the fell. Joan was with the calf in the byre, crying. Sarah was just a bairn and their mother, groaning deep and awful to hear, was in a bad way. Then, with one horrendous cry that issued from the very depths of her being, Mary Robson gave birth to a lusty boy.

'Merciful Father.' Joan, on her knees besides the calf, stuffed her fingers into her ears. 'Save and protect our mother. Don't let her die.'

'What's she doing to our ma!' yelled Sarah indignantly and Hannah leapt for the cottage door.

It opened before she could reach it and

6

Widow Dodds stood there with a look on her face that froze the girls to instant silence. With huge authority she pointed a finger at Hannah. 'Get you up yon hill and fetch your da as fast as them legs'll carry you. Tell him he's got a fine son but I divvent like the looks of the mistress. Off with you!'

Hannah needed no second bidding. 'Go to Joan in the byre!' she yelled over her shoulder at the bawling Sarah and raced across the yard. Before her eyes was the terrifying image she had glimpsed through the open door, of white legs and a spreading pool of blood. 'Oh Da,' she whimpered, bending double to grab the heather on the steep short cut up the hill, 'Come quick—I think me muther's ganna die.'

Nicholas Robson had been half expecting the summons all morning. Three ravens were circling the crags when he left the cottage at first light. Always a bad omen, that. He raised his arm in recognition of his daughter's 'Coo-ee-ee' and strode over the heather with his dog at heel.

Bairns. Nicholas cursed them all. A grief when they came, a grief when they died. Four of his lay in Eglingham churchyard already. But what's a man to do? His wife's labour had been overlong this time, she had been in no condition to bear this

7

latest child. If she were to die now—may the Lord forbid—he'd be in a fine mess. Left with a babby as well as three lassies. The hopeless pattern of his life weighed like a millstone about his neck; the struggle to survive, to pay his taxes and, more important than anything else to him, to hold on to his land.

There was no keeping up with the slight figure ahead of him. He thundered down in her wake, striking sparks from the rocks with his iron-tipped clogs. Hannah leapt down the hill with the agility of a goat, her long black plaits bouncing behind her. She reached the cottage door while he was still crossing the burn.

The midwife hurried across the yard to meet him, reassurance on her kindly face. 'Be of good heart!' she called. 'I have stemmed the flux that was like to have carried her away.'

'The Lord be praised.' Breathing heavily after his headlong rush downhill, Nicholas crossed himself devoutly and followed the nurse into the birth room.

'You'll not go nearer to being Widower Robson than you've been this morning.' The old woman dabbed her sweating face with her apron. 'But see, she's all right now.'

Nausea threatened to overwhelm him as he stood at the foot of the bed where his wife lay. The cleansing fumes of burning juniper barely overlaid the thick odour of female secretions in that overheated room. His wife, poor wretch, was drained white, as weak as any bled ewe and scarce able to lift an eyelid. He saw, with wonder, how hollow-eyed she had become in the space of twenty-four hours.

Unaccustomed to showing his feelings, like all men of the north, Nicholas nevertheless believed his expression to be one of concern. Maybe the steel of his eyes softened for a brief moment but his weary wife saw only the familiar black-browed, unsmiling image. 'Darkie Robson from out-by', was how he was known in these parts.

'A fine boy,' she whispered. 'Nigh was the death of me.' She closed her eyes, neither expecting nor receiving any show of affection. Her husband stooped to peer into the cradle.

'What a crop of hair,' marvelled the midwife. 'Never seen the like on one new-born.'

Nicholas remembered a certain laundry-maid who had hair like that, the colour of beech leaves in winter, but the exhausted woman on the bed bore little resemblance to the merry maid who had so captivated him years ago. A sad drab was what she had become. Life was a cheat. Without

9

a word, he turned on his heel and left the house. Hannah, on her knees on the stained rushes at her mother's bedside, began to cry.

'Come, lassie,' the widow spoke kindly and, taking Hannah by the hand, led her to the hearth where pots were bubbling. 'Don't thee go upsetting thy ma. She must rest. Do you stir this pot for me while's I wash the poor dear.'

Gratefully, from her seat by the fire, the child watched the old woman going about her business, yet the tears still flowed and sobs too deep to be checked caught at her breath again and again.

'If thee weeps more into that pot,' the widow chided gently, 'the broth will be too salt to drink. See, there's colour in thy ma's cheeks now. All's well.'

Hannah nodded vigorously and blew her nose. 'I was feared that she was ganna die.' She wanted desperately for her mother to comfort her with reassuring words but the figure on the bed still had not spoken to her. When she knelt with the porringer of broth and held a spoon to her mother's lips, Mary Robson turned her face away, withdrawing her hand from Hannah's timid touch.

'She'll take it later.' The widow missed nothing. 'Do you help me lay clean rushes. What a capable lassie ye are, to be sure.

Thy ma's lucky to have such a sensible helper.'

When Joan came in a little while later, holding Sarah, big-eyed, by the hand, Hannah had recovered herself and was her usual brisk and cheerful self. 'I divvent kna where it's ganna sleep,' she tossed her head in the direction of the cot whose occupant interested her not in the slightest. 'For sartain sure there's nee mair room in wor bed.'

2

Much of England in the seventeenth century was covered by fen, moor and forest but no place was more remote than here in north-west Northumberland where high and windy wastes went shouldering up to the Cheviot Hills and the Scottish border. It was a lonely landscape of moorland, craggy outcrops and black, peaty bogs.

Nicholas Robson had his freeholding here, a forty-acre piece left to him by his father, lying south-east of the market town of Wooler, fit only for sheep and goats on the heights but arable enough for barley, peas and turnips on the lower slopes. He had a good stone cottage and grew enough meat and grain to ensure that his family did not starve although their fare was mean enough.

As he trudged back up the hill to finish his interrupted work on a new fold for the sheep, he reminded himself that there was now one more mouth to feed. He had reason to be thankful, however, that the babe still had its dam. This child, he told himself, must be the last. His wife would never survive another labour such as this.

Nicholas's only other son apart for the new-born infant was a great disappointment to him, showing no aptitude for cultivating the land nor in caring for stock, but wasted his time carving bits of wood, making dolls for his sisters, while the sheep in his charge strayed out of sight. Beating brought no improvement and, in despair, Nicholas sent him away at thirteen years of age to learn the craft of a potter. In so doing, he put a greater burden of work on Hannah, who was more reliable than her brother Tom although she was two years younger. Tom, he saw, was following the breakaway streak in the Robson family who could not abide working on the land. His own brother, Samuel, had relinquished his share of the family holding at their father's death and had gone to join his Uncle

Jacob, to work the boats on the River Tyne.

Tom had been gone two years now and the smallholding was running quite well without him. The women saw to the vegetable garden, herded sheep and gathered firewood. They reared a pig every year, milked the cow and kept the hens and geese. They spun and wove while Nicholas, blessed with the strength of two men, drained the bogs and hawked out bracken in order to improve his land. He built barns and byres with stone he quarried himself from the Great Whin Sill. Already he could run more sheep, sell more wool, salt more meat than his father before him and would do more if the king's taxes did not drive him into a pauper's grave.

For centuries, these border lands had seen bloody feuding against the Scots. Every mountain pass had its gory legend and, even now, in the year 1683, when Scotland and England shared the same crown, men barred their doors at night. Cattle were herded within the shelter of the villages at dusk for fear of marauding moss-troopers; travellers using the lonely inns slept with primed pistols by their sides. The secret caves in the hills were home to many a fugitive from justice and most folk chose to live in the hamlets and villages for protection.

Not so Nicholas Robson, nor, for that matter, witless Auld Ned the shepherd of Blaw Weary who shared the lonely moors of Harehope Hill with Nicholas. Both men would rather starve than rent a cottage from the lord of the manor and work for a wage. Seasonal work was fine as long as there were peas to pick and hay to be cut but winter brought empty bellies and a hole in the ground. And when a man fell into arrears with his rent, he could be thrown on to the charity of the parish. So Nicholas stayed where he was and kept a sharp eye open for vagabonds and ruffians. His father's musket hung over the fireplace with flint and powder and a match of rope always handy.

His father, like most husbandmen, had fought for Parliament in the revolution but soon sickened of a war where father fought against son. His own brother, Jacob, a keelman on the Tyne, was on the king's side and their sainted mother would turn in her grave were her sons to harm each other. Jack Robson waited until harvest time then deserted from the army and headed for home in time to cut his barley, taking his musket with him.

Not all of those who sought refuge in the hills were criminals. Covenanters fleeing from Scotland and other Dissenters from

14

the established Episcopalian religion hid in the caves and secret places and would come begging for food at lonely cottages.

Nicholas would have no truck with them. In his opinion, a man was a fool to have his knees ground to a pulp on the rack and wheel over a matter of taking the Sacrament or no. Nicholas said his prayers, attended Eglingham Church on a Sunday, but he'd change his faith tomorrow if his neck depended on it.

The freeholding of Burnfoot had been his ever since his father died of the plague in 1665. At that time, there was scarcely a family in the district that did not mourn a death. Nicholas and his brother Samuel carried their stricken father to a lonely hillside set apart from any dwellings. Here, under rough shelters made of broom bush, sufferers were left, usually to die, rarely to recover. Each day, the brothers placed food outside their father's shelter and when, at last, it was left untouched, they set fire to his pyre. Broomie Bank, as it came to be called, glowed for months.

Urged to take a wife by his mother, Nicholas paid a visit to Chillingham Castle where he had delivered a load of fleeces earlier in the year. On that first visit, he had spied a bonny maid with chestnut hair hanging out the washing in the courtyard. When she bent to her basket he was transfixed by her neat ankles, her shapely legs and her broad, homely bottom. She had straightened at his stare and tossed her head.

'Who might ye be to stare so boldly?' she called and he had smiled at her imperious tone.

'Nicholas Robson,' he had answered, 'and who be you?'

'That'd be telling,' she flung back, picked up her basket and walked away.

Now, at his mother's suggestion, he paid a second visit to take her for his wife. His brother Samuel stayed at Burnfoot just long enough to welcome his pretty sister then picked up his bundle and went off to join his uncle on the River Tyne.

The laundrymaid, suddenly afraid of her dark, silent man, found herself glad of the company of his mother. The two women became the closest of friends despite the difference in their ages. When Mary Robson's first confinement drew near she was reassured beyond measure to know that her husband's mother would be at hand to advise and comfort her throughout the ordeal of childbirth.

'The services of a midwife are not needed,' Nicholas told his mother. 'You will be here to help her and I will be nearby.'

Filled with misgivings as she was, his

16

mother was unable to prevail upon him to change his mind. She forbore to mention her own ill-health but it was a source of continual worry to her that she might not be well enough to help her daughter when the time came. She was becoming increasingly out of breath with the slightest exertion and, on occasion, was forced to smother a cry of pain when sharp paroxysms grasped her chest.

Mary did not have an easy pregnancy. Sickness throughout the early months and, later, swelling of the legs made every household chore a labour. Nicholas showed her no consideration, only impatience with her complaints. Her time was near when Nicholas's mother awoke one night with the sensation of a red hot poker being thrust inside her chest. Gasping for breath, she crawled to the top of the ladder. Since her son's marriage she had given up the bed in the alcove downstairs and slept on a pallet in the garret. Still gripped with the knifing pain, she made to descend to the room below, caught her foot in her shift and fell headlong down the ladder. She was still conscious when Nicholas reached her but unable to speak. The plea in her eyes as she looked from her son to his weeping wife was not understood. Defeated, she died and Mary went into labour that same day, alone and terrified.

Nicholas brushed aside her fears. He spread his huge, capable hands, hardened and calloused by weather and work. 'Have I not safely delivered many a score of lambs? Think you I cannot bring forth my own children?'

All that was old history now. Mary had just given birth to her ninth child but the painful memory of that first confinement gave Nicholas no peace of mind. Every time he looked upon his firstborn, the only creature on earth whom he loved, eighteen-year-old Joan with her pale, triangular cat's face and huge violet eyes, her humped back and misshapen legs, he was reminded of his stubborn folly.

A midwife was engaged for all Mary's later confinements, but the hurt that Nicholas had done her could never be undone. If he could have brought himself to take her hands and beg her forgiveness, Mary might have found it in her heart to pity him and perhaps forgive, but Nicholas was incapable of such an admission of failure. The sight of his weeping wife tending her malformed baby merely enraged him further. Well might he wonder what became of the merry maid he married. With his own tyranny, he stamped out the very qualities that had so delighted him in Mary the laundrymaid. Her independent spirit, lively wit, the graceful self-confidence with which she carried herself, all these he relentlessly destroyed. For the rest of her life Mary lived in daily dread of his black humours and violent rages. The time for laughter was over.

3

Widow Dodds, after spending the night on a straw pallet at Mary Robson's bedside, pronounced herself satisfied with mother and babe and prepared to return to her home in the nearby village of Eglingham. Nicholas, still scratching after a night spent in the barn with the dogs, went off to the new fold, leaving Hannah to take the midwife home.

Joan, with her crooked back and withered leg, could not keep her seat on a horse and many tasks fell to Hannah that would otherwise have been the responsibility of the older girl, a situation which created a curious ambivalence of identity for Hannah. Too knowing for a child of twelve but without adult experience, she managed to displease her parents both by her precocious opinions and by her childlike caprices. The five-tailed leather strap that hung by the kitchen door seemed to be reserved especially for her. Sarah was too young to carry blame in any shared misdemeanour and her father would never lay a finger on Joan even though he struck their mother from time to time. When Tom was at home, he had diverted his father's wrath from his two young sisters, but Tom was gone and Hannah was left to learn about life the hard way.

With her accustomed fortitude, she accepted the situation, which to her seemed to be in no way extraordinary. Her father was a hard, cruel man and she hated him but she loved her mother deeply and sought constantly—and mostly in vain—to please her. Mary found this devotion tiresome. Hannah was too eager, too demanding of affection. She was almost thirteen. It was time she grew up.

In one respect only was Hannah certain of commendation from her mother. While in service in Chillingham Castle before her marriage, Mary had been taught by a benevolent mistress to read and write and do simple sums. This knowledge she sought to pass on to her own children in the hope that, thus equipped, they might rise to a better station in life. Hannah, with her quick intellect, scored here and astonished her mother with her aptitude for learning.

The only chance of employment for a girl of humble birth was as a servant in one of the big houses in the district. With her brains, however, Hannah might find herself a place above that of a common kitchenmaid. Some of Mary's own ambition which had withered and died at her marriage went into the encouragement she gave to Hannah.

Today's errand, to escort the midwife to her home, was much to Hannah's liking. She desperately wanted to get away from the scene of yesterday's horror. To be sure, her mother was much restored, though still of a most unnatural pallor. The widow had laid her in sheets made fragrant with lavender but Hannah still saw scissor legs and a hideous void. Joan and Sarah seemed able to forget their mother's recent agony in their joy over the new babe but for Hannah the room was still full of menace. Bloodied clouts steeping in a pail of water were enough to bring back the waves of nausea once more. She left Joan and Sarah cooing over the cradle and went to fetch her pony.

There was salt on the breath of the north-east breeze for the sea was no more than six leagues away as the crow flies. Horses' tail clouds were kicking up over the brow of the fell, streaming across the sky and pattering the slopes with shadows. There would be no rain today. She would get the old woman home in good shape.

Properly grateful for the widow's services, Nicholas had given her a new sheepskin in addition to the customary shilling. Ever since that first disastrous confinement he had been careful in his dealings with Widow Dodds. She was the guardian of his conscience and she knew it.

This morning, with the child at the pony's head and the sheepskin beneath her, cosseting her old bones, the midwife set off contentedly enough. Gingerly she turned her head from side to side and was relieved to find that the warmth of the sun on her neck was soothing away the stiffness that came from lying on Mary Robson's kitchen floor all night. Yet a stiff neck was a small price to pay for saving a woman's life. Never one to dwell on personal conceits, she nevertheless allowed herself a degree of pride this morning for, without her knowledge of nature's cures, this child bobbing along in front most assuredly would have been motherless today.

This lassie had a bad enough time as things were if the weals on the backs of her legs were anything to go by. Some of the scars were old and healed. Some were more recent. They showed beneath the frayed hem of her frock as she walked and no doubt there would be more hidden from view. Everyone knew that Darkie Robson had the devil's own temper but there was nought a body could do. A man might beat his child as oft as he felt was fit and 'twas no concern of anyone else.

The burn was all light and lively this morning, creaming against boulders worn smooth by winter's floods and falling from time to time into the peaty pools where Tom had taught Hannah to fish. She often thought of her brother. He had been her best friend despite being two years older and she was desolate when he went away. On mornings like this, they used to sit by the water where dragonflies flashed and dippers flitted in and out of their bankside nests. He showed her how to tease and trap the quick brown trout. He taught her how to swim in the deep brown water of the Devil's Pot that was always icy cold because it had no bottom, or so folks said. Burnfoot was lonely without him.

Out here, in the open air, the tense drama of yesterday seemed far away. Hannah looked back over her shoulder at the old woman joggling like a sack of potatoes on Dickon's broad back. 'Tell me again, old wife,' she pleaded, 'once again for truth, that me ma will be all reet now.'

Mercy on us, mused the midwife, what a worrit the bairn is. Aloud she said, 'She'll mend soon enough if you and your sisters help as much as you can until she gets her strength back. Just now, Sarah's little kitty-cat is stronger than your ma.'

Hannah nodded gravely. She would do it all. In her imagination, she heard her mother's praise— 'Whatever would I do without my Hannah—' She had many such imaginary conversations with her mother. They helped to compensate for the less acceptable reality.

' 'Tis swarming weather. Look at them bees.' The widow drew her attention to a wild plum tree thrumming with the sound of a thousand agitated wings. ' "A swarm in June is worth a silver spoon," ' she quoted.

'And what say you of a swarm in July?'

'Not worth a fly. Mark the tree well, child, and tell your da when you get home. They'll wait for him there till sunset.' Nicholas's hives straddled the hillside like a company of foot soldiers on the march. 'Tell him I'll have a pottle when it's ready. Remarkable cures I've had with honey.'

The widow's herbal remedies as well as her skill as a midwife earned her the respect of everyone in the parish. Many were the fevers and scrofulous afflictions that she had cured with her possets and unguents.

That Mary Robson was alive today was due to her knowledge of the magical properties of a certain type of diseased rye, purplish in colour and malformed to resemble a cockspur from which it took its name. The powerful tincture extracted from this plant had the ability to stop bleeding when all else failed but a drop too much would kill as surely as the loss of blood. The widow used it only as a last resort.

The little party reached the lower levels where hazel and alder greened the valley floor and the sound of tumbling water told the widow that she was nearly home. Eglingham Mill, faithful servant of all who lived hereabouts, came into sight, proclaiming its unchanging service to the community in the rhythmic creaking of its great wooden wheel. Here the farmer brought his grain, the potter his flint, the tanner his bark. The mill, the church and the Big House were the sinews of the village of Eglingham and Widow Dodds was glad to be home. She could not abide those high bleak places where the Robsons lived.

Dogs barked. Cockerels crowed. The clang of hammer on iron rang out from the blacksmith's hut as Hannah led the pony into the village street. Children mimicking the joggling seat of the nurse were caught in the act when she turned her head.

'Just wait till you have a bellyache, Master Cleversides, and we'll see if you like my medicine!'

Women called out, 'How went the birth?' and she answered, 'All's well. A boy.'

One of the brown stone cottages was her home, provided rent free by a grateful parish. 'Set me down here, Hannah,' she instructed. 'This is where I live.' She slithered to the ground in a flurry of petticoats.

'Have you got a sore bum?' Hannah enquired solicitously.

'And if I have, 'tis no concern of yours,' the widow replied testily. 'Give your pony a drink at the trough then come inside when you have washed your hands. Maybe I'll find some refreshment for you before you go home.'

Within the cottage, the air hung still and heavy with the scent of drying herbs. Bluebottles drugged with rosemary and lavender drowsed at the sunny window.

Hannah pushed the damp hair from her brow. ' 'Tis terrible hot in here and you haven't half got a lot of flies.'

'Leave the door open, then. The place has been shut up these last two days and mebbe it's a mite close.' The widow brought mugs and a jug of cider to the table. 'Sit ye down, hinny. You shall have a slice of spice cake for your trouble in seeing an old woman safely home.'

Hannah regarded the kindly face with interest. 'You never had any bairns of your own?'

Widow Dodds was amused. The child was pert but not artfully so. 'No,' she said. 'I was not blessed with children. My man went off to fight for the king in the revolution and got his head knocked off with a cannon ball.'

'Mercy on us,' Hannah murmured piously. 'God rest his soul,' and her eyes roamed around the room. It was simply furnished with a chair by the hearth, table and stools and an oak dresser. Behind a hempen curtain she glimpsed a bed, and a jug and ewer for washing. 'Never mind,' she said consolingly, 'at least you get a bed to yerself. At wor house, Joan snores and Sarah kicks. Never a night goes by without me giving one or the other a clout.'

The widow studied her thoughtfully. The girl was the living image of her father, eyes like blue lamps beneath a thatch of black hair. There was something of his aggressive character, too, that sat strangely on so slight a frame. The widow was reminded of strong potions in gallipots that must be diluted before use. She was perched warily on the edge of her chair as if ready for flight at the first alarm. A child accustomed to trouble, the widow

27

deduced. Those scarred legs came to mind again.

'What are ye looking at me like that for?' Anxiety drew the girl's black brows close so that the resemblance to her father was even more marked.

'I was just thinking,' the widow dabbed at frothy lips with her apron, 'that you look a spry kind of lass.'

The cake was halted halfway to Hannah's mouth. She would hear its price before she ate more.

'You could be of use to an old nurse if you have a mind to help me. I grow old and have no daughter to follow me.' The widow was in her fifty-seventh year. At her mother's knee, she had learned the mysteries of healing, the alchemy of distillation. The question of who would guard this knowledge after she had gone to her Maker was of growing concern.

'How help you?' There was alarm in Hannah's voice. 'I want nowt to do with babbies. It's a terrible business, that.'

'Why no, hinny, I wouldn't ask you to help with childbirth. I need someone to help gather plants for my medicines, the wild things that grow in the hedges and the woods.' She pointed to a row of bottles on the dresser shelf, winking ruby, emerald and amethyst in the sunlight. 'I need coltsfoot for croup and bronchitis.

Teazle and Solomon's Seal, feverfew and bark from the oak tree for all the afflictions that poor folk suffer, but my knees grow stiff and I cannot walk so far nowadays to seek them out. What say you, lassie? I could pay a penny or two.'

At once interested, Hannah nodded. 'That I can do, Mistress Dodds. Wor Joan knows the name of all the wild plants. She'll help me.'

After Hannah had taken her leave, with a pot of balsam for the weals on her legs, Widow Dodds turned thoughtfully away from her open door. She had inherited special gifts from her mother and there was no doubt in her mind, when she went back into her quiet kitchen, that a force had gone from the room. The chair where the child had sat was no more than a chair with a rush seat and ladder back but, a moment ago, it had shone with its own importance. It was clear to the widow that, housed within the unlikely frame of that undersized child was a spirit that many a man might envy. How long, she mused, could such energy be contained without violence?

Widow Dodds never spoke of her special powers lest they should be associated with witchcraft. Although she was highly thought of in the district, there were always some evil folk who rejoiced in the misfortunes of others who would gleefully swear all manner of falsehoods to prove she was a witch.

In her mother's time, a rogue had come from Scotland professing to be a detector of witches. Every farmer whose crop failed, every woman who gave birth to a stillborn child demanded that the witch in the community be exposed. For the enormous sum of three pounds a head, he agreed to root them out. Eventually the charlatan was brought to justice by the intervention of good Sir Henry Ogle of Eglingham Hall, but not before fourteen innocent women had been hanged on Newcastle Town Moor.

All this happened more than twenty years earlier but Widow Dodds was still careful to give no cause for gossip. In other parts of the country, women accused of witchcraft were still being burned or rolled down a hill in a barrel pricked with nails. Not far away at Alnwick was a ducking pond for mischievous women where, if the poor wretch did not drown, she died of inflammation of the lungs. So Widow Dodds never spoke of revelations and intuitions. She kept these to herself. She would not even keep a cat lest it was thought to be her familiar, though she would dearly have loved a little Tibby for company.

Joan was hanging out the washing in the yard at Burnfoot when Hannah pulled her lathered pony to a halt. 'Our ma's been asking for you,' Joan called. 'Da's hung a pair of pigeons in the barn. You're to ploat them and put them in the pot with a couple of onions. And mind you save the feathers this time.'

Hannah slid from Dickon's back and turned him loose. 'What's wor Sarah doing?'

'Spreading muck.'

4

Summertime was nearly over. The long days spent in the sweet-smelling hayfield, raking and turning the fresh-cut grass, the delicious cooling of sunburned legs in the waters of the Devil's Pot, were over. Now was the time for laying in wood and peat for the winter, lifting turnips and preparing surplus stock for sale.

The biggest sale of the season was held each year on October 17th at Wooler. This year Nicholas would be taking a good fell pony, a score of sheep and a year-old calf. There was enough feed to overwinter the cow but the pig would be killed before long and salted away for the lean months ahead. Throughout the long dark evenings the women would occupy themselves very profitably with spinning, knitting and weaving.

Clothing merchants from as far away as Newcastle visited the country markets to buy tweeds and flannels such as Joan wove and even the coarse stockings knitted by the younger girls fetched a penny-ha'penny a pair in Bewick, which was the nearest market for Burnfoot. Mary herself spun a wonderfully fine thread on her distaff. From no more than an ounce of fleece, she could produce a thousand yards of gossamer tissue which she knitted into fichus much prized by the gentry. Ladies were prepared to pay as much as ten shillings for such finery. Together, the womenfolk of Burnfoot made an important contribution to the income of the smallholding.

The three sisters were industriously occupied in this way one evening in late September while Mary tended the baby by the fireside. She who had learned from bitter experience never to become too fond of infants who might not survive their first year, was surprised by the rush of love that came unbidden to her heart whenever she held this latest baby in her arms. He was a lusty little fellow with sound limbs and mop of chestnut curls who did not lie quiet like other infants but demanded food, demanded attention, demanded love. This one, she told herself as she nosed into the milky sweetness of his warm flesh, would, with the will of God, survive the perils of infancy to care for her in her old age.

The radiance that he brought to her mother's face was not lost on Hannah. 'I hope you're not going to have nee more babbies, Ma,' she said sternly. 'You var nigh died with that one.'

Frowning with irritation, Mary put the hungry baby to her breast. The girl's eyes were always upon her, like a collie bitch, fawning, following her around. 'There's no choice,' she said shortly. ' 'Tis a woman's lot to bear children once she is wed.'

'Why can't she tell her man, "I divvent want nee bairns."?'

There was a muffled giggle from Joan but her mother's frown deepened. 'You are a stupid girl, Hannah, and should not talk of things you know nought of. Because of their original sin, women are duty bound to have children.'

Hannah put down her knitting. 'What sin?'

'The sin of Grandmother Eve,' her mother said impatiently. ' 'Twas her wickedness that tempted Adam, and all women must bear her blame from the day they are born.

You, Hannah, with your prideful ideas, are no better than the rest of us. We are all steeped in sin and will suffer damnation on Judgement Day unless we follow the Word of the Lord. The Bible says "Be ye fruitful and multiply" and I commend you to think on that.'

'And what if a woman does not marry? What of wor Joan?'

Mary gritted her teeth. The child was really past bearing. 'Joan prays every day for absolution,' she said tersely. The regular thud-thud of Joan's loom did not slacken. 'Now get on with your knitting. 'Tis no wonder you never get two feet the same size in your stockings for your attention is not on your work.'

'I shall never multiply,' Hannah declared. ' 'Tis a dirty business, no better than the beasts in the field.'

'Hold your tongue!' Once again, Mary found her anger rising against this impossible child. 'I will hear no more childish nonsense from you.'

'I'll not take a husband,' Hannah said doggedly, determined to have the last word, 'then I canna multiply.'

Sarah at her spinning wheel piped up smugly, 'You need have nae worry on my account, Ma. I shall find mesell a rich husband and have twenty or more bonny bairns.'

Mary made no response. With set face, she reached to the hearth for a dry diaper. She, too, had once cherished such fancies but the fairy stories were wrong. It was the handsome prince who turned into a toad, not the other way round.

Joan, never one to be near the heat of the argument, spoke now. 'You'll have to find a husband, Hannah, or who will keep you? Father and Mother have to support me since no man will take me and they cannot provide for you an' all.'

'I'll earn me own living,' Hannah answered stoutly, undeterred by the arguments ranged against her.

Sarah giggled. 'Girls can do nowt, silly!'

Angrily, Hannah turned on her younger sister, 'I can do owt a lad can do so shut your gob!'

'Be quiet, Hannah!' Had Mary not been holding the baby at that moment, Hannah's ears would have been boxed. She did not see Sarah gleefully stick out her tongue.

Thus provoked, Hannah leapt to grab her sister by the hair, scattering wheel, stool and bag of fleece across the floor. In the ensuing pandemonium of Sarah bawling, Mary shouting and the baby screaming, the door opened and Nicholas stood there glowering. There was an immediate silence apart from the baby's hiccupping whimper as his comfort was restored to him.

'What's this?' The steely tone in her father's voice made Hannah's heart contract. Here was trouble and the end of it would be the strap as usual. Her legs began to tremble uncontrollably in dread of what would surely follow. Nicholas waited in silence while Joan set the stools to rights, then he rounded furiously on his wife who sat with head meekly bowed over the baby at her breast.

'Can ye not keep order in my hoose, woman!'

And Hannah, even though she was filled with fear, had to speak out for her mother. ' 'Twas me and Sarah, Da.' Her voice quavered in spite of her resolution. 'It wasn't owt to do with wor ma.' Then she found she was facing her father alone for Sarah had scuttled for safety behind her mother's stool.

Nicholas did not see standing in front of him a twelve-year-old girl trying not to cry. He saw a brazen chit, head thrown back, defying him. He reached for the leather.

'I'm sorry, Ma,' Hannah whispered as the lash cut into her bare arm but she would not say 'I'm sorry, Da'.

Mary, watching her daughter take the cruel punishment with never a cry escaping from her tight lips, felt the rush of curdling go through her breasts. She knew that her milk would do the boy no good that day.

Alone in the byre, behind the gentle cow, Hannah wept the tears her father never saw. In the warm dark amid the steaming platts, she sobbed out her wretchedness. In a few weeks she would be thirteen years old. She was thin and ugly and her mother said she was full of sin. Aching for love, confused and disturbed by emotions for which there was no vent, she was left to stumble unguided into womanhood. There was no Tom. There was no one who cared a straw about her, least of all her mother. Joan was her mother's close companion. Sarah was spoilt. The baby was smothered in love. Only she, in the whole family, could do nothing to please.

On the following day, while the two younger girls were out cutting peat, Joan was at her loom as usual. Deftly she interwove the wools dyed with bracken, lichens and rowan berries which gave the colours of the countryside to her plaids but her mind was still on the angry confrontation of the previous day. She looked across at her mother sitting quietly by the hearth, fingers flying over her distaff.

'Da should not beat our Hannah so. She's only little.' But the support Joan looked for was not forthcoming.

'She provokes her father,' Mary said

shortly. 'He's got an evil temper and she should mind her tongue.'

'Sometimes thy bruises are without provocation.' Mary did not answer, so Joan persisted with sudden fire, 'Why dost take his rages so meekly, Mother? Lash him with thy tongue if thee can find nought else.'

Angrily, Mary's head came up. 'And be thrown out of my ain house?'

Joan frowned. 'He couldna do that.'

'A man can do as he pleases with his wife. A woman has nought, is nought,' she said resignedly. 'In the eyes of the law she is his chattel, of no more importance to him than his cow and rarely as much as his horse. When a woman marries, all her worldly goods pass to her husband. See how they get the better of us? They might just as well put chains round our feet. Not that I, as a laundrymaid, brought any great dowry but what I had was taken from me. Without money or goods there is no escape for a woman. All that is left for her is endurance. Be her husband cruel as Satan, stupid as a tadpole, she must obey him. Yet,' she added gravely, remembering, 'there are good men about.'

' 'Tis a lottery,' Joan protested, 'and I begin to think our Hannah is right, after all, to choose not to marry.'

'A ranting pauper spinster will end up in

the ducking pond. As for thee, Joan,' Mary added more gently, 'there is the comfort that only the Lord may bring but thy father hath made provision for thee since thy infirmity is none of thy doing.'

'The child in the womb know nothing of the options facing it,' Joan spoke with bitterness. 'Will it be a bold young master or a feeble woman? Sound in wind and limb like our little Ben or crooked like me? Into the fine sheets of my lady's chamber or under the hedge to a pauper wench? 'Tis with a wanton hand that Our Lord distributes His favours and infirmities.'

'Nay, daughter, you speak like a Leveller and other such ranters. Read your Bible. There you will see that a Paradise awaits such as you in the life to come and the tyrants on this earth will be cast down into the fiery furnace amongst the serpents. At the Judgement Day we will get our reward.'

'And mebbes our revenge,' said Joan.

Few callers came to Burnfoot, sometimes a travelling tinker or a Covenanter on the run. Mary made them all welcome for they brought news of the outside world. Ed Freeman, the carter from Eglingham, was a favourite with everyone since he brought sweetmeats for the girls, brandy for Nicholas and sometimes news of her elder son for Mary.

His waggon was standing in the yard when Hannah and Sarah returned from cutting peat. Dragging behind them the bogey Tom had made, piled high with turves, they broke into a run over the last few yards. Ed turned round from his seat at the fireside as the two girls burst into the kitchen, their cheeks aglow, their eyes alight with expectation.

He was a little man with legs so bandy they might have given him an inch or two in height had they been straightened. Beside Nicholas he was a gnome, but a gnome with a friendly twinkle in his eye.

He laid an arm about their shoulders. 'My bonny lasses!' Bonny they were not! Their faces were streaked with mud. Their long plaits were lank with the dampness of the day. He fumbled in his pocket. 'I've summat here for thee.' They took the proffered tablets of treacle toffee eagerly.

'See to the horse.' Their father cut short the greetings. 'Give it oats and water. Master Freeman will stay the night.'

The glow on Nicholas's face was not entirely due to the heat of the fire. Ed had powerful connections with foreign gentlemen who visited some of the quiet harbours on the north-east coast on dark nights and a keg of brandy, already broached, stood on the table. Mary could read the signs. There would be some heavy drinking before the fire burned low that night. She would sleep upstairs with the girls.

'Are we never to eat, woman?' The look Nicholas directed at his wife was not lost on Joan. Thus would a man address his servant. Her mother's words returned to her mind.

Forestalling Mary, Joan began ladling mutton broth into porringers and set them at the table with bread and spoons. Her father came immediately, taking his seat like an obedient schoolboy. She knew very well that she was her father's favourite, a position that gave her more embarrassment than pleasure.

Ed was not a native of these parts and traces of his Kentish origin could still be detected in his speech. As a youth, he had fought in Parliament's army, travelled the length and breadth of the country and finished up here, in Northumberland, when the armies were disbanded. Untrained for any work but soldiery and having neither home nor family, he would have starved but for women like Nicholas's mother who would not turn him away from their doors without a bowl of porridge and a crust of bread.

He earned a living as a carrier. His back was bent with the heavy loads he had toted before he made the money to buy his first cart. His wind was not good these days when he needed to outrun a nosy excise officer but life for him was what it had always been, risky, and he never lacked friends.

He remembered Mary Robson from the day that Nicholas brought her home as his bride. He'd seen the babies come and go. Some thrived. Some died. He remembered when this little hunchbacked maid with the beautiful eyes was born and how he had done his best to comfort the distraught mother. He'd watched the pretty young wife lose her bloom and seen Nicholas turn to a man of stone. This, Ed told himself, was the way of a man with a wife the world over and he was thankful that he had never felt inclined to approach a preacher with any of his lady loves.

Ed had news of Tom. The master potter was exceedingly kind to his apprentices and treated them like sons. Ed looked across to where Hannah and Sarah were eating their supper by the fire. 'I hear tell that somebody here is soon to have a birthday?'

'That's me,' Hannah nodded happily with a mouth full of bread. 'Coming up thirteen on All Saints' Day.'

'Your brother sends his remembrance lest ye may think he has forgot.'

This was as good as the treacle toffee. Hannah beamed with delight. 'He'd nae forget. Not Tom.'

Ed turned his attention to Nicholas. 'There's bad news an' all. The chimney man is hereabouts.'

Of all the taxes levied by the king none was more unpopular than this tax on every hearth. It singled out the poor most cruelly for its keenest effect. Folk could not exist without a fire to warm them and cook their food, yet they must pay this levy, no matter the circumstances, or surrender its value in goods. The king's agents, for the most part uncouth bullies, were entitled to invade the privacy of a man's home and take whatever they had a mind to if money could not be found to settle the dues.

'In a hut in Seahouses,' Ed continued, 'he could find nowt but a pillow and he took that though it was under the heed of a poor woman in labour.'

With unaccustomed fire, Joan spoke up. 'I'll warrant the king never wants for a pillow to lay his head on.'

Ed cocked a shrewd eye upon her. 'Ay, hinny, but ofttimes a king wants for mair than a pillow. T'was a heed wor merry boy's father lacked, not a place to put it.'

Nicholas poured more brandy. 'How long since he was seen at Seahouses?'

'The day afore yesterday and making this way. He'll be banging at thy door afore long.'

'And there he'll stay.' Nicholas drained his tankard. 'Let him but set one foot over my threshold and, b'God, I'll hang for him.' The crash of his fist on the table made the porringers dance.

Mary picked up the sleeping babe and signalled the girls to follow her upstairs. Both men would be roaring drunk ere long. She could be thankful for a man like Nicholas, however, knowing that he would permit no chimney man to invade her privacy. By dint of careful husbandry, Nicholas always made sure that, before all else, he could pay his taxes. Though it grieved him sorely to part with his hard-earned silver, the risk of forfeiting goods or land was unacceptable.

In the low space beneath the rafters, Mary and her daughters settled themselves for sleep. 'Get ye up rare and early the morn,' she instructed Hannah and Sarah, 'and go to Auld Ned. Tell him to hide whatever he has left in that old shack of his or the chimney man will have it.' She made the babe comfortable in a nest of blankets at her side and closed her eyes though sleep was impossible as long as the men continued their carousing.

'Y'd best put a clothes peg on yer

snitch,' Hannah confided to Sarah, 'for Auld Ned stinks like a poke of divvils.'

'You're not that fond of water thyself, milady, that you can mock an old man,' Mary said sharply. 'And mind thy talk. You speak no better than a beggarmaid.'

'Ma! She hasn't said her prayers,' piped Sarah and earned a pinch on the arm from Hannah.

5

With the coming of winter, colour drained from the hills leaving only the bronze and black of dead bracken, spent heather and bog. Blaeberry clumps shed their last tiny touches of flame and high crags that, in summer, detained for a while the rays of the setting sun, stood now shawled in salty sea fog. Nicholas's flock of sheep, reduced in number since the Wooler sales, came down to the lower slopes and each morning the cow rent the air with noisy protests until one of the girls came to break the ice on her drinking trough. There would be snow. You could see it in the heavy sky. Village children gathered kindling against the bad weather that was to come.

Winter, taxing the very old and the

very young alike, brought full employment to the pauper wench whose melancholy service it was to lay out the dead and for Widow Dodds it was the busiest time of the year. The going was hard on lanes that were axle-deep first in snow, then in mud, and ofttimes slippery with frost. So the old woman was delighted and somewhat surprised when Nicholas Robson gave his consent for Hannah to accompany her on some of her outlying visits. As long as her work on the holding was not neglected, he had no objection to Hannah helping the widow. In his opinion, all women should be able to dress wounds and treat common ailments and he did not in the least resent the curious bond which had sprung up between the old woman and his daughter.

The widow had become quite fond of this blunt and naïve child who was as easy with her as if she had been her own kin. For her part, Hannah warmed to the kindliness which she did not find at home. To feel needed was a new and pleasant experience. Whenever the blacksmith could spare his pony cart, Hannah would drive the widow to those places which could not be reached on foot, lending an arm when necessary, carrying the basket of poultices and cures and the pitcher of broth for those in need. She saw how the paupers of the parish lived in their mean turf hovels and how the lethargy of starvation robbed them of the will to help themselves.

The widow made no charge for her services at such places, preferring instead to ask an extra penny from those who could afford it more easily. Under her direction, Hannah learnt to make linctus for babies with bronchitis and cooling draughts to bring down a fever. Her respect for the old nurse's knowledge grew as almost every ailment responded to her treatment, from a festering thumb to a scythe wound and even, on one unforgettable occasion, the terrible injuries of the man who was flogged.

He lived with wife and child in a hovel of turves on a strip of poor land that lay between Eglingham and Old Bewick. Smoke from a fire of damp twigs almost obscured the figure of a woman with a child on her lap who sat by the dirty straw pallet on which her man lay, face down. Her lacklustre expression did not alter as the widow pushed open the door and came in, followed by Hannah.

'Come, come, Kit Spencer.' The widow spoke briskly to the man as she unwound the shawl from her head and rolled up her sleeves. 'Rouse thyself! This will not do. Raise up and take off thy shirt.' Over her shoulder, she spoke to Hannah, 'Stir up

47

the fire, Hannah. Put the pot close.'

Without a word, the woman, holding her child, crept off to the farthest corner of the hut as her man, groaning deeply, made an effort to do as he was bid. Painfully, he lifted the ragged shirt over his head. Hannah caught her breath with horror. Angry, festering stripes crossed and recrossed his back from the base of his neck to his waist.

'Who has done this?' she demanded but the widow merely handed her a bowl.

'Fill that with hot water from the pot on the hearth,' she said. ' 'Tis not anger he needs now but something to ease his pain.'

Into the bowl of water, the widow shook a few drops from a bottle. 'Tincture from the bark of oak will take the heat from the cuts.' She handed Hannah a pad of wool. 'Do you bathe the weals, gently now, for he has agony enow without our making more.' As Hannah got down on her knees beside the man, the widow turned to his wife. 'Canst not find summat useful to do that you must sit and stare while your man lies groaning?' She flung the dirty shirt at her. 'Wash this shirt. He's better with no shirt at all than this filthy garment. Give him a shift of your own if ye have one.'

She looked at the ailing child, the dulled

eyes of the woman. 'Have ye ought to eat in the house?'

The woman shook her head. 'I've nae flour to make bread, nae meat for soup. The parish sixpence is long since spent. Now my man canna work.'

The widow applied a cloth spread with balsam to the man's back and tied it there with strips of linen. 'Fetch the broth from the cart, Hannah.'

Angrily she berated the woman. 'There's wild turnips and parsnips in the hedgerows do ye but take a spade and dig for them and Spanish root to keep you clear of sickness. Had ye been less feckless, ye'd have gathered mushrooms and chickweed in September and dried them against the winter.' She poured broth into a pannikin and set it by the fire. 'Keep yersells fed or y'll all be deed the next time I come.' Digging deep into her pocket, she withdrew two pennies and put them into the woman's ready hand. 'And it wouldna hurt to clean your house!' was her parting shot as she gathered together her things and climbed back into the cart with Hannah.

'Lazy baggage,' she grumbled and then bethought herself, 'but when ye're half-starved, ye've no mind to do owt abut owt. Gee-up the pony, Hannah. We'll get on our way.'

'What happened to his back?' Hannah could not put the ugly sight out of her mind.

'He was punished by the law for trapping game on his own bit of land, and ye can make what ye like of that, my girl.'

'How can that be? If 'tis his land, then he can do owt he likes on it. We catch pheasants, partridge and all sorts of game on wor land, else we'd be living on oats and dripping for most of the time.'

'Your da, then, is either breaking the law, and if so y'd best keep quiet on't, or else he has the income of a gentleman.'

'Nay, he has not that.'

'Then keep thy mouth closed. The king in his wisdom now that we have put him back on the throne, rewards poor folk by depriving them of a dinner that is rightly theirs. If a man's income is a hundred pounds or more, that makes him a gentleman in the eyes of the law with entitlement to hunt game. The poor peasant, though he owns the plot of land that the deer runs over, will be flogged if he is caught with venison in his pot. That's how Kit Spencer got his stripes.'

'That's not fair!' Hannah was outraged. 'How can the king be so cruel?'

'Chanticleer is too busy with his pretty hens at court to give a thought to folk like us. Haste ye home now Hannah. 'Twill take more than a lass like you to put the country to rights.'

Hannah was approaching her fourteenth birthday when her mother brought up the subject of her leaving home to seek work. Surprisingly, her father refused to consider it.

'I'd ha thought you'd be glad of one less mouth to feed.' Mary's voice betrayed her pique.

'I need her on the land. She'll go next year when Sarah's older.'

That summer, Hannah had been working more closely with her father, trudging after him to snare rabbits and repair walls. She had a natural knack with dry-stone-walling so he left the construction to her while he split rocks.

He drove her hard. Now, with winter approaching, she was always the first out of bed in the morning to mend the fire and cook porridge for both of them. She was ready to leave the house with him, her legs wrapped in straw against the cold and the mud, before the rest of the household stirred. Together they rescued sheep from the deep clefts in Corbie Crags and sometimes had to pull them from the flood waters of Harehope Burn, well nigh drowned by the weight of their sodden fleeces.

He never told her he was pleased with her. She never knew. His dark looks never lifted and father and daughter could work all day alongside each other without a word being spoken. Yet she was aware of an easier relationship between them. She no longer feared him as once she had done. On one occasion only did he give her praise. When he would have destroyed a ewe with a broken leg, she stayed his hand, applied a poultice of comfrey and tied up the injured limb in a splint as she had seen Widow Dodds do with a child. The ewe's leg healed and when, in due course, she produced healthy twins, Nicholas acknowledged Hannah's skill and Widow Dodds's instruction.

Because of the extra work she was required to do on the land, Hannah had less time to help the old nurse. Joan took over the gathering of herbs and making of simples for her. Nevertheless, though she might envy Sarah on cold winter's nights seated cosily by her spinning wheel while she went with her father to search for sheep in the snowdrifts, she was loath to relinquish this new position of trust. More often than not, Sarah was now the one to feel the sting of the cat-o'-nine-tails although the sharp edge of her mother's tongue was still reserved, exclusively it seemed, for Hannah.

In the dark days before Christmas a message arrived from Tom. Mistress Reay, wife of his master potter, would be pleased for Hannah to visit Buckton in the spring. This news threw Hannah into transports of joy. In high spirits, she rode to Eglingham to tell Widow Dodds the good news.

'Me da says I can go. Now I am wishing for the winter to pass quickly. I have nae seen me brother for three long years,' and she added wistfully, 'I wonder if he's changed.'

'One thing is sure,' the widow said, 'that he will find thee changed. You're not the skinny little scallywag he will remember.'

In truth, Hannah's figure had plumped out. The pinched elfin face was taking on a mysterious bloom that might one day turn into something more than mere prettiness if coarseness did not mar it.

Before the promised visit could take place, however, the whole country was thrown into confusion by the death of King Charles. Ed Freeman brought the news to Eglingham. Out of breath, on a horse that was lathered in sweat, for he'd ridden hard all the way from Alnwick. He slithered to the ground in the market place, calling his news with the last of his wind.

'I had it from the driver of the London coach. He swore on the soul of his departed mother that 'twas the truth. The king has

53

died of a seizure and his brother James will take the throne.'

King Charles was not old. In his prime, you might say judging by the number of bastards he fathered. Yet, while seeming to be in perfect health, he had been struck down. For five days he had lain helpless while his panic-stricken physicians tried every known remedy—and some unknown—to restore the royal personage to former vigour. They purged him and bled him, held a hot iron to his head. They made him drink a vile potion concocted from human skulls. Notwithstanding all their efforts, their patient died, on February 6th 1685, leaving no legitimate issue. His brother James would inherit the throne: James the Catholic.

Ask a Scotchman and he would say James the Cruel. During his time as Governor of Scotland, James had relentlessly persecuted Dissenters and Covenanters, taking such sadistic pleasure in their torment on the rack that even his supporters were sickened. Charles, extravagant and pleasure-loving, had few enemies. His brother had many, though Catholics throughout the kingdom rejoiced. It was their turn to come out of obscurity, perhaps to settle old scores. The calm that had prevailed since the revolution was suddenly threatened. The new king's assurances that he would not interfere with the religion of the land were only half-believed.

'The Scots'll not have him,' was Ed Freeman's declared opinion. 'I hear tell that Argyll is back from Holland with an army and means to put one of Charles's bastards on the throne. Make nae mistake, there'll be blood shed ower this.'

Secretly, Nicholas agreed with him. The outlawed Dissenters who were usually to be found skulking in the hills had gone. To join Argyll, he surmised. He cautioned Hannah and Sarah to keep a sharp watch when they were out-by with the sheep. 'Any sign of trouble, bring the sheep in and get yersells haem. D'ye hear me?'

They were up on the heights of Bewick Hill, on Hanging Rock, when they saw the soldiers. From this great outcrop of sandstone, they could see the whole countryside laid out beneath them, the winding valley of the River Till and Bewick Bridge where it changed its name to Beamish; the pele towers, topping every rise, used for defence in the border raids and crumbling now into ruins, and the gap in the hills through which, for as long as anyone could remember, armies had marched to and from Scotland.

Sun glinting on steel caught Sarah's eye. 'Look yonder, Hannah! The militia!' A long, wavering line of redcoats was moving up the valley floor towards the Wooler gap. On the clear mountain air came the faint notes of fife and drum. 'They're awa to fight the Scots.' During the following weeks, there was rumour of rebellion over the border, of clan set against clan, of bloodshed not only between the Scotch Protestant leaders and the English militia but also amongst the Highland chieftains themselves. Hannah despaired of ever being able to ride to Buckton. With trouble at the border and soldiers abroad, there was no possibility of her taking to the roads to visit Tom.

'Thee'll bide here until the Scotch matter is settled,' said her father and she had to be content with that. In the meantime, she helped her mother and sisters in the making of new clothes for Tom. His own would be in a sad state by this time and he would have little money for replacements since he was not yet out of his apprenticeship. A flannel shirt and a jerkin of cowhide, two pairs of woollen stockings and a leather purse went into the bundle that Mary put together for him. She missed her easy-going son. His sunny nature had lightened many a dreary day for her but she had always known that he would have to leave. Two such different men as Tom and his father could never share the same roof.

Hannah, unconcerned with the rights and wrongs of the Scotch rebellion, hoped for an early return to peace and was glad when news reached Eglingham that the rebels' cause had collapsed and the Duke of Argyll and his supporters were in Edinburgh prison awaiting execution. Now she could prepare for her journey.

Buckton was a small village north of the market town of Belford situated on the Great North Road. Hannah had never travelled so far away from home before and the prospect filled her with excitement. Comfortably seated on Dickon's broad back with her bundles tied about her, she took leave of her parents.

She has a good seat, her father reflected. Head up, knees close. 'If thee happen upon the militia, have nae truck with them. Stand well back and let them by.' But she was not one to be frightened by a redcoat, that he knew. More like a lad she was than a simpering lass. The look of approval on his face as he turned away was not lost on his wife.

She waited until he was out of earshot. 'Do nothing to cause offence.' Her voice was sharp with spite although she knew that her anger was unreasonable. 'Give Mistress Reay whatever help you can.'

Hannah gathered up the reins; a last look at Joan and Sarah, still calling out messages for their brother, and then she was off down the burnside track.

6

Leaving the village of Eglingham behind her, with Widow Dodds waving farewell from her doorway, Hannah gave Dickon his head over the moor to Shipley Burn and on to the hamlet of Charlton. This much of the way was known to her. The real adventure started when she joined the Great North Road, that thoroughfare of coaches, waggons, pony-trains, riders on horseback and travellers on foot, tinkers, pedlars, vagrants and highwaymen.

Stretching from London to Scotland, its condition worsened the further north it went. Here in Northumberland, it was reduced to a narrow causeway with a quagmire on either side that was the dread of all coach travellers. An encounter with another vehicle which forced one or the other to leave the surfaced strip was an invitation to disaster as the many broken wheels lying at either side testified. Many were the sloughs and potholes waiting to trap an unwary rider. Hannah kept Dickon to a careful trot.

She had a journey in front of her of some twelve leagues and had left home at an early hour in order to reach Tom before the day was far spent. He had promised to keep a watch on the road and would come to meet her at first sighting. Her heart warmed at the thought of her brother but not without a tinge of apprehension. He was seventeen now. Grown up.

Such doubts as she had were pushed to the back of her mind by the sudden sight of the sea. The road lay along the broad coastal plain, curving to within a few miles of the shore from time to time to show her a wide expanse of water shimmering silver on this early June morning. Previous glimpses of the sea had been from the distant heights of Bewick Moor, appearing as a vague grey-blue space. Now, for the first time, she could discern its running, white-topped waves and the bobbing, dipping progress upon it of a ship in full sail. A fresh and salty breeze smacked her in the face and sent Dickon's head up with a whinny of delight.

Everything around her was excitingly different. Cattle, much fatter and sleeker than the cows at home, grazed on pastures that sloped right down to the pale golden sands. Women sang as they worked in the fields. A party of faws came by in a covered waggon jingling with pots and pans, led by a brown-skinned young woman in a green silk frock with a monkey on her shoulder. Hannah laughed out loud at its antics and when rich merchants went by, she could not contain her admiration for their splendid mounts, magnificent horses sixteen hands high, bridle and martingale of plaited leather decorated with filets of gleaming brass.

'A fine horse you got there, sir! Nae mistake about that!' But her compliment went unacknowledged by haughty milords who had no time for peasant girls.

She passed many a small dwelling built on common land at the edge of the road where curs yapped at every passing traveller. Children played in the sun at open doors surrounded by dusty hens, their mothers keeping an eye on them from washing line or spinning wheel. From time to time the tall chimneys and gable ends of a great house would show through a noble stand of trees but when, at last, a square church tower set amongst other substantial buildings appeared on the skyline, Hannah knew she was nearing Belford.

Carts began to crowd the road. There were serving maids in waggons packed with butter, cheese and eggs, and tidy matrons in gaily painted dog carts whipping up their high-stepping ponies. All exchanged a greeting with her and it seemed to Hannah that the world was full of the most amiable people imaginable until the London coach came by, careering through pools of stagnant water, fouling the clothes of those on foot and sending them leaping into the ditch for safety. Dickon reared in alarm, almost unseating his rider and Hannah was spattered with gobs of mud from the kerchief at her neck to her new white woollen stockings.

In a fury, she pricked Dickon into pursuit of the coach. Standing in the stirrups, shaking her fist and roundly cursing the coachman, she provided considerable entertainment for the passengers. But Dickon was no match for the team of four galloping greys and disconsolately, she was forced to give up the chase. She was in no fit state now to go visiting and must needs stop awhile in Belford to clean herself up before continuing to Buckton.

Belford market cross stood on a slight rise in front of the Blue Bell Inn which was the scene of much activity as Hannah trotted into town. Ostlers and farriers were busy with buckets and brushes and jingling harness. Their clatter filled the yard and through the open door of the inn a babel of voices gusted as the people came and went.

Hannah slipped down from Dickon's back and looped his reins over the water trough while she attempted to wash the dirt from her face.

Aware that she was being watched, she turned her back on a youth lounging at the inn door who seemed to find her plight amusing and he promptly laughed out loud.

'Here,' he said kindly, offering a square of cambric, 'use my handkerchief, else you will only make the damage worse.'

His tone was so inoffensive that Hannah thought better of her first impulse to tell him to mind his own business and took the proffered handkerchief, though with little grace.

' 'Tis a pretty trifle indeed for wiping clarts but I'll take it nonetheless and thank thee for thy kindness.'

'How didst come to be in such a plight?' He was looking at her soiled white stockings. 'Didst have a fall from thy horse?'

By his speech, Hannah could tell he was from over the border and, from his courteous manner, a gentleman, although his clothes were ordinary enough. She recounted the tale of her mishap as she applied the wet cloth to her face.

'That bully will feel the rough edge of my tongue were I to meet him again. Just look at my frock! I am on my way to visit my brother whom I have not seen these three long years and I am loth that he should find me in this sad state.' She turned her scrubbed face towards the young man for his approval. 'Is my face clean enough?'

'Good as new,' he assured her and would not take the wet kerchief back. 'A keepsake of your ride to Belford.'

Making herself comfortable by the pump, Hannah took her bait of bread and cheese from her bundle. She would not arrive hungry like a common beggar at the house of Mistress Reay. The young man declined to share it with her saying he had important business on hand and indeed Hannah noted that he kept an alert eye upon the road leading into the town.

A sudden burst of noise announced the departure of a coachload of travellers from the inn. Their coach, equipped with fresh horses, stood ready for them as, much refreshed by the Blue Bell hospitality, they trooped out into the sunshine. At the sight of their driver, Hannah jumped to her feet.

'Why, that's the man! That's the scoundrel who almost ran me off the road!'

Before the young man knew what she was about, Hannah had sprinted across the market square to confront the driver who, whip in hand, was already taking his seat.

'Hi! Thou knave! Dost think the Great North Road belongs to thee! By rights, ye should buy me a pair of new stockings for these are covered in mud after ye drove past me like a madman.'

The driver turned in some surprise, then laughed to see a maid in such a temper, which only served to increase Hannah's anger.

'Darest laugh at me after putting me in such a plight!'

'Oh, aye,' he grinned, 'thou'rt a sight indeed. Be off with you ere I call the watch.' He was not averse to giving his passengers an entertainment at the expense of an impertinent chit. He raised his whip. 'Be off, I say, with your dirty stockings, or this leather will make thee even more of a spectacle than thou'rt already.'

The young man, reading Hannah's intention as she bent to pick up a stone, reached her side in a quick stride and laid a restraining hand on her shoulder. To the driver, he spoke with surprising authority.

'Keep that whip for your horses, driver. This maid has some justice in her complaint but I'll not detain thee for an apology as thy passengers grow restive. Go on your way and have a care for other travellers on the road.'

The coachman's face purpled. To be made to look foolish in front of a whole coachload of passengers was almost too much to bear, and that by a mere youth. Caution whispered to him, however, that the young man was nobly born, 'twas plain to see, and who could tell what his family connections might be. With an ill grace, he brought his whip down heavily on the horses' rumps, sending them clattering over the cobblestones and on their way.

'Good riddance to bad rubbish!' Hannah yelled after him and, with some reluctance, dropped the stone from her hand. 'You should ha let me hoy this at him,' she chided. ' 'Twas only fair.'

The youth shook his head with a smile. 'A word of advice, young maid. Do not seek out trouble for it comes easy enough without the need to look for it, and 'tis usually the weakest in the argument who will suffer. If a woman sets herself against a man, count upon it, justice will not go her way.'

Hannah looked at him curiously. 'That's an odd thing for a man to say. But I'm not weak!' she added. 'I could outrun that pig's bladder any day. Yet I should thank thee for speaking on my account,' she said, on reflection. 'A whole coachload of trouble might have undone me,' she burst out laughing, 'though, in truth, it would have made good sport to try!'

She regarded her companion with fresh interest. There was not much to him, apart from his handsome looks. He was slightly built with delicate hands and feet. 'What is thy name? Mine is Hannah.'

'Well, Hannah,' he said seriously, 'I admire your spirit if not your diplomacy. Wait on—' his eye alighted on a rider who was entering the square at that moment.

Following his glance, Hannah saw the postman, leather mail-bag over his shoulder, a red-faced man on a steaming horse. He clattered to a standstill outside the inn and threw his reins to a waiting ostler before disappearing inside.

'I must leave you now.' The young man spoke softly. 'The man I seek a rendezvous with has arrived.' With that, Hannah's new friend followed the postman into the dark interior of the inn.

'And he never told me his name,' thought Hannah, as she set Dickon on the road again, then she put the events of the morning behind her. A little less than a league to go and she would be riding into Buckton. She tried to imagine Tom grown older but the image persisted in her mind of a thirteen-year-old boy with freckled face and snub nose. What would he think of her? She looked down at her spattered stockings. There was no help for them.

The salt air drenched and scoured her lungs for the road here lay close to the sea. What manner of house was the potter's house that had so much wind and water about it? How would she be received?

The potter's house lay on the west side of the road between the hamlets of Buckton and Fenwick, a three-storeyed house, solidly built of sandstone, facing the sea with the Kyloe hills at its back. Hannah's attention was first caught by the kilns, shaped like great beehives, and then she saw Tom, on horseback, standing in the stirrups, waving his hat in the air and hallooing. Gathering Dickon up beneath her, she put him into a wild canter over the last stretch of road to pull up short in a flurry of dust when the two horses came face to face.

Tom had grown. How he had grown! Would the shirt she had brought fit him? He was nigh as big as their da, but his embrace, when they dismounted, was reassuringly warm. He took her hand in his and they walked together over the cobbled yard at the back of the potter's house and she had to hitch an extra step to match his stride.

Emma Reay was a motherly soul whose only child had died in infancy. She filled the space left by the empty cradle by caring for her husband's apprentices as if they were truly her own family. Over the years, unschooled boys had come to the pottery and had left as craftsmen, and all would remember the warmth of their welcome at Mistress Reay's fireside. It was she who suggested to Tom that the sister whose name was often on his lips might enjoy a few days spent at Buckton and she stood now at the kitchen door, beaming a welcome as he led Hannah across the yard.

'So this is sister Hannah.' Who would have thought them to be kin? The one so strapping, ruddy-blonde and the maid a miniature with hair as black as the night. She sat them down with scones and milk at the kitchen table.

'And I swear she has not grown an inch since I last saw her,' teased Tom, 'though she's turned marvellous quiet.'

Hannah blushed, feeling strangely shy. Tom was so grown-up in his manner, so much a man now with his big laugh and easy way with the mistress.

'In times past,' Tom went on, 'I could scarce squeeze a word in edgewise when she was about.'

'The lass has travelled far and is tired,' said Mistress Reay. 'I'll warrant she left home at an early hour.'

'Six of the clock, ma'am,' answered

Hannah, recovering herself a little, 'but I had an argument with a coachman at Belford which hindered me.'

Tom groaned. 'Ah, then, my little sister has not changed after all for she'd pick a quarrel with the King of England if she thought him in the wrong.'

The potter himself came into the kitchen at that moment, a short, stocky man with tufts of woolly hair sprouting at each side of an otherwise bald pate. Overhearing the last remark, he sagely wagged his head 'And there's many might join her in these troubled times.'

'Now, Joshua,' Emma warned.

'Quite right, quite right, my dear.' Her husband acknowledged the reproof good-naturedly. ' 'Tis not the moment for such opinions.' Wiping his hands on his apron, he turned to Hannah. 'Welcome, little maid.' His huge, work-worn hand enclosed her little spread of fingers. 'If ye love thy brother as we do, then we shall all get along splendidly.'

Such openness took Hannah by surprise. There were no closed faces in this house. The comparison with her own parents was unsettling. She looked to Tom to see how she should behave in this unfamiliar relationship.

Tom's marrer, Daniel Fergusson, joined them at supper to complete the circle

69

around the kitchen table. A year older than Tom and already out of his apprenticeship, Daniel was a solemn young man, content to leave the conversation to others after his initial polite acknowledgement of Tom's sister. The two young men, Hannah reflected, were as different as pie from pottage but that they were good friends was plain to see. Daniel's home was in Edinburgh and he had the way common to many Scotchmen of speaking only when he had something of substance to say. Yet he was not aloof. His composed features were rescued from dullness by the crease of humour at the corners of his straight, firm mouth. When he raised his head from the saying of Grace, Hannah looked into eyes like deep brown lakes, reminding her of the patient old cow back home.

Next to him sat Tom, sharing jokes with their genial master, throwing back his head in unrestrained laughter, showing his strong white teeth. His rosy face was as mobile as Daniel's was still but the bond between them was strong and that was enough for Hannah to accept Daniel without reservation.

At the top of the table sat Mistress Reay, contentedly dispensing stew to her family in which, Hannah realised with surprise and pleasure, she herself was now included.

7

Of the many delights to be found at the potter's house, one that gave Hannah great pleasure was her bedroom. Mistress Reay had been to considerable trouble to make the little attic room comfortable for Tom's sister. She had frilled the oak bed with daffodil yellow duroy to match the muslin curtains and covered the floorboards with a wool mat. A ewer and jug stood on a table and beneath the bed was a chamber pot, all in glazed white earthenware made by Joshua himself and decorated by Emma with yellow roses. Hannah had never seen such luxury and took to washing herself all over every night lest she soil the white linen sheets on her bed.

Living so close to the sea was a new experience. She went to sleep to the sound of waves breaking on the shore and awoke to the clamour of seagulls circling the chimney pots. Her bedroom was filled with the sea's reflected radiance, a bright, white light never to be found amongst the fells. Her eyes, accustomed to the rough moorland of Burnfoot, delighted in the distant horizons and limitless skies to be seen from her bedroom window.

Mary had taught her children all she knew of the ancient saints of Holy Island and here was the sacred place itself before Hannah's eyes. The castle, held first for the king and then for Parliament during the revolution, reared up from a spectacular formation of rock. Cattle now grazed on an emerald sward amongst the rose-pink ruins of a once magnificent abbey that had been destroyed in the reign of Henry VIII. Cut off from the mainland twice a day by the tides, the island lay like a jewel in the sea.

King Henry was not the last to plunder the abbey. Hannah's own grandfather used to tell the story of a greedy nobleman in his day who loaded a ship with everything left of value in the ruined abbey, including the lead from the roof. The Lord Almighty exacted awful vengeance for such sacrilege and caused a great storm to arise. The robber's ship was tossed this way and that by mountainous seas and, laden as it was, sank to the bottom of the sea taking all hands with it.

The saintly Cuthbert himself had chosen to live as a hermit on the tiny island nearby and ofttimes Mistress Emma would speak his name as if he were still there, in his tiny cell with his pot of boiled onions to sustain him through long hours of prayer.

Ancient times and present days kept easy company here and fishermen spread their nets to dry over the tumbled cloisters of yesteryear.

There was much at Buckton to interest and entertain Hannah. Trading ships under full sail constantly used this busy sea lane between Newcastle and Berwick, carrying coal and wool and barrels of salt fish, glass from Newcastle, oysters from Scotland, timber and tar from faraway Sweden. She fell in love with the sea and never fell out again and Tom felt the same.

'Farm work is not for me,' he told Hannah. 'Pottery is my craft, clay my master and my home is here, by the sea.'

Hannah watched him at work alongside Daniel, slamming and kneading the cheesy blocks of freshly dug clay, fashioning it with dripping hands on the wheel into bowls and pots and tall-necked bottles. A deft touch with the fingers produced a spout on a pitcher. A handful of clay drawn down into a tail became a handle.

'Lids must fit,' said the master potter, discarding any work that was not up to standard.

Daniel was the more experienced of the two young men producing domestic ware that bore the stamp of functional perfection, enough to gladden the heart of any discerning wife. Tom, striving for originality of design, had not yet perfected the basic disciplines although some of his pots achieved an inspired beauty that was quite beyond Daniel's talent. Joshua recognised their different qualities and counted himself lucky to have such dedicated young potters under his instruction.

Short in stature, he was almost as broad as he was long. A lifetime of pounding clay had developed a powerful spread of chest and shoulder. The well-turned calves showing beneath his sacking apron testified to long hours spent at the kick-wheel. Every day except the Sabbath day he spent in the worksheds, trying out new techniques, experimenting with glazes, passing on to Daniel and Tom his knowledge of the craft he loved.

'A glaze must marry with the clay it sits on,' he insisted, so each new glaze was tested and tested again before being applied to finished pots. When Daniel and Tom were eager to open the kiln after firing to see the results of their work, he curbed their impatience. 'Let the pots soak,' he'd tell them, 'and bide till they're cold. To hasten them will serve only to splinter the glaze.'

With his spectacles on the end of his nose and clay splattered all over his shiny domed head he went from shed to shed all day long, never failing to discard his clogs before entering Emma's flower-fresh, whistle-clean kitchen.

Joshua's special skill lay in the making of tiles and platters inlaid with clays of contrasting colours. These found their way to many a nobleman's house and were much sought after by the merchants of Newcastle. Emma made her own contribution to the pottery, skilfully decorating glazed ware with paintings of the flowers that grew in her garden. Hannah, who had no artistic ability whatsoever, could only watch in admiration.

On the morning after her arrival, Tom was to ride to Belford to settle a bill and would take his sister along with him. It was market day and there would be much to entertain her.

'Hast any money to spend, sister? There will be ribands there the like of which ye've never seen before. Satin and velvet ribands from France.'

They were in the stable, saddling the horses, the sturdy grey Galloway that Tom would ride and Hannah's Dickon.

'Tuppence I got from Widow Dodds,' said Hannah, 'but I might buy summat else than ribands. A chapbook if I see one.'

'You and your books!' Tom swung into the saddle and led the way out of the yard, past Daniel standing at the door of the workshop, shyly returning Hannah's cheery wave. 'There are books in the parlour that ye could nae doubt have a read of if ye but ask.'

The morning was bright and brisk. Mistress Emma's dishclouts were already washed and spread over the raspberry bushes to dry. Men and women were making hay in the fields, the men scything and the women, with their petticoats tucked up out of the way of fleeing mice, raking the fresh-cut grass. The growth was taller and more lush than anything produced at Burnfoot, Hannah reflected. Da would jump for joy over a crop of hay like this.

'Is not this a bonny place, Hannah?' Tom took a deep breath of the sharp, clean air.

'Though Harehope is a pretty burn,' Hannah reminded him with a stirring of loyalty.

'Yet never a sight like that,' Tom pointed to the sea, as smooth as a pond today with no hint of a breaker to disturb the prospect of blue. A ship in full sail approached, borne lightly as a feather on the breath of the wind.

With admiration in her eyes, Hannah reined in. 'Let's watch it come ashore, Tom. Please?'

Tom laughed. 'No ship aims to come ashore here unless the crew be drunk or dead, though many a fine vessel has been blown, willy nilly, on to the evil rocks that be out yonder. In fog, the mariners canna get a bearing on St Nicholas,' he turned in his saddle to point to the ruined church standing on the high ground behind them. 'They've no means of telling how near the land is till their keels strike the rocks, then it's ower late.' They pricked up their horses and continued. 'A terrible dangerous bit of coast this is, though ye might not think it today. We light a barrel of pitch on the headland on stormy nights but even that's not easy to sight sometimes.'

Hannah tightened her reins. Such tales were indeed hard to believe when the sea slept docile as today. 'Race you, Tom! That auld fat mare of yours canters like a donkey!'.

Before Tom left home, they used to charge over the fells like this together but they'd scarcely got going on the highway, with Dickon leading and the heavy Galloway clattering behind when a shout from Tom called Hannah to a halt.

'Hold a moment, Hannah!' There was a note of urgency in his voice that made Hannah wheel about. 'See yon clump of trees?' He was pointing to a stand of pines and bushes on a slight rise at the side of the road just ahead of them. 'Do you see a horse tethered? I spy a man hiding in the bushes.'

Hannah screwed up her eyes. There was indeed a man lying half-hidden in the long grass. 'What can he be up to, Tom?'

'No good, of that I am sure. I carry Master Reay's silver in my pouch and I want no mischief. We will skirt the road and take the path by the sea.'

Hannah was about to follow when the half-concealed figure raised himself on one elbow to peer in their direction. Seeing her hesitation, Tom called sharply, 'Quickly, Hannah! We divvent meddle with highwaymen.'

But Hannah had seen that slim young man before. 'This is no highwayman,' she said, 'this is my friend.' Whereupon she stood in the stirrups and waved excitedly, 'Coo-ee! 'Tis Hannah!' She put Dickon to a canter and sped down the road leaving Tom no option but to follow her though with little enthusiasm. As they reined in at the side of the road, the young man rose to his feet, somewhat reluctantly, it seemed to Tom.

'The same little maid,' he said politely and bowed, 'but with a clean face.' His smile took away any hint of ill manners.

'And this is my brother Tom I tellt thee about yesterday when we met in Belford.'

Tom, noting the speech and manners

of the young man, touched his forelock politely but said nothing. The fact that Hannah's new friend was in a state of some agitation, however, did not escape his notice and was confirmed by the stranger's next words.

'I fear, Tom, that you surprise me in a most urgent business and, though I do not wish to seem lacking in courtesy, I must ask you to hurry on your way and tell no one of this chance encounter.' The young man was clearly anxious to be left alone. ' 'Tis a matter of life and death that I am engaged upon, one which puts me on the wrong side of the law, but I asure you, for a most worthy cause. You must believe me. The life of my dear father hangs upon the success of my enterprise. I await a certain personage who may appear at any moment along the road from Belford and, since I would not involve you in my wrongdoing, I must beg you to be on your way, with my regrets that our acquaintance is to be thus curtailed.'

Tom gathered up his reins. 'We'll be off without further ado and will respect your secret. I took ye for a common highwayman but can see I am wrong in this. Goodday, sir, and good luck in your undertaking if, as you say, God is on your side though the law is not.'

Greatly puzzled, Hannah followed her

brother's example and trotted off down the road to Belford leaving the young man to take up his position of concealment once more.

'How in the name of all the saints did ye get mixed up with that young gentleman, Hannah?' This was another instance, one of several since her arrival, of his sister surprising him.

'He took my part when that scurvy coach driver threatened me with his whip.'

'And why would he raise his whip to you?'

'Because I gave him the rough side of my tongue after he'd covered me with clarts.'

Tom grinned. 'Mebbes your friend should have taken the driver's part when a great bully like you is roused.'

A swirl of dust rising from the road ahead attracted Tom's attention. 'See, Hannah, a horseman coming this way. Can this be the man thy friend awaits?'

They saw, when he drew closer, that he wore the king's crest on his hat and on the leather bag slung from his shoulder. Fat-necked and rosy-faced, sitting very straight with his nose in the air, he went by without a greeting.

'The postman,' said Tom, wonderingly.

'That's right,' Hannah nodded. 'My friend said he had business with the postman at the Blue Bell Inn.'

'Seemingly his business was not completed to his satisfaction then and he means to finish it this morning. Gee-up your pony, Hannah. Some plot is afoot here that we'd best know nowt about. Haste we to the town.'

'And yet,' said Hannah, complying somewhat reluctantly, ' 'tis a pity we do not tarry to help him if his father's life is at risk?'

'Listen to me, Mistress Busybody,' Tom spoke with all the authority of seventeen years, 'since I left Burnfoot, I have learned a thing or two about life and I know that folk like us are of little concern to anyone. Were we to meddle in the affairs of the gentry, 'tis not they who suffer when events turn out ill but us; so, Hannah, we will say nowt about this, only keep your ears and eyes open amongst the gossips of Belford and we might glean something of the business.' Tom's face wore a thoughtful look. 'Thy friend is young to challenge the law in this way for I'll warrant that chin ne'er saw a beard.'

The traffic of carts on the road increased as they drew nearer to Belford where every square foot of ground in the market place was occupied by a stall of one sort or another. The sleepy village of the day before was transformed into a hubbub

81

of selling and buying. Sharp-eyed, shrill-voiced wives clutching their tight purses jostled beneath gaily striped canopies hung with geese and rabbits, baskets and cooking pots, oil lamps and ropes. Vendors calling out their wares offered casks of oil and sacks of seed, tubs of butter and cheese, bundles of coarse soap, leather aprons for a blacksmith, saddles and bridles for a horseman. Ripe cherries. Sweet lavender. Fresh fish from Seahouses. Salt cod from Boulmer and French dolls from who knows where.

'Makes Bewick Market look like a sale in somebody's backyard, don't it?' said Tom as Hannah stood speechless with surprise.

Dogs barked. Sheep bleated. Pigs squealed. From a clearing further down the road came the sound of the pipes and Hannah's face lit up. 'Oh Tom! There's dancing!'

'I must see to my master's business first,' Tom pushed her towards the market stalls. 'Do ye take a look here whiles I'm gone then we'll have worsells a dance. All the lassies in Belford have wooden legs and I have nae danced a jig since I left Burnfoot. Pick no fights, mind, while I'm away!'

She spent her tuppence on a little book of poetry because the words, many of them new to her, sounded right and then, when a dark-skinned faw wanted to tell her fortune, she had no money left.

'The oil burns bright in your little lamp,' croaked the old woman tracing the lines on Hannah's palm with her finger, 'but 'tis a glim that casts a shadow. Here's one to blow it hot and one to blow it cold. A penny, my pretty. I'll tell thee all for a penny.'

Shaking her head, Hannah withdrew her hand 'I have nae money left, old woman.'

The old woman continued to peer after her, a question in her glittering black eyes but Hannah had forgotten her in anticipation of the dance. Back home, in the old days, Hannah had always partnered Tom at the Bewick hoppings. No one in the neighbourhood could touch the pair for grace and lightness of step and, for both, dancing was the greatest pleasure imaginable. Now, as they took their places amongst the other lads and lasses on the stretch of common land by the court leet, Hannah was amused to see admiring glances directed at Tom by the girls. Many a maid would be content to partner such a strapping, handsome fellow. None would guess that she was his sister and there was envy in their eyes.

The piper drew the first commanding note to pull the pairs into circles, a maid at the side of each youth. Then in came the fiddler with his twinkling bow to accompany the pipes, telling the beat, calling the tune, filling the summer's afternoon with careless gaiety. Hannah was away with the rhythm, toes tapping, spinning, twirling, changing hands in a chain of dancers, linking arms in a gyrating whirl like a spinning top on its point. Finally, the piper begged a rest and the dancers drifted away to seek refreshment.

'We'd best make for home,' Tom led his sister back to their tethered horses, 'though I've nae doubt ye could dance all night long and never grow tired.'

Hannah's face was flushed. Her eyes shone with happiness. His little sister, Tom reflected, was growing up. She was well favoured in her looks and the time must come when she would choose someone other than her brother as a dancing partner.

A noisy crowd had gathered in the yard of the Blue Bell where they had tied their horses. Tom frowned.

'Summat's amiss,' he muttered, taking a firmer grip of his sister's arm. 'Stay close.'

At the centre of the disturbance was a red-faced man in such a state of excitement that he could scarcely speak coherently. Egged on by the crowd, he struggled to unburden himself amid much puffing and blowing and mopping of brow.

'It's the postman,' whispered Hannah.

'Three or four rogues—' the man stuttered, waving his arms about, 'I cannot rightly say how many—all armed to the teeth—frighted my horse with their muskets. I was thrown to the ground—' and certainly his coat was covered in dust. 'You may be sure—' his voice rang out with sudden authority, 'that I put up a good fight! As bearer of the king's mail, I count my life as nought beside my sacred duty.' This brought a cheer from the crowd and a pot of ale to his hand. 'But the odds were devilish high against me!' His audience had to wait until he had quenched his thirst before he could continue.

'Count upon it,' he went on, warming to his theme, 'I gave the villains plenty to take away with them in the shape of a broken nose or two and a few black eyes. They did not go unmarked! They will remember the folly of waylaying the postman for many a long day. Upon my word!' He had to stop to dab at his eyes and drain his pot. 'But, try as I might, they overpowered me.' His bravado drained away and the rest of his tale was told in a whimper. 'They set my horse loose to run wild into the woods and left me to walk back to Belford. Alas, what a misfortune to befall me.' He fell to wailing and dabbing his eyes. 'I shall pay dearly for this. It will appear as negligence to my masters.'

'Were ye robbed?' the crowd wanted to know.

'Robbed?' he rolled his eyes to the heavens. 'Aye, I was robbed and now no doubt I will be robbed of my head by the king though no one could have protected his warrant with more valour than I.'

'They stole the king's warrant?'

'For a rebel's execution, no less!'

This was indeed a serious affair. The crowd about him shuffled and murmured in sympathy as the poor man, now quite overcome, gave way to tears which ran unashamedly down his plump cheeks. The landlord laid a supporting arm across his shoulders.

'Didst wound any of them with your pistols, Courier? If so, we'll send a search into the woods. A wounded man will not get far.'

'I was prevented from doing so,' the wretched man went on aggrievedly, 'for while I slept last night—in your hostelry, sir—the charges were removed from both my pistols. I found myself defenceless under attack. Your hospitality, sir,' he shook off the friendly arm, 'is questionable.'

Tom led Hannah away leaving the landlord to his protestations and the postman demanding to know who would succour his wife and children when he was sent to the gallows.

'What think ye now of thy young gentleman, Hannah?'

'I know not what to think,' Hannah confessed.

'Seemingly, he had hidden accomplices. He takes great risk upon himself when he interferes with the king's orders.'

' 'Twas to save the life of his father,' Hannah reminded him, not wishing to think ill of the man who had befriended her. He had asked her not to condemn him, no matter what she heard. 'He did not tell me his name,' she added regretfully.

Tom shrugged. ' 'Tis not wor business. Howay home. There's nowt much hurt about that postman but his pride. Hark at him! Still bleating.'

Their tale of the postman's misfortune was received with great interest by the potter and his wife although Tom and Hannah cautiously withheld mention of their encounter with the young man.

'A death warrant stolen, you say?' Joshua exchanged a meaningful glance with his wife. 'And he was bound for Edinburgh. Then maybe one of our friends has been spared.'

'A postponement only,' sighed Emma,

'for the king can sign another warrant easily enough.'

'Why does the king seek to kill your friends, Master Reay?' Hannah asked in astonishment but Tom bade her be silent.

' 'Tis none of wor business, Hannah. Did I not warn thee not to meddle in other folks' affairs?'

'Easy, Tom,' Joshua Reay said soothingly. 'There's nowt wrong in the lass's question, only in the answer. The brave men who lie in Edinburgh's Tolbooth under sentence of death are the leaders of the Scotch rebellion. There are many like them, and I am one of them, who would not stand by and see the lawful religion of the country threatened by papists. We, who have the true faith, would replace Catholic James with a Protestant but our cause has collapsed. The Duke of Argyll has already gone to the scaffold and more are like to follow him. We have shot our bolt but no one will make a papist out of me. I follow the religion which my heart dictates and put myself in the hands of God.'

'Amen,' said Emma.

'These are dangerous times and what I have said must not go beyond these four walls.'

His listeners solemnly nodded.

'But all is not lost,' Emma reminded him. 'Though the Scotch rebellion has failed, the prince has support in England.'

'Aye, the prince.' It was a rueful smile that the potter conjured up. 'A bonny lad who has the virtue of being a Protestant but the misfortune to be a bastard, one of Charles's litter.'

Tom brought up the subject again some days later when he and Daniel were packing a kiln ready for firing with Hannah looking on. Their master was taking a bath in front of the kitchen fire so they were free to talk.

'I fear for our good master if his religious beliefs become known. King James is cruelly hard on Dissenters.' Tom said gravely.

Daniel agreed. 'No hint of the master's beliefs must reach King James's ear.'

'Is not Master Reay a Protestant like the rest of us?' queried Hannah.

'Only more strict,' said Tom. 'He'll nae take the Sacrament, which practice is accepted by most Protestants. Nor can he abide any other rites which he thinks do smack of popery. He would never recant. Not even on the rack.'

Hannah shivered. 'I'd take the Sacrament rather than be tortured.'

'Not so wor Joshua,' said Tom.

Daniel looked up with a serious face from his painstaking stacking of pots. 'We must keep close counsel lest we put the master in danger unwittingly. There are spies about. Redcoats have been spotted in the Kyloes looking for deserters from Argyll's army.'

Instinctively, Hannah looked over her shoulder at the craggy heights of the Kyloe hills, grown over in places with patches of woodland. A man might well seek refuge there; better than lying in Edinburgh prison awaiting execution like the father of her highwayman friend.

In the pleasures and novelties of the following days, however, Hannah forgot about such troubles and concerned herself with helping in any way she could, both in the pottery and the running of the household. Under Emma's serene management, no task was too tedious. Hannah tried her best to please this kindly woman in whose company mean thoughts or rough words seemed to melt away before they were spoken. Those dark places of her own inner self, long shut away from the casual observer, opened to Emma's affection like a flower in the sun. In so doing, she became each day more lovable herself.

'My saints, thou'rt a willing help, Hannah.' Mistress Reay's round apricot face dimpled with pleasure. 'A good pair of hands for thy ma.'

Hannah made no answer for she was

not so willing to do these chores at home, yet here in this bright kitchen; with Emma singing as she baked, she was content to do whatever was asked of her.

'You have other brothers and sisters, Tom tells us?' The touch of longing in Emma's voice was lost on Hannah.

'There's Joan who's eighteen and Sarah turned ten and Benjamin the babby.'

'Thy mother is blessed indeed with so many children to comfort her.'

Hannah straightened from the hearth where she knelt. ' 'Tis no blessing,' she said earnestly. 'Me ma was nigh dead of the last one.'

With the passage of time she had learned to close her mind to painful memories, to steer clear of any thought that might lead her back to that dread vision of her mother. Now, however, talking to this gentle woman, she dropped her guard. The nightmare vision appeared once more. White legs. Dark blood. The sickly smell. Tears sprang to her eyes and, although she had more to say on the subject, no words came. She got to her feet and would have left the kitchen had not Emma stayed her with a kindly touch.

' 'Tis a woman's great privilege to bear children, Hannah. This is the Word of the Lord.'

'And if she should die while she's about it, is that, too, the wish of the Lord?' Angrily Hannah brushed the tears from her eyes.

'Her reward awaits her in heaven' Emma paused. 'Thou'rt thinking,' she continued, divining the unspoken thought, 'what can Mistress Emma know about such things, but I, too, had a child. Our little son was only lent to us. The Lord gave and the Lord took him away before he had even learned to walk.'

Discomfited, Hannah hung her head.

Emma patted the dark hair. 'There, 'twas a long time ago and the hurt is healed. But I know the joy of bringing forth a child, despite the travail, as one day you will, I am sure.'

'Not I!' The head shot up, denial written on every line of Hannah's face. 'I have made plans against such a thing for I am resolved never to let a man come near me.'

The sound of the men's clogs on the cobbled yard brought the conversation to a hasty close.

'Here come the men for their porridge, Hannah. Quickly clear away the pail and dirty clouts.'

Putting away her troubled thoughts, Hannah tidied the hearth and served the men with their breakfast.

'Hurry up, dreamer!' called Tom. 'Why so solemn?'

Daniel looked across the table at her. 'Our little cook is deep in thought this morning.'

And Emma, seeing her blush at Daniel's shy smile, consoled herself that this little maid was like any other after all.

The men were firing. Both kilns were loaded with raw clay pots and vessels and the fires lit under them. Tom had been up all night overseeing the first stage of the operation when excess moisture was released from the clay and allowed to escape through an aperture in the kiln doors. Now the gaps in the door would be sealed with bricks and mud and the temperature raised to the point when the clay vessels inside changed their composition to a hard material suitable for glazing. The fires needed constant feeding and so, while the men ate their breakfast, Hannah was sent to fetch wood from the woodpile.

It lay some distance from the house adjacent to a little spinney of ash and birch. Hannah had just begun to load the bogey with logs when a roughlooking man rose up to confront her from the far side of the pile. His garments were in rags, his bearded face hollow-eyed and grey. Hastily he put a finger to his lips to silence the cry that rose to her lips.

'Have no fear, little maid...'

Another Scotchman.

'I mean no harm. Pray tell thy mistress Rob McNab is here with news.'

Hannah found Mistress Emma head down amongst the gooseberry bushes. She put down her basket at once.

'Bring him to the kitchen, Hannah. Make sure he is not seen by any passing coach or waggon for his life may depend on't.'

The Covenanter, for such was he, was welcomed with great kindness, given a tub of hot water with soapwort in which to bathe his bleeding feet, a tankard of ale and bread and meat. An hour or so was spent in close conversation with Joshua and Emma before he was sent to rest on a pallet of straw behind stacked clay in the workshed. Hannah, as well as Daniel and Tom, was instructed to keep a close lookout and raise the alarm at the sight of any redcoat. She was milking the cow in the late afternoon when Tom came to her in great excitement.

'Wor visitor brought news, Hannah! A strange tale that will set thee laughing as it must for all who hear it. Thy brave young man who led the attack on the postman was no man at all but a lassie!'

In her astonishment, Hannah squirted a stream of milk up her bare leg. 'Ow! What's that ye say?'

'A Scotch lass, Griselda Cochrane, daughter of Sir John Cochrane under sentence of execution in the Tolbooth. She got word that the warrant for her father's death was on its way and so would hold up the postman. Dressed as a man. Her old nurse who lives hereabouts helped her with clothes. I thought she was a mite ower bonny for a man!'

Hannah clapped her hands in delight. 'Did ye ever hear the like!'

Daniel joined them in the byre. 'King James can easy write a second warrant,' he reminded them soberly.

'Aye, but the maid has given time for her grandfather to bribe those at court who have the king's ear for a pardon.'

'That would be Lord Dundonald,' said Daniel. 'He'll nae grieve over a bag of silver if it'll buy his son's life.'

When she returned to the kitchen with the pail of milk, Hannah found Joshua in high good humour. 'Here's a jest indeed! The three armed rogues who attacked the postman now turn out to be one young maid.' He roared with laughter. 'The king's courier will be the laughing stock of Belford for evermore!'

The tale was still being discussed at

supper that night, Hannah's last night for she was to return home in the morning. The Covenanter had taken himself off as secretly as he had come. Only the pallet behind the sacks of clay remained to show that he had been, but his news would be talked of for many a day.

'I'd ha thought you fit to tell a maid from a man, Tom,' Daniel said slyly. 'But perhaps she was a brawny lass with a beard?'

Hannah fished in her pocket and brought out a square of cambric edged with lace. The letter 'G' was embroidered in one corner. 'I did think this awful fancy for a man.'

8

On her last morning, Hannah was loth to open her eyes, reluctant to leave her white and yellow bedroom with its smell of the sea and soda soap and the holy picture hanging on the wall.

'But ye shall come again when ye may be spared at home,' promised Emma, clasping Hannah to her well-filled bodice that smelled of lavender, baked apples and hay. 'And shall read me more poetry.'

'Come again. Come again,' Joshua bustling off to his mortars and pestles, his sieves and measures.

Daniel, holding Dickon while she mounted, smiled his slow smile. 'Safe journey.'

Kindness, she decided, was infectious, like smallpox. You could pick it up from a neighbour. Here at Buckton, there was plenty of it. She wondered, as she rode away at Tom's side, if she, too, might have caught the smit.

'They have all been good to me, Tom. I never was so happy in all my life.'

He was to set her along the way for a mile or two. 'They are like that with everyone, Hannah. 'Tis my good fortune to live with such folk.'

The road ahead was long and lonely after Tom had turned his horse about and said farewell. There was no telling when they might meet again. That would depend on whether the da would let her go a second time. Her mind ran back over the happy days at Buckton. Singing in the parlour on the Sabbath, riding along the sands below the tottering ruins of Bamburgh Castle with Tom and Daniel, even braving the sea to swim. It was colder than the Devil's Pot by far and the drag of the tide was scary until she got used to it. She had swum in her shift. The lads moved away while she dried herself behind the rocks then they all raced home, Tom on the potter's Galloway, Daniel on Mistress Emma's neat little chestnut mare and Hannah on Dickon. Oh, what times to remember for ever.

Her eye lingered on the sea. She would have to turn away from it soon to take the way inland over the heights to Burnfoot. There were white-topped waves this morning, bouncing the fishing cobles about so that from time to time they disappeared from view entirely, but the breeze was light and the sea good tempered. Tom was indeed fortunate to live in such surroundings.

Before she reached the place where she must turn off the Great North Road, she came upon a company of soldiers, straggling in unmilitary fashion without any rousing accompaniment on fife or drum. The reason became clear when she drew near to them for she saw that most had heads and arms tied up in bloody rags or else limped on sticks. Yet they were not so downcast that they could not raise a greeting as she trotted by.

'Hast been fighting in Scotland?' she called out, quite forgetting her father's warning not to tangle with the militia.

'That we have,' they called out, in good

heart, 'and left them in a worse state than ye see us just now.'

Aye, she thought, and no doubt helped to put Grizzy's father in jail.

With the sea now left behind her she turned Dickon's head inland, over gently rising land where the afternoon light blazed the gorse and shimmered amongst the silver birch saplings. The familiar peaty smell of the moor brought a hint of home and sent Dickon's head tossing in anticipation.

There was no sign of the widow as they rode through Eglingham though her door stood open. Hannah would have liked to dismount and gossip but had no time to stop. She was eager now to tell her news back home. Up Harehope Hill they went. The going was rough but Dickon had no wish to slacken pace. Finally, all in a lather and a clatter, they reined to a halt in the yard at Burnfoot where Mary was splitting firewood.

'So you're back.' Mary disengaged herself from Hannah's impetuous hug. 'I trust ye caused no trouble at the potter's house.'

It was a cold welcome. No smile. No embrace. Not the smallest hint of affection. That part of Hannah which had flowered in the warmth of Emma's kindness curled up close like a bud caught by the frost.

'Carry this wood inside for me,' her mother continued. 'We've all been doing thy work while ye've been away enjoying thysell.'

In the familiar kitchen once more, so drab after Emma's bright place, so lacking in any attempt to grace its plain, limewashed walls, the tales she meant to tell of embroidered linen cloths for laying on the table, or burnished copper serving pots, all seemed out of place. What was the use of describing to Sarah her pretty white and yellow bedroom by the sea when the garret where they slept was shrouded in cobwebs and littered with mouse dirt. The fountain of her excitement drained away. Already the visit was beginning to take on an air of unreality.

After questioning her on Tom's progress, her father showed more interest in the potter's family than did his wife. What was his house like? Was he a godly man?

'He says the Lord's Grace before we eat,' she told him, 'and prayers at night before we gan to bed. It's a holier house than wors.'

Her father let that pass. 'I trust he's nae papist?'

This she was quick to deny. 'Popery he cannot abide. He was one who sided with the Scotch rebels against King James but since their cause is lost, he says we must make the best of a Catholic king.'

This roused Nicholas. 'Let me hear nae more! Such talk can put a rope around a man's neck. Learn to keep thy mouth close.'

Miserably Hannah recalled that this had been Master Joshua's instruction also. Thankfully she had checked her tongue before mentioning the meeting with the Covenanter and she waited until her father had gone outside before relating the story of Grizzy Cochrane. She had a rapt audience in Joan and Sarah but praise of any sort did not come easily to Mary Robson. She dismissed Hannah's tale with characteristic acrimony.

'Things have come to a pretty pass when a highborn lass plays the highwayman and frights a poor postman out of his wits.'

'He was witless to start with,' was Hannah's surly rejoinder which earned her a box on the ears. She was back in the old ways again, the loveless days. The happiness which had possessed her was fast evaporating and after a while it was as if she had never been away.

'Hannah has gone all moony since she went to stay with Tom.'

There was some truth in Sarah's complaint, for Hannah's glimpse of a world outside Burnfoot had opened her eyes to many things which gave her food for thought. Dissenters were not wrongdoers as she had been led to believe, but honest men and women like Master and Mistress Reay who merely sought to worship according to their beliefs.

Not all husbands beat their wives. It would be unthinkable for Master Reay to take a leather to Emma! Lastly and importantly, she had put her mother alongside Emma and drawn the only possible conclusion. Her mother did not love her, nay, did not like her even. Acknowledging at last the futility of trying to please, she withdrew within herself. The passionate attachment she had long held for her mother, who gave nothing in return, withered away leaving only indifference. She found she was looking forward to November when she would be fifteen years old and ready to seek work outside the home, although the nature of that work was not yet clear.

'I divvent want to be just somebody's servant, Joan.' Joan and Hannah were out in the garden picking raspberries, discussing Hannah's future. 'A lad can do as he fancies. For a lass there's nowt but weshing and cleaning.'

'What do ye want to do?'

Hannah considered this. 'I could teach little bairns to read or summat.'

'Make up thy mind to do it, then. Thy

fine lady, Mistress Cochrane, showed ye what a woman can do if she sets her heart upon it.' She corrected herself with a short, humourless laugh. 'I mean normal women, like you and Sarah. There's no independence for a mishap like me.'

Joan's deformity was never spoken of in the family, least of all by Joan herself. For a moment, Hannah glimpsed the wound that was usually concealed. She put a timid arm about Joan's thin shoulders.

' 'Twas unfair of God to disable thee when the rest of us are all well-made.'

With a sigh, Joan turned away. ' 'Tis not God I blame.'

Hannah frowned. 'Surely not the Widow Dodds?' Everyone knew she was the best midwife in the north.

'I have lately learned,' Joan said indifferently, 'that there was no midwife.' She limped away with her basin of raspberries leaving Hannah more confused than ever. There were no neighbours near Burnfoot who might have helped her mother. Who, then, had brought Joan into the world, and maimed her?

The matter was not raised again. There was a reserve about Joan that deterred further questioning but sometimes, when Hannah watched her father bring forth a calf from its straining dam, she wondered. Was this the reason for the curious influence Joan had over her father? She was the only one that he would heed, the only one he would never strike. Only Joan dared speak up when his explosions of temper silenced the rest, though Hannah was beginning to discover that his angry outbursts, violent as they were, had lost the power to terrify her. Secure in the knowledge that this would be her last summer at Burnfoot, she was able to distance herself from family quarrels. She was deeply sorry for Sarah, however, who would be the butt of all blame once she herself had left.

'Divvent anger him with back answers,' she advised. 'That's where I went wrong for I couldna keep me mouth shut and he laid into me all the harder with the strap.'

The two girls were up on the top of Bewick Hill, herding sheep, knitting as they went. Sarah was twelve now, nearly thirteen and more of a companion for Hannah whose new air of independence she greatly coveted. There were other noticeable changes in Hannah which impressed Sarah, like washing herself every day and cleaning her teeth with sage leaves. One day she even took a broom to the garret where they slept then painted the whole place with whitewash! All this had come about since the visit to Buckton.

'I wonder if me da'll let me go to Buckton when I'm older?' she asked wistfully.

'It's manners to wait till ye're asked,' Hannah said curtly and then regretted her sharpness when she saw Sarah's face fall. She remembered how she had found kindness infectious at Buckton. It seemed that unkindness was just as easily picked up.

'Howay!' She reached out to take Sarah's hand. 'Put yer knitting down. Race ye to the top. Let's see what the dog is fashed about.'

When they arrived, dishevelled and out of breath, they saw why Gyp was barking. Down in the valley, where the girls had seen them earlier, the militia were returning from Scotland.

'All higgledy-piggledy,' said Sarah. 'No drums. What think ye, Hannah?'

'Why, I think it be a train of wounded. See, they're carried in carts, most of them. And they're calling a halt.'

'At the auld pele.'

The fortified tower which had garrisoned fifty men at the time of the border raids had fallen into disrepair but roof and walls were still intact though its battlements had crumbled.

'Let's away down,' said Hannah, 'And see what's afoot.'

But Sarah hung back. 'What aboot the sheep? Wor da will kill us!'

'Put Gyp to keep them. They'll not stray far and we won't be gone long.'

Reluctantly, Sarah followed her sister down the hill to meet other curious folk making their way up from Old Bewick village.

' 'Tis the wounded from the Scotch fighting,' one old goody told them. 'They must bide here awhile afore going doon to London.'

These were more seriously wounded men than those Hannah met on the Belford road. Some, not yet adjusted to recent blindness, were being helped out of the carts by orderlies. Others, seemingly on the point of death, were carried inside the pele on stretchers.

'Get a move on!' bawled a sergeant with a face as coarse as a pumpkin. 'Any of yez that can walk, get yourselves inside.'

Inside the pele, women were stuffing palliasses with straw. 'Hark the way they talk,' said one of the Bewick wives. 'They divvent belong around here.'

'Clear out, ye idle loafers!' The sergeant advanced threateningly towards the watching crowd. 'If gawping is all ye can do, be off with ye!'

The women made a token shuffle but did not leave. Hannah, emboldened, sneaked round the back of the sergeant to peer inside the tower and was confronted by the familiar figure of Widow Dodds, with cap askew and apron streaked with blood.

'Why, Hannah!' she cried 'Art come to help? We can use another pair of hands.'

But Hannah shrank back. The scene inside the building was horrific. Men were crying out, swooning with pain, as orderlies laid them none too gently on the ground. The stench of suppurating wounds and soiled bandages made her clap her hand to her mouth in dismay.

'Oh no, Widow Dodds, that I cannot do!'

'Then get out of the way,' the widow said sharply. 'It's dark enough already in here without you folk blocking the door.' She raised her voice to reach all those who stood outside. 'Harken to me, ye Bewick and Eglingham women. If ye'll help here, ye're welcome. If not, take yersells off but leave yer petticoats behind ye for we're gey short of clouts to bind the wounds of these poor souls.'

Uncomfortably aware that she had not lived up to the widow's expectations of her, Hannah was preoccupied for the rest of the day. That evening, after their father had been served with his meal, she spoke of what was on her mind.

'The auld pele at Bewick is full of

wounded soldiers, Da. I want to help Widow Dodds look after them.'

Mary's eyes widened in surprise but Nicholas made no hurry to answer. At length, without raising his eyes from his platter, he spoke, in the cold, flat tones that all his family feared.

'How ist ye know aboot the men in the pele?'

'We saw them from the top of Bewick Hill.'

'How came ye to speak with Widow Dodds?'

He was playing with her as a cat plays with a mouse. The exchange would probably end with the strap.

'I tellt Sarah we should go doon and see what the militia was at and I saw the widow in the pele.'

He looked up then. He had got what he wanted. The ice in his light blue eyes froze his four womenfolk to silence. A log settling on the hearth sounded like a thunderclap. Hannah took in a deep breath and waited.

'You were charged with my sheep.' Her father spat out the words.

At this point, girls were supposed to give way to tears as Sarah was preparing to do. Mary closed her eyes. Joan bent low over her work.

'We left Gyp on guard.' Hannah's face

was set. She would not be put down like a naughty child. 'We were not gone long and all was well on our return.'

Nicholas pushed away his empty platter and drained his mug of ale. Is he never going to speak of the matter of helping the widow, thought Hannah. If it is to be the strap, then lay on and have done with it. Nicholas wiped his lips on the back of his hand. 'For neglecting the sheep,' he said at last (miraculously, his anger appeared to have cooled), 'you will go to bed hungry.' He shot a glance at Mary. 'See to it, wife.'

So there was to be no strap. 'What aboot the wounded soldiers?' she asked again.

Joan, anxious for no further confrontation, jumped in with, 'You would be in the way, Hannah. What can a girl like thee do to help those poor souls?'

Strangely, it was Joan's words that turned Nicholas to favour Hannah. For once, Joan irritated him by dismissing her sister's request so lightly. If the girl wanted to help, there was no reason why she should not.

Chubby-faced Sarah, catching his eye, gulped hastily, 'Not me, Da. I divvent want to go. That place is all muck and mess.'

Sternly, Nicholas addressed Hannah, sitting straight-backed on her spinning stool. 'Once ye've put thy hand to a task, there's nae backing away till the job be done. As long as ye ken that, ye can go.'

By the next morning, Hannah was already half regretting her decision to help Widow Dodds and secretly hoped her father would change his mind, but pride would not allow her to back down. She had only to call to mind her heroine Grizzy Cochrane and all thoughts of retreat vanished.

Her mother saw her off on Dickon. 'Drink no water but what you have in your flask. There's mebbes cholera amongst the troops. Keep thy hair covered with a kerchief and wear thy smock at all times.' She paused and, with a touch of unaccustomed concern, added, 'God go with thee, child.'

As Hannah went on her way down the burnside track to Old Bewick, conjecture as to what she might be expected to do for the wounded men occupied her thoughts. Most fervently she hoped it would not be more than she could stand.

On nearing the pele, she was not reassured to see orderlies slinging corpses wrapped in canvas into a waiting cart. Some of the more grievously wounded had not survived the rough journey from Scotland and found their final resting place in Bewick churchyard. Steeling herself, Hannah tethered Dickon and went into the pele in search of Widow Dodds.

Amongst the litter of equipment, boots and buckets, water bottles and tinderboxes, men in various stages of distress lay on palliasses, their muskets propped against the walls behind them. Over all was the stench of excrement and sepsis.

Some half-dozen women who were not known to Hannah were attending to the men's needs but Widow Dodds was not amongst them. Shyly she approached one who, by her bright expression and ready smile, brought a ray of sunshine to these dismal surroundings.

'She's over there,' the young woman pointed to a table set at the back of the building, 'preparing salve for these poor souls.'

Her voice, sweet and light, carried inflections that were strange to Hannah but she followed her directions and came upon the widow, busy with mortar and pestle. She greeted Hannah with surprise and pleasure.

'Ye've thought more on the matter? Ye're more than welcome for there's plenty here that needs to be done.'

But when a terrible scream rang out from behind a nearby curtain, followed by the sound of a relentless saw, Hannah almost took to her heels and fled. Only the thought of her father's scorn kept her there, holding hard on the widow's table to steady her shaking legs.

'Old fool,' the widow said savagely. 'The surgeon-major is a mite too handy with his saw. He knows only three remedies; bleed, purge or cut off. There's many a boot would still have a leg in't if they'd leave the healing to me. Look ye, Hannah, take water to the men. They've been begging this last half-hour and me with no time to see to it. Here are pannikins and when the pitcher's empty, fill it from the pump outside. Go to Polly if ye need help, Polly with the red skirt.'

Lacklustre eyes followed Hannah's progress, with pannikin and pitcher, between the pallets. Men too weak to help themselves could only mouth the word, 'Water', so that Hannah must sink to her knees beside them and hold the vessel to their lips. One who lay propped against the wall of the pele, a blood-stained bandage spiralling his chest, was unable to hold his head upright and most of the water she offered was spilled down his naked chest, turning the dried blood on his bandages to a spreading pink. His eyes, dark with laudanum, met Hannah's in mild reproof at her ineptitude. Shyly she slipped a hand beneath his sweaty neck to support his lolling head while he drank and when his thirst was quenched, he gave a little nod, rewarding her with a look of gratitude. Gently and with budding confidence, she laid his head against the wall. His breath was foul, his tongue thickly furred. His body smelt of urine and sweat but at that moment Hannah loved him as a mother loves her baby. She went in search of Polly-with-the-red-skirt to ask if she might have a pillow for her very first patient.

Polly was the cheerful young woman Hannah had spoken to on arrival. 'You're a kind lass to come and help these poor men,' she said in her funny way of speaking. 'There's flour bags and straw under the tarpaulin by the steps. Make your man a pillow then give the poor fellow a wash, what's left of him that's not wrapped up in bandages and I'll tell the orderly to shave him.'

'What's the matter with him, ma'am?' Hannah found the courage to ask.

Polly laughed. 'No "ma'am-ing" me, my love. I'm just plain Polly. As to what mischief your man has suffered, why, I cannot rightly say for the surgeon-major does not tell me his secrets but 'tis my belief a musket ball has gone clean through his lungs for he do breathe terrible bad. You'll not hurt him by washing his hands, face and his feet and that will bring him the greatest comfort. The sergeant has issued clean shirts, not before time, I can tell you, and I'll help you put one on your man when you've washed him.'

'Who are these women, Mistress Dodds?' Hannah asked as she sought a bowl of water and a flannel rag.

'Soldiers' wives,' replied the widow, 'and yet some are not truly wives. They have to follow their men, even with babies at the breast, or they'd starve while waiting for His Majesty's paymaster to make provision for them.'

'Is Polly's man here?'

'Aye, he's here. Now get along. There's more than one here needing to be washed.'

Hannah lived through a nightmare that first morning at the pele. Her first sight of a bad wound sent her scurrying outside to vomit in the bushes but she recovered herself. Under Polly's supervision, she fed gruel to helpless men, bathed their feet that had marched in waterlogged boots for weeks. She held the stump of a man's leg while Polly applied a poultice. She emptied the slops and mopped up the vomit of men made senseless with brandy before the ordeal of amputation. The burly major, emerging from behind the curtain from time to time to drink a pot of ale, looked more like a butcher than a doctor.

The agony of the dying was almost too

much to bear. The screams she would never forget for as long as she lived. At the end of the day, she was exhausted, physically and mentally drained, but nourished by a new self-knowledge of unsuspected strength.

That night at Burnfoot over supper, she had nothing to say. Her father seemed to understand that her experiences had overwhelmed her and silenced the questions of the others. All he asked was, 'Will ye go back the morn?' and seemed pleased when she answered yes.

Knowing what faced her, Hannah found it even harder the next morning to present herself at the pele. Nothing but her own determination took her back to that place of misery, but Polly was there, cheerful as ever.

'Which is your man, Polly?' she ventured. Polly seemed to attend to all the men with equal care, joking and laughing with all of them.

Her man was the red-headed giant with powerful shoulders, sinewy arms and no legs. Hannah flushed crimson with confusion.

' 'Tis all right, love,' Polly said gently. 'A soldier's wife is prepared for anything, as her man must be.'

'What will become of him, Polly?'

Polly went over to her man and rumpled his shock of fiery hair. 'We're going to make a little cart on wheels, aren't we, Rob? You'll go down Box Hill a good deal faster than me with two legs.'

Shocked and inadequate, Hannah had to turn away from Rob's empty gaze. Polly's cheerfulness amazed her.

'If I didn't laugh, I'd cry,' Polly said simply, 'and what would be the good of that? I thank the dear Lord I have not been blessed with children,' she continued, 'nor am I likely to be now. Do you take a couple of pitchers and come with me to the pump.'

All but one of the six large pitchers had been emptied during the night. Hannah did as she was bid and followed Polly into the yard.

'King Charles's hospital for soldiers is not yet risen above its foundations,' Polly went on. ' 'Tis a bonny site, amid the hayfields by the River Thames at Chelsea, but will not be ready for my Rob and others like him for many a day. I daresay 'twill be too late for some of the brave lads.'

'How will ye look after him?' The problem seemed insurmountable to Hannah.

'I must earn enough money to keep us both and find a roof to cover our heads. Rob will get a pension when the paymaster sees fit; not the eight pence a day that he got as a fighting man but whatever it is, it will help.' Polly laughed at Hannah's glum face. 'Come! Cheer up! 'Tis not the end of the world. Hurry up with those pitchers for the slop pails are to empty.'

With full pitchers, they struggled back to the pele past the lascivious eyes of the horse-handlers. 'I'm young still,' Polly continued, 'and strong. I can sell chestnuts in the streets of London or hops in their season, like any other woman. I'll get by.'

'What makes a man go for a soldier?' Hannah asked wonderingly. 'I'd rather be a herdsman. There's less chance of getting your legs cut off.'

'They're mostly pressed men, love, or tricked by the recruiting officer with the king's shilling, like my Rob. When you're starving a shilling means bread. The gunpowder and cannon come later.'

With sharpened interest, Hannah looked at the other women. They seemed weary beyond words. Some had small children clutching at their skirts. What would be their future without a soldier's pay? Would they all end up begging on the streets of London? Did no one care about soldiers' wives?

Those men who were not seriously disabled, who would be sent back into the line when their wounds healed, were happy to jest and chat with the women. They had plenty to say about the Scotch campaign.

'Scarce need for us,' they said. 'Argyll was betrayed by his own folk.' The rights and wrongs of the affair were not soldiers' business but Hannah was again reminded of Grizzy's father.

Three days later, when some of the wounded were showing the benefit of rest, a rider from London brought dispatches that threw the surgeon-major and the sergeant-in-charge into hasty conference. The Duke of Monmouth, Pretender to the throne, whose cause had been lost in Scotland, had landed on the south coast of England and the populace was flocking to his standard. James was mobilising a large force to meet the usurper and all the signs pointed to a great battle to be fought before many more days had passed.

The thought that he might miss such a confrontation was exquisite agony to the sergeant who loved the art of war above all else on earth. So plausible were his arguments that the surgeon-major was quite won over to the idea that the sick train should move off forthwith, staying in Newcastle only long enough to place the wounded in the care of the infirmary there while the sergeant and the surgeon, with all fit men, would take ship for London and join King James's troops without delay.

Hannah helped Polly prepare the men for the journey though whatever they might do for them would not lessen the discomfort of travelling in a bumpy cart over rutted roads.

' 'Tis a terrible shame they cannot bide another day or so. The folk here are kind and caring. But our sergeant makes a poor sort of nurse and would have done with this whole train of wounded as soon as may be.'

There was not room in the carts for all the women and some would follow on foot, changing places at the second leg of the journey after spending the night at Morpeth. That the train was going by Morpeth had thrown the surgeon-major out of temper, for he knew of a certain hostelry in Alnwick with a superb cellar and would have preferred to take that alternative route to Newcastle. As the sergeant pointed out, however, they were honour bound to take the shortest route and that, indubitably, was via Morpeth.

When the last man had been helped into the carts and the muskets and powder were stowed safely away; when the orderlies had put on their red coats and formed a line; when the sergeant was astride his frisky chestnut gelding at the rear of the column; the surgeon-major, paunchy in

119

tight breeches and braided tunic, took his place. Mounted on a splendid grey as proud as himself, he raised an imperious white gauntlet for all to see and the shambling cortège of foot soldiers and creaking carts moved off.

Polly had drawn a lucky straw and was up in the cart alongside Rob. Hannah, standing at the roadside by Widow Dodds, looked to her for a last goodbye but Polly had forgotten Hannah. With her legless man beside her propped on a sack of straw, she stared unseeing into the distance, all gaiety gone from her pretty, hopeless face.

The watching women stayed in the road until the last waggon disappeared from sight and the prancing sergeant was swallowed up in dusty distance. The train would cross the ford over the River Breamish below Old Bewick and take the rough track to Percy's Cross and the Morpeth road. There would be many aching bones before shelter for the night was reached.

'Ye did well, Hannah,' the widow nodded approvingly. 'Now, if you will see me home on that nag of thine, I'll split a barrel of herrings which the sergeant gave me and you can take half home to yer ma.'

As Hannah turned aside to saddle up

Dickon, paupers hired by the parish to clear away the rubbish left behind came trudging up the hill with besoms and pails.

That was the end of it, then; three days that had seemed like three weeks and had changed her into a grown-up.

9

There were many in the north of England who had sympathised with the Duke of Argyll's rebellion in Scotland, the nobility excepted. In the view of these more prominent subjects, James's legitimate claim to the Crown could not be denied. His position was unassailable and they would have nothing to do with plots to overthrow him, despite his religion. They would not put one of Charles's bastards on the throne of England though he be a Protestant and as charming a fellow as the Duke of Monmouth undoubtedly was.

Northern gentry such as Sir Walter Heslop of Bewick, the Walton's of High Heugh and others put their faith in the king's coronation oath to respect the religion of the country and were considerably relieved when couriers brought the news of

Monmouth's defeat by the king's forces at the battle of Sedgemoor. They wanted no more revolutions.

'The king has triumphed,' Sir Walter, a man of substance and temperate opinions, told his wife. 'That foolish young man who sought to snatch the crown has paid for his treason with his head. Now we must pray that our faith in James is not misplaced.'

'More heads will roll,' forecast his wife. 'A man of his unforgiving nature will see to it that those who supported the rebellion will suffer.'

Lady Heslop was a woman of considerable stature. She had earned the respect of her household, during the civil war when, as a young bride, she had managed her husband's estate while he was away fighting for the king. At one point, though the household was under siege and suffering considerable hardship, she had defied Cromwell's troops most valiantly. Her acute assessment of James's character was to be quickly proven.

With unbridled savagery, the king exacted full revenge against all who had taken sides against him, beginning with the Duke of Argyll's estate in Scotland. Every house upon it was burned to the ground. Honest labourers who had lived there for many years under the duke's protection paid dearly for their allegiance to him. Three hundred were transported as slaves to the Barbados, some with ears cut off, the women branded on the cheek. The lucky few who escaped sought refuge over the border, taking with them a tale that would be handed down from generation to generation of the rape of Inverary.

Next, it was the turn of the rebels in the west of England who had flocked to join Monmouth when he landed at Torbay. The king set in motion a circuit of assizes to tour Dorset and Somerset, to seek out and try every peasant who had ever held a pitchfork for Monmouth. The man he put in charge was the cruellest judge of all, Judge Jeffreys.

A wave of terror spread through the west country as hangings, drawings and quarterings were carried out without due trial or considered judgement. Carts bearing dismembered bodies trailed their horror across the countryside. Every crossroad had its gibbet with its rotting corpses. Even the nobility of the land who had supported James were stunned by the barbaric licence he allowed. The question in everyone's mind was—what manner of man was their ruler who would permit such atrocities. Such thoughts were not voiced in public, however. Spies were everywhere.

Huguenots who had fled to England from France to escape persecution by a

Catholic king were filled with alarm at rumours filtering down from the court of King James. They prayed that this Protestant island, last bastion of the Faith, would not be corrupted by Catholicism.

The Huguenot glassmakers on the Tyne were old friends of Sir Walter Heslop and of his father before him. Sir Walter fully understood their present apprehension and whenever his business took him to Newcastle an invitation to dine with the glassmakers at their elegant house in nearby Howden was extended to him. Here, in the privacy of their sombre parlour where thick carpets and tapestry-hung walls muffled their discreet voices to little above a whisper, matters of importance could be discussed without fear of being interrupted or overheard.

They met here one brisk October morning, the two senior partners, brothers Hubert and Ernest Gustave, their cousin Guy de Colonnières and Sir Walter, their grave faces reflecting the serious nature of their discussion.

Reports were reaching Newcastle daily of fresh atrocities permitted by King James and of his increasing persecution of Dissenters. But there was another reason for the Huguenots' present anxiety. Louis XIV of France, their implacable enemy, had just revoked the Treaty of Nantes by which, since 1598, some measure of protection was afforded to Huguenots. This gesture of toleration, such as it was, had now been withdrawn and the glassmakers feared greatly for relatives still in German Lorraine as Louis sought to dominate Europe.

The forebears of the glassmakers had fled Paris after the massacre of Protestants on St Bartholomew's Day in 1572. Three families, the Tyteries, Henzels and Tyzacks had accepted an invitation to come to England and set up their industry near the Tyne where there was a plentiful supply of coal for their furnaces. Other members of the Huguenot community took refuge in tolerant Alsace and Lorraine but these lands were now under the control of Louis' armies and there was no safe place anywhere in Europe for Huguenots.

The Gustave brothers were the direct descendants of those early settlers on the Tyne and had recently been joined by their cousin, Guy de Colonnières, from Alsace. At fifty, Guy was much younger than his two sedate cousins and spoke with passion this morning, thumping the table in front of him.

'Even Strasbourg is overrun by Louis! Life is unsupportable for Huguenots. I tell you, he billets his crude soldiers in Protestant homes and gives them licence to do what they will—aye, and even corrupt the wife and daughters if they so wish—until the wretched family swears to convert to popery.'

He mopped his brow with a pocket handkerchief. The room was hot, for despite the autumn sunshine pouring through the window, a fire burned in the hearth. Guy had already stripped to his elegant shirtsleeves, all ruffles and fancy bands. The older men had removed their wigs and sat with waistcoats unbuttoned, reflectively puffing on their pipes.

'My cousin Albert and his son are not allowed to practise their trade and so are prevented from making a living. Their goods have been confiscated and my cousin's wife is in delicate health. I beg you, gentlemen, to help them as you so nobly helped me. Albert is a skilled glassblower and his son has great talent fashioning beautiful windows of coloured glass. They will not be dead wood here and, I promise, will repay handsomely any benevolence you might show them.'

Sir Walter extended his hand towards Guy. 'Depend upon it. You have my word. I will help in any way I can.' As a young man, he had undertaken the fashionable tour of Europe. A letter of introduction to his father's old friend, Guillaume de Colonnières had enabled the young English nobleman to enjoy the unstinted hospitality of Guy's parents who lived in some style at that time in Lyons. A member of that family was in need of help now and Sir Walter saw his obligation quite clearly. He committed himself as he had done previously when it was Guy himself seeking to escape from Alsace.

Hubert, the elder of the two Gustave brothers, was already embarking upon the details of an escape plan. The bottle of Madeira was pushed out of the way to make room on the table for a map of Europe to be unrolled and displayed.

'Let the skipper put into one of the small northern harbours where no questions will be asked,' suggested Sir Walter. 'Beadnell is such a one.'

Ernest, who had remained silent so far, said drily, 'I do wonder if our cousin doth exchange the frying pan for the fire in leaving Alsace for England.'

'King James hath made a promise concerning the established religion of the country,' Sir Walter said doggedly, 'and will not be allowed to break it.'

Ernest bowed respectfully. 'Then I will try to share your confidence.'

Remote from such affairs of state, the common people of the land went about their seasonal tasks. At Burnfoot, the pig had been killed, the puddings made, the hams hung in the chimney. Hannah's thoughts turned to her imminent departure when she would go out into the world to seek her own living. 'That's the last time I'll drive a bullock to Wooler Fair,' she told herself. 'The last time I'll waterproof the byre. Someone else can do it now.'

Her fifteenth birthday came and went and, as the end of the Martinmas term approached, she prepared herself for the hiring line at Bewick Fair.

'I mean to be mair than somebody's servant,' she told Widow Dodds, 'but I divvent ken what.'

'What's wrong with being a servant?' queried the widow. 'You'll be fed and given a roof ower your head. I canna see owt to quarrel with in that.'

Hannah sighed, 'I would fain write letters for a gentleman than scrub floors for his wife.'

The widow chuckled, 'Such ideas! Where will they take you?'

'Not varry far,' Hannah replied bitterly. 'Girls are expected to do nae more than sew and spin and clean the house. I wish I'd been born a lad.'

Hannah had brought a bundle of tripes for the widow. Mary Robson never forgot others who had no pig to kill. Widow Dodds, pleased as always to see the young girl, had taken her inside the cottage for a warm-up before she rode home in the November fog.

'Thou'rt no lad,' the widow nodded placidly over her posset of warm ale, 'so content thyself with what God made thee. Be not scornful of lowly tasks, hinny, but seek every chance to better thysell. I know thee to have many good parts and if ye can curb thy impatience these will one day bring you to a good station in life, but at Bewick Market in a sennight I doubt ye cannot be too choosy and must perforce take whatever is offered.'

On Hiring Day, Hannah helped Joan and Sarah load up the cart as usual with eggs, butter and cheese and lengths of plaid. Now that the moment of departure was upon her, she could not stay the churning of her stomach and ate no breakfast that morning. Joan, quieter than usual, was not prepared to discuss what opportunities might lie ahead for Hannah and Sarah was inclined to be tearful. Most of the way to Old Bewick was passed in silence.

November 28th, being Hiring Day, was an important day in the year for traders and farmers. The market square was thronging with country folk, well wrapped up against the cold, for there was sleet in the wind and lowering grey skies hid the hills from view. Hannah helped her sisters set up their stall alongside regular stallholders from Eglingham and from further afield, from Wooperton and Beanley, then went to take her place in the hiring line. Farm hands and labourers stood together, each carrying the tool of his craft. The labourer held a shovel, the carter a whip, the woodman a bill and the weaver a wool comb. The women offered nothing but themselves, to be used at their employers' disposition.

Hannah was about to join them when a sudden thought sent her hurrying to a corner of the market place where a fat old body stood gossiping over a basket of dead geese. Suspiciously eyeing Hannah, she was yet loth to turn aside from her crony until Hannah picked up one of the birds from the basket.

'Now then, Hannah Robson. What are ye after? Divvent maul my birds aboot unless ye mean to buy.'

Hannah gave her a winning smile. 'Nought but a feather from its wing, Mistress Fraser, which the bird will not miss since its flying days are over. Neither will the loss of feather spoil the stew.'

'What do ye want a feather for? Some work of the devil, nae doubt.' Hannah Robson was a queer one. Folk had seen her dancing all by herself on Cateran Hill, but then, look who sired her! Bad blood will out.

'To write with,' Hannah wheedled. 'These are fine quills.'

'Aye, take it then.' Goody Fraser was more interested in her neighbour's gossip than in Darkie Robson's forward lass. 'Only one, mind. Folk like a good wing to clean their chimneys with.'

The other girls giggled when they saw Hannah up for hire with a feather stuck behind her ear. 'What's thy trade, Hannah? Flying like a bird?'

'Do ye not ken the sign of a scrivener, dolts!' Hannah answered fiercely, but though foremen came to claim ploughmen and ropemakers, tilers and ditchers, nobody seemed in need of a clerk. Other girls were led away by haughty ladies and screw-eyed housekeepers but no one came near the cross-looking girl with the goose feather stuck in her black hair. A tedious hour passed during which the sympathetic glances from Joan and Sarah only added to her mortification.

Lady Heslop of Bewick Grange was a regular customer at the Burnfoot stall for Joan's cloth and Mary's fichus. She knew Hannah to be a sharp and lively girl and it was with a gleam of interest in her brown beady eye that she picked her way through the puddles to the hiring line.

She was a tall woman at any time but today, in her pattens, she towered above the diminutive Hannah.

'Are you seeking employment, Hannah?' She was prepared to engage this girl if a place could be found within the domestic requirements of the Grange.

'Yes, my lady.'

'How old are you?' The girl was undersized but looked healthy enough. No sign of consumption.

'Turned fifteen and 'tis time I sought my own living.' She pointed to the quill behind her ear. 'I am a clerk and this is my badge.'

Lady Heslop could not suppress a titter. 'Are you indeed! Well, I will see what can be done. I will visit your mother within the next day or two.'

Thankfully, Hannah took the feather from her hair and returned to her sisters.

'Will Lady Heslop engage thee, Hannah? I saw her stop by thee.'

'She promises some employment though I'm not sure what.'

Hannah was cutting peat with Sarah a few days later when Joan's 'Coo-ee' called them back to the house.

'There's a horse tied up outside,' said Sarah. 'We've got a visitor.'

Hannah recognised the decorated pommel and bridle of the handsome bay. ' 'Tis my Lady Heslop. Come about my situation, I shouldn't wonder.'

Inside the cottage, Mary, in a welter of embarrassment was trying to quieten the screams of an indignant Benjamin who was determined to get his hands on the fine plumed hat lying on the table. She turned in relief as Hannah and Sarah appeared at the door. My lady sat stiffly upright in Nicholas's chair, waiting for peace to be restored.

'Come, Ben. Come to Jo-Jo.' The cripple edged forward and took the fretful child from its mother.

Hannah, her mother thought despairingly, looked like a witch, her unbound black hair in a cloud about her dirty face, smock and bare legs soiled with peat. 'Wash your hands and face, Hannah,' she snapped. 'Lady Heslop has come to see thee and you looking like a beggar girl.'

Hannah, serene in the knowledge that this was her affair, was unmoved. 'My lady kens as well as any that ye canna keep clean when ye're working in clarts.' She dropped a perfunctory bob before following Sarah to the pump.

'Wait till she goes!' tittered Sarah. 'Ye won't half get wrong for answering back.'

Mary was indeed aghast at Hannah's

effrontery. Lady Heslop, however, seemed not to have taken offence but nodded agreeably, suppressing a tiny yawn in an exquisitely embroidered handkerchief.

The position offered to Hannah was second laundrymaid at Bewick Grange. She was bitterly disappointed. 'I'll be of more use writing your letters than washing your clothes,' she said shortly.

The response exhausted my lady's patience entirely. An angry flush mounted her fleshy cheeks. She knew very well that the child was bright and for that reason had made the journey to this miserable hovel to offer her help. Nicholas Robson was not one of her husband's tenants. She owed no benevolences to his family. In the face of such ingratitude, she almost withdrew her offer, but the anxiety on the wretched mother's face dissuaded her. She got to her feet, rearranging her long skirt with a swirl of irritation. ' 'Tis time you learned your station, girl,' she snapped.

'She'll come, and gladly,' Mary said grimly, 'and grateful we are for your ladyship's kindness.'

'Very well,' Lady Heslop picked up her hat and riding crop. Ignoring Hannah, she spoke to the mother. 'She will be provided with livery and a good feather bed with three blankets. She will be fed well and given religious instruction. In addition, she will be paid four pounds after one year's service if she prove satisfactory.' She turned to Hannah, standing miserably by. 'You may present yourself to my housekeeper on Sunday coming. Goodday to you, Mistress Robson.'

'Hold her ladyship's horse, Sarah!'

The interview was over and Hannah was left to face the anger of her mother.

Two days later, she left Burnfoot, carrying her small bundle of possessions. Dickon had now passed to Sarah and she must go on foot over the tops to Bewick Grange. Mary had been glad to see the back of her. Let someone else try to hammer some discipline into that obstinate head.

Her mother's rejection no longer bothered Hannah. Childhood devotion had withered away through lack of any response and she set off now across the fell without a backward glance. Strangely, it was her father who came closest to understanding her unhappiness.

He had stopped her at the cottage door. 'What ist that sends ye off with this glum face? All birds leave the nest. 'Tis natural.'

' 'Tis the shape of my future that angers me. I had hoped to be something more than a laundrymaid.'

'Then 'tis up to ye to reach for it,' he had replied. 'There's none will do it for thee.'

135

She recognised the truth of her father's words but the hostility of the world she was about to enter filled her with apprehension. Doors leading to better prospects were closed against her and her resources for gaining entry were pitifully few.

With Burnfoot and her sister left behind, she was aware of total aloneness as never before. She was walking away from them all, from Tom, Mistress Emma, even from Widow Dodds. The morning was almost spent when the fine avenue of beech trees leading to Bewick Grange came into view. Unconsciously, she quickened her step. This was her new home and she must make the best of it. With head high she walked purposefully across the rear courtyard of the mansion where stable boys were making a great noise over currying the horses and swilling the stalls.

'Watch out them ducks divvent gobble thee up,' they called out as Hannah picked her way through a procession of ducks. 'They eat morsels like thee for their breakfast!'

Their banter took on a more malicious tone when Hannah, nose in the air, ignored them. 'Jump for it, Titch!' they yelled and a pailful of liquid manure came streaming in her direction, sending her leaping into the air to avoid splashing her stockings with the noisome douche.

Furiously, she turned on her tormentors. 'Keep your horse shit where it belongs,' she screamed, 'up your arse, you ignorant bastards!' And before a second pailful could follow the first, she leapt for the back entrance of the house and rapped loudly on the door, well aware that she had made a deal of trouble for herself in the future.

A solemn-faced girl with crossed eyes, wearing cap and apron, opened the door and led Hannah silently along a cold stone passage to the housekeeper's office. Hannah's term of service had begun.

10

Work in the laundry began at an early hour each Monday morning. Other serving girls who shared the long dormitory with Hannah were still sleeping soundly when squint-eyed Peg, Hannah's superior in the laundry, came to waken her. Cross and shivering in the chill dark hour before dawn, she pulled the blankets from Hannah with little ceremony.

'Get yersell OOT!' she hissed as Hannah, suddenly exposed, curled up inside her shift. ' 'Tis ye should be first up. Not me. I'm the gaffer of ye and ye'd best not forget it.'

Sleepily, Hannah went to the jug and ewer that was shared by all the girls and splashed a little water over her hands and face.

'Howay,' grumbled Peg who dispensed with such vanities and was already dressed in chemise, skirt and bodice. 'Ye're not going to a ball.'

The rest of the household at Bewick Grange still slept. Trenchant snoring issued from the butler's quarters as the two girls crept down the squeaky back stairs to the kitchen. A vagrant who had found shelter for the night on the rushes by the fireside stirred at the girls' approach and tail-wagging hounds came to nose their skirts as Hannah followed Peg to the pantry.

'Is that wor breakfast?' In some dismay Hannah took the proffered mug of milk.

'We get wor porridge later when we've got the fires going.'

Hannah pulled her shawl close and followed Peg across the yard, her wooden-soled shoes slipping on cobbles still rimed with frost. In the east, the first streak of light in the night sky edged up over the hills, fingering the sodden heather, jewelling the blaeberry bushes. A gorgeous cockerel flapped to the top of a stinking midden to salute the rising sun with ear-splitting clamour and a troop of glad pigs ran chortling from their steamy sty.

'Howay!' nagged Peg relentlessly. 'Div-vent stand there gawping. If them boilers isn't brimful of boiling water by the time the sheets come doon, we'll have wor free time on a Sunday stopped by the housekeeper. She's mean enough for owt.'

While Peg got the fires going beneath each of the boilers with embers from the kitchen hearth, Hannah, with hands numbed by the cold metal of the pump handle, carried pailful after pailful of water to fill them. There was soap to be shredded and lines to be slung across the yard and the nearby meadow before they could join the other girls at breakfast in the servants' hall where porridge, cheese, barley bread and hot milk awaited them. Lady Heslop was as good as her word and kept a good table for her staff.

Heads turned as Hannah came into the hall behind Peg and took a seat at the long benches.

'Stuck-up nobody,' was the thought of the other girls, resenting Hannah's proud aloofness, and 'Would she come easy?' thought the boys. But Hannah was thinking of that other household over the hill where Joan would be stirring the crowdie and her

139

father warming his socks by the fire. Sarah, always last, would still be abed. And her mother? Seeing to Ben, nae doubt, with never a thought for Hannah.

Work in the laundry was hard. Washing for the whole household was taken there to be thumped with a heavy poss-stick, rubbed till the knuckles of the girls' hands were raw. Wringing made their wrists ache. Carrying the heavy baskets of wet linen made their backs ache. At the end of Hannah's first day, which went on till sundown, she was so weary she could scarce drag herself upstairs to bed.

Tuesday was easier. This was the day set aside for fine laundering which was much less now than in the days when six daughters were at home. Then, Peg told Hannah, there would be six or seven dresses, petticoats and fancy drawers, embroidered mantles, all flimsy-flamsy stuff. Nowadays, with only Lady Ursula at home with her mother, the Tuesday load was light although there was always a frilled shirt for Sir Walter who insisted upon a change every week.

All laundry must be dry for folding on Wednesday. On Thursday it was mangled and any gophering was done on Friday. By Friday afternoon the weekly cycle was completed. Peg set off hopefully for an assignment with a lusty lad in the hay

140

at the back of the barn leaving Hannah, with her swollen feet soaking in a pail of hot water, to contemplate her first week at Bewick Grange.

About her, the scoured stone flags steamed faintly in the weak December sunshine. Sheets airing on the indoor lines swung lazily in the draught from the open door. The copper boilers, burnished so that you could see your face in their rosy gleam, stood with lids askew to let in the air. Mops, pails, brushes, clouts, all clean, laid out in a neat row, ready for Monday when the ritual would begin all over again.

The life of a laundrymaid, Hannah decided, was tedious beyond belief and very hard work. She wished with all her heart that she was back at Burnfoot, herding sheep.

She was to discover, however, that Saturdays brought a welcome change. Sir Walter was in the habit of inviting friends to dine on a Sunday and, on that day also, her ladyship saw that every servant was treated to a good dinner of roast meat and dumplings followed by cakes and ale. Hannah found that she was required to help Mrs Nan, the cook, with the preparation each Saturday. She did this willingly enough, happy to take a rest from Peg's mean tongue.

The kitchen was huge, big enough to contain the whole of her father's cottage bar the chimney. Wooden dressers, their shelves filled with platters, meat covers, porringers and pitchers occupied most of the wall space and racks for spoons and knives. In her mother's kitchen there was but one sharp knife and that well worn away with the stone.

The spit on the ample hearth was big enough to turn a full-grown pig and the long working table made from the trunk of an ancient oak would have borne the weight of an ox. From the high rafters hung venison and hams, strings of onions and dried apple rings. The stone shelves of the great larder were neatly stacked with pickles and preserves and on the floor stood tall earthenware bins, like those Daniel made from coiled clay, fitted with wooden lids. These, Mrs Nan told her, kept the bread fresh and wholesome from one baking to the next.

Mrs Nan herself was the greatest comfort to Hannah. Fat and easy-going, unashamedly lazy, she was of such an amiable temper that Hannah was put at her ease on her very first day. She was an extraordinary shape. There was no telling where bosom ended and belly began nor at what point the legs might make contact with this unimaginable trunk. Always on the brink of merriment, her fat, dimpled cheeks a-tremble on the verge of laughter, her brown eyes were never without sparkle. Laughter was infectious in Mrs Nan's kitchen. It was not only when she was peeling onions that Hannah had to dab her eyes.

Kitchen chores here were a pleasure and Hannah did not mind in the least when Mrs Nan would collapse perspiring on the settle, as she often did, leaving Hannah to do all the work. The attraction seemed mutual. After one merry interlude when their imagination ran riot over the anatomy of the gingerbread men they were making, Mrs Nan was left gasping for breath.

'Oh my! If thou'rt not the greatest treasure a body could ask for! I'm going to have ye oot that laundry and into my kitchen permanent. Just ye bide a bit.'

Lady Heslop was surprised and somewhat gratified by the cook's request. Her own judgement in employing the girl was thus justified despite her disastrous performance in the laundry. Indeed, Mrs Nan should have permanent help for she suffered terribly from the dropsy. If Mrs Nan had taken a fancy to the Robson girl, she could have her.

So Hannah was moved from laundry-maid to kitchenmaid. No great promotion, she told herself, but her world had suddenly become a happier place. Mean Peg could find someone else to bully. She, Hannah, was happy to be Mrs Nan's right hand.

There was not a single department of the household at Bewick Grange where Lady Heslop's influence was not keenly felt. From the dairy to the sewing room, vegetable garden to medicine chest, her rules prevailed. A formidable woman in every way. Broad-bosomed, stately as a galleon, she controlled the household with firm benevolence. Although she was now in her sixtieth year, her energies had not slackened. The welfare of her servants was her particular concern. Every spring, she dosed them against worms and fevers with medicines of her own making. She assisted the women in childbirth and gave instruction upon rearing their infants. Situations in her life were dealt with in the same forthright fashion that had earned her husband's respect during the civil war. Now, when he was increasingly concerned with affairs at court, he was happy to leave all domestic affairs to his estimable wife.

The marriage, launched in the troubled waters of revolution, developed into a partnership of mutual respect. She bore him six daughters but, to their great sadness, no son arrived to carry on the honourable name. When Hannah joined the establishment, all the daughters were suitably married and gone from the home except Ursula, the youngest.

Conceived at a time when Lady Heslop believed herself to be past the age of childbearing, Ursula lacked the quick intellect of her mother and the stable personality of her father. She was undeniably plain, into the bargain, and any prospective husband would reasonably expect a handsome dowry for taking such a daughter off their hands.

Hannah met her for the first time in the herb garden. Hearing voices close at hand, Hannah straightened from the clump of parsley which had managed to survive winter's frosts and came face to face with the young lady whom she knew to be the Lady Ursula. Her mistress's daughter had been talking to her little dog and jumped with fright at Hannah's sudden appearance.

'Forgive me, my lady,' Hannah bobbed. 'I did not mean to affright ye so,' for indeed, Ursula's protruding light blue eyes seemed about to pop out of her head. But she recovered herself and Hannah would have taken herself off had not Ursula stayed her with a hand upon her sleeve.

'Do not hasten away, little maid. May I know thy name?'

' 'Tis Hannah, my lady. Pray excuse me for the cook awaits this parsley for a stew.' So saying, Hannah grabbed the herbs and withdrew, uncomfortably aware of the disappointment she had caused by her brusqueness. She had heard talk in the servants' hall that this daughter was half-witted. Perhaps that was so. All Hannah had seen was a lonely young woman and she felt ashamed at her flight.

Happy in her work in the kitchen, Hannah became more kindly disposed towards the other serving girls and they, in turn, were prepared to be friendly. One or two of the stable lads attempted to carry friendship too far for her liking, but a little hot broth spilled down a neck while she served them at table invariably put a stop to wandering hands. The scratch down the face of one more bold than the rest who cornered her in the woodshed was enough to deter his more prudent fellows.

'Thou'rt a perky one!' chortled Mrs Nan. 'I declare every one of them lads is ready to lick thy boots if ye'll let him.'

Hannah shrugged. 'Boys are stupid. I canna be fashed with their silly ways.'

'Ye'll not catch a husband that way.'

Deftly, Mrs Nan disembowelled a pile of rabbits.

'I divvent want a husband,' said Hannah. 'I'll make my own way and take no man for my master.'

The cook sniffed. 'So ye say now.'

Hannah looked up from the cabbages she was shredding. Mrs Nan was fat and greasy, with sparse, untidy hair and a red nose from too much tippling but she must have been young and good to look upon once. 'Do ye have a husband, Mrs Nan?'

'Ye might say I have and ye might say I haven't. I sartainly had one once but I cannot rightly tell if I have one now. He went off and left me when I was but twenty and me with his babby on the way.'

Hannah was aghast. 'And ye've never seen him since?'

The cook tossed her head in a show of bravado. 'Not from that day to this and, if he was to walk in here now, I'd likely slit his throat with this knife. So I would. But he'll be deed by now for sure. On a gibbet as like as not.' With one quick slash she severed a rabbit's head from its body. 'May he rot,' she chuckled wickedly.

'How did ye live, after he left?' Hannah was unable to take her eyes off the jolly butcher at work before her who treated

147

calamity so lightly.

'The parish paid me threepence a corpse to look for signs of the plague and when they ran oot of corpses, they had me filling potholes in the road. Four pence a week they gave me for that. Not enough to keep a cat alive. Then the babby began to show and that was the end of that.'

'How d'ye mean?'

'They threw me oot of me hoose and chased me oot the parish. Oh aye! The good wives as well as their men! They'd no wish to have a pauper's brat as a charge as well as its mother.' Mrs Nan's customary expression of good humour vanished. When she pushed up her lower lip like this and narrowed her eyes, Hannah saw a bitter, ugly woman.

'They ran me oot their parish,' Mrs Nan continued, 'and into the next one. I didna get far for my time had come. I had the bairn under a hedge one bleak morning in March when the dykes were running slush and that's where good Sir Walter found me and fetched me here. Here I've been ever since.'

'What aboot the babby?'

'A little girl. She died. A wet hedge is no place for bringing babbies into the world.'

148

'Oh, Mrs Nan.' Hannah laid down her knife and dabbed her eyes with her apron as the tears ran down her cheeks.

The cook looked up in surprise. 'Now the Lord save me if the little thing isn't as soft-hearted as a kitten! Tush, child, it all happened long ago.' Mrs Nan was her usual self again. 'No call for anyone to shed tears over me. Now hurry with them vegetables for I'm waiting to make the pies.'

She regarded Hannah thoughtfully as the girl hastened to do her bidding. 'Take heed of my story, hinny. That's how the world treats a poor woman on her own.' There was fondness in her glance. 'Ye've got summat to learn aboot life afore ye go making grand plans. It's like climbing yon fell.' She waved her knife at the window. 'Ye no sooner pull yersell oot of one bog when ye're up to the hocks in another and there's not many folk like the master and mistress here who'll put out a helping hand. You mun pray to the Lord Almighty, lass, for He's your only help. And sometimes He's too busy to help an' all.'

'If I were to get doon on my knees at this minute,' said Hannah, ' 'twould be to beg the Lord to give men a turn with the womb, for there never was such a handicap that He has given to women.'

149

'Some women rejoice in the womb,' Mrs Nan sniffed. 'They sit at home and coddle it and bring forth children like a row of peas in a pod.'

'Like a sow with her litter.'

' 'Tis different when ye fall in love,' Mrs Nan conceded, her eye wandering for a moment from the rabbits in the fleeting thrall of remembered romance.

'Love has nowt to do with it!' Hannah protested. 'My father cares not for my mother. He beats her.'

Mrs Nan gave up. ' 'Tis a hard world for women,' she agreed. 'Now let's have them carrots.'

The kitchen at Bewick Grange was a sociable place. Sir Walter's orders were that no traveller, be he ever so humble, be turned away without food and drink. Strangers warming themselves at the fire were a common sight. Pedlars selling needles and laces, buttons and sticks of licorice, tinkers and their pots, all were old friends of Mrs Nan and would join her in a jug of ale or something a mite stronger. The flush on her cheeks was not always due to the heat of the fire.

Their tales were of the adventures that had befallen them as they travelled the length and breadth of the kingdom, of swamps where a man could sink up to his knees and his bundle disappear from sight, and open heaths alive with highwaymen. They told of towns like London, crammed tight with people all making a living from selling and buying. Though scarce twenty years had passed since the Great Fire reduced London to ashes, so many new dwellings had been built, each squeezed against its neighbour, that there was scarce room in the narrow streets to lead a donkey.

Hannah, working quietly nearby, missed not a word.

More furtive-looking men came from time to time, men who took their food hurriedly, ever and anon casting anxious looks over their shoulders.

'Dissenters,' sniffed Mrs Nan, 'for the long drop if they're caught. Never ye breathe a word, my girl, for our master's in mortal danger if it be known he befriends these outlaws.'

Hannah was on the point of telling the cook of her good friends, Master and Mistress Reay who were Dissenters, then she thought better of it and held her peace. News of the potter was to come, however, from an unexpected source before many days had passed.

Hannah was coming from the henhouse with an apron full of eggs when she encountered Ed Freeman unloading his

151

wagon of peastraw in the yard.

'Why, Master Freeman! Here's a face I know. What brings thee here?'

The carter had not expected such a welcome. 'As to my face, why, I'm glad it pleases for I have none other to offer, but my business is best left as a matter between thy master and me.' With a huge wink he lifted a firkin of brandy from its place of concealment under the straw. 'Come, sit ye doon awhile aside me for I have news for thee.'

Mrs Nan nodded acquiescence. Ed was a regular and a popular visitor. 'Sit ye doon with yer supper, hinny,' she told Hannah, 'and have a bit crack with Ed.'

The carter brought sad news from Buckton. 'I met thy brother at Belford Market Tuesday sennight and he bade me tell thee how the potter, his master, is thrown into prison by the officers of the king. Spies, it seems, did inform against him that conventicles were held at his house. They were all caught at their devotions and taken off to prison, the preacher, the potter and all who worshipped there.'

'What of my brother? What of Mistress Emma?' A terrible fear gripped Hannah.

'By the grace of God, they were not taken. Mistress Emma was in the byre seeing to a sick cow, otherwise she would be with her man in Morpeth jail. Thy brother and his marrer were busy at the kilns and not accused with the rest. They are left to carry on the potter's trade until he returns—if he returns,' he added darkly, 'for King James detests nothing so much as a Dissenter.'

Stunned, Hannah could only whisper, 'My poor Mistress Emma! She will be grieving so.'

' 'Tis as I told thee, Hannah,' Mrs Nan interrupted gruffly, 'this king will have the liberty of every Dissenter in the country and of everyone who helps them. A close mouth, my girl. Heed my warning! Eddie's right. Spies are everywhere.'

Hannah could think of nothing but the genial potter languishing in prison and of his despairing wife. 'I beg thee to remember me to Mistress Reay through my brother when next you meet him, Master Freeman.'

'Your brother, in his turn, asks me to report upon his little sister and how she fares in service at a noble house,' said Ed. 'What am I to say, other than that ye are the bonniest lass I ever set eyes on, my oath.' In very truth, Darkie Robson's skinny little brat had taken on the looks of a quite bewitching damsel. His eyes strayed to the white bosom swelling above her bodice.

Hannah brushed away the groping hand from her knee and meaningfully bunked a few inches further down the bench. Giggling foolishly, Ed took the rebuff in good part.

'All men are bad, hinny,' he counselled her. 'Have nowt to do with any of them.'

Mrs Nan roared with approval. 'Sartainly divvent trust this one!'

The carter got to his feet wiping his mouth clean of froth from the ale. 'Mebbes I'll take thee to Belford with me one day to see thy brother, if ye'll trust an old rogue that far.'

Hannah tossed her head. 'No more nor less than I'd trust me grandfather if I had one.' Ed Freeman, who she had known since she was a baby, presented no threat to her.

'Grandfather is it?' Ed put on a mournful face. 'And me in me prime.'

'Will he come again, Mrs Nan?' asked Hannah, sad to see the carter go.

'He will,' Mrs Nan spoke with conviction, 'for the master will not go short of his brandy and tobacco.'

'He's a smuggler, isn't he?'

'Whisht!' Mrs Nan said crossly. 'D'ye want to see the little fella strung up on a gibbet? Folks round here would be in a poor way without Ed Freeman, I can tell ye. Without his drop of brandy to keep oot

154

the cold in winter, the churchyards would be gey full.'

There was a flurry at Burnfoot when the arrest of the potter became known.

'That's Hannah's God-fearing man for you.' Nicholas chose the occasion to drive home a lesson to his family. 'Grace-before-meals and family prayers did him no good when he went against the law in the manner of his worship.'

'Who's to say which religion is the right one?' Joan unexpectedly challenged him. She was twenty-one years old now and lately her father had noticed this streak of defiance in her hitherto compliant nature. 'It seems to me that what is right one year is wrong the next,' she went on. 'Ist God who changes His mind, d'ye think?'

'Hush, Joan!' Her mother was horrified at such outspokenness.

'We'll have nae more of this talk,' her father growled. 'Look at the land around ye. The birch tree bends with winter's storms and lives on. The ash that stands fast is torn up by the roots in a tempest. Take heed, woman. Seek not to oppose the law, even in thy thoughts. Thy prayers, when and how ye choose to say them, should be for thy brother Tom, that he be not infected with his master's base religion.'

11

Sir Walter rarely visited the kitchen and Hannah was taken by surprise one day when, looking up from the dough she was pounding, she was confronted by this handsomely dressed gentleman. Genially, he put them at their ease as Hannah followed Mrs Nan's example and dropped a hasty curtsy.

'My lord.' Mrs Nan pulled up a chair and wiped it clean with her apron. 'Wilt take a glass of brandy?'

Hannah had not had the opportunity to observe her master at such close quarters before and she was impressed with the strong, handsome features of a man who was no longer young.

'Brandy, Hannah,' hissed Mrs Nan, jolting her out of her reverie and sending her scuttling to the cupboard where such spirits were kept.

'I have a favour to beg of thee, Mrs Nan,' Sir Walter began, 'to extend your warm hospitality to some rather unusual guests who may arrive at any time, more than likely in the middle of the night.'

'Sartainly, sir.' Mrs Nan was unmoved.

Her loyalty to her benefactor was unquestioning and total. 'Whatever ye want, will be my pleasure.'

'You may not understand their speech for they are French by birth.'

'Mercy on us!' Despite herself, the cook caught her breath. The French were well known to be demons. Whatever next!

'They are devout people who flee from the persecutions of the Catholic king who has overrun their land.' Sir Walter continued, cosseting his brandy glass in the warmth of his hand. 'I cannot say in what unhappy plight they may arrive. The lady in their party will surely be exhausted after a perilous journey across land and a sea trip in a small boat. They will be brought secretly to our shores and I must ask you not to speak of this matter to anyone or we may be responsible for their imprisonment by the militia.' He looked up. Mrs Nan and Hannah nodded vigorously. 'They will be in need of warm food and a good night's rest.' He sipped his brandy reflectively. 'The housekeeper is preparing accommodation for them in the east wing and I would ask you to serve them in their rooms as soon as possible after their arrival.'

'Yes, my lord. Hannah and me will see to that.'

For the first time, Sir Walter turned his

attention to the dark little maid standing quietly by Mrs Nan with floury dough still sticking to her arms, and wondered fleetingly where his wife had found her. He got up to go. 'Remember, they have done no wrong. Their only crime is that they are Huguenots.'

After he had gone, Hannah looked across at Mrs Nan. 'What in heaven's name is a Hugono?'

They came a fortnight later on a moonless night when the strip of water that separated England from Europe was lashed into mountainous waves by wild March winds. The butler and the housekeeper had done their night rounds, checked the fires and snuffed out the candles. The great doors were bolted and barred when a rider came thundering up the drive to tell Sir Walter that the ketch from Amsterdam had landed.

The watch had just cried the hour of midnight when Hannah was awakened by Mrs Nan shaking her roughly by the shoulder.

'Wake up, lass, and get yersel dressed. Them furriners have landed at Seahouses and the master's away with a coach and pair to meet them.'

Mrs Nan by the light of a candle was a fearsome enough sight to rouse any girl

158

from slumber. Red-rimmed and rheumy eyes peered through a tangle of grey hair. Her dewlap trembled with agitation. With her free hand she held aloft the folds of her long flannel nightshift disclosing ankles distorted and overhung by the dropsy. Hannah sat up.

'They'll be here within the hour,' Mrs Nan urged. 'I mun put me claes on.'

Hastily donning skirt and apron, Hannah made her way downstairs in the company of a chambermaid who had been roused to light fires in the guests' apartments and put hot bricks in the beds. Pantry boys were already busy with bellows at the fire when Hannah entered the kitchen.

'Shred some mutton into the pot, Hannah,' Mrs Nan called out from the little room adjoining the kitchen where she slept. 'Sweet Jesu! I've lost me stockings! And a tasting of marjoram, handful of onions, barley to thicken. Oh! The uproar in me bowels. It'll take a fair drop of brandy to set me right this night and no mistake.'

In a matter of minutes, the kitchen was transformed from its night-time stillness to a scene of busy preparation. Tapers lit up the shadows and sent the puzzled hounds to seek oblivion under the table. Logs on the hearth crackled and blazed under Hannah's cooking pots.

' 'Tis a foul night.' One of the stableboys

had been sent to set a lighted flare at the end of the drive to aid the travellers and now stood drying himself off by the fire. 'They'll be froze to the marrow when they come, I shouldn't wonder.'

Lady Heslop herself appeared, wrapped in a fur-trimmed mantle. 'What can you offer the visitors, Mrs Nan?'

'Good mutton broth, my lady. Cold sirloin of beef with pickled plovers' eggs. Fresh-baked bread and compote of apples, if it please you.'

The butler, in immaculate livery—Hannah wondered if he slept in it—approached Lady Heslop carrying a decanter and glasses on a silver tray.

'In the hall, Johnson. By the fire.'

All was ready and most of the household awake although the watch had just told two of the clock when the doors were thrown open and Sir Walter led in his guests; two men, one younger by many years than the other, both heavily cloaked and, on Sir Walter's arm, a poor pale lady who seemed scarcely strong enough to walk across the hall to the seat that awaited her by the fire.

'She's fair gone,' breathed Mrs Nan in Hannah's ear as they stole a peep through the door, 'and wet through the lot of them.'

When, a little while later, Hannah carried

food to their apartments, the woman was nowhere to be seen.

'Madame has retired.' The older man, speaking in heavily accented English, indicated the bedroom. 'I will serve her.'

Both men had taken off their wet outer garments and sat close to the blazing fire. Unwigged and in disarray though they were, their dress was enough to proclaim them gentlefolk. The lace failing from neckband and wrist of their soiled and crumpled shirts was of the finest quality, but it was the beauty of the younger man's face that held Hannah's eye as she laid food before them. Heroic statues in Sir Walter's garden bore such features as his, the straight nose and finely curved nostrils, the shapely head set so proudly on a slender neck. He was about Tom's age, she guessed, but there any similarity ended. The hand that took the bowl of soup from her was long and narrow. Laces fell back to reveal a wrist as slim and white as a maid's.

She banked up the fire, moved the brandy bottle closer and bade them a good night's rest.

'I wouldn't want the job of laundering their shirts,' was her report to Mrs Nan.

The visitors stayed abed until the afternoon of the following day when they arose, looking considerably refreshed to take a light dinner before their cousin Guy de Colonnières came with a carriage to fetch them. The meeting was emotional, their thanks to Sir Walter and Lady Heslop heartfelt.

The sight of the two ladies in animated conversation by the waiting coach, each speaking in a language unintelligible to the other, brought a smile to Hannah's lips as she crossed the yard to the barn. When she returned a few moments later with her bag of turnips, she saw that the honours had gone to Lady Heslop who had clinched the matter by shouting louder than the little foreign lady.

As Hannah made for the kitchen, she almost collided with the young man of the party, hurrying, head down against the wind. He stopped short at the encounter, meeting her eye. Gravely, he raised his beaver hat. Recollecting herself in time to make a quick bob, Hannah turned to watch him cross to the carriage. Kitchenmaids were rarely accorded such courtesies and she was left with a warm feeling at the compliment.

When the lady had been settled within amidst rugs and cushions and the travellers' possessions stacked away on top of the carriage, Guy de Colonnières spoke for them all as he shook Sir Walter warmly by the hand.

'England is our refuge,' he said with utmost sincerity, 'and will have our loyalty from henceforth. She will not regret opening a door for Huguenots.'

'You bring your talents with you,' Sir Walter answered. 'England is the richer for your weaving, your silk and glass manufacture. 'Tis not a bad bargain for England.'

At the coach door, Guy lowered his voice. 'I pray with all my heart that such harmony between us will continue. My doubts concerning your Catholic king I keep to myself.'

Sir Walter laid a hand on his shoulder. 'Be comforted. There is a point beyond which Jamie dare not go. And, remember this. He has no heir by this second wife and is not likely to father one now. At his death, the succession passes to his Protestant daughters by his first marriage. So you see, my friend, we have only to wait.' He raised his hand with a signal to the driver. 'Patience and fortitude be our watchwords.'

With a jingling of harness and scraping of carriage wheels, the coach, with its inscription—HENZEL, TYZACK AND TYTERIE. GLASSMAKERS—artistically painted on the back, set off down the tree-lined drive.

Spring stole over the countryside and the lanes around Bewick Grange were starred with golden celandine. One day when Hannah's work was done, she was preparing to take a walk when Mrs Nan bore down upon her, a clothbound book in her hand and she saw, from the glint in the cook's eye, that Mrs Nan had other ideas for her.

'Answer me this, Hannah, for ye make yersell oot to be a scholar of sorts; is a trader a rogue or a genius who sells a book to a body who canna read?'

Hannah laughed outright, for she saw straight through Mrs Nan's deviousness. 'Why, Mrs Nan, I do suspect you want me to read to you this tale sold by a crooked genius and indeed it would please me to do so.' Travelling pedlars often brought tuppenny chapbooks for sale but Hannah, having no money, could not buy them.

She took the book. 'By the looks of it, this will keep us occupied for many a day.' The print was small and closely written. 'Come, Mrs Nan, we'll make a start.'

With great satisfaction, Mrs Nan settled her great bulk on the bench outside the kitchen door where a wall cut off the wind but allowed the sunshine in. Hannah drew up a milking stool for herself and, with scavenging hens clucking about her feet, began to read.

Sir Walter, passing by a little later, was struck by curiosity. 'Nay,' he motioned them to remain seated, 'pray do not let me disturb your pleasure. What ist you read, little maid, that so enthrals our worthy cook?'

The incident stuck in Sir Walter's mind. 'We have a maid in the kitchen,' he told his wife, 'who reads John Bunyan's *Pilgrim's Progress* to the cook. 'Twould seem she deserves a more worthy employment than peeling onions for old Baggy Nan.'

'I am of the same mind, my lord.' Lady Heslop was quick to acknowledge the truth of his remark. 'Yet we will incur Nan's awful wrath if we take her away for the two, ill-matched though they may seem are good company for each other.'

'Where didst find the lass? She hath a familiar look about her, yet I cannot exactly place her.'

'She's one of Nicholas Robson's brood at Burnfoot,' she told him, 'with a will of her own, like her father, but she managed the trading at their stall in Bewick Market very well and hath a quick brain, to be sure.'

'Maybe,' said her husband thoughtfully, 'when Ursula is indisposed...'

'Which is often,' cut in his wife.

'...the girl might read aloud to her, enlivening an hour or two for our poor daughter.'

Hannah's qualities had not gone unnoticed by Lady Heslop. Of the group of tittering wenches whom she endeavoured to instruct in reading and writing, only Hannah showed genuine interest and application. Remembering the child's disappointment when she was first hired as a laundrymaid, Lady Heslop was honest enough to admit to herself that Hannah would indeed make an adequate clerk. She resolved, therefore, that the girl must be helped to improve herself, in spite of Mrs Nan's undoubted opposition.

In truth, Mrs Nan was not pleased when the occasional summons came for Hannah to attend Lady Ursula in her room. 'Leaving me, with my feet the shape they're in, to do all the fetching and carrying. See to it that ye come back as soon as ye can.'

Hannah looked forward to these diversions as did the sickly Lady Ursula, who greeted her with pleasure every time she appeared. In lacy cap and beribboned nightgown, the wan figure raised herself from her pillows and stretched thin arms towards her visitor.

'Dearest Hannah, you will shift the ache in my head better than all my mother's potions. Come sit by me and pass the time with stories.'

To be greeted thus warmly touched Hannah deeply and helped her to contain the impatience which sometimes rose within her when confronted by her mistress's frequently foolish behaviour. In any case, to sit in clean cap and apron on a softly padded stool in an elegantly furnished bedroom while she read from any book she chose to borrow from Sir Walter's extensive library was bliss indeed.

When Lady Heslop saw them like this together, Hannah with neat black braids framing a lively face rosy with health alongside dough-faced Ursula, she felt sorely cheated. Had the roles been reversed, suitors would be battering the door down to seek the hand of her daughter, whereas the truth was that, if a husband was to be found at all, Ursula's dowry would need to be greatly increased and that before many more months had passed lest a more disagreeable situation developed. Ursula's devoted attendance on the gardener's boy had not gone unnoticed.

Hannah saw that an opportunity to improve herself was at last within her grasp when Lady Heslop informed her that she would be entrusted with the marketing on the following day. She would take the pony and trap and a list of requirements from housekeeper and cook and would be judged on her performance.

Mrs Nan was surprised and not a little proud that her Hannah could be trusted with a purse of money, but there was some resentment amongst other servants who had been in the employ of Sir Walter long before Hannah—especially when Hannah, unable to resist a little bragging, was more than a little condescending when she asked, 'Is there owt at the market I can get for ye lasses?'

Part of Hannah's excitement lay in the fact that she could see her sisters again and hear the news from Burnfoot, perhaps news of Tom and of Master Reay. Six months had passed since the potter had been taken by the militia and thrown into Morpeth prison where, as everyone knew, conditions were vile. Pray God he might be released soon. As she flicked up the pony and bowled smartly along the Bewick road, it pleased her to see kerchiefed serving girls turn and stare. Who could this be, they would be thinking, driving Lady Heslop's trap, unmistakable with its coat of arms and padded leather seats? Hannah smiled to herself, imagining what they might say. 'Why, that's Darkie Robson's lass. She's come up in the world and nae mistake!'

'Why, Hannah!' Sarah gasped in surprise, 'How grown up ye are!'

'That's a bit of good stuff,' Joan fingered Hannah's cloak. 'Ye did right to leave home and better thyself. We go on much the same at home with Father's tempers and Mother's tears. Thou'rt missed, Hannah, for all thy wilfulness.'

There was more change in Hannah than in themselves. Six months at Sir Walter's generous table had worked wonders. There was about her a glow of health and she had assumed a certain dignity that befitted Lady Heslop's deputy at the market.

'Wor Ben fell in the burn and var nigh droonded,' chattered Sarah, 'and now he has the croup.'

'I make all the potions for Widow Dodds now,' said Joan. 'The parish pays me sixpence a week for helping her, and Father's brother, our Uncle Samuel, who he has not seen these forty years, paid us a visit.'

'He's nice,' piped up Sarah, 'not cross like wor da and he says we're to visit him on Tyneside.'

'We've two cousins there,' said Joan, 'that we know nought of.'

'What news of Tom and his master, the potter?'

'Ed brings news that Tom and the other apprentice are looking after the business. Master Reay is still in prison and in bad health.'

169

' 'Tis not right,' Hannah frowned. 'The poor man has done no wrong in the eyes of the Lord.'

'Seemingly, 'tis the eyes of the king that count for more in these times,' Joan spoke with bitterness. 'Were I a man, sound in wind and limb, I swear I'd find fellows of a like mind and lead them to London to chop off his head, the like of his father.'

'Why, Joan,' Hannah was astonished, 'art become a ranter then?'

'Nay,' Joan said shortly, 'nor a windbag. Have ye come for her ladyship's shawl? I have it ready.'

'What about me ma? I did not ask about me ma.' The oversight was intentional but, in spite of herself, Hannah found herself enquiring.

'Her pains are bad,' said Joan. 'Widow Dodds says she's got a prolapse.'

'What's a prolapse?'

'Her insides are coming down because Ben was too big for her to have borne.'

'Holy Jesus! Whatever next! What's to be done?'

'The widow pushed them back and keeps them there with a contraption but she still gets pains.'

Hannah turned to Sarah. 'Do ye help the da in my place?'

'Oh aye, and I get the strap in your place too. I cannot wait to get away from home like you did, Hannah. You look so fine in your smart claes and your pony trap.'

Truly, Hannah reflected as she drove back to the Grange later that afternoon, her circumstances had changed for the better. From the bottom of her heart she pitied her sister, Joan, who must be confined to Burnfoot for the rest of her life.

12

Hannah's firm bargaining and scrupulous accounting won unqualified approval from Lady Heslop. After that first occasion, she was frequently given the task of marketing. The first market of the Michaelmas term was always well attended. All the fruits of autumn were here, apples rosied with a rub, chestnuts, cobs and walnuts. In the makeshift pens, live pigs, squawking their last before slaughter, added their squeals to the hubbub. Hannah was here to buy all that Joan had to offer.

Meeting with her sister and with other old friends such as Widow Dodds had become a regular occurrence and it was while she was talking with the old nurse that Hannah was reminded of Lady Ursula's ill health.

'She is sorely troubled with the bile from time to time, Mistress Dodds. Canst give me a cure for her?'

' 'Twill be the green sickness ye speak of,' said the widow, 'and will mend when she has her first baby. Is she wed?'

'No. She is twenty and one years old and has no suitor even.' Hannah paused. 'In very truth, I do believe it is the green sickness for her skin does take on a most horrid greenish hue at these times.'

'I will bring thee a potion of elderflowers and dill seed that will relieve her. If she is sore distressed, do you put her in a bath of warm water in which crush a bulb of garlic, yet this will not work so well as her first lying-in.'

'Then I pray for a suitor for the poor thing,' said Hannah.

Some commotion was distracting the widow's attention. 'Look yonder,' she nudged Hannah with her elbow. 'Excisemen.' Uniformed men on horseback were approaching the market place at a quick trot. 'Looking for trouble,' the widow sniffed, 'and they'll nae doot find it.'

At that moment, a young man sprinted through the market at such speed that Hannah could only be certain of one thing, that he had red hair.

'Stop that man!' the officers called out

172

and brought their horses cantering up in a cloud of dust, scattering hens and dogs and children. At the same time, Ed Freeman appeared from nowhere and dived under the widow's capacious skirts, almost knocking her off balance before taking cover under Joan's stall, quite hidden by draped lengths of plaid.

'Not a word,' he hissed to the startled women, 'or I'm a dead man.'

Hurrriedly dismounting, the excisemen ran through the market square, knocking folk off their feet, upsetting stalls, and the women, protesting loudly as they retrieved their dishes of potted meat and fat round cheeses from the dust, somehow contrived to cause the maximum hindrance.

'Look to yourselves, ye idle loafers.' The red-faced officers turned on the tittering crowd when it was obvious that the quarry had escaped them. 'We be not so blind as some may think. We know your little game and any who dabble in contraband will smartly learn what the inside of His Majesty's prison is like.'

A silence fell. Even the yapping dogs were quiet as the disgruntled excisemen remounted and galloped away. But not for long. No sooner were they out of sight than the hubbub broke out once more and Ed Freeman crawled out from beneath Joan's stall, gallantly planting a grateful kiss on

Widow Dodds's hand.

'The Lord's looking to ye, Ed,' the old goodies called out, 'for He kens well I canna do wi'out my drop of brandy nor yet pay the king's tax on't.'

'Let him tax them as can afford fifty pound for a satin coat like the gentlemen at court, not poor working folk like us.' Labourers and herdsmen who would find it hard to raise fifty pounds in one year by the sweat of their brow went grumbling away and the business of the market was resumed.

Ed took a mug of ale from Joan. 'Didst see a fellow come by here in a hurry ahead of me?'

'Aye,' said Joan, 'a stranger, but I couldna get a peek at him, he was running that fast.'

'He had red hair,' said Hannah.

'Aye,' nodded Ed, 'and not so much of a stranger at that, for he is the son of thine Uncle Samuel that left the land for the sea some time back.'

'A cousin, then?' said Joan with interest.

'He's hereabouts, hiding in the woods nae doubt from those asses that wear the king's uniform. If ye should meet him on thy way home, Hannah, ye could be of service to him. I tellt him ye'd have a cart and would mebbes lift him.'

'And mebbes I won't,' Hannah said

tartly, outraged at the suggestion. 'What would my lady say to that!' Choosing to ignore Ed's crestfallen expression, she took her leave of her sisters and prepared for home.

In the event, the decision as to whether or not she would help her unknown cousin was not left to her. The pony had just settled to a steady pace when a hand reached out from under a pile of produce that she had stowed away earlier in the day and grabbed her by the ankle. As she opened her mouth to scream, a man revealed himself and she knew him at once by the colour of his hair.

'Hold, sweet coz! I mean no harm. Will Robson is my name, the son of thy father's brother and as such I do beg a favour. Drive on, if you will.'

He had something of Tom's open features and a wide, confident smile, but there was an impudence about him that immediately affronted her. She brought the pony to a halt.

'What mischief are ye up to, sitting in my cart?'

'Ssssh!' He held a finger, ringed with gold to his lips. 'Not so loud. The king's men seek me.'

'They've gone,' Hannah said, 'in bad fettle because you and Ed got away.'

He looked relieved. 'They didna get Ed?'

'He hid behind my sister's flannels.'

Her new relation laughed. 'Trust Ed to seek safety under a lassies's skirts!'

'Not her skirts,' Hannah frowned crossly, 'the cloth on her stall. So what are ye doing in my cart, Cousin Will, if so ye be?'

'Prithee, drive on and I will tell thee as we go.' He rolled his eyes appealingly. 'I see by your tender looks that ye have a heart of gold.'

Angrily, Hannah started the pony with her whip and the cart rolled forward once more.

'Take me, for kinship sake, as far as Ed's barn in Eglingham and ye'll have my heart for evermore.' As Hannah's frown deepened, he saw that he must try a different tactic. 'Else my blood will be on thy head, sweet lass and my poor old father dead of grief to lose his only son.'

'Then shouldst thou have thought on him before adventuring thus.' She found his cheery insolence hard to resist, however, and when they reached the turning for Bewick Grange, she put the pony towards Eglingham instead. The deviation was no more than half a league but, 'We'd best make haste,' she said firmly, 'else my mistress will wonder what has become of her servant and her purchases.'

Assured now of a safe passage, Will lay back, half-hidden from sight, amongst the bundles of rope and tubs of tallow, and treated her to an amused inspection from head to toe. 'What's thy name? I've tell't thee mine. Is't "Moon-eyes" mebbes, or "Kiss-me-quick"?'

'My name is Hannah,' she answered tartly, 'and I'll take nae nonsense from thee so keep thy lecherous eyes to thyself.'

' 'Tis nought but my friendly way with maidens,' he sighed, 'forever bringing me trouble.'

For all his banter, Hannah noticed that he kept a sharp eye on the woods and thickets about them. She was curious about this man in spite of her disapproval. 'How will ye go from Eglingham?'

'I'll lie there till night falls then make my way to the sea. My sister's man will come on the late tide for me.'

'Are ye all rogues, then?'

'Aye,' he grinned, 'some of us more than others.'

'My Uncle Samuel?'

'The worst of the lot, but he canna run fast nowadays and sends me in his place to do his business.'

'Yes,' Hannah agreed. 'Ye're fast. Fast as my brother Tom. Does my father ken his brother is a smuggler?'

Will laughed quietly. 'Why, man, he's up to the neck in't himsell. How else would he get his baccy and his spirits?'

'It seems the whole of the land leads the taxman a dance,' said Hannah, remembering Sir Walter's cellar.

Will pulled a wry face. 'The dance will be ours if we're caught, a dance at the end of a rope. So keep this talk to yoursell, little coz.'

'I've a mind to run thee in right away,' Hannah teased. ' 'Tis only that ye resemble my brother a little that I help thee, though he is nae carrot-top. Ye'd do well to dye it black for 'tis a sure giveaway, that poll of thine. But here is Ed's barn and I'll thank thee to climb doon and let me be on my way.' They had come to a halt outside the large barn where the folk of Eglingham stored their fodder in winter. 'Go quickly. There is no one aboot.'

Swift as a shadow, he slipped over the tailboard. 'Farewell Cousin Hannah. I'll not forget thy help.' He was gone in a moment, swallowed up in the dark interior of the barn.

Hannah turned the pony about and made for Bewick Grange at a brisk trot. The day was drawing in and she must be home before dusk. Lawless men preyed on lonely travellers at night and she carried the household purse upon her.

'There's news,' Mrs Nan told her as they unpacked the victuals together. 'A suitor for Lady Ursula has come forward.

A nobleman, they say, and he's coming here for the harvest feast so there's plenty work for thee and me, Hannah, my lass.'

The news seemed to please Ursula. Hannah found her young mistress possessed of a new dignity.

'I have a suitor, Hannah,' she said gravely. 'He is to visit shortly.'

Hannah bobbed. 'If this news gladdens your heart, my lady, then it pleases me also.'

'Of a certainty it gladdens me! Can you think otherwise? All my sisters are married. Now, at last, here is someone who wants me. I am fortunate in that he is a nobleman of excellent family, so I am content, though my heart doth indeed yearn for another who is denied me.'

Hannah knew all about the gardener's boy.

'At the harvest feast, my lord and I will meet and doubtless the betrothal will be arranged at that time.'

This was a new Ursula. Silly, vacillating chatter was replaced by a sensibility of opinion that Hannah had not heard before. As the day of harvest celebration drew near, all who saw Ursula remarked on the new sparkle which lit her face, the fresh colour in her usually wan cheeks.

Every year, as a reward to his tenants

for labour well done and a harvest safely garnered, Sir Walter gave a feast in the great hall of the Grange. The estate consisted of some six hundred acres given over to sheep and goats on the higher slopes, oats, barley, peas and turnips in the low fields. His workforce lived with their families in cottages on the estate for which they paid a rent of twenty shillings a year. Like all wage-earners, they were dependent on the will of their master for their livelihood but Sir Walter's employees had little cause for complaint as their welfare was of continuing concern to him and to his wife.

Preparations for this forthcoming celebration kept Mrs Nan and Hannah, and some extra hands as well, fully occupied for the next few weeks. Special efforts were to be made this year since the company was to be honoured by the presence of that august gentleman, Sir George le Flemont of Budle Hall, suitor to Lady Ursula.

Maids with brooms scoured the high walls of the hall free of cobwebs. Pantry boys were set to clean the family silver which Cromwell's men had failed to find, an exquisite punchbowl and wonderfully wrought candlesticks, the set of figurines that the young Sir Walter had brought back from his tour of Germany.

The master and the butler spent long

hours together in the cellar discussing wines for the guests and ale for the workers, neither party would go dry. Mrs Nan and Hannah and three extra kitchen hands produced batches of pies and puddings while the spit turned endlessly over the fire.

The day of the feast arrived and still none of the curious servants had set eyes upon the honoured visitor. Children with scrubbed and shining faces took their places beside their parents at tables that stretched the length of the hall, tables laid with round fat cheeses, custards and hot bread, platters heaped with slices of roast beef and pork and portions of fowl. Hot pies were still being carried from the kitchen. There was room for everyone and food for everyone. Laughter and chatter filled the air as Hannah went from place to place with a pitcher of ale, filling the mugs and tankards, exchanging a joke with the stable boys, curbing the children's antics.

Impressive as ever in his handsome livery, Master Johnson, the butler, surveyed the scene with critical eye. The wooden dais from which Sir Walter would make the expected announcement of his daughter's betrothal was decked with evergreens and symbolic white lilies. All was in readiness.

At the sound of footsteps approaching from the private apartments, he raised a white-gloved hand and was accorded a respectful silence.

'Everyone will stand for my lord and his lady, for the lady Ursula and the honoured guest, Sir George le Flemont of Budle.'

His powerful voice was still echoing round the hall as men and women put down their spoons and platters and scraped to their feet. Sir Walter, with his lady on his arm, led the party but everyone's eyes sought the stranger who would marry the master's daughter. Their gaze quickly travelled to the young lady herself and there discovered that the air of contentment which had surrounded her of late had evaporated. Pale as death itself, she mounted the steps to the dais, pointedly ignoring Sir George's proffered assistance while he, with irritation plainly stamped upon his aristocratic features, took his place beside her.

'Sweet Jesu,' Hannah breathed, 'not that old crow!'

He was certainly old enough to be her father. Thin as a cord, topping Sir Walter by a head or more, Sir George held himself in a perpetual stoop to avoid low beams. Glittering black eyes beneath stern brows showed little potential for affection and Ursula's lack of enthusiasm was understandable. Nevertheless, when Sir

Walter made the expected announcement, tankards were filled and a hearty toast was drunk to the happiness of the now betrothed couple. Feasting was resumed with undimmed enthusiasm.

When Sir Walter's party had left the hall and lavish spread of food had been all but demolished, the tables were pushed aside and a space cleared for dancing.

'Dancing!' groaned Hannah. 'My feet are swollen to the size of pumpkins for I have been working them overhard since first light this morning. I couldna dance a step.'

Yet, when the day was quite done and the great fire had sunk low, when children who had fallen asleep by its embers were being warmly wrapped and carried home by their weary mothers, Hannah was still dancing.

The maids with their skirts kilted up, their wooden shoes discarded and the men with loosened hose falling around their ankles, still whirled and swung. Many a bare pink toe was crushed beneath a heavy boot earning the clumsy culprit a box on the ear. At last, the piper cried an end to his exertions, drank up his gin and staggered off into the night, leaving the maids and pantry boys to put the hall to rights. The harvest feast was over.

Hannah, flushed and happy, her shoes and stockings in her hand, went to the open door to cool her hot cheeks. Carried on the still night air, the muted voices of departing labourers and fretful children making their way home over the fields marked the end of the day.

An autumn mist drifted up, carrying on its chill breath the pungent scent of wormwood and of rotting leaves. This was the back end of the year, summer's ending, winter's prelude. The midnight garden was retreating as the earth took back into itself the force of all growing things. The sombre note of a cruising barn owl, the rattle of a disturbed pheasant echoed through the stillness of the night. In the west tower where her mistress slept a lamp still burned. A feeling of melancholy, at variance with the evening's gaiety, stole over Hannah. What thoughts were keeping the bride-to-be awake on the night of her betrothal?

The butler, doing his round, pulled her roughly inside. 'Off to bed with ye.' He closed and bolted the heavy door. 'It'll be cockcrow soon and ye'll nae be wanting to get up.'

In their own apartment, as they prepared for bed, Sir Walter and Lady Heslop were discussing the marriage transaction.

'Undoubtedly, she will come to see that it is all for her own good.'

Sir Walter, not yet undressed, was sitting disconsolately on his wife's settle, listening without conviction to her reasoning.

'She knows that, on our demise, this estate and everything in it passes to Simon D'Aveney, being the eldest son-in-law. Her life here as a spinster under him would have little to recommend it. No, dear heart,' she removed the rings from her fingers and jewelled drops from her ears, 'believe me, 'tis better that she be mistress of her own home even though—' she lowered her voice mischievously—'her husband be an arrogant bore.'

'He has a noble lineage,' Sir Walter conceded, 'more ancient than the Heslop family tree.' He cocked an eye for his lady's reaction. 'And a useful man to know in matters of trade for he is in business with the East India Company where huge profits are to be made.'

'And dost hope a little drops into thy pocket, perhaps?'

Sir Walter chose to ignore the tart sally. 'There is another consideration, perhaps more important than all.' He took off his powdered wig and ran a hand through his sparse grey hair. 'This news I have not burdened you with until now.' He held his wife's indirect gaze in the mirror

185

with sudden seriousness. 'My friends at court grow increasingly alarmed at the king's conduct. By devious means and despite his fine promises, he is gradually replacing all his Protestant advisers with Catholics. Our common concern is that the evil campaign which he presently wages against Dissenters will one day be extended to include all Protestants, non-conformists or otherwise.'

'My lord!' Lady Heslop put down her comb and faced her husband in alarm.

'We must pray that day never comes,' her husband continued soberly, 'and bear in mind always the fact that James is not immortal.'

'Amen to that,' said his wife fervently.

'Evil days, if they come, will pass when his Protestant daughters ascend to the throne. For the present, however, we may take heart for Ursula's sake. Sir George's family have always changed their religion as easily as they change their clothes. Sir George supports the king in everything he does and will jump any way to save his skin. Count upon it, our little daughter will always be on the winning side.'

There was a thoughtful pause while Ursula's parents considered her betrothal which, in truth, was too far advanced to be retracted with any shred of honour.

'Taking everything into consideration,'

Sir Walter concluded, 'I think we have done the best we can for our daughter.'

'My own feelings exactly,' said his wife with satisfaction.

13

Despite Widow Dodds's simple against the bile which Hannah had been allowed to administer, Lady Ursula's bouts of indisposition increased after the visit of Sir George. Hannah found herself in continual demand to attend her whenever she could be spared from her kitchen chores.

'She doth rack herself with dry vomiting and weeps continuously,' Hannah told the cook. 'I am no apothecary yet to me the reason is clear. 'Tis the fear of sharing the bed of that old man that doth bring out these malignant humours in her body. If he were a kind old man, she would not take it so hard, but he is horrid as a toad with long thin legs like a spider.'

'Toad or spider,' Mrs Nan snapped with unaccustomed sharpness, ' 'tis the business of my lord and lady. Thou'rt nowt but a kitchenmaid and would be better served to keep that in mind.'

Ursula regarded Hannah's lowly status

with envy. 'Would I were a kitchenmaid like thee, Hannah, then I would wed whomsoever I pleased.'

Aye, thought Hannah grimly, but Spotty-face the gardener's boy might not have thee without thy riches. She had heard his cruel jesting when he was with his cronies. Aloud she said, 'Ye would not find my station in life endearing, milady. Poverty is a cruel master.'

'Not so cruel as wealth beyond my reach,' said Ursula with unexpected acuteness. 'Think thee I will see a penny of the handsome dowry my father will pay? 'Tis my husband's fee for relieving my parents of me.'

Hannah, asking herself honestly what she would do in Ursula's position, what Grizzy would do, found no solution other than taking herself off to a nunnery, but Ursula lacked purpose for such a desperate gesture. She would be blown this way and that by whichever wind was the strongest, lacking any real will of her own.

'I must do as my parents command,' she spoke more to herself than to Hannah, 'but I believe I shall die of a broken heart.'

Unmoved by her daughter's tears, Lady Heslop set in motion preparations for the forthcoming marriage and lectured the reluctant bride on the duty of all wellborn ladies to marry into other noble families for the purpose of providing heirs of good stock.

'You may not enjoy the intimate duties of the marriage bed but that is not the whole of married life,' she told Ursula. 'You will live at your ease in luxurious surroundings. You will be mistress of a great house and, after a while, you will know the untold joy of children.'

None of this talk impressed her daughter. Neither did it ring true as Lady Heslop knew as well as any. Sir George was a widower. His household was already ordered by his first wife's mother. As for the heirs, he already had two grown sons by his first marriage.

'No,' Ursula told her shocked mother, 'he simply wants a young woman for his bed to spare him from the pox of bawdy houses.'

Lady Heslop's sense of decency was outraged by this frank confrontation of matters that were best left undisclosed. Nor had she expected such acute observation from her slow-witted daughter. Ursula, she saw, must be carefully handled. For the problem ran deeper than she had first supposed.

Hannah was at work in the kitchen when she was summoned to Lady Heslop's cabinet.

'Running off again,' grumbled Mrs Nan, 'leaving me with all the work.'

' 'Tis none of my wishing, Mrs Nan.' Hannah slipped out of her stained apron and tied back her hair. 'Mayhap her ladyship will not keep me ower long, then ye shall sit and Hannah will finish all the chores.' She had become genuinely fond of the old baggage and circled her large girth in an affectionate squeeze.

'Sweet talk ne'er cooked a fowl. Be off with ye.'

Lady Heslop was seated at the desk where she was accustomed to arrange her household affairs. On the window seat sat her daughter, an unheeded embroidery frame on her lap. The eyes of both were upon Hannah as she closed the door behind her and waited expectantly for instructions. Suspicion darkened her face as she met her ladyship's keen scrutiny.

Mercy on us, thought Lady Heslop, she can look quite as fierce as her father.

'You sent for me,' Hannah reminded her when the silence became oppressive.

'How old are you, Hannah?' asked her mistress.

'Turned sixteen, milady.'

Lady Heslop's strong, capable fingers tapped the desk in front of her. Her agitation was not lost upon Hannah, nor Ursula's pathetic look of entreaty, though the reason was beyond her imagination.

'I believe you to be a good girl with plenty of common sense,' Lady Heslop continued.

Hannah bobbed.

'I know that I can trust you with my marketing and the household purse. Can I trust you with something more precious to me than gold and silver?'

Puzzled, Hannah asked, 'What treasure is this that concerns me?'

Lady Heslop smiled. 'The word is well chosen. For "treasure" is what our dear daughter is to her parents.'

Hannah's eyes darted to the window seat for enlightenment.

Lady Heslop continued. 'Our daughter's marriage to Sir George le Flemont will take place in six months' time. She will become mistress of a great estate. She has requested that she might take you with her as her personal maid.'

Astonished, Hannah opened her mouth but no words came.

'Before I agree,' the tapping of the fingers quickened, 'I must have your sacred pledge that you will look after our youngest daughter well, see always to her comfort and obey her wishes.'

Perplexed, Hannah looked from her imperious mistress, the very embodiment of authority, to Ursula's pleading face.

'Come, Hannah,' urged her ladyship, 'what say you?'

Clutching her embroidery to her bosom, Ursula rose from her seat and came over to Hannah. 'Oh please, dear Hannah, say you will come?' she entreated.

Hannah's thoughts were in confusion. To rise from kitchenmaid to lady's maid was a piece of great good fortune, but to exchange the benevolent household of Bewick Grange for that of the forbidding Sir George was not to be undertaken lightly; yet she could not but be moved to pity by Ursula's plight.

'I would fain know where the Lady Ursula would take me,' she said calmly. 'Is it near or far?'

'Budle Hall is a stately residence overlooking the sea near Bamburgh, no more that a day's ride from here. I would insist that you be given a suitable room of your own, near my daughter's apartments. Although you would wear Sir George's livery, your upkeep would be the expense of my husband which he undertakes willingly for the sake of our daughter's contentment. What say you?'

Bamburgh and the sea! The words rang like bells in Hannah's ears. 'Why then, milady, the answer is yes,' she said delightedly. 'My brother lives not a league from Bamburgh at the village of Buckton.

I have already visited him there and like the place well enough.' She had scarcely finished speaking before Ursula clasped her in an impetuous embrace and Lady Heslop, sighing with relief, allowed herself momentary relaxation, head in hands.

'But milady,' Hannah laughed, 'I am a kitchenmaid not a lady's maid.' She turned to Ursula. 'How shall I dress thy hair with these onion-chopping hands? I ken more of the mysteries of pickling pork than I do of powder and patches.'

'You have done with such menial tasks.' Composedly, Lady Heslop regarded her kitchenmaid. 'You will receive instruction from my own servant. I have watched you grow from an impertinent urchin, Hannah, to a sensible wench. Take this charge upon you seriously, and who knows what might follow. A high position in Sir George's household would not be out of the question. Now go and tell Mrs Nan she must choose another to help her in the kitchen.'

Mrs Nan's reaction was to retire into a fit of sulks which lasted several days during which she scarcely spoke to Hannah; neither would she name anyone to take Hannah's place. At length, however, after a comforting session with the brandy bottle, she threw off her gloomy disposition and faced Hannah frankly.

'Thou'rt right to better thysell when the chance is offered,' she said, ' 'tis only that your poor old Nan is going to miss thee sorely in the kitchen.'

As Hannah hugged the old woman, bleary-eyed as she was with tears and alcohol, she reflected that she, too, would miss the warm companionship that had grown up between them.

'If I make a poor showing at the business, I'll nae doubt be sent back to you,' she said consolingly, 'for I know not if I have the makings of a lady's maid.'

The wedding date was fixed for June 10th of the following year, 1687. Bewick Grange took on an air of frantic activity. Suites of rooms, unused for years, needed refurbishing before Ursula's five sisters, their husbands and children, as well as the party from Sir George's household, could be accommodated.

Plasterers and carpenters came to restore cracked walls and rotten wainscotting, block up the rat-holes and mend broken latches. Mrs Nan complained she could scarce get near her own fireside for the legs of journeymen and tinkers. Hannah noticed the glassmakers' wagon from Howden in the yard one day but there was no sign of the young man with the sloe-black eyes, just a churl carrying panes of glass for window replacements.

Clothiers from Newcastle brought bales of silks and velvets, bolts of linen and packs of ribbons for Lady Heslop's approval and soon every wench who could hold a needle was busily employed in the making of Lady Ursula's wedding apparel.

Only one figure seemed to be untouched by the air of excitement and that was the young woman at the centre of it all. The bride-to-be was measured, pinned, draped in silk, bedecked with ribbons. Her bosom was enticed into more alluring curves, her somewhat wandering waist forcibly confined. All of these attentions she submitted to with total lack of interest, preferring to spend the last days of her freedom in walking her little dog in the garden, never very far from the strapping lad whose job it was to weed the flower beds.

She would frequently seek out Hannah in the kitchen, much to Mrs Nan's disapproval. It was, 'My lady will mark her gown if she sits there' and 'Have a care for the hot fat, my lady,' until she was driven away, but not before she had obtained Hannah's assurance that she would not go back on her promise to accompany her mistress to Budle Hall.

The prospect of her impending responsibilities weighed heavily upon Hannah
but she drew much comfort from the
knowledge that she would be near Tom
and her beloved Mistress Emma. There
had been no news of the imprisoned potter
for many months and Hannah never failed
to mention him in her prayers at night
along with Grizzy Cochrane, her heroine,
and Joan with her crooked legs.

The third Sunday after Lent was Mothering
Sunday when every servant girl was given
a day's holiday to visit her parents with a
simnel cake in her bundle baked by Mrs
Nan and Hannah. On a sparkling spring
morning, Hannah took leave of the cook
and set off with a light step to cross the fell
to Burnfoot. Wait till her mother heard her
news. A kitchenmaid no longer. A lady's
maid now. She walked proudly amongst
the daffodils, a smile on her lips as she
imagined the astonishment with which her
news would be greeted.

Her mother was pleased. There was a
nod of approval and Hannah knew better
than to expect more. Joan and Sarah were
wide-eyed with astonishment.

'But ye canna dress a lady's hair,'
objected Sarah.

'I can now,' retorted Hannah and,
indeed, her own appearance had improved

since Lady Heslop's personal maid had taken her in hand. Her father, showing neither approval nor disapproval, said nothing until she was about to leave.

Her mother, thinner in the face than Hannah remembered, came to stand at the door beside Joan and Sarah to see her on her way and it was then that her father broke his silence. Taking her roughly by the arm, he took her aside, out of hearing of the others.

'Ye'll remember ye come from decent stock. If I hear owt of ye lying with a man afore ye're wedded, I'll flay the last shred of skin off ye're back, so help me God.'

As though stung by an adder, she jerked her arm away from his touch, his carnal, defiling touch, her innermost privacy violated by the lewd overtones of his words. She made no answer, but for a moment the blood in her veins ran icy cold. She picked up her bundle, waved goodbye to her mother and sisters and turned her back on Burnfoot.

By the time she reached the top of the hill, some measure of calm returned. A clean wind filled her lungs and cleared the anger from her mind. 'Oh Jesus,' she murmured to the comforting, rustling trees, 'Friend of Little Children, where do I belong?'

The sun shone for Ursula's wedding. June was lavish with her gifts that year. Campion, meadowsweet and honeysuckle and in the shady places grouped foxgloves made a charming setting for a notable social occasion. There were roses everywhere. Decently dressed labourers and their families, making their way along country lanes to the Grange, plucked wild roses from the hedgerows to stick in their caps and bonnets. The gardener's boy, in a last gracious tribute to his admirer, had brought each cultivated rose in the flower beds to perfection. Inside the hall itself, every urn and pitcher was filled with roses. The air was saturated with their perfume on this memorable day when two noble families of the north were to be joined by marriage.

Sir Walter's line might not go back to William the Conqueror as was Sir George's boast but that it was a noble house was plain to see. No great castle, this, bristling with fortifications, but domestic architecture at its elegant best. Graceful columns, now somewhat scarred with Cromwell's muskets, flanked a wide sweep of steps leading to the great hall where waxed floors gleamed in the sunlight. Rich tapestries covered the plastered walls between silver candle sconces. Tables laid with embroidered cloths and sparking with glass and silver awaited honoured guests. Over the deeply recessed fireplace hung Sir Walter's sword and scabbard alongside that of his father, both of which had earned their wearers honour in the service of their king. Ursula had no cause to feel ashamed of her parentage.

But this daughter of a noble lord had no room for pride in her heart. On this day of joy and feasting, she, alone, was leaden with misery. Nevertheless, she carried herself with a quiet dignity that surprised and pleased her mother. As the long day of ceremonial progressed, through the sacred service in the private chapel where the sweet music of viol and gamba should have soothed her, to the feasting and drinking afterwards, Ursula was unmoved. She sat at the head of the flower-decked table, her sisters and their husbands noisily merry around her, and watched her husband grow coarsely drunk.

Outside on the summer lawn, Hannah danced with the stable boys and chamber-maids and put aside all misgivings about the future. Tomorrow she would move on, leaving behind these oafish lads, squint-eyed Peg and Mrs Nan. Tonight there was dancing and merrymaking until the stars faded and Mistress Ursula was bedded.

'My sister Hannah is now a serving maid at Budle Hall.' Tom looked up from the note in his hand. 'Is that not fortunate? 'Tis less than a league away across the flats.'

The face of the old man sitting by the hearth brightened. 'Maybe we will see the little maid here once more. That would surely gladden my poor wife.'

His Majesty's prisons were evil places where men were left to rot in their own ordure in cells that lacked both air and light. Eighteen months in captivity had aged Joshua Reay almost beyond recognition. Once a robust, merry fellow, he was now so emaciated that his bones were barely fleshed. The joints, swollen with the ague, were grotesquely distorted. A racking cough that fetched up blood told its own tale of consumption of the lungs. This much mercy had been shown to him, that he might return to his home to die.

Yet there was still a bright intelligence in his eyes. The punishment he had endured so steadfastly for his religion had wrecked him physically but left his wits undimmed. Many of his fellow Dissenters had fared worse than he. Their shrivelled heads on city gates were a dire warning to those who would defy the king's wishes. Some survived only to be fettered with ball and chain and sent to work as slaves in the Barbados Islands.

Joshua, his faith unshaken, had come to terms with his fate and daily offered thanks to God that two such young men as Daniel and Tom were at hand to help him in his time of dire need.

Emma was indeed cheered by the news of Hannah's presence at Budle Hall, but it would take more than a visit from Tom's sister to lift the pain from her heart. She no longer sang as she churned the butter. Her merry laugh which in happier days would be heard in kitchen and in dairy as she went about her work was silent now. A desolation seized her every time she looked upon her husband for the truth was there for all to see. His days upon this earth were numbered.

No longer able to work the clay, Joshua nevertheless was at pains to advise and instruct his two assistants in all the finer points of the craft, sharing secret glaze recipes with them and many techniques which he had perfected over a lifetime of working with clay. Daniel, now twenty years old, was pledged to return to his parents in Edinburgh, there to set up his own business but Tom would stay. The assurance that Emma's welfare would be secure in the young man's hands after he himself was no longer there to look after her, brought peace of mind to the sick man.

Upon Daniel's departure, Tom was to be given two new apprentices to help him run the pottery under Joshua's supervision. Eventually, at the demise of his master, he would be manager of the business with a generous share of the profits, accountable to Mistress Emma in all things.

Tom was nineteen years old now, a trained potter, yet there were moments of panic when he contemplated the future without Joshua and without Daniel to assist him. Joshua and Emma had taken him into their house and treated him like a son. He prayed that he would not disappoint them. Thankfully, the accounting side of the business would rest in Emma's competent hands as it had always done. Tom was only too well aware of his shortcomings in this respect.

As to the charge laid upon him to look after Mistress Emma's comfort, Tom had sworn with his hand on the Bible before the old man, that her wellbeing would be his constant concern. Looking at Joshua now, huddled over the fire though the day was warm and sunny, Tom knew that the day of his increased responsibilities was not far distant. He resolved to arrange a visit from Hannah at the earliest opportunity.

Budle Hall with its massive keep and curtain walls had none of the gentler aspects of Bewick Grange. Built as a fortress by the edge of Budle Bay in 1168, it had been enlarged by successive generations of Le Flemonts. Though it bristled with defensive abutments, it had never endured the rigours of a siege. There were no marks of cannon on the eight-foot thick walls, unlike the ruined Bamburgh Castle nearby, for the family motto, 'What I hold, I keep', had been carried out to the letter by succeeding generations of Le Flemonts, often at the expense of loyalties and principles. But no Le Flemont head had ever graced a city gate.

Unfortunately for the residents of this formidable building, little thought had been given to providing domestic comfort. At all seasons here, the women went warmly clad. Truly magnificent views over the sea to the ancient island of Lindisfarne were enjoyed at the cost of permanently rattling windows and whistling draughts. In wintertime, capricious winds romped through the great hall causing more smoke than heat to be distributed from the burning logs on the hearth. To Ursula and her maid, newly arrived from the Grange, their new surroundings seemed utterly dreary.

While his first wife was alive, Sir George, saw fit to provide her widowed mother with apartments at the Hall. Her air of refinement which could be attributed to her descent from a lesser scion of the Irish aristocracy added a certain gloss to his rough and ready household. The formidable Mrs Sedgecombe amply repaid his largesse by assisting her daughter in the running of the household and by sundry other favours of a more personal nature, since Lady Le Flemont was in a continual state of pregnancy. At her daughter's untimely death, Mrs Sedgecombe was persuaded to stay on in her role as housekeeper for Sir George and his two grown sons, Harry and Cecil, the only survivors of ten infants borne by Ursula's predecessor.

News of Sir George's intention to remarry understandably threw the redoubtable Mrs Sedgecombe into confusion as to her future. She need not have worried. Sir George had no wish to involve himself in the affairs of his northern household. His interest lay in the coffee houses of London and the opportunities they presented for making advantageous financial transactions.

Plainly, his new wife was incapable of ordering a household but it was not for this talent that he had married her. A certain recklessness at the gaming tables in Soho, London, had lately put him in queer street; not a cause for any great concern, for the next returns from his investments in the East India Company would surely settle any temporary embarrassment. For the immediate present, however, the generous dowry offered by Sir Walter saved his face. The London debt could be honoured leaving a comfortable balance in credit.

At the same time, he was quite prepared to carry out the undeniable duty which rested with him to provide more heirs for the Le Flemont line. He was not yet sixty, a man in his prime, spry and active. His loins groaned pleasurably at the prospect. The fact that he had a plain wife worried him not in the least and could be considered an advantage. There would be neither competition nor jealousy amongst some of the sweet boys in his employ.

He informed Mrs Sedgecombe, who was eminently suitable in every way, efficient, discreet and masterful with lesser servants, that she would be continuing in her position as housekeeper.

Thus reassured, Mrs Sedgecombe prepared herself to meet her new mistress and could scarce refrain from laughing aloud in relief when she encountered Ursula and her maid standing unattended in the hall where Sir George had deposited them on arrival. The new mistress, she saw at once, was a simpleton, a scared rabbit.

There was nothing of the servant

about the tall figure who advanced with unhurried steps towards the new arrivals, seemingly unmindful of the fact that she was keeping them waiting. Her robe of grey cloth was plain but well-cut. The white lace at her throat was held by a cornelian brooch of rare distinction. Her head, with its smoothly coiled black braids was tilted just enough to allow her to regard the new mistress of Budle Hall straight in the eye. By contrast Ursula seemed to shrink within herself, or so it appeared to her anxious maid.

In the circumstances, Mrs Sedgecombe could afford to be gracious. Affecting a thin smile which, Hannah noted, was in no way reflected in the dark glittering eyes, she placed one angular arm about her new mistress's waist. 'Come, my lady. I will show you to your room,' and Ursula, reassured, allowed herself to be led away, leaving Hannah, alone and full of mistrust, with the baggage in the hall.

Tom's reaction was similar when he called at Budle Hall a few days later and asked if he might speak with his sister. The housekeeper took several minutes over her assessment of him, from the crown of his head to his sturdy countryman's boots. He disliked intensely the arrogant set of her chin but, stretch as she might, she must look up to him for he had the advantage of several inches.

At length, with an irritable jingling of the keys at her waist, she addressed him. 'You do not resemble your sister.'

Tom smiled, 'For satisfaction on that point, ye must seek my mother,' he cocked his head cheekily, 'for I had nowt to do wi'it.'

Frowning at his impertinence, she turned away. 'The serving maids will tell you where to find her.'

Hannah had carried cushions to a secluded corner of the grounds sheltered from the sea breeze by a stout wall and was reading to her mistress when Tom found her.

'My lady!' she shrieked, dropping the book from her lap as she sprang to her feet, ' 'tis my brother Tom!' His arms went around her in a great bear hug.

'Mercy on us,' complained Lady Ursula, 'you almost frighted me out of my skin!'

'I beg pardon, milady.' Instantly contrite, Tom disentangled himself from Hannah's clasp. ' 'Tis so long since we met.'

Ursula pouted. 'My brothers, that is to say, my sisters' husbands, do not embrace me thus.'

'Then that is their misfortune.'

She smiled at his gallantry. 'I like your brother, Hannah. But do not tell me he has come to take you away from me for that I could not bear.' She turned an appealing face to Tom. 'Your sister is my only friend in this horrid place. My parents have abandoned me and I have no comfort but Hannah.'

'Nay, my lady,' Tom was quick to reassure, 'I come only to seek permission for her to visit my master who lives hard by and has fond remembrances of her, whenever it might suit thee.'

'I would like to come too,' said Ursula surprisingly. 'I dislike this ugly fortress.'

In some embarrassment, Tom turned to Hannah. 'Master Reay be mortally ill, Hannah, and not fit for my lady's company, being so recently released from prison.'

'Prison!' Ursula was horrified. 'He has done wrong?'

Hannah took her hand. 'My lady, Master Reay is a good and saintly man, his only crime being that he chooses to worship as his heart dictates and not as the king would wish. And, because he hath offended the king, 'tis certain Sir George would not allow thee to visit him.'

Ursula sank back on her cushions resignedly. 'Sir George would not allow it,' she repeated dully. She agreed, however, that Hannah should visit the sick man as soon as possible and a day was decided upon.

On the following morning, Hannah was in the washhouse attending to her mistress's personal laundry when one of the chambermaids stopped to speak to her, a plump and bonny lass, fair and freckled.

'I met thy brother yesterday,' she said shyly. 'I tellt him where to find thee.'

Hannah nodded. 'I think he was glad to meet thee for Mrs Sedgecombe saw him first and was none too friendly.'

'Pooh!' the girl snorted derisively. 'Old Gripes, we call her. Her face 'ud turn the milk sour. My name's Betsy Lisle,' the girl offered. 'What's yours?'

'Hannah Robson.'

There was a pause then, 'What's thy brother's name?'

'Tom.' Hannah looked directly at the girl. What was Tom to her?

With studied nonchalance, Betsy flicked a ladybird from her downy arms. 'Is he courting, this brother of yours? I suppose he's got a girl. All the nice ones have.'

Hannah laughed out loud. 'Why Betsy Whoever-ye-are, I believe ye've taken a shine to my brother!'

Betsy tossed her head in instant denial then promptly joined in the laughter.

'Whether he's courting or not,' said

Hannah, 'I cannot say, for yesterday was the first time we have met in two long years. Shall I ask him?' she teased. 'Shall I tell him Betsy fancies him?'

'You dare and you'll feel the weight of my hand across thy face,' Betsy threatened. 'I like him though. He's a proper sort of chap.'

When Tom came one week later with pony and trap to collect his sister, it was no accident that Betsy happened to be drawing water at the well in the courtyard. 'Goodday, Tom,' she said perkily, 'I'll fetch Hannah for thee.' And it seemed to Betsy that Tom returned her smile.

Although Hannah had been warned of the decline in the potter's health, she was not prepared for the great change in him. The once rotund and jolly fellow with rosy cheeks and luxuriant whiskers could not possibly have turned into this old and emaciated creature huddled by the fire. When he saw Hannah, however, his eyes lit up with their old kindness, bringing a lump to Hannah's throat. Dear Mistress Emma, too, was shrunk from her former plump comeliness and had need of a brooch now to hold her blouse together across the bosom.

They welcomed her as if she were their own, true daughter, yet more than that for such love was never hers at Burnfoot.

'To see thee again, Hannah, and you grown into such a fine young lady, brings gladness to us all,' said Emma.

'To tell the truth,' jested Tom, 'I could scarce tell which was maid and which was mistress when I called at Budle Hall, so grand has our little Hannah become.'

Daniel, standing apart, said not a word but smiled the slow, warm smile she always remembered. But the sight of the poor potter, all a-tremble in his chair, became more than she could bear. With tears in her eyes, she dropped to her knees beside him and took his hands in hers.

'I have prayed for thee, Master Joshua, with all my might and yet it seems the Lord has not listened to me.'

'Nay, Hannah, do not say that,' Mistress Emma interrupted as her husband searched for words. 'We have much to be grateful for. The preacher who was here the night the militia came and others who did lead us in prayer are banished to the Barbados with the mark of the branding iron upon them. My Joshua is at peace now and for that we must thank God.'

Joshua laid a hand on Hannah's bowed head. 'The Lord has answered thy prayers, child.' Though his voice shook, there was still strong purpose there. 'All the torments of hell await the black soul of the king, yet we who were persecuted rest in perfect ease of mind knowing that we have not betrayed our faith.'

'Amen,' said his wife devoutly.

14

Built on rising land, Budle Hall stood fair and square in the path of the north-east wind that blew untempered by any land straight from Scandinavia. At its side ran the Waren Burn which turned the wheel of the Waren mill, carrying out this service to the local community before emptying its waters into the wide inlet of Budle Bay, from which the Hall took its name.

Hannah was overjoyed to be near the sea once more, its attraction outweighing by far the disadvantages of draughty passages and weeping walls. Almost every window in the great keep, narrow though it might be, gave a view of the sea. As she went to and from her mistress's chamber, her eye would be held by a fishing coble or a stately schooner, by a great arching rainbow dipping into the horizon or momentous skies that foretold storms.

The brisk wind that blew even in midsummer brought its own benefits to the Hall, sweeping the courtyards clear of rubbish, ventilating the noisome closets of a building that was home to some thirty servants as well as the noble family. Nevertheless, the thought of winter brought a shiver to Hannah's spine.

'Get yersell a flannel binder afore the back end.' Betsy was Hannah's mentor in all things. 'Ye've got to keep yer kidneys warm.'

Sir George kept a much larger establishment than Sir Walter had aspired to. Mrs Nan would have been amazed to see the gaggle of scullery maids and at least a dozen stable boys who looked after the mounts for Sir George and his two sons, his two carriages and the pony trap.

Hannah's new duties were not so arduous as those of laundrymaid or kitchenmaid at Bewick Grange though she was required to be at hand for most of the day to entertain her young mistress.

She had learned to dress Ursula's hair in the current fashion after a few lessons from Lady Heslop's personal maid and could wire the rather coarse, tow-coloured hair into side bunches neatly enough after combing the central portion straight back to make a flat bun. She dressed her own hair in a simple yet elegant style very different from her previous heavy plaits, and her hands, until now reddened and coarse, were beginning to lose their roughness. Almost imperceptibly, she was taking on the gloss of refinement.

She was on good terms with most of the other serving girls though she kept the ogling boys at arm's length. Betsy Lisle, however, was her especial confidante and they would walk together in the evening when Ursula was occupied in the drawing room, playing cards with Mrs Sedgecombe or doing her needlework. Hannah would not be needed until her mistress was ready for bed.

Betsy's family were fisherfolk. She came from the little fishing village of Boulmer, some two leagues south of Bamburgh. Born and bred by the sea, the sound of its waves was the music of her living.

On summer evenings, with shoes and stockings tied around their necks and their petticoats kilted up 'oot the wattor' as Betsy termed it, they explored the rock pools left by the receding tide perhaps to catch a glimpse of a pale scuttling crab or the flash of a shoal of minnows. They teased the tendrils of rubbery anemones into frantic fibrillation and studied the painstaking progress of a winkle on a dripping rock face.

'I couldna bide away frae the sea,' Betsy declared, ' 'tis as much a part of me as my big feet and freckles.' The sea was her friend in all its moods and she drew Hannah within its thrall.

There were wild flowers growing on the sand dunes that Hannah had never seen before and Betsy knew them all by name, storksbill, seapink and spicy lovage and the tamarisk bush bending to the wind. They walked to Budle Point where the waters of the bay met the sea and watched the spurning breakers crashing over Harkness Rocks.

'Them's the Farnes,' Betsy pointed out the rocky islands ringed with surf, 'And doon there,' she swung her arm to the south, to the scalloped coastline veiled in smoke from the limekilns, 'past Bamburgh Head is Seahouses, Craster and Boulmer. That's where I come frae.'

Close at hand the ruins of Bamburgh Castle reared up majestically from slabbed basalt cliffs.

'Who knocked that down?' asked Hannah.

Betsy shrugged. 'There's always folk ready to knock a castle doon and others ready to build it up again.'

'Naebody's mended that one.'

'It belongs to Squire Forster and he has nae the money. He lives in the manor hoose with his bonny daughter, Dorothy.'

In such pleasant evenings spent together,

a warm friendship quickly developed between the two girls which, as far as Hannah was concerned, compensated for the many drawbacks of life at Budle Hall.

Betsy was an amiable, uncomplicated girl some two years older than Hannah and had been in service at Budle Hall since she was fourteen years of age. Now she occupied a position of some importance in the household, being responsible to Mrs Sedgecombe for the cleanliness and maintenance of the bedchambers. When Hannah sought her opinion of Sir George, Betsy replied in her usual forthright manner that he was a randy old devil and it was best to keep out of his way.

'Lucky he likes pretty lads as well as lasses so he's got plenty to choose from, but pay heed, Hannah. If the auld ram gets ye into a corner, yell for Mrs Sedgecombe. That'll douse his fire. She's the only one he minds.'

Sir George's two sons had hoped for a pretty stepmother to liven the rural scene and felt badly cheated with Ursula. At nineteen, Harry was only two years younger than his new stepmother and having decided that she was a nincompoop, took great delight in tormenting her. An elegant young man with superior airs, as befitted Sir George's elder son, he was a student at Oxford University and consequently was away from home for most of the time, which was fortunate for Ursula. She had never met anyone as false as he, who concealed such exquisite mockery behind a smiling exterior. During her first few weeks as the new mistress of Budle Hall she was frequently reduced to tears.

Cecil, the younger son, received instruction at home from an impoverished priest of covert Catholic persuasion and, though he was cast in the same mould as his brother, he lacked nerve to bait Ursula without the support of Harry. On more than one occasion, he had suffered a humiliating rebuke from his stepmother's sharp-tongued maid when Hannah could no longer stand by and see her mistress reduced to tears.

Sir George did not seem to object to his sons' behaviour and, though he did not join in the cruel banter, he did nothing to discourage it. The boys' grandmother, displeased as she might well be, cannily followed Sir George's example since her own preservation was of more concern to her than that of his simple wife.

Accustomed to the always courtly behaviour of her father, Ursula was daily affronted by the offhand manner in which her husband treated her. He spoke little and, by his lack of soft words when he lay with her, emphasised the animal in him. His insensitive exploring hands about her person filled her with disgust. Nevertheless, she would do her duty as she had been bred to do. This much of Lady Heslop's character was in her daughter, but nothing in the world would ever make her love this man who was now her husband.

There was no one that the unhappy mistress of Budle Hall could confide in but Hannah and she, knowing herself to be ill-equipped to deal with such a responsibility, begged leave to write to Sir Walter to acquaint him of his daughter's unhappiness. Would he not demand that Sir George show his daughter more respect?

This brought an immediate stiffening of Ursula's resolve. 'Nay, Hannah,' she dabbed her red eyes, 'that will not do. 'Tis Sir George who owns me not my father. I must make what I can of my life for 'tis of concern to no one but myself.'

'And me,' said Hannah stoutly. 'It maddens me to see you treated so.' Roundly cursing Ursula's tormentors, she went to fetch the rouge pot and powder to repair her mistress's ravaged cheeks. Yet she was careful not to let her anger show when in the presence of Sir George. He would not hesitate to send her away if she were to cause offence and, if that were to happen, Ursula would lose her only ally.

'Listen to me, hinny,' Betsy's advice was practical as usual, 'divvent meddle with the affairs of the gentry for 'twill be ye who comes off worst.'

The two maids were sitting on rocks still warm from the sun, dangling their bare feet in a pool. Salt water was good for your corns, Betsy said. Rubbery thickets of oarweed caressed their white legs with slippery fronds and tiny fishes buffeted them with no more impact than the touch of a feather. At the base of the pool, a patch of sand picked out by a refracted ray of light, rearranged itself into the form of a crab.

'There is no one here who cares about her,' Hannah said sadly, 'so I must stay by her.'

'Ye've a good situation here, Hannah,' Betsy gave her friend's waist a comforting squeeze, 'so just keep thy mouth shut and eyes closed to what's going on and let milady look to hersell.' Betsy leant forward casting a shadow on the light water and dropped a pebble into the pool. With a flicker of sand, the crab disappeared from sight. 'Keep oot o' trouble, like that wee crab.'

With the affairs of the gentry dismissed, Betsy launched herself into a more congenial subject. Her slightly prominent blue eyes rested on Hannah with affectionate curiosity. 'Have ye got a sweetheart, Hannah?'

Hannah shook her head.

Betsy leaned forward confidentially. 'Ye ken Sam Diggle the forage lad?'

'No.'

'He's got his eye on thee. Ye've only to give him the nod and he'll come running.'

Hannah lifted one neat foot and watched a string of crystal drops shatter the clear lens of the pool. 'I divvent want a sweetheart, Betsy.'

Betsy shook her head disapprovingly. 'Ye're a queer one. The way ye go on, ye'll never got yersell a man.'

'I divvent want one. I can manage fine on my own.'

'And die an old maid with nae bairns to look to ye? Ye're daft! I hope that sweet brother of thine is not of the same mind.'

Hannah laughed, 'That thee must find out for thysell.'

'I have three bachelor brothers back home in Boulmer, all looking for a canny wife.'

Hannah could see the workings of Betsy's mind and made haste to turn the subject. 'My cousin works in Boulmer.'

Betsy looked up with interest. 'A

fisherman? What's his name? For sure, I'll ken him.'

'Nay,' said Hannah, suddenly discreet, 'as to the nature of his business, I cannot say but it is not catching fish. His name is Will Robson, son of my father's brother.'

Betsy burst out laughing. 'Why all the world kens Will Robson, and Sam, his father and the rest of the crew from Tyneside. No,' she winked, 'he is no fisherman but in Boulmer we keep a close tongue aboot other folks' affairs. Ye'll mebbes see him at Belford Fair, flirting with the lasses.'

'May we go to the fair?' Hannah's face lit up. What a break in the monotony of daily life this would be.

'Oh aye,' Betsy nodded, ' 'tis the last of the summer festivals before Harvest Supper and all of us servants are given leave to go. There's a waggon to take us there and fetch us back.' Her eyes sparkled. ' 'Tis a great day, Hannah. There's a faw with the second sight who'll tell thee true as true who thee'll marry and folk come from miles around for the hoppings. 'Tis summat to look forward to, I can tell ye, and it's three weeks on from now.'

As the sun set behind them over the distant hills, shadows crept over the rocks to the pool where the girls were sitting bringing a chill reminder of the passing

221

time. Betsy, drying her legs on her petticoats, urged haste. 'Howay, thy poor little mistress has suffered Old Gripes's company for long enough. Time we went back.'

'Aye,' said Hannah drily, 'now she must change it for that of Old Randy.'

As they neared the Hall, a coach, much ornamented and scrolled and drawn by four fine greys, clattered to a halt outside the main entrance.

' 'Twould seem we have a noble visitor,' Hannah remarked. 'Whose crest is that?'

'My Lord Crewe, Bishop of Durham,' said Betsy offhandedly, 'a frequent visitor.'

'For a churchman, he picks strange company, for I find no sign of godliness in our master.'

'They are birds of a feather for all that.' Betsy led the way through the rear door to the servants' quarters. 'He, too, has his eye on a young wife, having lost his first.'

Hannah was to recall the bishop's name a few days later when she was given leave to visit the potter's house once more. Tom collected her in Emma's pony trap and they were driving along the narrow lane from Budle Hall when the same coach overtook them at great speed, forcing Tom, cursing loudly, into the ditch. When he saw the coat of arms, he hastily set the trap back on the track. 'The Bishop of

Durham!' There was a note of urgency in his voice. 'We must see which way he is heading. Hold hard, Hannah!'

At a rattling pace, he set off in pursuit and, where the road forked north and south, he was in time to see the bishop's coach disappearing in the direction of Belford.

'And good riddance,' Tom took the opposite direction. 'We want none of his ilk at Buckton.'

'What has he done to ye that we must chase him so?' demanded Hannah.

'His Grace likes to hunt and little harm in that, but where other men chase foxes, he seeks out Dissenters. Vose the Covenanter is in hiding hereabouts. What a catch for my lord the bishop! Mistress Emma risked her freedom by giving him food and shelter last night.'

'What of Master Reay? Is he no longer in any danger?'

'He is threat to neither king nor bishop now for they have broken him. We believe 'twas the bishop's spies who brought him to this sorry state.'

'What wickedness to mistreat a good man so,' Hannah grieved.

'He is in the hands of the Lord now. Each day he grows weaker.'

The reason for this, Hannah's second visit to Buckton, was the occasion of

Daniel's departure for Scotland. Mistress Emma had roasted a sucking pig and insisted that Hannah be invited to supper. She was there to greet Hannah when she stepped down from the trap and shook her head in answer to Hannah's immediate enquiry.

'Failing, my dear, but tonight we must put our tears behind us and make a happy farewell for Daniel.'

The table in the bright kitchen was laid with some of Joshua's most prized painted platters, but their gifted creator in his seat by the fire seemed scarcely to belong to this world any more, so transparent was his frame, with the bones clearly showing beneath his parchment skin. Yet his welcome to Hannah was as warm as ever.

'Go seek Daniel for me, Hannah,' begged Emma. 'He's putting his tools together in one of the sheds. Tell him the food is on the table.'

Hannah found Daniel in the clay shed, dressed not as usual in sacking apron over ragged shirt and breeches but in a coat of good broadcloth and linen at his neck. There was a faraway look on his face as he tuned to Hannah's call.

'Art saying farewell to thy clay shed, Daniel?' she gently teased.

Whereupon he turned his dark eyes full

upon her, for once unshielded by lowered lids and shockingly vulnerable.

'With a tug of war in my heart, Hannah, for though I rejoice to see my parents again and to set up my own business, yet are there many reasons why I am loth to leave.'

'Of a certainty,' Hannah agreed, 'kind folks like the master and mistress are not easily left behind.'

'And others,' his glance was meaningful.

A tiny nerve jumped beneath Hannah's calm exterior. 'Aye,' she parried, 'and Tom will miss thee too.'

'And wilt thou miss me sometimes, Hannah? Wilt ever think on me?'

Abruptly, she turned to leave. 'I surely will and I wish thee all prosperity in thy new venture, but now Mistress Emma bids thee come to the table for meats are cut and wine is poured.'

'Hannah—' Even as Daniel reached out to detain her, she shrank back as if menaced. The alarm which had been slowly stirring within her turned to anger which, though she knew it to be unreasonable, she could not control. The easy companionship which she had always shared with Daniel turned to a violent physical revulsion as he stood before her, blatantly, it seemed to her, offering his maleness. To her distorted vision the set of his strong shoulders now was unbearably brutish; the stance of his parted legs threatening and crude.

'Don't touch me!' she cried wildly and fled from the shed leaving Daniel to follow, crestfallen and puzzled.

That Daniel had long cherished a love for Tom's sister was no secret to Mistress Emma and she had hoped by asking Hannah this night to provide Daniel with the opportunity to declare himself. She was quick to realise, however, when both returned to the kitchen that whatever had passed between them, had brought no joy to Daniel who was silent throughout the meal.

When it was time for Tom to take Hannah back to the Hall, Daniel accompanied them into the yard. Tom, not usually renowned for tact, must needs return to the house for his jerkin, leaving Daniel alone with Hannah for a final farewell.

'Hannah,' Daniel appealed to the tense figure seated in the trap, 'please believe me, I meant no harm. I wished only to ask if, when I have established my business, I may see thee again?'

He was as putty in her hands and she squeezed him as if she would revenge herself on the entire male population for being as they were. 'Why, yes,' she said rudely, 'providing I am not become invisible and thee not blind, then thou mayest see me, but I have no further use for thee, Daniel, except ye be the friend of my brother.'

'Dear Lord,' muttered Tom as he drove away, leaving Daniel a forlorn figure in the empty yard. 'What hast said to Daniel, sister? I have never seen such a look on his face, nay, not in all the six years we have been together.'

Hannah had the grace to feel a twinge of shame. 'He was talking stupidly. I had to speak my mind.'

'And in so doing have hurt him deeply, I fear. He is an excellent fellow, Hannah, and loves thee deeply though ye're too young to comprehend—I might say appreciate—such devotion as his.'

They were racing along in the gathering gloom. The first stars were making their appearance in the night sky, but it was not simply the chill air that made Hannah shiver.

'Oh, Tom, divvent ye start lecturing me an' all. I want nae husband EVER. My flesh creeps if a man so much as brushes against me, yet I do need a brother. Do not turn away from me.' Her voice faltered so that Tom cast a hasty glance at his unpredictable little sister and saw that her eyes were bright with tears.

'Nay, little sister, thou'lt always have thy

brother Tom. Yet trust me, one day ye'll meet a man who will turn all these strange fears and fancies of thine upside down and inside out. That day ye'll fall in love. Till that day, I'll hold my tongue, only this do I ask; that ye think not hardly of Daniel for he is my truest friend, a man of most excellent qualities.'

Hannah said nothing until she had regained her composure. 'I have behaved like a shrew, Tom. I am truly sorry and will write to Daniel and tell him so. I would fain have him as a friend if he will be content with that.'

15

Belford Fair fell on the second Saturday in September. All the young servants at the Hall were out of bed at an early hour in order to complete as many of their duties as possible before handing over to those on the staff who were too old or who had no inclination to go. Betsy was in a state of high excitement.

'We're gannin in the big waggon and we divvent come home till nigh on midnight.'

'I canna leave my mistress that long,' Hannah objected.

'Then bring her with ye. She doesna get overmuch fun.'

Hannah sought out Mrs Sedgecombe since Sir George was away in London. That lady was pleasantly surprised to find Lady Ursula's usually uncommunicative maid seeking her advice. Most certainly, she agreed, it would not be fitting for Lady Ursula to travel with the servants in the waggon, but since Master Harry and Master Cecil had both announced their intentions of going to the fair, they should take their stepmother along with them if she chose to go.

Ursula did. She was almost as excited as Betsy. Harry and Cecil were less so. They meant to cut a dash, show off a little with the pistols perhaps; might even enter the boxing contest and certainly make the acquaintance of the prettiest wench there. What neither had planned was to take their dull stepmother along with them. Nevertheless, though Harry might let it be known that he was master of Budle Hall in his father's absence, he knew he was deluding himself. His grandmother held the true reins of authority in the household when his father was away. Although Mrs Sedgecombe was careful to pay lip service to Harry as elder son, he knew and she knew who was master. Thus, on the morning of the fair, Harry, with very bad grace, found himself driving Ursula in the trap while his brother Cecil followed on horseback.

His ill temper and sarcastic wit, however, were quite lost on Ursula who, for once, was in high spirits. Her husband was far away in London. She knew she was looking her best in fur-trimmed tippet and hood of rich green velvet over a long woollen mantle of matching green. She waved delightedly to villagers in the nearby hamlet of Outchester who came to stare, as Harry, in a vain attempt to frighten his stepmother, sent the trap careering wildly around the narrow lanes. He was forced to adopt a more sober pace when they reached the highway with its burden of traffic: farm waggons carrying giggling maids and lusty youths, merchants in their carriages, tinkers on foot, all bound for Belford Fair. Summer with its plentiful food and clement weather was drawing to a close. This was the last festival before Harvest Thanksgiving and everyone was determined to make the best of it.

A pleasant surprise awaited Hannah as she climbed down from the waggon on the outskirts of the fairground, for she almost fell into the arms of her brother.

'I said to mesell that all them pretty lasses from Budle Hall are bound to be at Belford Fair and was I not right?'

The girls giggled and bridled, making great play with their eyes. For Hannah's brother, with his thatch of chestnut-coloured hair and his manly form was enough to catch any maid's fancy, but it was Betsy who took his free arm as he led Hannah away into the noisy hubbub of the fair. The complaining bleat of sheep in the saleyard, the whinnying of over-excited horses, the cries of toffee-apple vendors and chestnut roasters all combined to make the heart beat faster on this fine autumn day. The early morning mists had cleared and the girls were already untying their shawls, showing pretty bosoms above their bodices.

There were horse races and foot races, quoit-throwing, post-heaving and wrestling on a greasy pole over the duckpond. In a roped-off corner of the field a red-faced manager introduced a hairy brute of a man called Samson and invited the onlookers to punch his nose. 'A guinea if ye last a minute!'

'But he gets the guinea if ye go doon,' laughed Tom.

The faws were here in their brightly coloured tents, come all the way from their traditional camping ground at Horseley Moor; and the serving girls from Budle Hall, with pennies in their pockets that Mrs Sedgewick had advanced, crowded around the trays of trashy jewellery and bright ribands that were for sale. Enid bought a brooch made from the eye of bird that was certain to bring her luck and Mab bought a riband for her curly brown hair.

A woman whose wrinkled face had weathered to the colour of a walnut grabbed Hannah by the arm, 'Cross my palm, my pretty,' she wheezed. 'There's a tale writ on thy bonny face that none but Old Fan may read.' She wore a head kerchief of the finest silk of a deep and royal purple. Tiny gold moons jingled from her ears. Her eyes, black and glittering like chips of coal, bored into Hannah's.

'Be off with ye,' Tom pushed the old crone away. 'My sister hath no need of soothsayers.'

'True enough,' the old faw called out to their departing backs, 'for what will be, will be; but none but the seventh daughter of a gypsy queen hath the sight to see it afore its time.'

Hannah shivered despite the sun's warmth. 'I wonder what she saw.'

'Would she tell, d'ye suppose, who I shall marry?' asked Betsy, ogling Tom.

He was in the best of spirits, with a girl on each arm. 'Come,' he laughed, 'I know just the man for thee for he will not answer back nor leave thee for another wench.'

232

'Then take me to this treasure without more ado,' instructed Betsy and roared with delight when Tom stopped a pedlar to buy two gingerbread men.

Hannah, seeing her brother and her friend on such good terms, was content. When, a few moments later, she passed her young mistress walking with Master Harry, any misgivings she might have had were put at rest. She would enjoy this holiday to the full.

Later, when the fiddler called his first tune, Betsy was a mite put out as Tom took Hannah for a partner in preference to herself. Yet she, too, was soon clapping with the crowd as sister and brother drew all eyes, the slight, dark girl with movements so light she seemed to float and her brawny swain who despite his size stepped as nicely as a hen in a fowlyard.

The dusk of an autumn evening closed in around the dancers. Tarry flares over the faws' stalls threw weird shadows around the dancing figures as the fiddler still sawed away at the old favourites, 'Gathering Peascods', 'Shepherd's Hey', 'Strip the Willow'.

An occasional youth staggering by, voices raised in argument, proof was all around of much ale being drunk. Hannah, resting from the dance, looked about her in sudden concern for her mistress. She was further alarmed by a glimpse of the two young masters of Budle Hall passing by, unaccompanied by Lady Ursula.

Abruptly, she turned to Tom. 'I must go seek my mistress. 'Twould seem that both her escorts have deserted her.'

Anxiety gripped her as she moved out of the lighted circle. Who knew what villains lay concealed in the dark shadows behind the tents. It was beyond comprehension that Sir George's sons could desert a defenceless woman in a place where, as everyone knew, thieves waited to rob the unwary. When a sudden scream rang out, piercing the night air with its note of terror, Hannah's blood ran cold. She picked up her skirts and ran to join the men and women who were hurrying in the direction of a barn in the opposite corner of the field. So fixed in her mind was the notion that the person in distress must be her mistress that she almost ran past a lonely figure seated on a bench beside a chestnut brazier.

'Why, my lady!' Hannah gasped, in relief and astonishment, 'why dost sit here and where are your escorts gone?'

'They left me some time ago,' Ursula explained. 'I looked for thee, Hannah, but could not find thee. I am cold and I want to go home.' Indeed, she was shivering with cold.

At that moment a horse bearing two riders went by at a furious gallop, caught for a moment in the glow from the brazier before disappearing into the darkness. That brief glimpse, however, had been enough to establish that the riders were Master Harry and Master Cecil.

'There go your stepsons, my lady, heading home it seems, and in a great hurry with no thought to your safety.' Hannah put an arm around her mistress's waist and led her away. 'Come, we will find my brother. He will know what to do. Where is thy fur tippet?' A chill breeze had sprung up, flapping at the faws' tents and sending paper pokes from the toffee man's stall bowling across the ground. ' 'Tis no wonder thou'rt cold.'

'A poor woman came by with four small children and begged for money so that she might buy food. I had no money so I gave her my tippet that she might sell it.'

' 'Twas nobly done,' Hannah nodded approvingly. 'Pray God she was a deserving woman and not some whining thief.'

The screaming, Hannah noted, had ceased and the crowd was returning to the dancing ring. 'What's amiss?' she asked of a passer-by, although now that she was assured that her mistress was in no danger, her concern was less.

' 'Twas nought,' the toothless old goody

235

grinned. 'Some lover a mite rough with his lass, nothing more.' The old woman peered more closely at Lady Ursula and touched her velvet hood. 'Why, my lady, 'twas thy fine fur that was stolen, was it not? For 'tis the match of thy hood. But they catched her! Never fear. They have her. Trying to sell it, she was, but the Belford Watch has it now, and her an' all. In the Belford lockup. Ye'd best go claim what's yours.'

Ignoring the crone's outstretched hand, Hannah hurried Ursula away. Alarmed at the increasing drunkenness around her, she was anxious only to get her mistress safely home before some mischief befell her.

'But Hannah,' Ursula protested, 'I gave the poor woman that tippet.'

'We must find Tom,' Hannah insisted. 'The other matter can wait.'

They found Tom and Betsy in the barn with the rest of the serving girls from Budle Hall gathered in a subdued group around Enid. Enid, pretty little Enid, lay half-swooning against a bale of straw, her face blotched with tears, her bodice ripped apart.

'Is Enid hurt?' gasped Hannah.

'Say rather she has been ravaged,' said Tom grimly, 'by one who would have us call him "gentleman".' He turned an angry face to Lady Ursula. 'Thy stepson, milady,

Master Harry Le Flemont take his pleasure where he will and then runs away.'

Ursula buried her face in her hands and, seeing her distress, Tom was quick to repent. 'Forgive me. I should not have spoken to thee thus but anger got the better of my tongue.'

Lady Ursula's tears, however, were not for Enid but for herself. Her own plight was no different from that of this poor serving wench. It was rape by another name that she herself suffered every night when her lord was at home.

The affair was not made much of at Budle Hall for it was a common enough occurrence for a man to take advantage of a maid. There was even a touch of admiration for Harry in the stable boys' glances when he collected his mount the following morning. The young master must have his pleasure and if any were to criticise his behaviour his response would be, 'Why, she enjoyed it! Led me on, the little faggot.'

If he had thought to seek out Enid before returning to Oxford, he would have found her hiding in the dairy behind the butter churn. Naturally enough, no such thought was in his mind.

Ursula's concern was with the beggar woman to whom she had given her tippet. Mrs Sedgecombe agreed with her that a visit should be paid to the court leet at Belford without delay in order to retrieve it.

'Perhaps thy maid will do this business for thee,' suggested Mrs Sedgecombe. 'She has her wits about her.'

But Ursula was surprisingly firm. 'And I wish to accompany her. We will take the pony trap.' At Hannah's suggestion, she wore the same green mantle and hood in order to prove ownership.

She confessed to feeling nervous. 'I have never been inside a courtroom before, Hannah. I'm glad of thy company.'

'Ye could say the same of me, my lady, yet we have the good fortune to be on the right side of the law. Not so thy poor pauper woman.'

The hearing had already begun when they entered the building and were shown to a place at the back of the room, properly distanced from vagrants and commoners awaiting trial. A message sent to the magistrate on the bench caused him to raise his eyes in surprise and bow in the direction of the wife of Sir George Le Flemont. She had come to identify the stolen tippet which lay before him now and he would be brisk about the business so as not to detain her ladyship overlong.

The wretch in the prisoner's box would hang, of course, but it seemed she meant to have her say before she was taken away.

She had four children, she said, the eldest but seven years old.

And where was her husband, if husband she had? Titters from the clerks. Mayhap she had four 'husbands', a different one for each child? The clerks enjoyed the wit of the magistrate.

She said that her husband had found work in another parish which paid for his keep but not for her and the children. They had been left to starve.

Had she tried to support herself? Could she not spin? Spread manure? Did not the parish give her generous help?

She had no money to buy fleece to spin and already there were enough spinners to keep the weavers busy. She had spread manure. She had gathered stones from the fields and filled potholes in the roads. For this she had been paid six pence a week to support herself and four children.

'Six pence!' she cried, with desperation in her voice. Her thin face was the colour of putty, her eyes dark with fright. 'Do my lords know what can be bought with six pence? Scarce enough to feed one child for a week let alone their ma and three more.'

'So you took to stealing.' It was smoothly said. There was cruel cunning behind the magistrate's smile. He was set upon giving a good account of himself today when the property of the wife of the influential Sir George was involved. This was an opportunity to advance his career and he meant to make the most of it. Lady Le Flemont would see justice done and her tippet returned to her while the miscreant would be adequately punished.

'I am an honest woman, my lord,' the woman's voice wavered, on the verge of tears, 'and have never stolen even an apple in my life and yet—'

The magistrate leaned forward, the better to hear. 'Yes? Speak thy heart so that thy conscience may be clear.'

'And yet I would not see my children starve. Rather than that, I would steal and own it frankly, for my first duty is to the children whom God hath entrusted to my care.'

'Ha!' exclaimed the magistrate delightedly, 'now we have it from thine own lips. You would steal in order to feed your children. I say you have stolen!' He pointed to the tippet. 'This beautiful piece of apparel, for which I would pay ten pounds and not feel robbed, was found in your possession. The proof of your crime is here, woman, the damnation that will hang thee from Belford gibbet before the sun sets this night. Ye may well grow faint, for the noble lady from whom you stole is here to claim what is rightfully hers and in so doing condemn thee utterly.'

At this, the woman gripped the side of the box and looked up in sudden surprise.

The magistrate continued. 'I will ask the clerk to escort Lady Le Flemont to identify and claim her property.'

Hannah was amazed at her mistress's calm. Turning aside all offers of assistance, Ursula rose and walked slowly and composedly down the aisle to face the magistrate who was all honeyed smiles for her.

'I am most honoured that you should come in person to our humble court to settle this disagreeable affair, my lady. I will not detain you long. Only identify this tippet which all can see is a match for your charming gown, then I will sentence the prisoner and all will be done.'

His obsequiousness was quite lost on Ursula who turned instead to the woman in the box, her plain features uplifted by a gentle smile.

'She is no thief. Pray release her. Since I do not carry money, I gave her the tippet that she might sell it to buy food for her children. She is a good mother, as all here can see.'

The woman's tears came in a flood of

relief and there was pandemonium in the courtroom. Clerks and ushers, idlers and prisoners all set up an excited chatter.

'Silence in the court!' Humiliated and angry, the magistrate thumped his gavel. 'I will not tolerate interruption. My lady,' he began patronisingly, but Ursula was there before him.

'Since you expressed a desire to buy this tippet, my lord, then I am of a mind to sell it to you and at the price you name thyself. Though I know this court is no market place to conduct such an exchange, I will accept thy ten pounds now, for my maid and I are in some haste to be away.'

Hannah was as dumbfounded as the magistrate and watched in disbelief as Ursula picked up the tippet and handed it to the blustering, helpless man. Now was seen something of the mother's spirit in the daughter after all. 'Ten pounds,' Ursula reiterated firmly, 'that is what you offered, is it not?'

There was a pause while the whole court held its breath. Then the magistrate, having no option, fumbled for his purse, his face convulsed with chagrin. As he counted out a heap of crowns he could not resist a tiny threat. 'I trust Sir George will not take offence at your selling your wardrobe to me,' he said slyly, but Ursula was not to be cowed.

'This much is mine,' she said loftily, 'to do as I please with.' Then she walked to the prisoner in the box and emptied the money into her hands. The woman was too overcome to speak.

'Let her not be molested. She must go to her children.' Though Ursula spoke calmly, she could not control the trembling of her limbs. Only Hannah knew what this noble effort had cost her. Turning to the woman, Ursula continued, 'If any try to harm you, you are to send me word.'

'Release her,' ordered the magistrate sourly, and the woman stepped free. With a look of intense gratitude towards her benefactor, she hurried from the building.

Oh, my lady would pay for this outrage! The magistrate was not to be humiliated in his own court by any woman, highborn or not and he would have his revenge. Waiting prisoners trembled to see his anger which would undoubtedly prejudice their own forthcoming trial.

Hannah hurried to Lady Ursula's side and led her away, out of the oppressive atmosphere of the court into fresh September air. 'Oh well done, my lady,' she cried delightedly. 'Well done indeed.'

Ursula glowed with pleasure at Hannah's praise.

'For certain it is that ye have saved that poor woman's life.'

On their way home, they passed the very gibbet where the woman would have hung but for Ursula's intervention.

'Supposing she had been hanged,' Ursula mused, 'what would have become of her children, Hannah?'

'The parish pays four pounds a year to foster parents.' Hannah knew of such children in Eglingham. 'In this way, some evil folk come by a slave and are paid into the bargain.'

Ursula shivered. 'When I lived with my parents at Bewick Grange, the world seemed a kind and friendly place. I have learned otherwise since.'

'I had not your advantage of gentle birth, my lady, and discovered quite early that life is a box of tricks. The good do not always win. The die is loaded against the poor from the start and especially is a poor woman wronged, for she bears a double misfortune, her poverty and her sex.'

'How sagely you talk, Hannah.'

Hannah shrugged. 'I have given the matter much thought. See how justice works against the woman you have just saved. Her husband abandons his wife and four children, yet does a hue and cry go out to find him and make him face his responsibilities? Nay. The judge says, "Hang the woman. Board out the children," and the matter is closed.'

It was past noon when Hannah turned the gig into Budle Hall's tree-lined drive.

'We have taken all morn to settle that dispute, Hannah,' Ursula sighed, 'and I fear I have made an enemy of that magistrate.' An involuntary cry escaped her lips as they turned into the courtyard. Grooms were unharnessing a pair of greys from Sir George's carriage. 'My lord is back. Now must my misery begin all over again.'

The discomfited magistrate who had been forced to part with ten pounds made quite sure that Sir George was immediately informed upon his return. In the angry scene that followed, Ursula faced a man quite out of his mind with rage.

'To sell your clothes like a common slut! And in a courtroom, of all places!' In his fury, he would hear no explanation.

The magistrate would have been mollified to see the marks left on Ursula's body by her husband's riding crop. It was left to Hannah to try and comfort her mistress and bathe the weals, to conceal the ugly bruises on her face with powder and paint.

There was nothing to be done. Ursula dried her tears resolving never again to court the anger of her husband. She would endeavour to please him in everything she did, as was her wifely duty. Nevertheless

she would for ever cherish the memory
of her victory over the magistrate and
on those occasions when her misery was
almost too great to be borne, the look of
gratitude in the eyes of a poor peasant
woman would return to lift her spirits.

16

Apart from the irritation caused by his
wife's folly, Sir George's mood on his
return from London was one of barely
suppressed elation. He had found his
business affairs in a most satisfactory state.
Undreamed-of profits were accruing to his
credit as a result of the popular demand
for imported spices, eastern oils, silks and
taffetas. As a shareholder in the East India
Company and part-owner of one of its
vessels, Sir George was well on the way
to becoming a very rich man. He could
begin to think seriously of refurbishing his
residence after the manner of the fine
houses in London. Some classical sculpture
might be introduced into the great hall. A
painted window similar to one he had seen
in Chelsea would enhance the library and
he intended to engage a painter to depict in
oils a likeness of himself and his sons. The

fortunes of the Le Flemont family were in the ascendancy once more.

He had used his time in London to his advantage, gleaning what information he could from the gossip of the coffee houses. Rumour and intrigue abounded, tales of bribery and corruption. He marked them all but kept his own counsel, even in drink, when many a man had been brought to ruin by a loose tongue.

The king had grown bolder during his two years on the throne and now made no attempt to conceal his Catholic preferences. To the growing concern of hitherto loyal Protestant supporters, almost all influential positions at court were now in the hands of Catholics. Even the highly respected Cavalier families, whose loyalty to the monarch was traditionally the cornerstone of their creed, were beginning to voice their disquiet. They could be seen, heads together, in earnest discussion in the coffee houses. Sir George was never invited to join them. He was not a popular man. When he appeared, such conclaves fell silent and did not resume discussion until he left.

'Le Flemont,' the word went, 'will run with the hare and hunt with the hounds and go for cover when times are bad.'

Smarting from the snubs, Sir George comforted himself with the knowledge that the days of Protestant supremacy were over. His contacts at court assured him of that. The high and mighty Cavaliers, most of whom were Protestants, were riding for a fall and Sir George Le Flemont intended to be at hand when discredited nobles were stripped of their lands. In this mood of extreme content, he returned to his Northumbrian fortress and applied himself to correcting his wife's waywardness.

In the capital, however, public disquiet increased and when James demanded of Parliament the money to raise a standing army for his own protection, there was a storm of protest. The excesses of Cromwell's army were still too fresh in men's minds for such a statute to be approved.

With every day that passed, James was demonstrating that he meant to rule as an absolute monarch and only the knowledge that his legitimate heirs were Protestant kept the lid on the ferment that was brewing in the city of London.

Great was the consternation, therefore, when, in October of that year, 1687, James let it be known that his queen was pregnant. There was general astonishment for the king was no longer young and many barren years had passed since Mary of Modena suffered her last miscarriage. This unfortunate obstetric history, however, did offer hope to the Protestants. The queen had miscarried many times before and would no doubt reach the same fruitless climax with this her latest, and most surprising pregnancy.

The Protestants hopes were to be dashed. The pregnancy advanced without complications and the threat to the established religion of the country could no longer be ignored. If the queen produced a live heir, he would certainly be brought up as a Catholic.

The Huguenots who had sought refuge in England from just such a bigoted Catholic monarch as James were thrown into the deepest despair.

'First Paris,' moaned Albert de Colonnières, 'then Strasbourg, now England. There is nowhere left for us to run to.'

Sir Walter could find no words of comfort now to lift the hearts of his Huguenot friends. He sat silent as they contemplated the chilling future.

'He will close the Protestant churches,' Guy de Colonnières predicted. 'There will be nowhere for us to worship. Protestant midwives will be forbidden to practise and what Catholic nurse will cherish a Protestant infant? Will James's dragoons make themselves easy in our houses as Louis' did?'

Madame de Colonnières buried her face in her hands.

Sir Walter tried to offer reassurance. ' 'Twill never come to that,' he said quietly. 'Englishmen will stand so much and no more. Nevertheless, I see dark days ahead for all of us until this matter is settled.'

The prospect of a Catholic heir in the near future was good news for Sir George at Budle Hall. Congratulating himself upon his choice of a Catholic tutor for his sons, he found he could look upon that seedy individual with something like warmth when he considered the advantages that might result from such employment.

When the Protestant cause was as dead as mutton, preferment would lie with those of Catholic persuasion. Nevertheless, the situation needed delicate handling. A move too far, too soon, could undo him. There was much to consider. Cloaked in black with his hat pulled low against the wind he paced the seashore plotting his own rise to fame and the destruction of his enemies.

'Like a greet nasty daddy-long-legs wi' boots, on,' Betsy would scoff at him when she was safely out of his reach. The simile was apt for the master's feet did seem uncommonly large for the long thin legs to which they were attached. This inequality of substance produced an extraordinary kicking movement when he walked as if he meant to shed the cumbersome weight from each spindly ankle. Startled serving girls coming upon his solitary figure crossed themselves and ran. None were game enough to meet his cruel, lusting stare.

News of the queen's condition affected Betsy and Hannah not in the least. Their preoccupation was entirely with two other pregnancies much closer to home, both of which should have been of concern to Sir George. His wife was expecting her first baby and his dairymaid was carrying his son's bastard.

Hannah had failed to identify the reason for her mistress's recurring sickness and when Widow Dodds's usually infallible receipt of rosemary pounded in a glass of wine failed to alleviate the distressing symptoms, she sought the help of Mrs Sedgecombe. That grandmother's instant diagnosis came as a complete surprise to Hannah.

'Why so amazed, girl? Your mistress is a married woman and Sir George is no cripple. 'Tis wholly natural and God's blessing that she should be carrying his child.'

The fact that Enid was in a similar condition was even more disturbing to Hannah.

'Three months gone.' Betsy confirmed. 'She fell first time, poor lass.'

'Does Master Harry know?'

'She tellt him when he was home last week and he sent her away weeping. He says the bairn's not his and that others had been there before him which is not true. He forced her, that night in the barn. Enid had never lain with a man before and well he knows it.'

'Why does she not tell Sir George?'

'And what would he do? Take his dairymaid for a daughter? Nay. He'd send the wanton packing, then she and her bairn would have nae roof ower their head.'

'What's to be done, then?'

'She must marry any lad that'll have her, and that quickly, before her apron declares that the honey has already been tasted.'

'When a babe is born six months later, what will he think?'

'Why then, Hannah, my simpleton, my green-as-grass little innocent, he will find that the age of miracles is not past.'

Hannah frowned. 'That's not fair.'

Betsy shrugged. 'Nowt's fair. For Master Harry 'twas but an afternoon's pleasure but see what a pickle he puts our Enid in.'

Hannah found Enid in the dairy amongst the creaming pans. The sight of her thickening waist and swelling skirt caused Hannah's stomach muscles to tighten involuntarily. There was only six months difference in age between herself and Enid. She could relate all too easily to the present situation. Confronted by the shocking evidence of rape, Hannah wanted to turn away as if the very sight were contagious, as if Enid herself were unclean, someone to be shunned.

Then Enid, so poignantly vulnerable, turned to her friend, with a helpless gesture, 'Oh Hannah.'

Hannah's base thoughts fled. When she spoke, there was true concern in her voice. 'Can nought be done, hinny? I used to help an old nurse. We made potions of pennyroyal which ofttimes expelled an unwanted infant.'

The ready tears brimmed over. ' 'Tis too late. I've tried all the herbs and potions I know and still I carry that beast's brat within me. I swear now, before God, that I will never, never love that child even though it be my own flesh and blood.'

Hannah took her hand and stroked it gently, searching for words of comfort. 'Hast sought advice from the old goodies who live by Waren Mill?'

Enid sniffed. 'They told me to go to the crone who burns kelp by the shore. A few blasts from her pump and she'll get rid of the baby all right and me along with it, like many another poor girl in desperate straits. And she charges a crown for her evil work! Nay, Hannah,' Enid withdrew her hand and adjusted her apron strings. 'I thank thee for thy concern,' she spoke more calmly now, 'but there's nought anyone can do unless it be Old Nosey the coachman. I'll wed him the morn if he'll have me.'

Thomas the coachman was twenty years her senior, a fat, coarse man with a nose like a beacon.

'He's desperate for a wife,' Enid continued, 'before he falls off his perch with the ague and old age.'

'Ye canna mean to marry him!' Hannah was aghast.

'I'll marry anyone who'll give my bairn a name and me a roof ower my head.'

In spite of herself, Enid blossomed. Her firm skin had the bloom of a peach. Her rounded little body was as cuddlesome as a kitten. Thomas the coachman could hardly believe his luck as he led his sonsy bride down the aisle of Bamburgh Church. Later, at the feast generously supplied by the master, the sniggers of the stableboys passed him by. His restricted wits did not allow him to comprehend more than one fact at a time. The wonder of possessing a wife, a young and lovely wife, was enough for Thomas at the moment.

As Enid bloomed, so Ursula wilted. Nausea persisted until Sir George himself began to take an unwelcome interest in the plates of food she left untouched.

'Starve thyself if thee have a mind to, but not when thou'rt carrying my child. Stay with her,' he commanded Mrs Sedgecombe. 'Make sure she eats. Since the infant stands a good chance of being weak in the head like its mother, at least let it be strong in body.'

To Hannah's relief and surprise, Mrs Sedgecombe showed real concern over Ursula. Circumspect in all her actions, the housekeeper would not risk her position by directly opposing the master's wishes when he was present, but in his absence she occasionally went out of her way to show Ursula many small acts of kindness. The long narrow face common to many Irishwomen would visibly soften with pity as the young wife, weak and wretched from continual bouts of sickness was helped from the table by her staunch little maid. On one occasion she went so far as to voice a criticism of her master. 'I know him of old.' She spoke softly, as if talking to herself. 'There is no kindness in his nature. He can be cruelly hard.' This remark was invested with such dark implication that, for the first time, Hannah paused to wonder how Sir George's first wife, the housekeeper's own daughter, had met her end.

'Please write to my mamma, Hannah,' Lady Ursula begged, 'and seek a remedy for this sickness.'

Lady Heslop's reply came swiftly, conveyed in person by the young artist whom Sir George had engaged to design a painted window for the library.

Mrs Sedgecombe presented the fashionably dressed young man to Lady Ursula in Hannah's presence. 'Mounseer Alphonse de Colonnières,' she announced, 'from your respected mother.'

Hannah rose from her stool and came forward to relieve the young man of a bottle of physic and a poke of oranges. His clothes were more elegant, his bearing more confident, but it was the same dark-eyed young Huguenot who had rested with his family at Bewick Grange after fleeing from Europe.

He was explaining himself to Lady Ursula. 'You will not remember me, my lady, but my father, mother and myself are forever indebted to your parents for sheltering us when we were in dire trouble.'

Lady Ursula smiled, a wan gesture on a face grown thin and pale yet one which still carried the warmth of her affection. 'Who would not remember such a handsome youth?' He gracefully acknowledged the compliment. 'Now our roles are reversed,' Ursula continued. 'You were ill and weary then. Now that is my lot.'

'It is the deep concern of your parents that you quickly regain your health, my lady. Knowing that I am to carry out a commission here for Sir George, they begged me to bring these comforts to you myself so that I may report truthfully on your state of health and happiness.'

'And what will you tell them?' Ursula's voice was sad and flat as though the question was of no import.

Alphonse hesitated. 'Why, that I believe I have seen you in better spirits...'

'Aye,' said Ursula sharply. 'You may say that in all truth. Tell me,' making an effort to deflect interest from herself in a way that compelled Hannah's admiration, 'what is the nature of my husband's commission to you, Mounseer Alphonse?' Though in no mood for idle chat, Ursula behaved with unhurried courtesy.

'It is to design a circular window in the library and depict there, by means of coloured glass, an heroic scene such as might be found in a Greek temple.'

'Though somewhat unlikely in Northumberland?'

He smiled his agreement but ventured no opinion.

'You may visit us here in my apartments whenever you choose.' Ursula was drawing the interview to a close. 'Hannah and I welcome a new face in this dreary round of days before my child is born.'

For the first time, he turned and looked at Hannah who smiled to see him struggling to identify a memory.

He came on two more occasions and Hannah would catch a glimpse of him from time to time as he worked at his easel in the library. Sir George had not seen fit to light a fire there for his comfort though winter held the countryside in a cruel grip. From the open door, Hannah could see that his hands were blue with cold as he covered sheet after sheet of paper with bold charcoal drawings. He never looked up, being intent upon his work.

In truth, the library was no colder than any other room in Budle Hall. Passages that had been cool in summer were achingly cold now and the coughing, grumbling residents wore all the clothes they possessed in order to keep warm. Mrs Sedgecombe had scarce been able to put on a shoe for rheumatism of the toe joints until Hannah came to the rescue with one of Widow Dodds's salves. It was warmer to be out and about than huddle within dank walls and Hannah was glad to escape from the sickroom to walk with Betsy from time to time.

'Ye've no cause to worry so,' Betsy comforted her.

' 'Tis a natural thing after all and the midwife will move in when your lady gets near her time.' But the sense of foreboding stayed.

The two maids would walk, well wrapped up, by Budle Bay, where thousands of Arctic birds sought to overwinter on the mud flats. They were a memorable sight; whooper swans calling their wild, evocative cry, whistling widgeon and flocks of waders searching the incoming tides for scraps. Adrift in this wet world of salt mists amongst the piping, wailing birds, Hannah could forget for a while the depression of the sickroom, and the forthcoming ordeal that faced her mistress.

In deep midwinter, the sea showed another side to its character. Waves that had lapped dulcet, thick as cream, at the foot of the great tower all summer long now hurled themselves in icy swathes at its weathered stones, bleaching against the lowermost windows on occasion.

'Howay to Budle Point,' said Betsy. 'I'll show thee a rough sea!'

It was a day when none but the young and foolish ventured out without cause.

Sudden sleeting showers stung the face like knives. The wind, scooping up veils of sand as it raced along the shore, turned the girls' skirts into sails and almost bowled them off their feet. At Budle Point, they could scarcely make their voices heard above the roar of the elements, the punch of obdurate rocks into columns of green water and the screech of seabirds as they searched the curtains of foaming spray for food. There was no telling where the grey sea met the grey sky. The horizon was an arm's length away, a league away.

'There's a sea for you!' Betsy shouted with proprietorial glee.

Hannah put her mouth to Betsy's ear. 'What's that booming noise?' An irregular thumping as if someone were dragging a heavy chest across the floor of the ocean itself, sent a shiver down Hannah's spine.

'The sea breaking over the Farne rocks. Pity any sailor oot there.'

'What chance for a ship in this!' cried Hannah. 'Tom Tiddler's luck in a trout pool.' As she spoke a point of flame pierced the mists over Bamburgh head.

'They've lit the beacon,' said Betsy, 'but it'll nae show much on a day like this.' She took Hannah's arm. 'Howay. We'd best be making home. Mind ye,' she went on as they reached quieter stretches of the bay, 'there's some who like nowt better than a shipwreck. Storm treasure is what they're after. There's good pickings from a harvest of corpses! Not me!' Betsy hastened to answer Hannah's accusing stare. 'I'll have nowt to do with dead man's gold for 'twill bring ill luck for sartain.'

After such outings Hannah could face her sickroom duties with increased resolve and, by her own cheerfulness, was able to lift the flagging spirits of her mistress. She never tired of reading aloud to Ursula though the choice of books available was limited. The chaplain did not hold with educated servant girls and was reluctant to lend any books until a command from Lady Ursula herself released a few heavy tomes, some in Latin which he knew would not be understood. There were, however, several books of poetry which could be read over and over again and still yield fresh enjoyment.

As winter gave way to the more kindly airs of spring, the thinness of Ursula's limbs was emphasised by her swollen belly. Her face, hollow-cheeked and white as a lily showed a woman who was clearly in no fit condition to go into labour. Hannah, unable to effect any improvement, was appalled at her own inadequacy and longed for the arrival of the midwife.

When she came, she brought little comfort. Hannah could have wished for Widow Dodds's reassuring presence in place of the stout old goody in musty black who never stopped talking from the moment she stepped down from the pony trap. Her nose was large and red and Hannah, who had some experience of this condition after working with Mrs Nan, suspected that it was not entirely due to the bracing sea breeze.

She was to move into Hannah's room next to Lady Ursula's bedchamber and Hannah was to share a room with Betsy and the other chambermaids.

'What a time it is for bairns to be born!' The old woman bounced Hannah's mattress for comfort. 'I'm on the go from morn till night with scarce time to draw breath twixt one babby and the next.' She raised her hands to take off her bonnet and Hannah, who had become particular over such things, noticed her dirty fingernails. 'The old books do say,' the midwife went on, 'that if a woman is to conceive at all, 'twill be at Michaelmas and ye can see the truth of that. The king himself was a proper fellow that night! Now, where am I to put my bonnet? Then ye can take me to the little pet who waits for me.'

17

If Hannah had introduced a trundling sow into the bedchamber it could not have created more disturbance than did this uncouth woman hired to deliver Ursula's baby. The air of calm that Hannah had been at pains to preserve for her mistress's peace of mind was shattered by the midwife's non-stop clacking. The clatter of her boots on the floorboards, for she would not put on slippers, brought Ursula hands to her throbbing head.

'Headaches, is it?' the midwife observed cheerfully. 'A bit of blood letting will soon cure that.'

With eyes as big as brandy balls, she came to Hannah one day. 'Ye've a queer one there and no mistake,' here a conspiratorial dig in the ribs. 'She wants to know how the baby will get oot of her belly!'

'I tried to tell her,' Hannah said lamely, recoiling from the offensive breath, 'but midwifery is nowt to do with me.'

Ursula's labour began prematurely on the ninth of June. She watched the square of sky framed by her window change from

263

dawn's pale flush to the hot blue of noon then the indigo of night before her travail came to an end.

Men and women of the estate went about their daily work. Maids gossiped beneath her window. Grooms confided lovingly to their cherished horses and the smell of new-cut hay wafted in through her lightly stirring curtains. The summer sea crumbled gently on the shore while Ursula, totally unprepared for this ordeal to which her body must submit, sank deeper and deeper into a lonely abyss of pain.

From the depths of despair, she cried upon God to help her and when a great white tern appeared at her window, she interpreted this as a messenger sent to give her strength. Again and again the great bird, mistaking its own reflection in the glass for an adversary, attacked and buffeted the window with its wings. Ursula's eyes never left it as her infant made its unhurried way down the birth canal. The tern flew away as the baby girl was born.

Hannah, crouched outside the door with her fingers in her ears, still heard the agonised cry of achievement.

'Wake yersell up, girl.' The midwife shook her roughly. 'Tell the master it's a girl. All that fuss,' she grumbled, 'and it not the size of a kitten.'

Ursula's baby was indeed a puny little thing. After one look at his latest offspring, Sir George gave it little chance of survival.

'It's her first,' he said curtly to the midwife. 'She'll take more care next time.'

Had he visited Enid's humble cottage he would have found a lusty new-born boy, the dead spit of his eldest son and as robust an heir as he could have desired.

'Why, what a man y'are, Thomas,' joked the stable boys as they drank the coachman's health in flagon after flagon of ale. 'A great boy like that after only six months of marriage!'

Thomas, gloriously drunk, chuckled delightedly. 'Just ye wait and see what I can do after nine months! A bairn strong enough to pull the coach, I shouldn't wonder.'

Twenty-four hours after Ursula and Enid were safely delivered, the queen gave birth to a son. Now were the worst fears of England's Protestant majority confirmed. The rightful heir to the throne was a Catholic. Wild rumours born of desperation suggested that the baby was a changeling, smuggled into the queen's bed in a warming pan. Rational thinking reasserted itself, however, and those powerful Cavaliers who up till now had refused to contemplate any action against the lawful king, now agreed that steps must be taken to prevent the established religion of the country being overturned.

The king's eldest daughter by his first wife was the obvious choice to supplant James. A Protestant herself, Mary was married to William the Prince of Orange, that stalwart defender of the Protestant faith in the Low Countries and the greatest thorn in the flesh of the Catholic King of France, Louis XIV. Without more ado, they offered him the crown of Britain.

Ursula's tiny baby was christened without delay. Amelia Georgina was a pitifully small scrap of humanity, but to her mother she brought transports of joy. Hannah was astonished at the wholesome change in her mistress. Ennobled by motherhood, Ursula radiated a confidence that was in sharp contrast to the depression of her pregnancy. Propped up on pillows with her baby in her arms, she was the very picture of happiness.

'Is she not adorable, Hannah?'

The midwife sniffed. 'Bide awhile afore ye jump ower the moon,' she warned. ' 'Tis early days.'

Her words were tragically prophetic. Ursula's pride and joy lasted no longer than forty-eight hours. The babe would not suckle, had scarce the strength to cry and died in its mother's arms.

As in a lamp turned low, the radiance drained away from Ursula. Still holding the cold little creature to her breast, she stared about her with eyes from which all intelligence had fled. Hannah's heart was rent to see Fate mistreat her sweet mistress so.

'Take the babby away from her,' grunted the midwife. 'It's deed.'

When Hannah, with infinite tenderness, waited upon her mistress the following morning, she found a stranger. Ursula's somewhat protruding light blue eyes regarded her with hostility. Her voice, when she spoke, was cold and curt.

'Go away, girl.'

Hannah was preparing to wash and dress her mistress. 'My lady,' she said gently, ' 'tis I, your own Hannah, come to make you comfortable.' But Ursula would have none of her ministrations and the washing had to wait.

'Shock,' said the midwife, 'I seen it many a time. It'll pass.'

With Ursula, it did not. Clearly, the young mother's mind was deranged by the tragedy and, long after the midwife had taken her leave, Ursula walked the grounds of Budle Hall, ceaselessly seeking her baby. Enid and other mothers, seeing the look of cunning on the face of the poor demented creature, took care to hide their own babies at her approach lest she do them a mischief or even steal them away. To Hannah fell the thankless task of guarding her.

Ursula, previously so guileless, became sly in her ways, taking great delight in escaping from Hannah's supervision. When she took to rising from her bed in the night to wander the corridors, Hannah placed her own mattress at her mistress's door and many times led her back to bed without receiving a civil word.

' 'Tis Hannah, my lady,' she would say but the response was always the same.

'I do not know thee. Go away.'

The words struck like a knife. Her mistress's welfare had been Hannah's sole concern ever since arriving at Budle Hall. What had been done in the name of duty at first became an act of devotion for she truly loved her sweet mistress with all her heart. Now she must stand helplessly by and watch that face of sweet innocence transformed into a mask of cunning. An evil spirit had taken possession of her charge. This new Ursula was hateful towards her, breaking into scornful laughter whenever she perceived the tears in her maid's eyes.

At last, on Mrs Sedgecombe's advice,

Hannah wrote to Sir Walter and Lady Heslop, since Sir George chose to ignore his wife's condition.

'I fear the loss of her baby hath unhinged my mistress's mind,' she wrote. 'I pray thee, if it be at all possible, to visit with all speed.'

Sir Walter read the letter with an uncomfortable feeling of guilt. He had been so involved with affairs in the Netherlands where Prince William was even now raising an army, that he had given little thought to his daughter's bereavement beyond a letter of condolence.

'We will make arrangements to go there three days from now,' he told his wife, 'upon my return from Newcastle. That's a wise little maid to write such a letter.'

Lady Heslop occupied herself during those three days in airing Ursula's old bedchamber. She meant to bring her daughter home again until she was re-covered in health, Sir George or no Sir George. In her present mood, she would brook no stay or hindrance. She gave instructions for the bed to be made up with lavender-scented sheets and vases to be filled with roses. Caring for others was at the very root of her nature. The gap left by Ursula's departure had taken her by surprise.

'A week or two here,' she told the

sympathetic chambermaids, 'with proper food and physic and we'll soon have the roses back in her cheeks.'

She need not have been concerned about Sir George's reaction. Tired of the sight of his silly wife, he had taken himself off to London once more. Harry was away in Oxford leaving only Cecil at home in the charge of his tutor and Mrs Sedgecombe.

If Ursula's parents had come at once, if Sir Walter had cancelled the Newcastle visit, the young mother's tragic end might have been averted, but Fate ruled otherwise.

On a brilliant, blustering day when white horses were running the ocean for as far as the eye could see. Ursula, in her wandering, came upon Cecil discoursing on a bench with his tutor.

'Now for some fun,' tittered Cecil and the chaplain's mouth twitched as Ursula approached, peering this way and that. Her long hair fell unkempt about her shoulders for she would not allow Hannah near her. Her face was streaked with the juice of blackberries plucked from the hedges as she passed.

'Excuse me, sir,' she addressed the cleric politely, provoking Cecil into a fit of giggles, 'have you seen my baby? A little girl, with starry eyes? I believe she passed this way.'

Piously, the chaplain lifted his eyes to the sky. 'Madame,' he intoned, 'thy baby rests in heaven.'

'Perhaps Sweet Jesu hath given her wings,' sniggered Cecil, pointing to the top of the high tower where seabirds, mewing and wheeling, flashed white against the summer sky.

With stained fingers, Ursula brushed the hair from her eyes and peered in the direction he indicated. One bird in particular held her attention. Its forked tail set it apart from the chunky herring gulls. A bird like this, she remembered, with black cap and red legs had borne her company during the long hours of her confinement. A look of determination stole across her vacant features. Somewhere in her confused brain, bird and baby became hopelessly interchangeable. She hurried away in the direction of the tower.

'Poor creature,' the chaplain shook his head sanctimoniously.

'She's an idiot,' scoffed Master Cecil, 'and should be put away.'

Hannah found Lady Ursula beating upon the tower door with bare fists. 'Oh, my lady, you must not run away from me.' She was out of breath from running. 'I am your friend.' But the look that Ursula gave her was of pure dislike. 'The tower is locked,' Hannah said gently. 'What ist ye seek here?'

Ursula pointed to the birds circling over their heads. 'Dost not see her? There. She rests on the parapet. There sits my little darling. See how she preens herself so prettily?'

Confused, Hannah stood silent.

'Why so glum!' Ursula rounded upon her. 'Stupid girl. I like not your black looks. Go away.'

'My lady,' Hannah faltered, ' 'tis nought but a bird you see.'

The sudden blow across her mouth was so unexpected that Hannah was almost knocked off her feet. Surprise that a weak woman could deliver such a blow mingled with the hurt she felt at being thus treated. Tears filled her eyes, but her deranged mistress must be humoured.

'You are right, of course. I beg my lady's pardon. Come away now for the tower is locked and we may not go in.'

'My baby is looking for me,' Ursula muttered as she allowed herself to be led away.

The incident upset Hannah greatly. 'She has no love for me now,' she told Betsy with a heavy heart. 'I trust her parents will come ere long.'

On the night following Ursula's attack upon her, Hannah slept but fitfully, awaking at the slightest sound from her mistress's chamber. In the morning, filled with a growing uneasiness, she checked that all was well and that her mistress was still soundly sleeping before she herself went downstairs to the kitchen to prepare breakfast.

The household was just beginning to stir. Sleepy kitchenmaids blew on grey embers to raise a blaze. Porridge that had stood by the hearth all night needed but a jug of cream and a stir to make it ready to serve. Thinking that some fresh raspberries might tempt her mistress's fickle appetite, Hannah took a bowl and went into the kitchen garden.

She was head down amongst the bushes when the cows passed by to milking, nudging and mooing into the yard. The whole world seemed slow and easy at this early hour, calming her troubled spirits. Here in the garden the air was fragrant with phlox and gillyflower and lemon-scented thyme. If only Lady Ursula might be persuaded to rest here while Hannah read aloud to her, she might regain some peace of mind. Since the death of her baby, Ursula had lost interest in stories and poetry.

A sudden raucous cacophony amongst the birds brought Hannah's head up with a jerk. Some disturbance was causing them to wheel in agitation about the top of the tower. A great tern amongst the lesser gulls was the reason for the uproar and Hannah was about to resume her picking when a sight made her blood run cold, made her drop her half-filled basin, pick up her skirts and run, crying out for help as she went.

Standing on the battlements of the tower with arms outstretched, wildly snatching at the shrieking birds, was Lady Ursula in her nightclothes. Even as she ran, Hannah saw the slight figure propelled dangerously close towards the edge of the parapet as the roistering wind made a sail of her cotton shift.

'No! No! No!' Hannah's legs felt as if weighted by lead. Her heart beat within her breast like a caged bird as she raced to the tower.

The door stood open, the key still in the lock.

'She must have taken the key while I slept,' panted the butler, buttoning his shirt as he ran.

'Fetch mattresses, pillows, straw-bales—anything!' Mrs Sedgecombe, scarcely recognisable in flowered velvet mantle over her shift and her hair hanging down her back, was still in command, her voice ringing out like a bell over a suddenly thronging courtyard.

Hannah, a prayer on her lips, was already

halfway up the spiralling stone stairway. Funnelling down towards her, beating against her ears, the hideous cacophony of bird cries added to the nightmare of the moment. It seemed that she would never reach the top but at length she tumbled out into the daylight just as a great groan rose up from the courtyard below.

The parapet was empty save for the birds circling unconcernedly above her head. Then she knew that she was too late. The kindly breeze, taking up the folds of Ursula's nightgown, had let her go as lightly as a falling leaf but the paving stones of the courtyard were obdurate and final. She lay like a spatched chick eighty feet below Hannah's horrified eyes.

18

Before leaving Budle Hall for ever, Hannah paid a last visit to Mistress Emma and Tom. That household was sadly reduced. An empty chair now stood by the fireside where Joshua was wont to sit.

Disease had quietly diminished the potter until, at the last, only his fever-bright eyes showed signs of life in his wasted body. Devotedly, Tom carried him from the couch where he slept to his chair by the fire and back again at night until the day he died.

There were other changes. Daniel's absence affected Hannah more than she had expected. Quiet and retiring by nature, he yet left a significant void. In the evening, at the long kitchen table, the old harmony was somehow flawed without him. Impatiently she shrugged off the prick of shame at her remembered rudeness towards him. She had meant to write to him but all that belonged to a world now gone, to a time of lighthearted, carefree days which seemed lost to her for evermore.

As though reading her thoughts, Mistress Emma said, 'Daniel rode down from Scotland to pay his last respects to Joshua and see him buried.'

'I trust that Daniel's affairs prosper.'

Hannah's subdued manner did not escape Emma's notice. This maid had been badly shaken by the tragedy at Budle Hall.

'Come. I will show thee where my dearest now lies in peace.'

She led Hannah to the clump of rowan trees on the rising land at the back of the house. 'He would not suffer the liturgy of the Episcopal church to be read over him, choosing rather to be buried here in

276

unconsecrated ground.'

Hannah stood silent beside the narrow mound of earth bordered with pansies, all that was left to remind her of the kind and jolly potter she once knew.

'I thank God daily for Daniel and Tom in my hour of need.' Emma dabbed her mild blue eyes with a scrap of cambric. 'In truth, Hannah, I would be lost without your brother now that Joshua and Daniel are both gone.'

Tom had indeed taken upon himself the double charge of caring for the potter's widow and managing the business, though Mistress Emma was no deadweight and continued to handle the accounting with her usual skill.

When the tragedy at Budle Hall became known, Emma's immediate thought was for Hannah and an invitation for her to make her home at Buckton had been dispatched without delay. Such a tempting offer was hard to turn away but Hannah reviewed in a more sober light her first glad impulse to accept.

There was little money to spare after the fine had been paid to secure Joshua's release from prison. Tom and his two young apprentices would need to work hard to mend the fortunes of the pottery. She could contribute nothing to Mistress Emma's income and would not take the bread from her mouth.

'But what wilt do, Hannah?' Tom was filled with anxiety over his sister. Since the death of her mistress, Hannah had changed from a gay and lively companion to a sad and morose figure. 'Father'll nae keep thee at home.'

'I have money to pay my keep at home for a little while,' Hannah said. 'After that, I do not know what I shall do.' She shook her head helplessly in a gesture so foreign to her character that Tom would rather have seen her in tears.

'The Lord will take thee by the hand and show the way,' said Emma, 'yet there is for ever a place for thee beneath my roof.'

Hannah was speaking the truth when she said she had no plans for the future. An emptiness within her denied any constructive thought. Try as she might, she was unable to conjure up the face of the gentle mistress she had loved. That beloved image was usurped by a mad creature with staring eyes and unkempt hair. In her imagination Hannah could hear the spiteful voice railing endlessly against her, giving her no peace. Night and day the vision was before her of a shattered body in lacy nightclothes spreadeagled on the courtyard.

She had lived through a nightmare since that dreadful day. Lady Heslop's attitude at her daughter's funeral showed clearly that she held Hannah to blame for her daughter's death.

'I could not be with her all the time, my lady,' she had protested, for the accusation of negligence was too cruel to be borne. 'There was none other but myself to prepare her breakfast and in that short time she left her bed and climbed the tower.'

Unexpectedly, Mrs Sedgecombe came forward with words of support. She, who was not given to intervene on another's behalf, found that she was unable to stand silently by and see Ursula's dedicated little maid so wronged. 'I have never seen such devotion in a maid for her mistress,' she declared. 'Truly she must not carry blame.'

But neither the kind words of the housekeeper nor Betsy's loving sympathy could wipe away the sting of the undeserved rebuke.

If Sir Walter could have found it in his heart to speak, he might have suggested to his wife that her anger was but an indulgence to quieten her own conscience. As parents of the dead girl, both had failed to concern themselves over her welfare until it was too late. Her young and inexperienced maid had been left to bear the burden.

But he said nothing. He was under great stress on another account. While grieving at the shocking death of his daughter, he was, at the same time, deeply involved in the plot to bring Prince William of Orange to England. On the previous day, he had put his name to a charter that would cause him to lose his head and everything he possessed if the plan failed. The personal problems of a serving wench were therefore outside his concern at the moment.

The final leavetaking between himself and Sir George was chilly, made more so by secret information which confirmed what Sir Walter had long suspected, that Sir George would take the king's side in any confrontation, even to the extent of turning Catholic. The Le Flemont coat, he noted grimly, which had been turned many times in the past, was showing its lining once again. He was at some pains, therefore, not to disclose his own hand and to make their leavetaking as brief as possible.

Sir George, on his part, was quite obviously glad to see the back of the party from Bewick and made no secret of the fact that he considered himself to have been put to a great deal of expense and trouble over the marriage for small gain. Here he chose to ignore the generous dowry provided by Sir Walter and not reclaimed.

Hannah was to be returned to her home. She would travel with the Heslops to the point where the track for Burnfoot left the Bewick road. What happened to her after that was of no concern to Lady Heslop. Further employment was out of the question.

The dreary task of packing Ursula's belongings fell to Hannah. Each garment brought its own memory of happier days to rekindle her misery and when Lady Heslop, in a conciliatory tone, offered her one of the flowered cotton day dresses, she almost screamed her refusal. How could she put next to her skin the garment worn by her dear, dead mistress? But Lady Heslop had been affronted and Hannah lacked the words to explain her feelings.

After a last tearful farewell to Betsy and Enid, Hannah climbed inside the Heslop carriage. Because of the unsettled weather, she was being allowed to sit inside although she would rather have braved the rain than endure the chilling presence of Lady Heslop.

The coachman cracked his whip. The team of four picked up their feet and clattered away down the drive leaving behind for ever the gaunt forbidding walls of Budle Hall. When the last glimpse of Betsy and Enid was lost in shrubbery, Hannah shrank back into her corner, fixing her eyes on the passing countryside to avoid the malevolent stare of her ladyship sitting opposite. Her heart was full but she would make no public display of her grief.

Her ladyship saw only a silent, sullen young woman and she wondered how she could have been so mistaken as to engage her as a companion for her darling Ursula. She was not often wrong in her assessment of character but in this case, her judgement had been tragically at fault. The girl had been well cared for and not hard worked. Sir Walter himself had paid her wages as Sir George saw no reason why his wife should be indulged with a personal maid. All this kindness had been repaid with a negligence and careless dereliction of duty which had cost her daughter her life.

A tiny tear squeezed out from Lady Heslop's bird-bright eye. This righteous grief obscured for the moment a certain uneasiness in the deepest recesses of her heart. Later, she would face the truth since, by nature, she was too honest to allow self-deception to persist but, for the moment, Hannah was the scapegoat.

Distancing herself from the tension around her, Hannah's eyes sought the sea, wild and free, gunmetal slashed with silver on this day of sunshine and showers. She recalled the happy times spent with Betsy plodging in and out of the lapping waves, their petticoats above their knees, the walk home in the sunset. Waiting for her, with her undemanding affection, would be her sweet lady but that was before the baby died, before her mistress was bewitched. At this point, Hannah had to bite her lower lip to stop its trembling and Lady Heslop, noting this, told herself angrily,. 'See how the little minx sets her face. I do declare she feels no sorrow at all for I have yet to see a tear. Oh, I'll have no more to do with her or her family. Kindness is wasted on such as they.'

Bamburgh Head and the Farnes were left behind and the distant outline of Dustanburgh Castle. As the coach turned off the Great North Road and made for the moors, Hannah wrenched her thoughts away from Budle Hall and directed them towards whatever might await her at Burnfoot. She did not think of it as home. It was just another place, with other problems. What kind of a reception could she expect? Discharged in disgrace from her employment. Seventeen years old and no nearer to earning her own living than she had been at fourteen.

Lady Heslop broke into her thoughts. 'Have your belongings to hand, girl. We are almost at the point where you will get out.'

Sit Walter, helping her down from the carriage, could not let her go without a word of comfort. 'Put it all behind thee, Hannah. What's done cannot be undone.'

Her nod was noncommittal. She shouldered her bundle and set off without a backward glance along the old familiar track through gorse and birch. Her belongings were scant and she stepped out easily enough in the strong boots that Lady Heslop provided for all her servants.

No salt breezes here to whip the cheeks but the heavy smell of peat and rotting bracken and the tangy vapours of tumbling burns. A curlew called from craggy heights. The feeling of aloneness was total and bleak. In a rare mood of self-pity, she allowed the unshed tears to fall but not for long.

Catch Grizzy Cochrane crying? Not likely. The memory of that now dim figure made her dry her eyes and face the future with fresh resolve. In a small linen bag sewn into her petticoat were six gold guineas, wages paid to her by Sir Walter. These she intended to hand over to her father for her keep. In addition, she had saved from occasional allowances doled out by Mrs Sedgecombe, silver coins to the value of five pounds. This, her safeguard against the future, would not be surrendered.

From the top of the next, rise she caught her first glimpse of Burnfoot. Washing fluttered on the line. A wisp of smoke meandered lazily about the chimney. Cockerels crowed and a sudden crescendo of barking erupted as Robbo and Gyp, the sheepdogs, caught her scent.

'Oh Mother, Mother,' she breathed, 'please understand.'

Mary Robson did understand but could not find the words of comfort that Hannah longed to hear though there was pity in her heart when she looked upon her daughter's troubled face. The story of Lady Ursula's death had spread by common gossip long before Hannah's own letter of explanation reached Burnfoot. It was a subdued reunion. Even Sarah was shocked into silence by the withdrawn and melancholy figure who had taken the place of the harum-scarum sister she remembered.

Nicholas went straight in. 'Didst push thy mistress off the top?'

That brought the old fire to her eyes and a shocked denial.

'Then that's the end of the matter,' he said curtly. 'Get yersell oot of them good claes for there's work to be done if ye're biding here.'

Hannah was intensely grateful for his matter-of-fact acceptance of her return and for the sympathy of the others.

Sarah was growing up fast. 'Thee's not to blame,' she said. 'Thy lady was demented.'

'How long ist since ye did some spinning?' Joan demanded. 'I'm sorely in need of thread for flannel.'

In this way, she was absorbed into the daily routine while the anguish within her slowly healed. She worked willingly to help her father with the harvest. Dressed in an old skirt of her mother's, she scythed and threshed the barley, led hay from the bottom pastures with Dickon between the shafts of the old hay bogie and stacked it in the barn. Her recent occupation as a lady's maid was no preparation for this kind of heavy manual labour. Her back and shoulders ached at the end of the day, but she made no complaint.

No one asked how long she would stay or where she would go when she left but Hannah knew she must make a decision soon. The transition from castle to cottage was not easy. She had grown fastidious in her ways and was accustomed to keeping her clothes and her body clean.

Folks at Burnfoot rarely bathed. The stink of her father's feet in the kitchen at night when Sarah pulled off his boots was worse than a fox's earth. Ben had nits in his head. Everyone scratched at the fleas. The porringers they ate from were cracked and stained and the butter was thick with hairs. Before her time as a lady's maid, she had noticed none of these things. Now they grated on her every day but the change was in herself, not in her family.

Her mother saw all this and felt a perverse pride that Hannah had so risen above her station. Her hands were white, her hair well-groomed. Joan and Sarah looked like paupers beside her. With her refined ways and speech from which all coarseness had disappeared, she might yet find the high position that Mary had dreamed about. Or a good marriage.

'No,' said Hannah.

Was there not a young man, Mary suggested, a friend of Tom's with good connections in Edinburgh who had shown an interest in her?

'I'll not marry,' Hannah reiterated.

But Mary refused to believe that her accomplished daughter preferred to remain a spinster. A suitable match would no doubt come about in due course for this most gifted of her children.

'Take your time, lass. Look for some employment with a good mistress. There's plenty of gentry hereabouts forby that lot at Bewick Grange.'

Hannah felt that there was no need to tell her mother at this stage that she had no intention of ever going into service again.

She would be nobody's servant, call no one 'Master'. Noble families who sold their daughters to the highest bidder sickened her. Young gentlemen whose sport it was to collect the maidenhood of simple girls as proof of their virility yet never be called to account, enraged her. Nobility, it seemed to her, was simply a matter of wealth entailing no refinement of character and she would have no more to do with it. The way ahead was not yet clear but her resolve to be independent grew with each day that passed.

Yet when she looked at Joan, she was humbled that she should have such aspirations when so much was denied to her elder sister. Now aged twenty-two, Joan seemed more shrunken than Hannah remembered, the hump on her back more pronounced.

Nevertheless, Joan's interest in matters outside Burnfoot was avid. Hannah was plied with questions about Tom and Mistress Emma, about life at Budle Hall; of wainscoted dining rooms, windows of painted glass and walls hung with rich carpets brought from the East in Sir George's ships.

'Still,' Joan glared at the hard stools, the floor covered in muddy rushes and rain blowing in at the window, 'I daresay it's cosier here.'

Benjamin, at five years old, was a spoilt and peevish child, over-indulged by his mother who left any correction to Joan. Ever since his birth, she had known indifferent health and sought to avoid confrontation of any sort.

Man's assumption of superiority, Hannah saw, began in the cradle, fostered by the same women who would later suffer from his tyranny. Benjamin got short shrift from Hannah when he tried his tricks, so that within a very short time he set up a howling at the very sight of her.

'Spoiled brat,' Sarah agreed. 'Me ma can do nowt with him.'

The summering was over. Hannah and Sarah together tramped the high crags as of old, bringing the sheep down to winter quarters. Sarah was fifteen now, plump and bonny and glowing with calf love for a certain young herdsman.

'Where does this fine laddie of thine live?' Hannah asked indulgently.

'His da has the run of Stonyhaugh.' Sarah pointed to a distant fellside. 'Ofttimes I hear him on a still day for he's a canny hand at the flute.'

'Doth he sing thee love songs then? Or pen his heart in a poem?' Hannah teased.

'Divvent be se daft!' Sarah blushed, then, with a sideways glance at her pretty sister, 'I bet ye've got a sweetheart an' all.'

But Hannah's attention was on the breathtaking view which suddenly confronted them as they topped a rise, of the wide coastal plain with its hamlets and castles, woods and watermills, and beyond, to the sea itself. She could identify Bamburgh Head and the island of Lindisfarne with its castle. Further out lay the Farnes, ringed in white even from this distance. How many times had she stood with Betsy on Budle Point and admired this same view. A wave of nostalgia engulfed her.

'Oh Sarah, ye've no notion of the wonder of the sea!' As she spoke, she suddenly knew where she wanted to go. To the sea, to the majesty of its deeps, the modesty of its crystal pools and to its ever-listening ear.

'That's where I'm going. Back to the sea.'

Sarah laughed. 'Ower much wattor for me. What'll ye do there, wor Hannah? Catch fish?'

Aye, she thought, I will. She thought of Betsy's family at Boulmer who lived by fishing. Betsy had said there was always work to be had there, salting herrings.

'Howay,' Sarah interrupted her dreaming. 'We'll get wrong if we're late.'

They turned for home by way of Blaw Weary but nought there remained of the shepherd's cottage except crumbling walls and a chimney stack. Hannah stopped in surprise. 'What's become of Auld Ned?'

'They found him deed, beside his dogs,' Sarah said matter-of-factly. ' 'Twas the cold or hunger. Nobody could rightly say which.'

Hannah frowned. 'Who pulled his house down?' It had been a good house, built of stone by Ned's father once the heathen Scots had done with raiding. Twenty pound it had cost him.

'The parish feared some vagrant would take up and live there and be a charge on the rate so they pulled it down.'

The kitchen, once the pride and joy of Auld Ned's mother, stood open to the weather now and the hearth, so beloved of Ned's dogs, was littered with rabbit and sheep droppings. Goats had devoured most of his flock-filled pallet and the slabbed window ledge where he would sit and watch his cabbages grow was already green with lichen.

'Pity they had to pull it down,' said Hannah. 'Such a bonny view.' Below them, Harehope Burn could be seen dropping in smoky waterfalls to the valley floor below.

Sarah shivered. 'It gets cold up here once the sun goes down. Let's away.' Mists were rising from the rapidly cooling earth. 'They're killing the pig the night. We'll be wanted.'

The light was almost gone when they reached Burnfoot. Mary and Joan had a great fire going in the yard beneath a tub of water in preparation for the pigs carcase. After slaughter, it would be lowered into this to loosen the bristles. Mary looked up at the girls' approach.

'You're late.' Her eye rested suspiciously upon Sarah. 'Where've ye been?'

'Blaw Weary,' said Hannah. 'Sarah showed me what is left of Auld Ned's cottage.'

'Fetch the salt from the barn. If thy da finds nowt ready for him there'll be trouble. And mind ye spill nae salt,' she called after Sarah, detaining Hannah with a motion of her hand, 'for 'tis like gold dust with the tax upon it.'

With lowered voice, she turned to Hannah. 'Didst stay with Sarah all the while?'

'Aye, Mother.' Hannah marked the note of urgency.

'She saw nought of that herdsman?'

'No.'

Anxiety creased Mary's brow. 'She spends ower much time up there an' I ken weel she meets him. If her da finds out, he'll kill her.'

Something of her mother's concern communicated itself to Hannah. A vision of Enid passed through her mind. That night, in the garret she shared with Sarah, she thought fit to warn her young sister.

'Whiles I have been away in service, Sarah, I have seen something of the ways of men and I tell thee now that thou'rt too young to be alone with that herdsman of thine.'

Sarah's eyes opened wide. 'But he loves me! And I love him.'

'Love!' Hannah's lip curled. ' 'Tis not love but lust. Men seek only to satisfy the animal in them. The sweet talk, the fancy speeches, these mean nothing.'

'My Donald's not like that,' Sarah said firmly and Hannah trembled for her, so totally innocent was she.

'Do not let him touch thee,' she warned. 'An afternoon's sport for a lad is a lifetime of sorrow for a lass should she fall.'

'But we only hold hands,' Sarah protested tearfully and Hannah, seeing how she had allowed herself to leap to unfounded conclusions, laughed and gave her little sister a hug.

'Well, keep it that way.'

The hams were salted, tripes and pluck washed. The bacon hung in the chimney, black and white puddings in the larder. When the barley was ready for grinding,

Hannah offered to take it to the mill at Eglingham in the hope of seeing her old friend, Widow Dodds, once more.

Her pony Dickon felt easy beneath her as he swung, heavy laden, down the burnside track. Despite the homely clothes she now wore, the thick flannel skirt with woollen shawl crossed over her bosom, something of the lady's maid still lingered in her appearance. A traveller meeting her would take her for no ordinary serving girl and he would think twice before making any advances towards her. There was a reserve about her that discouraged any such approach.

The alders by the waterside were showing bare red branches. Yellowing leaves tinkled from the silver birches with every breath of the breeze. Another autumn, Hannah reflected. Another year passing, and she swore out loud to Dickon and the scampering rabbits that, before winter broke, she would be off to try her luck as a fishergirl at Boulmer.

'Fishergirl!' Widow Dodds was astonished.

'I have a friend called Betsy Lisle who comes from a family of fisherfolk at Boulmer and mayhap they will give me employment.'

The widow was not alone. Beside her at the table, a pot of ale in front of him, sat

Ed Freeman the carter, as pleased to see Hannah as the old woman herself.

'Can ye no find easier work than guttin' fish, lass? 'Tis a far cry from a lady's maid.'

'I'll not go for a servant again,' said Hannah firmly. 'No more "Yes milady, No milady" for me. I'll be my own mistress if nothing else.'

The widow bustled about, fetching spicy cake and cider, happy to see Hannah again, whom she had loved in her own rough way, ever since this serious-minded young woman was a dirty-faced urchin.

'I heard tell ye were haem and hoped ye'd not forget to visit your old friend.'

Here in the familiar old kitchen amidst the fragrance of drying herbs, Hannah felt at ease for the first time in many weeks. Though no questions were asked of her, she found herself telling the whole story of the tragedy at Budle Hall, unburdening herself in a way that had not been possible with her own family. The firelight flickering on the faces of her listeners, showed only loving concern.

When she finished, the widow reached out and patted her knee. 'Put it all behind thee now, lass, for thine own conscience is clear.'

'I ken the Lisles of Boulmer,' said Ed. 'Ye could say we do business together.' He winked hugely at the widow.

'What think ye?' Hannah asked earnestly. 'Would they give me work?'

Eyeing her, Ed took a long draught of ale. He wished he were better looking, and younger and didna have such powerful sweaty feet. Such things put the lassies off. For the fact of the matter was that Darkie's lass had grown into the bonniest bit of woman he'd seen in many a day.

He put down his pot and smacked his lips. 'Oh aye, I've nae doubt they'll give ye work but they'll pay gey little for it. They're a rough lot,' he went on. 'The work's rough and the folks're rough. Ye'll be messing aboot in cold wattor come rain or shine wi' yer petticoats soaked and yer hands red raw. To my way of thinking, that's no life for thee.'

'I don't mind hard work.'

'Thee'll stink o'fish.'

'Nae more than the rest of them.'

Ed was clearly concerned. He screwed up his wizened monkey-face in an effort to put his argument. 'Thy Uncle Samuel that has boats on the Tyne could mebbes give thee a better job than the Lisles.'

'I'll not beg from my own kin.' Hannah had already considered this option and rejected it. 'When I've learned a trade at Boulmer and can keep myself, then mebbes I'll seek out my uncle.'

'Pigheaded as yer da,' Ed grunted.

Hannah threw back her head and laughed, the first time for many a day. 'Why so glum, the pair of you? I thought thee'd courage me on but thou'rt dismal as a wet week in Wooler!' Becoming serious, she went on, 'Do not fret, dear friends, for I have a little money saved to tide me over until I find work and,' she smiled, 'I'll nae starve for I can always eat fish.'

'Varry weel,' Ed nodded resignedly, 'since thy mind is made up, I'll help thee if I can. I go to Boulmer next week to seek kelp for the glassworks. There's room in my waggon for ye if ye so wish.'

19

'A common fishergirl!' Mary was outraged. Hannah, on whom she had built such high hopes, proposed to cast away all her advantages and seek work amongst women whose low life was a byword throughout the country. 'To curse like a fishwife' was a common enough saying and showed the low esteem in which such women were held.

'Where's all thy book learning now?' she demanded (and all the pretty graces and

297

nice ways of speaking). She changed her tune to one of pleading. 'Thee'll soon be eighteen years old, Hannah. With thy training, a better situation can be found. I did hear that Squire Strother and his lady of Fowberry Tower offer good conditions of employment. There's Ros Castle and Rock Hall; Chillingham, even, though my Lord Grey is dead now and his son is the master. There's a noble house for any lass with ambition. All these chances are thine, Hannah. Why choose to be a fishwife?'

'I've done with the gentry,' was all Hannah would say and her frustrated mother had to be content with that.

Hannah's last days at Burnfoot were put to good use in helping her father with repairs that must be done before the bad weather set in. Turves needed replacing on the roof of the barn. Cracks in walls must be sealed with pitch. They worked together as two strangers might, with little said between them, each uneasy in the other's presence. Hannah's imminent departure was not mentioned. It was as though she had already moved outside the circle of her father's concern.

At the finish of her last day's work, she hung back to cleanse her hands in the burn before following her father into the house. With a rough stone, she chafed at the tar stains on hands that were no longer smooth and white, a fact that worried her not at all. Where she was going, hands were meant for hard work. She marvelled that this, her last day at Burnfoot, meant so little to her. She was ready to leave it all for an unknown future with no more than a twinge of regret for things past. A new life was waiting. She rose from her knees, drying her hands on her petticoat.

At that moment, her father's voice rang out like the roar from a bull and was immediately followed by a piercing scream from Sarah. Hannah's heart contracted as she ran across the yard. Through the open door of the kitchen she could see Nicholas, made more huge by the plaid about his broad shoulders, standing with legs apart, the many-tailed strap in his hand. He was a sight to strike terror into any woman's heart and, indeed, that was the state to which he had reduced his wife and daughters. Sarah, sobbing as if her heart would break, held her face in her hands. Three long weals etched starkly on her white neck were already oozing blood.

'I saw thee!' Nicholas's voice was thick with loathing as if he addressed some obscene beast, not a fair little maid. 'Fornicating whore that thou art. My eyes are sharp as an eagle's. I saw thee with thy paramour!' He flung down the cruel leather 'cat' and crashed into his chair.

'Thought thee'd be safe in Auld Ned's place, but nought that goes on in these fells is hidden from me!' Mary hastened to pull off the muddy clogs from his outthrust legs. 'If thou'rt with child, 'tis oot this door ye'll go, bag and baggage.'

Had he seen Hannah's outraged face as she stood in the doorway, he might have paused in his tirade. Mary, looking up, was amazed at the resemblance between father and daughter in their fury. The whites of Hannah's eyes showed brilliant against her sun-tanned face, the pupils black and distended with an anger that matched her father's.

Hannah, aware of throbbing temples, knew well enough whence this passion came. She was her father's daughter. This rage was her inheritance.

'What wilt thou, Father?' Her level voice betrayed none of the tumult within her. 'Wouldst have another of thy daughters maimed? Is one cripple in the family not enough for thee?'

The barb struck home. Nicholas's face purpled. Involuntarily, he glanced towards Joan and met, not the gentle forbearance he had come to expect, but a look of cold condemnation that pierced him to the marrow.

Hannah pursued him relentlessly. Any fear she might have felt was overridden

300

by anger. She stooped to pick up the stained leather strap. 'I know not Sarah's error but nought that she could do would deserve that.' She flung the leather at him. 'Take a good look. The blood ye see is drawn from a fifteen-year-old maid, thine own flesh. Dost ever take a whip to grown men or are weak women thy only sport?'

The women's weeping tailed away on a whimper. Time stopped. A spurt of fear like summer lightning electrified the room as Nicholas jumped to his feet sending the chair crashing into the hearth.

'Jesu, Sweet Lord, save us all,' muttered Mary in anguish. The walls seemed to throb. Workaday pots and pans shivered before her eyes. Her knees felt weak beneath her.

Nigh on six foot tall, Nicholas towered above Hannah. To the watchers of this fearful drama it seemed that a violent charge emanating from the one struck a similar power in the other. Father and daughter held each other by their eyes, those brilliant, glass-blue eyes common to both, now brimful of hate for each other. What would be the outcome of this confrontation was beyond imagining. The moment was infinite with menace.

Coolly Hannah broke the spell. She let her gaze travel over him as if assessing a stranger, coming to rest on his great hairy hands, tensed at his side like the paws of an animal about to strike. The disgust she felt showed in her face.

Involuntarily, he followed her gaze and was shamed by the sight. A flash of restraint which sometimes came to his rescue, saving him from emotions he could barely control, surfaced at this moment, pulling him back from the violence that he would have regretted for the rest of his life. The brutish hands slackened. In his madness he had thought to choke the life out of the girl who dared defy him, to see that insufferably proud face turn blue and gasp for forgiveness.

'Bully!' she spat at him, having no pity, and he had to turn away so that he would not be goaded further.

Joan brought him ale. Mary served him food. Sarah and Ben crouched silent, as far away as possible from the table where he sat. When he spoke again, he was fully in command of himself. His voice was cold, impersonal. He looked elsewhere as he addressed Hannah.

'Thou'rt no kin of mine from this day forrard. Begone frae this hoose before I rise for I will not set eyes on thee again.'

When he had finished his meal, he put on his clogs once more, called the dogs to follow and went out into the night. Hannah looked from her mother, head in hands by the hearth and Joan sitting idle at her loom to Sarah's tearstained face. A curious calm now possessed her. The relationship with her father, always potentially explosive, was now at an end.

'What didst do to madden him so, Sarah?' Her tone was matter-of-fact, unemotional.

Sarah choked back her sobs. 'Donald brought his new lute to show me. He's been busy making it this last twelvemonth and me da saw us sitting on the big stones by Auld Ned's place.'

'Did ye mind what I told ye?' Hannah asked sharply, 'not to let him touch ye?'

Sarah began to cry again. 'We sat doon together and he played his lute. Nee mair than that. I swear it. But me da thinks evil of me just the same.'

'Put it behind thee, Sarah.' Wearily Mary got to her feet and carried food to the table. 'The child is an innocent,' she said to Hannah.

'I hate him,' said Sarah vehemently, 'even though he be me da.'

'Aye,' said her mother, 'mebbes. But ye'll hae to put up with him till ye're old enough to go into service.' She turned to Joan. 'I'll share your pallet tonight.'

When the rest of the family had retired to bed, Hannah stayed to have a last word with her mother. 'Did I do wrong to defy our da like that, Mother?'

There was something like respect in Mary's troubled voice. ' 'Tis what I should have done in the years gone by but I lacked the courage. Now 'tis all too late, but not for thee.'

'I leave in the morning,' Hannah said softly. She badly wanted to touch her mother's hand, stroke her cheek, make a small gesture; but she refrained, for she knew that this was what her mother hoped she would not do. 'Remember my virtues then, Mother, when I am gone, if virtues I have, and try to forget my shortcomings.'

Mary regarded her balefully. 'There has been little joy in my life. My husband has no love for me nor I for him. He deals in blows more often than kind words, yet even on the darkest days, one bright hope kept me going, that my children might raise themselves up and escape the wretchedness of our daily life here at Burnfoot.

'Of the five whom the Lord saw fit to save, only you, Hannah have the brains to improve your station. Here's the cruellest blow of all; that you should choose to throw away your gifts and lower yourself to an existence that is even more base than our own.'

'Believe me, Mother,' Hannah said soberly, 'I am as determined to improve myself as you would wish and I will do so, but this must be done according to my way and no one else's.' Boldly, she took her mother's hands in hers and, for once, the older woman did not draw back. 'My only grief is that I leave behind my mother and sisters to endure the moods and tempers of that evil man.'

'He is not always cruel,' said Mary. 'Life here will be easier without thee. Flint on flint will aye strike sparks.' She turned away. 'But I know he will never allow thee back and I shall never see my clever daughter more.' Tears misted her eyes.

With sudden insight, Hannah saw that roles were now reversed. The daughter had become stronger than the mother and the one to offer comfort. 'I promise thee now that when I have made my way in the world, I will come back. I am not afraid of my father.'

Mary, noting the toss of the head and the set of chin, remembered the young, bold Nicholas who had so won her heart many years ago.

'In truth,' she said quietly, 'I do see that. But remember this. Though ye may feel and act as bold as a man, thou'rt not a man and so will be disadvantaged in a world where women count as nought. Heed my advice, Hannah. Watch thy tongue. Ofttimes it runs away with thee and may put thee to a dismal end in the ducking pool afore thy goal is reached.'

There was a rare warmth in her voice as she mounted the stairs. 'May God protect thee, child. I will pray for thee and for all thine endeavours.'

Lingering downstairs only long enough to hang her wet stockings by the fire to dry, Hannah followed her mother to bed. She had no wish for another encounter with her father that night.

In accordance with her father's wishes, she rose at cockcrow. She had slept but poorly. Sarah's throbbing neck made her a restless bedfellow despite Joan's cooling poultice of yarrow.

As Mary had foreseen, Nicholas returned from the alehouse noisily drunk and spent some time hollering for his wife before sodden oblivion overtook him. As Hannah crept about the cold kitchen seeking bread and milk before starting her journey, loud snores from the curtained box bed proclaimed him still asleep. She cut an extra wedge of bread against hunger later in the day and, with a last look about her, drew back the bolts on the door. Whatever the future held, she told herself, would be preferable to enduring her father's tyranny here. She let herself out into the crisp, cold October morning, feeling no regret, only concern for her mother and Joan. Sarah would soon be away into service and out of reach of his tempers.

'When I have a place of my own,' she had told Joan, 'ye shall come and stay with me.'

Brave plans, she reflected ruefully as she stepped out across the still dark and sleeping countryside to Eglingham. She'd need luck and the intercession of Sweet Jesu Himself to help her carry them out.

Rain had fallen overnight and the burn was full, falling in joyous cascades of white water over the boulders, rushing through the narrows. Six weeks had passed since she walked this way after taking leave of Sir Walter and Lady Heslop. Then she had been in the depths of despair. Now Bewick Grange and Budle Hall were fading into the past although she would never forget her dear Lady Ursula, nor her terrible end.

There was nothing to be gained from looking over her shoulder, she must look to the future. When doubts assailed her, as they did from time to time, she called to mind the tale of Grizzy Cochrane. Grizzy, when she was only a little older than Hannah now was, had shown what a woman might do if she had a mind. She had said then, 'I must borrow a little of your courage, Hannah.' The recollection was a talisman for Hannah, a protection against any ill fortune which might befall her.

Since, in the event, her stay at Burnfoot had been so short, she had withheld some of her Budle wages. Kindly Joan had added a further two crowns to her little store of money which lay now in a linen bag against her waist. Without it she would be lost, a pauper and the friend of no one until such time as she could earn her own bread.

Nevertheless, her spirits were high and there was a spring in her step as she strode through the clumps of damp heather, sending pheasants into lumbering flight at her feet. She had eaten her last game pie for some time, she reflected sadly. From now on, the sea must provide her with a living. God willing, and if Ed Freeman met with no disaster on the way, she would be in Boulmer before this pale sun had set.

Every step away from Burnfoot took her nearer to freedom. As she approached the clanking wheel of Eglingham Mill a feeling of excitement gripped her. A flock of herons by the burn, disturbed at their fishing, took off in agitated flight above her head, trailing a shower of ice cold droplets from their spindly legs. Cheerfully she greeted them.

'Divvent fash yersells!' she called out, slipping easily into the vernacular as if the time had come for all the new-found graces to be discarded, 'I divvent want yer fish!' Swinging her bundle, she stepped lightly into the village street.

Ed Freeman was adjusting the harness on his team outside the big barn. 'A bonnie morn for a ride wi' a bonny lassie,' he greeted her. Despite the truths that faced him in the mirror, Ed still cultivated the image of a dashing gallant. 'Throw your gear in the back alongside the turnips and climb up on the board. We'll be off directly—'

Eglingham village was just awakening. The clatter of milkmaids' pails mingled with a cacophony from lordly cockerels. Widow Dodds was still abed.

'She lies in, these days,' said Ed. 'Her legs are bad.' He looked askew at Hannah, sitting all composed on the board. 'Ye'll nae be sorry to quit Burnfoot, I reckon?'

'It's time to go,' she answered guardedly.

'Aye,' Ed grunted, 'afore he kills ye. He's a murdering devil when the drink gets to him.'

Hannah, not knowing how much Ed knew of the previous day's disturbance, held her peace.

'Ye sent him to the alehouse last night in mighty bad fettle,' Ed went on, 'but, begod, he was a sight worse when he left. Darkie Robson's a guid one to have by ye in a fight,' Ed mused, 'but there's nane aroond here that's game enough to make an enemy oot of him.'

And that, thought Hannah, is exactly what I have done.

He threw her a blanket for the morning was chill with a mist that threatened to overwhelm the watery sun. Then he climbed up beside her. With a call to the leader and a crack of the whip, they were on their way, bound for the town of Alnwick and the coast. Manes tossing, harness jingling, their massive forequarters straining, his pair of sturdy draught horses pulled the loaded waggon out of the rutted yard and into the lane.

Their route took them along the vale of the River Aln through glades of alder and larch by hamlets where the women could be seen at work digging turnips or washing clothes. They all had a greeting for Ed.

'What fettle the day, Ed?' they would call out and he would answer with some enquiry about a sick child or an aged parent.

'It seems thou'rt well known wherever ye go,' observed Hannah.

' 'Tis my business,' Ed shrugged. 'When folks need a drop of brandy or a bag of salt they ken weel they'll pay nae tax wi' me.'

'Art not feared the excisemen will catch thee?'

Ed made a face. 'Blockheads, all of them. They'll have to get up early to catch Ed Freeman.'

Hannah looked curiously at the carter, cocky, self-confident, dressed in clothes that other folk had discarded. Nothing matched. Not even his stockings. 'And thou'rt content with thy life, Ed?'

The nearest horse chose that moment to lift its tail and fart. Ed laughed.

'There's yer answer, hinny. Nay, but life's a game and there's nowt in it for losers.'

By midmorning the road grew wider and much rutted with the passage of coaches and carts as they approached the important market town of Alnwick, the seat of the Percy family and home of many wealthy nobles. Progress was slowed by the increase of traffic; aristocratic gentlemen in periwigs on richly caparisoned horses, waggons like Ed's full of farm produce and pony trains transporting lead from the moors.

' 'Tis a marvellous town, Alnwick,' Ed promised, 'the like of which thee's never seen.'

Even so, Hannah was unprepared for

the grandeur of the buildings that lined the route into the town centre. Built of stone, embellished with porticoes, pillars and armorial devices, they formed an impressive introduction to a town that was bustling with activity.

Hannah gazed in wonder at the church of St Mary and St Michael with its massive pinnacled tower and the great castle which dominated the town. The drawbridge was overgrown with weeds now. Hart's-tongue and speed-well clothed the fallen walls of the ancient turrets. Still it stood in awesome majesty, despite its ruined state.

'To which great lord does such a castle belong?'

'Since ancient times, 'tis the seat of the Earls of Northumberland,' said Ed, 'though there's little enough left to shelter a mouse from the rain now. His lordship is well liked here, for though he fought for the king in the revolution, yet when he was beat, he did right well follow the orders of Parliament to make amends to the poor on his estate. There's none here will say a word against him.'

The wide market place rang with the cries of vendors. In the centre a bull tethered to an iron ring added its angry bellowing to the noisy pandemonium. 'There'll be sport with baiting after the trading is done,' said Ed. 'Hold on—'

312

He pulled the horses to a halt. 'Look yonder.'

Outside the Nag's Head Inn in Fenkle Street, a coach with a steaming, stamping team of horses was drawing an excited crowd.

'Summat's up,' Ed muttered. 'That's the London coach. Take the reins, lassie, and stay with the waggon whiles I discover the news.'

As light afoot as a young man, Ed slipped down from his seat and was lost at once amongst the plaids and bonnets of the crowd. When he returned, it was with the news that Prince William of the Low Countries had set sail for England and meant to take the Crown from James.

'Kings, queens and princes and their follies. What ha they to do wi' me?' He took over the reins again and gee-ed up the horses. 'These are dangerous times, Hannah lassie, and we're well oot of them. Let them chop each other's heeds off in Lunnon if they have a mind so to do and we'll ca' canny the whiles up here.'

Hannah could only agree with him. There was enough drama in her own small world without her concerning herself with affairs of state. 'Aye, Ed. 'Tis my future as a fishergirl I care about, not the King of England.'

With Alnwick left behind, they headed

towards the coast. Hannah lifted her face to the sudden brisk tang in the air. 'I can smell the sea!'

Ed pointed with his whip to distant masts in the river's estuary. 'Yonder's the port of Alnmouth. I carry seaweed there from Boulmer to be shipped to Newcastle. The Frenchies at Howden use it for making glass.'

In her mind's eye, Hannah saw again the young Huguenot who painted the exquisite window in Budle Hall library. Another time. Another place. Another life.

A league went by before Ed drew her attention to a bay of curving white sand backed by gently sloping sandhills and grassy dunes. 'Yon's Boulmer.'

A huddle of mean cottages and a few upturned boats at the edge of the sea. Boulmer. A quiver of apprehension ran through Hannah. 'I hope I get work for I'll be in a pretty fix if I don't. 'Tis a long walk to the next place.'

'Trouble comes soon enough without ye rushing to meet it,' Ed chided.

As the heavy-laden cart trundled along a sandy lane, women, closely shawled against the sharp sea breeze, greeted Ed warmly but Hannah's smile was not returned.

'Divvent rush them,' Ed advised. 'They'll take thee when they're ready and not afore.'

314

The people of Boulmer were poor. They, lived and died by the sea. Their trade was salting and smoking fish, herrings mostly, which were plentiful around these shores. There was a ready market for such delicacies in London and even places further abroad, such as Germany and Norway. And crabs. Boulmer crabs and lobsters were regularly exported to Newcastle and Berwick.

When the weather was right and the fish were running, the living was easy but when storms prevented the men from putting to sea, when the herring shoals failed to appear, when there was nothing in the larder but shrimps and seaweed, then the churchyard at Longhoughton claimed its toll of the very old and the very young. Death was a frequent visitor at the squalid, mud-walled hovels. Small wonder, then, that the women of Boulmer looked with suspicion on the lass Ed Freeman brought. There were enough paupers on the parish rate as it was.

This was not the only reason why strangers were not welcome at Boulmer. On nights when the moon hid her light behind the clouds and you could barely see a hand in front of your face, cloaked and masked riders, with their horses' hooves wrapped in clouts to deaden all noise, congregated here on the beach. Out at

315

sea a foreign ship, bearing no lights, would slide into the bay and drop anchor.

Those on the shore waited for the swish of oars and the low, quiet whistle of the boatman before wading out to unload precious cargoes of silks and spirits, tobacco and salt. Money changed hands swiftly. Kegs of brandy and sacks of salt were whisked out of sight into hiding places or carried on horseback through the night to places as far distant as Alwynton, Bamburgh and Rothbury.

The arrival of a strange young woman in this very secret community was looked upon with the gravest suspicion.

Ed pulled up outside one of the larger cottages. 'This is the Lisles' house. She'll be roond the back, boiling crabs.'

Pulling her shawl close about her, Hannah jumped down from the waggon and followed Ed to the yard at the back of the house, past coils of rope and lobster pots, buckets of tar and drying nets. Everywhere the old familiar smell of things to do with the sea called out to her to stay and make her home here if she could. She was about to come face to face with Betsy's mother. Would there be work for an untrained, inexperienced fishhand? The next few moments would decide her future.

20

Two women shawled in black, one young, one well into middle age, stood over a copper of boiling water. They looked up at Hannah's approach, unsmiling, their faces running with moisture and grime and waited for her to speak. Ed, Hannah reflected, had a way of making himself invisible at times like this. He was showing a deep interest in the contents of the pigsty.

She addressed the older woman. 'Am I speaking to Mistress Lisle?'

There was the merest suggestion of a nod. The younger woman's eyes raked Hannah's person from top to toe.

'I'm a friend of Betsy's,' Hannah persevered. 'I was in service with her at Budle Hall.' The silence deepened and Hannah plunged on desperately. 'I'm looking for work and Betsy said ofttimes you were in need of extra hands to help with salting and packing fish.'

'Hands, aye.' The woman's voice was gutteral having none of Betsy's sweet lilt. 'Hands that ken what they're aboot.' The woman thrust a stick into the boiling water and clattered the crabs around.

'I'm willing to learn,' Hannah said humbly.

'Haddaway back where ye came frae,' Mistress Lisle grunted disparagingly. 'I've nae use for the likes of ye.'

Ed sauntered up, the very image of studied nonchalance. ' 'Tis Darkie Robson's lass from Old Bewick,' he said casually. 'Cousin to Red Wull.'

The effect was instant. For a moment, Martha Lisle's face registered complete astonishment then a grin broke through the sweat and steam, banishing all surliness. She grabbed Hannah by the arm, peering this, way and that into her face. She was a big, raw-boned woman with a grip of iron that made Hannah wince.

'The auld divvil's lass, no less! Aye, there's a likeness there. I mind well them sooty eyes. Will ye break as many hearts, I wonder?'

Hannah stared in amazement at Betsy's mother. Wonderingly, she asked, 'Dost know my father then?'

Mistress Lisle grinned lewdly. The few teeth left in her head were stained brown with tobacco. 'Say rather that he knew me and many another spunky lass at Chillingham Castle, but it was yer ma he wanted, nice in her ways, clever as a cuckoo, and, besides that, she was a redhead. There's some men canna resist a redhead, but ye take after yer da. Hast thy mother's brains? Will ye take a look at that chin, Ed Freeman. Obstinate as the auld divvil himself, I do declare.'

Ed smiled slyly and fingered the stubble on his face.

'She's the dowter of her da all reet.'

Martha wiped her steaming arms on the sacking apron about her middle. They were as red as the perishing lobsters and the joints of her hands were swollen and distorted with the ague. She nodded, for Hannah's enlightenment, towards the younger woman. 'Betsy's sister, Meg.'

Betsy must resemble her father, Hannah decided, for these two were as black and swarthy as she was fair.

'Howay in oot the cold,' Martha slid her arm through Hannah's. 'A mug of hot ale is what ye need.' Rolling like a sailor as she shifted her weight from one swinging hip to the other, she propelled Hannah towards the back door of the cottage leaving Meg to follow sulkily behind.

The dwelling was as poor within as without and Hannah could not help contrasting Betsy's comfortable quarters at Budle Hall with the wretched circumstances in which her parents lived. The light from one small window made little impression on the inner gloom. Rags

319

stuffed into cracks in the walls did not cut off the draughts completely. Hannah's reaction was not lost on Martha.

'Most lassies would choose service rather than gut fish.' Her eyes narrowed. 'There's likely a good reason for leaving a comfortable place and seeking out Martha Lisle.'

'My mistress died,' Hannah said quietly. 'There was no place for me any more.'

Meg came up with pots of ale at that moment and spoke for the first time. 'I heard tell the mistress of Budle Hall hoyed hersell from the top of the tower and killed hersell.'

Martha's quick little eyes, sharp as earwigs, flickered over Hannah's face. 'Would that be her?'

Hannah, reluctant to go over the sad tale once more, said briefly, 'She lost her baby and went demented.'

'Poor lady,' Martha spoke soothingly, seeing Hannah's unease. 'A common enough affliction after childbirth. But there's more places than Budle Hall would employ the likes of ye. Did thee not try elsewhere for a post?'

Hannah fixed Martha with a glare. 'I'll be no one's servant ever again. If I have to salt fish to keep mysell, why then, I'll salt fish, or owt else that'll earn me a living.'

Martha threw back her head and cackled

with delight, presenting a red gape that was powerfully redolent of rum. 'Now I ken ye're Darkie's lass for sure!' She slapped her thigh. 'That could ha' been hissell speaking. My oath! The very words!'

Ed, quietly chuckling in the corner, drained his ale. 'What's it to be, Martha Lisle? I've got business to see to. Does she stay or come back over with me?'

Martha rubbed her chin. Money was involved here. Through narrowed eyes, she took in Hannah's slight figure. Not much to her. Skinny as a whippet but the set of her neck spoke of a strong back and there was no denying the character behind that chin. She stifled any lingering doubts.

'I'll give thee a go. It's gey hard work and if ye canna do it, ye'll have to go.'

Hannah nodded cheerfully.

'There's nae bed for thee here,' Martha gestured towards tumbled blankets in the alcove. 'There's fower men here forby Meg and me but Widow Murray will mebbes take thee for a few pence.'

Hannah was to be given sixpence a day and her supper if she proved her worth. This much achieved, she left with a light heart to make the acquaintance of Widow Murray. A glimpse of Meg's dark, disapproving face as she followed Ed into the yard convinced her that here was no amiable companion such as Betsy.

She would need to go warily with Meg.

Nell Murray opened the door of her cottage to them and bade them welcome. 'Any friend of thine, Ed Freeman, is good enough for me.'

She was a neat, thin woman whose dress showed none of the slovenliness of Martha Lisle. The shawl about her shoulders was painstakingly darned. Her skirt was free from stains.

She had been widowed earlier that year when a great storm deprived her of husband and two sons in one night of tragedy. The day had been fair, the herring running full and free, the wind no more than a light breeze. So busy were the men of Boulmer, laying out and pulling in their nets, that a handful of clouds gathering over the land above Kyloe Crags attracted little attention until the squall hit the water and the sky turned dark as night.

Too late, the alarm was raised. 'She's coming off the land! Get in-by afore she blows up hard!'

Nell and the other wives raced to the Point to light their tar-soaked flares, for the men at sea were already lost to sight in veils of blinding rain. Rampaging winds whipped up mountainous waves on a sea that only a moment or two earlier had been calm as a millpond. Nell's three men and the boy they took with them pulled on the oars till they thought their hearts would burst within them but relentlessly the land wind blew them out to sea. These four and twenty more from Boulmer were lost that night, never to be seen alive again though a contrite sea returned their corpses later with the matchwood of their boats.

The fine Latin phrases of the Longhoughton priest might help widows and orphans to pray to God for strength, but bellies were not filled this way. Nell, like the other bereaved women, strove to support herself with fish-curing and with spinning when she could afford a fleece. Hannah's contribution of a shilling a week for bed and lodgings was eagerly accepted.

Her cottage was superior to that of the Lisles for her men had been diligent householders. At the time of the disaster, they had been engaged upon enclosing the wooden walls with dressed stone and, although the work was unfinished, the seaward side was complete and a good roof of Allendale slabs defied the wind which periodically relieved meaner cottages of their turves. The kitchen was a cheerful place with a bright fire burning and a rag mat on the earthen floor. Hannah was given a box bed with a clean flock mattress and she moved in with Nell Murray right away.

Nell shook her head over Hannah's long woollen skirt. 'Ye canna push the boats oot in them claes,' she said. 'I've an auld pair of breeks ye can have.' Already, there was a warmth of feeling between the two women. Here was a friend when Hannah needed one most.

Martha met head-on the storm of protest which resulted from her hiring of Hannah. Her man, Big Wattee, sons Gregory, Dick and Young Wattee, huge, hairy men all of them, made their feelings plain.

'What business hae ye, Martha Lisle,' her husband demanded, 'to entice paupers into the parish? We've enough of wor ain without seeking mair.'

Martha thrust beneath his nose the swollen wrists and gnarled knuckles of her deformed hands. 'Take a look at these. Ye'd hardly call them hands any mair, now, wad ye? There's days I canna get a grip of the gutting knife, nor the needle to mend the nets. Ofttimes Meg and me are hard put to deal with one day's catch afore the next one is brought in. But there's not one of ye lot cares a tinker's cuss about me.'

With a grunt of impatience, Big Wattee lowered his tousled head to his porringer.

'There's nowt wrong wi' thee hands.'

'Aye. That's reet,' his wife mocked. 'Ye'll see nowt but what ye have a mind to.'

Her sons, dunking hunks of bread in their fishy broth, echoed their father's displeasure. 'Wor da's reet. We've enough to do filling wor ain bellies forby some fancy friend of wor Betsy's.'

'Dost ever think of owt beyond thy bellies?' Leonine in her scorn, Martha stood against the firelight, arms crossed over her plumped bodice. 'Ye're going to hear summat now.' She paused significantly to ensure their full attention. 'I'm telling thee all. I've hired this lass to help me. If she's good, she stays. If she's nae good, she goes straight back where she came frae. And that's that!'

Meg, bringing more bread to the table, ventured. 'She talks gey fancy for a fishwife.'

'She'll not last the week,' Big Wattee snorted. 'Wait till she has to shove her cuts in a barrel of brine! That'll send her screaming haem for her mammy.'

This sally appealed to his sons. Merrily they rocked on their stools as their mother, gouty, bandy-legged but magnificent in her authority, trundled off into the yard. She was the boss and they knew it.

Big Wattee had the wrong idea right from the start. Soon after her arrival, Hannah had a summons to leave her work in the yard and go to the kitchen. Big Wattee sat sprawled in a chair, his legs spread before him.

'Get these off,' he growled, indicating his long sea boots.

It was a telling moment for Hannah. To give in now would make her the servant of these men for the rest of her time at Boulmer. At the risk of losing her employment, she would make the situation clear.

'That I'll not do.' She kept the anger from her voice. 'I'll clean and salt fish for thee but if it's a servant ye seek, look elsewhere for I'll not pull the boots off thee nor any other man.'

Coolly she returned to her work in the yard while Big Wattee's disbelieving roars echoed around the kitchen. Martha, fully aware of the confrontation, smiled to herself. This was Darkie Robson's lass all right. If Darkie had wed her instead of Mary Packman, mebbes she'd have had a dowter like this. The memory of half-forgotten passions tickled her with a voluptuous quiver as she tipped a wicker pot full of scrabbling lobsters into the seething boiler.

Hannah had yet to prove herself, Martha

conceded, but, if things worked out all right, who knows but what one of her sons might take her for a wife. That would suit Martha. The two of them would get along fine.

Wearing the traditional navy blue breeches lent her by Nell, Hannah took her place amongst the wives and daughters of Boulmer but only Nell Murray offered friendship. The others kept apart, covertly watching as she grappled with unfamiliar tasks, quietly enjoying her inevitable mistakes.

Nets must be mended, leaky boats caulked and tarred and each day when the late afternoon tide filled the harbour with water, the barelegged women pushed the twenty-five-foot cobles over the sand and into the water. The sea was icy cold in October, gripping the ankles in a ring of pain but Hannah plodged in unhesitatingly, knowing that the women were waiting for her to complain. At the end of the day, Nell's cosy kitchen offered comfort and companionship.

When the boats returned with their catch at first light, the women were there to help pull them ashore and to unload. Then, while the men sought hot food and sleep, the women began the task of sorting, gutting, smoking and salting the fish. The gutting knives were wickedly

327

sharp and it was some time before Hannah learned to eviscerate a fish cleanly with two simple movements as the other women did. Their quiet scorn as she bound up yet another bleeding gash on her hands merely increased her determination to master the skill.

Martha's menfolk derived intense enjoyment from making life difficult for her but she developed her own methods of dealing with them. It was their delight to thrust out a foot and trip her up when she was passing by with a full jug of milk, to catch her bending and run a lewd hand up her skirts. Gregory, the eldest, a lard-faced loon, followed her into the pantry one day and blocked the way with his huge frame.

'I'll not let thee oot till thee gives us a kiss,' he chortled, dribbling from slobbery lips. 'Be nice to Gregory or thee'll stay where thou art.'

Impatiently, Hannah weighed up the options of dashing between his fat legs or upturning him, neither of which were practical. She turned instead to the ale keg at her back and turned on the tap. Ale poured out over the earthen floor in an amber flood.

Gregory was horrified. 'Look what ye've done, stupid wench. That's good ale going to waste!'

As Gregory lumbered past to turn off the tap, Hannah made her escape.

'Who's made the mess on the pantry floor?' demanded Martha.

'Gregory will tell thee,' said Hannah, but Gregory, red-faced and sullen, glowered speechless at his pudding.

The incident did nothing to endear Hannah to her employer's sons but when one day she was 'accidentally' pushed into deep water from a coble, they discovered to their surprise that their victim was far from helpless.

They were in no hurry to offer help to the girl in the water. They intended to wait until their drowning victim was in the last throes of terror before throwing a rope. Like most of the fisherfolk of Boulmer, they had a wholesome respect for the sea and could not swim. Hannah hugely enjoyed their discomfort when, after coolly declining the proffered rope, she struck out for the shore.

Their pride was badly shaken. From the bottom of her heart, Hannah blessed Tom for teaching her to swim in the Devil's Pot.

'I canna think what the boat was doing out there anyway,' said Martha with a glint in her eye. 'Boats are cleaned in the shallows.'

Hannah was quite prepared to leave

the matter there. She was not unhappy. The work was hard but rewarding and she did not intend to give up because of Martha's oafish men. At the end of every day, something had been achieved. Since her swim ashore from the Lisle boat, the women had become noticeably less hostile, except for Meg, whose dark, brooding face seemed for ever closed to Hannah.

Boulmer's very existence depended on the sea. The people got their living and sometimes their dying from it. From the cooper who made the barrels to the men who cast the nets, the pattern of their lives was governed by the sea.

When the fleet returned from its overnight trawling, the catch was carried to a long, stone slab to be cleaned and gutted then laid in shallow vats of salt. After an hour or so it was transferred to stout wooden barrels, layered in fresh salt, topped up then loaded on to the single-masted trading hoys which put into the bay from time to time.

When Hannah joined the community, the plentiful catches of summer were dwindling. There were days when the cobles came back with small catches or none at all and days when storms kept the fishermen ashore. As winter approached, the women went shrimping in shallow water or scraped whelks and limpets from the rocks to augment what smoked fish they had put by for their families.

On days when there was no fish to smoke or salt, no crabs or lobsters to boil, Hannah saw her usefulness fading and turned her attention to other aspects of the trade where she might be of service. She dreaded a dismissal from Martha who could afford no benevolence when there was no work.

She had already noted that all the business affairs in the Lisle household were dealt with by Martha. It was Martha who struck the bargains with trading seamen, Martha who took charge of the bills of payment.

' 'Tis mostly wives who see to that,' Martha agreed. 'The men care nowt aboot the money as long as their bellies are filled and there's ale in the barrel.' Big Wattee and all her sons were usually stupid with drink as soon as they set foot ashore.

Martha's so-called office was a counter in the drying shed, always in a state of confusion, notes written on scraps of paper, bills and invoices all mixed up with Martha's own painstaking attempts at letter writing. The way forward for Hannah suddenly became blindingly obvious.

331

'Will ye let me do the accounts for thee, Mistress Lisle? I used to keep the kitchen inventory at Bewick Grange and did all my lady's marketing.'

Martha squashed her in a bearlike embrace. 'I should ha kenned that Mary Robson's lass would be good with figures!' She crowed with delight. 'Here y'are, hinny.' She thrust a much thumbed notebook into Hannah's hands. 'Make what ye can of that for I get a headache every time I look at them figures and wor Meg's nae better. There's fish gone to Lunnon that's not been paid for,' she searched in the heap of bills for a scribbled note, 'and I'll nae let the rogues make a monkey oot of me.'

Hannah riffled through the pages of the notebook. Income was mixed up with expenses. There were bills that Martha owed for tar and salt and cooperage and money owed her for fish. 'I'll need a proper account book,' she said firmly, 'then I can sort out these monies for thee.'

'Ed Freeman can fetch thee one frae Alnwick,' Martha declared. 'He's due any day now.'

Meg, passing by, stopped short at the sight of Hannah seated at the counter. 'What's this?' she crabbed. 'A new boss?'

'Now, Meg,' her mother said soothingly,

'ye ken weel ye're no better than me at figures. Hannah here has done clerking for the gentry.'

The contrast, Hannah mused, between Meg and her sister Betsy was striking. Wistfully, when Meg had gone she turned to Martha. 'Does Betsy never visit here?'

'Oh aye. She didna come Michaelmas so she'll nae doubt come Christmas. An if she canna get for Christmas, then she'll come next Mothering Sunday. It depends on that housekeeper at Budle Hall.' She handled a heap of nets awaiting repairs. 'She'll come when she can. She's a good girl.'

'She was my special friend,' said Hannah. 'I miss her sorely.'

Martha's shrewd glance told her that Darkie's hard little lass had a soft centre after all. 'Ye'll ha company of a different sort when yer cousin comes.'

Hannah had forgotten about her cousin.

'Red Wull. Divvent tell me ye ha nae made the acquaintance of that fine laddie?'

A sudden memory of a cheeky face beneath a cap of ginger hair brought a smile to Hannah's face. 'Oh aye. I mind him now, hiding from the excisemen at Bewick Fair two years since.'

'And may they never find him,' said Martha piously, 'for he's the poor man's friend, is thy cousin Wull.'

21

Ed Freeman arrived with his cart full of turnips two days later. Night had fallen and Hannah was alone in Nell's warm kitchen, holding her blue feet to the fire. The sea coal she had collected from the shore threw out a wonderful heat, better than wood, better than peat. The talk of the day was that there was enough coal in Northumberland to make riches for all; all the landowners, that is. The only gain for folk like the fishermen of Boulmer was what the sea threw up.

Nell was not yet returned. Her supper simmered in the pot hanging over the coals. Not a sound disturbed the silence of the night but the rhythmical rush and retreat of the waves over sand. Then a footfall, voices, a hand on the latch and Nell came into the kitchen holding aloft a turnip. Peering around her shoulder was the genial face of Ed Freeman.

'Tuppence for this!' Nell cried aloud in mock dismay. ' 'Tis poor folks like us will make thee rich, Ed Freeman. What a rogue thou art, to be sure.'

' 'Tis a pleasure to see thy cheerful face

once more, Ed,' Hannah greeted him, 'for I swear I have never yet seen it miserable.'

Ed came to the fire and smiled down at Hannah. 'Wrap up thy legs, lass, or thee'll get chilblains.'

'Ye'll take a pot of mulled ale afore the night's work begins.' Nell went hurrying off to the outhouse.

Ed eyed Hannah with some curiosity. She looked well enough but the pretty conceits had gone, the nicely dressed hair, the pale hands he had so admired had all given way to a rougher image.

'I see thou'rt a proper fisherlass now, nae mair a lady's maid.'

'As I intended,' came the soft rebuke. 'What news do ye bring, for we hear nought of the outside world except what reaches us by the sea.'

Nell came up with a steaming mug. 'Aye, let's have thy news. Thou'rt the best gossip hereabouts.'

Ed pulled up a stool. 'To begin with matters close to thy home, Hannah,' he began. 'Last full moon the Widow Dodds did deliver a poor woman of a child with two heads which mercifully died soon afterwards.'

' 'Tis a mercy the child did not live,' said Nell, 'for it would have been fit for nought but the travelling fair.'

335

'Thy da's byre burned down but the cow was saved.'

Hannah groaned, ' 'Tis not long since we tarred and turfed it!'

'And there's news frae Lunnon...'

Nell cut him short. 'What folks get up to in Lunnon is nae concern of ours.'

'And yet,' mused Ed, 'the talk of revolution and riot comes closer to hand when I tell thee that Heslop of Bewick is arming his tenants to fight.'

'Sir Walter?' Hannah raised startled eyes. 'Who will he fight?'

'The king or the Dutchman. One or the other. Some would have the king stay, though he be a Catholic and his son to follow him. Some would have Prince William and the Princess Mary because of their proper religion. It seems there will be blood spilt, for the Dutchman has landed on the south coast and hath brought his own soldiers with him.'

'We want nae mair revolutions up here,' said Nell firmly. 'Little good but a deal of harm came frae the last rebellion.'

'What will my father do?' asked Hannah. 'Will he fight?'

Ed roared with laughter. 'Thy father says he'll fight for no one but hissell—and he does that gey well!'

Hannah frowned. 'My lord of Bewick Grange grows too old for such hazards.

This military fire befits a younger man than he.'

'There's no cooling his temper,' sighed Ed, 'and his lady would be up in the saddle alongside him could she but find armour to fit!'

'I wonder—what of Budle? Will he fight? And for whom?'

Ed laughed derisively. 'Budle brags but Budle bides. He'll let the smoke clear before he makes a move.'

Nell pushed away her empty supper platter and drew up her spinning wheel. 'Ist truly came to this, Ed? Another revolution? 'Twill mean more taxes and we are taxed enough already, God knows.'

'They say,' said Ed, 'that Prince William hath promised to do away with the hearth tax, should he become king.'

'Then he shall have my loyalty,' declared Nell, 'for that is the cruellest tax of all.'

'Speaking of taxes,' Ed lowered his voice conspiratorially, 'I hope to do thee a good turn tonight, Mistress Murray.'

Hannah's eye gleamed. 'Thou'rt smuggling tonight then, Ed? Art not afraid of thy neck?'

'S-sh-sh!' He placed a finger over his lips. ' 'Tis thy talk will string me up for spies are everywhere.'

A sharp rat-tat on the door at that

moment made them all instantly alert but the head that poked around the door was not wearing the king's badge but a black silk hat trimmed with ribbons perched upon a tousle of ginger hair.

'Stap me eyes!' Will Robson's gaze alighted on Hannah. 'Can this be my milky cousin? My little dimity-dolly turned into a fishgirl?'

'Howay in and shut the door,' Nell said briskly. 'Draw yersell some ale.'

'Last time we met, you were running away from the excisemen,' said Hannah. 'Are we to see the same game tonight?'

Will laughed, appreciating her move into the attack. 'Mebbes,' he called from the outhouse, 'and wilt hide me, sweet coz, as ye did afore?' Returning with a pot of ale, he slapped his bonnet on the table and slipped easily into a cross-legged position at her feet.

He was as she remembered him, lean, tense as a coiled spring, and playing the fool. He was wearing the traditional dress of the Tyneside keelman, yellow waistcoat, grey bell-bottomed trousers and blue 'bumfreezer' jacket over a white shirt. Around his neck he wore a knotted black silk kerchief.

Suddenly serious, he contemplated Hannah. 'They said I'd find thee here, Hannah Robson, and I did not believe them. Why did ye come? 'Tis a hard life for a woman.'

'I'll be my own mistress.' Doggedly, she repeated her creed and turned crossly away at his ill-concealed smile.

'Ye have kin on the Tyne,' Will went on more seriously. 'There's work for women on the keels. Come awa' wi' me. Ye'd be among thine own folk,' but he did not wait for an answer. At that moment, a long, low whistle sounded somewhere in the dark night outside. With one lithe movement, he was up on his feet, bonnet in hand.

'Howay, Eddie man, the boat's in.' Turning to Nell, he laid an affectionate arm about her shoulders. 'Stay indoors, Nellie Murray. Say thy prayers. Mind thine own business and keep my pretty cousin away from the Frenchmen. They make too bold lovers.'

'And no-good husbands,' added Nell.

'I'm not the marrying kind,' Hannah said coldly, angered by this cheeky cousin, but he responded with delight, slapping her heartily on the backside.

'Why, no more am I! So we will make excellent company.'

'Cut out the gab, Wull!' Ed called impatiently from the door, 'or we'll miss the boat.'

Hannah had a glimpse of dark figures

339

hurrying by. The scuttering of loose gravel and an occasional soft whinny betrayed the presence of horsemen.

' 'Tis as he says, none of our business.' Nell closed the door and slid home the heavy bolt.

'When I lost my men last January,' Nell said, returning to her wheel, 'I would have starved to death but for thy cousin. The little I had saved went to pay the chimney man's tax. There's nae work with the fish in January, as ye'll find oot, and I had nowt to eat but seaweed. Times I wished I'd perished with my lads.'

Hannah's face was full of concern. Despite their short acquaintance, a strong friendship had grown between the two. 'Whatever did ye do?'

'Begged, and I'll nae do that again. Everyone hates a pauper. Even the women in this village, that I've kenned all my life, treated me like the dirt beneath their feet. The parish gave me sixpence a week, enough for a dish of crowdie a day. For that I had to carry stones frae the shore and fill up the holes in the road, no matter the weather, no matter the bronchitis that lay like an iron bar across my chest. I couldna breathe for coughing and I knew that soon it would be a shroud and a hole in the ground for me. It grieved me to think of all the greedy folk that would swarm inside my cottage and help themselves to the things my Bob made for me.'

'Then, along comes Red Wull. He'd been the marrer of my eldest lad. He takes one look at me wi' my load of stones and tells the parish to find a man to make their roads. He brings a side of bacon for my larder and a bag of flour. He brings a good fleece so I can earn money with spinning till the fish start running. He nursed me, like a son, till I was well again.

'I tell all this for I see ye've taken against him for his plain speaking. Judge him not by outward show, hinny, for he is pure gold within.'

Taking up the carding comb, Hannah busied herself with teasing the buffs from a handful of fleece as she pondered Nell's words. It was with some humility that she eventually spoke.

'Seemingly I have misjudged my excellent cousin and for that I am truly sorry,' but she could not refrain from adding, 'yet I do find him uncommonly bold in his manner, though he be my father's brother's son.' Then she had to join in Nell's good-humoured laughter and the rest of the night was passed in companiable gossip with an ear always cocked for any untoward disturbances outside.

Boulmer presented a face of innocence

341

next morning. The women in the smoke-houses diligently threaded fish over smouldering oak fires while all the men except the very old or the very young were abed. Their dealings with the French barque had kept them busy for most of the night.

A stranger might have puzzled over the plentiful horse-droppings on the beach and the lines etched in the sand where barrels had been dragged, but there was no evidence to hang a man should the excise officer come this way. The horsemen had hastened away with their packs of silks and tobacco and many a kitchen floor now concealed a flagon of spirit. Of Ed Freeman and Will Robson there was no sign, but Nell found a sack of salt and a bottle of brandy at the bottom of her copper in the washhouse.

Ed's news of rebellion involving northern nobles created a stir even in this community which did not usually concern itself with outside affairs. If Sir Walter was arming, then maybe the Ogles would follow. The Spencers, perhaps, and other important northern families. The people of Boulmer, for their own sakes, needed to know what was going on. Visiting ships' captains were the men who might throw light on the issue.

What manner of man was this prince

who aimed to take the throne from James?

William had few personal charms in his favour. Far from robust, he lacked the gloss of good health. His long and dreary face was rarely enlivened by a smile, but his wife, the Princess Mary, made up for all his shortcomings in this respect. This amiable and much loved lady, being the elder daughter of James by his first marriage, was totally acceptable to the governing class of Britain.

In other respects, William, as the acknowledged champion of the Protestant cause in Europe, was the ideal choice to lead any opposition to King James. The northern squires, Sir Walter amongst them, were armed and ready, waiting upon William's strategy.

He was a prudent man, however. He had no desire to suffer the fate of his wife's grandfather, Charles; nor did he seek a personal and possibly bloody encounter with her father, so after landing at Torbay, he lingered in the West Country, giving time for his supporters to rally to his standard. Circumspect in everything he did, he would not take the Crown until it was constitutionally offered to him. So the northern squires held themselves in readiness and besieged every courier for news.

But if there was confusion in the north,

it was nothing compared with the scene in London. The king, it was said, had lost all control. Unruly mobs roamed the streets, burning down the homes of Catholics and settling many a personal grievance on the way. Rich and powerful masters, their past misdeeds lying heavy upon them, walked abroad at their peril. One amongst them in particular, the Lord Chancellor, formerly Judge Jeffreys of infamous memory and arguably the most hated man in the realm, was especially vulnerable. He found it expedient to move from his costly mansion in Duke Street to a small apartment in Whitehall where he might hope for protection from the king if need arose.

Any influence James once had was fast disappearing, however. When he hired Irish mercenaries for a personal bodyguard, he antagonised his few remaining friends. Then the navy declared for William and James's cause was lost. Abandoned by all the most powerful nobles in the land, he fled to France, throwing the Great Seal of the kingdom into the River Thames as he went, in a final gesture of defiance towards his son-in-law.

William's patience was rewarded, but until he could be formally installed as king, the country was without a head, without a government. Before he left, James had disbanded the army but neglected to pay them and undisciplined soldiers roamed the streets of London stealing goods and burning down houses at will.

Into this confusion came Will Robson on behalf of the keelmen of Tyneside and his equally naive marrer, Jacob Dawson, representing the fish-smokers of Craster.

Of late, wily London merchants, taking advantage of the present turmoil in the capital, had neglected to settle their bills for imports from the north. Will for the Tyne and Jacob for Craster had been elected to come in person to collect the dues owed. Neither had been to London before and would have been amazed, even in tranquil times, by the complexity of its streets and the multitude of people who lived there. Faced with the present disorder, they were stunned into speechlessness when they stepped ashore at Billingsgate dock into the pushing, shoving, ranting crowds.

Not without difficulty, they found the addresses they sought in Little Old Bailey and Threadneedle Street where the laggard payers, confronted so surprisingly by their creditors, paid up smartly.

Jacob, ill at ease in the great city, grabbed Will by the arm. 'We got wor money. Let's awa' back to the boat.' But Will was loth to leave the exciting streets of London without further exploration. He persuaded Jacob that it would be right and

345

proper to sample the ale of the great city before they left.

They tried two inns, the Crown Tavern in Leadenhall Street, and the Feathers in Fish Street. Both were crowded, unfriendly and dirty beyond belief. By their speech and Will's distinctive clothing, the two strangers were seen at once to be men from the north and more than one light-fingered rascal had his eye on the pouch at Jacob's belt.

'Howay, man.' Jacob drained his tankard. 'Let's oot of here afore we get wor throats cut.'

Reluctantly, Will allowed himself to be led back towards the dock. There were wonderful sights to be seen and he might never set foot in London again. Then a glimpse of Mother Susan's whorehouse, situated conveniently close to the quay where the collier was tied, put another thought into his head.

'I'll join thee directly, Jacob. Divvent let the boat sail without me,' and he clattered, full of beer and bravado, down the steps into Mother Susan's Respectable Establishment for Seafarers.

Polly, seeing Will stagger none too steadily into what Mother Susan chose to call her Conversation Room, got off her seat and grabbed him before any of the other girls had a chance to get their hands on him. He was the answer to a prayer. Earlier that day a stranger had presented her with a most unusual, but lucrative, proposition. Four crowns he had offered for a suit of sailor's clothes. And here was the very thing. This sailor, from the north by his dress, was already a mite befuddled so there would be no difficult in persuading him to undress.

She took Will by the hand and led him up the rickety stairs, smiling encouragingly over her shoulder and obliging with a girlish squeal when he nipped her bottom. A powder in his gin and he would sleep the sleep of the just, but she hoped he'd get his money's worth first. He was a nice-looking young fellow and Polly had a heart of gold.

Will saw none of the patches on her faded red satin dress, nor the lines and wrinkles that powder and rouge could not hide in her once pretty face. He saw a bonnie lass, full of promise. When he awoke, his head was splitting and his clothes were gone.

The boat that was to take him home to the Tyne was about to sail when he reached the quay. The gangway was already lifted and he had to be hoisted aboard on a rope but Jacob knew better than to laugh at Red Wull, Terror of the North, dressed in a woman's petticoats! He

347

contented himself with, 'Been to market, have ye, hinny?' as Will landed in a sprawl of skirts on the deck. But wait till he got back to Craster! What a tale to tell.

'I'll never trust another Londoner again as long as I live.' Will stood on the afterdeck watching London's skyline fade from view. 'She was a bonny, kindly lass an' all,' he added aggrievedly. ' 'Tis a mercy I kept me sark or she'd have had that as well.'

Polly split the four crowns with Mother Susan as her contract demanded and that night Rob, her man, almost upset his cart with laughing as she told the tale.

Polly and Rob had known hard times since his discharge from the army. At first, he had been given a place at the Savoy Hospital with the rest of the wounded from the Scotch campaign but once his stumps had healed, his bed was needed for someone in worse plight. His small pension was not enough to live on or put a roof over his head so Polly worked to support them both and, like most women in her position, she turned to whoring.

Mother Susan took pity on this legless soldier and his pretty little wife and gave them the garret at the top of her house, to be paid for out of Polly's earnings. This small room was now Rob's world.

His travelling days, which had taken the pair of them over the length and breadth of the kingdom, were over. From bed to bucket on his small wheeled cart was the limit of his adventuring now. He tended the fire and cooked food for himself and Polly.

With arms grown excessively muscular, he could hoist his torso on to a box by the tiny garret window which gave a view of one of the busiest ports in the world. Far below him were the schooners and frigates, brigs and hoys, loading and discharging on London's great river. In his imagination, at least, he could escape to wander at will over the oceans of the world.

He had been promised a place in the fine new hospital that was going up on the riverside meadows at Chelsea. Nell's idea, that—Old Chanticleer's little orange girl. But it would never be finished in his lifetime, Rob was convinced. The only way he'd go down Mother Susan's stairs would be in a box, a short square box to save timber.

Polly lived from day to day. 'Why worry about tomorrow?' she would say when some of the younger girls reminded her that she was getting on in years. 'Ain't there enough to worry about today?' The fact remained, however, that, though she was still pretty, she was thirty-two years old and most gentlemen preferred someone younger to entertain them.

Every day, she carried two buckets of coal and a bucket of water up the stairs. She emptied the slops and washed their clothes and endured Mother Susan's drunken tantrums in silence lest a hasty reply robbed her of employment and a roof over her head. On one occasion only, had her man caught her weeping. Most times she drowned her sorrows in gin.

'I know not who needs a sailor's costume so bad he'll pay four crowns for it.' Polly had bought beefsteak and oyster pies from the streetseller below and ale to wash it down. 'But we have to thank him for a good supper.'

'Good luck to him,' Rob lifted his tankard, caring not in the least where the money came from.

'I hope it was the right size. The gentleman's servant gave little enough to measure by.'

' 'An if it ain't, he cannot have his money back,' Rob scraped his platter, 'for we've ate it.'

As Judge Jeffreys made his way along the narrow streets of Wapping he knew very well that if anyone recognised him he was a dead man, The mobs were out looking for him. They'd string him up. He flinched as he remembered the countless quarterings he had ordered and witnessed. Dear God, not that. He must get out of the country with all speed. In his disguise as a sailor he would seek a berth on a ship bound for France. King James, his one-time protector, had already fled.

He turned into a low tavern where disengaged skippers were to be found and took a seat by the window. No one gave him a second glance. He was just one of many sailors come to wet their whistle or seek employment. Out of habit, his hands strayed to tug at the black curling eyebrows before he remembered his manservant had shaved them off that very morning. A giveaway, he had warned his master and rightly so. Well he knew that those fearsome appendages had added to his terrifying appearance in the courtroom and for that reason had cherished them. His forehead felt strangely smooth without them.

But the poor scrivener who happened to be passing by in the street was in no doubt whatsoever as to the identity of the evil face at the tavern window. This man had been tied to the tail of a cart and flogged through seven towns, even though his innocence was proven. He was not likely to forget the face of the fiend who sentenced him, with or

351

without eyebrows. To him fell the exquisite pleasure of revenge.

An alarm was raised. A mob arrived from nowhere. There was scarce a man who did not know some poor soul who had suffered at the hands of Judge Jeffreys or who had not a personal debt to settle. They cornered him. They threatened to tear him limb from limb until the terrified judge pleaded to be taken to the Tower, forfeiting his liberty by his own choice in order to save his skin. But the crowd was loth to let him go and it took a ring of pikemen to protect him as he was led away to London's great fortress. The infamous judge never tasted freedom again, dying in the Tower some time later.

The uproar in the capital died down. Law and order returned as William and Mary agreed to rule jointly within certain new statutory restrictions of longlasting effect. All future laws would be made, not by the monarch as previously, but by Parliament and no tax might be levied without the consent of Parliament. The Protestant religion was confirmed as the Established Church of the country. The revolution, for such it was, had been achieved without bloodshed.

Sir Walter and others of like mind put away their battle accoutrements. There would be no civil war. The tenantry went back to their fields in time for the winter ploughing and the Huguenots of Howden opened a case of rare Canary wine to toast the health of King William III and his good Queen Mary.

The story of Will's flight in petticoats from London was hailed with delight in the north.

'Thy cousin,' Ed Freeman told Hannah, dabbing his eyes as he doubled up with mirth, 'is a proper Nancy.'

The story was never forgotten. It was passed from father to son and, in time, to their sons too and many a frisky young blade was warned, 'Ha'd on to thy breeks in a whorehouse or ye'll mebbes come haem in a petticoat like Red Wull of Sandgate.'

Ed brought other news to delight Hannah. 'I met thy brother Tom in Belford and he bade me say that he and Betsy Lisle are now betrothed and he doth think this will please ye well.'

Hannah's shout of joy jerked Martha's head up from the nets she was mending. ' 'Tis thy Betsy and my brother betrothed, Mistress Lisle! Glad news indeed!'

And Martha was pleased. This union between the two families might make another match more likely. She'd caught

Little Wattee, the youngest, looking at Hannah with sheep's eyes on more than one occasion.

'And something else,' Hannah went on, 'They plan to visit here towards the new year at the beginning of March, perhaps for Old Year's Night.'

'There's nae room in wor hoose for any mair folk,' Meg announced with some truth, but Martha overrode all objections.

'He can make a bed in the stable. Betsy can lie with ye, Meg, like she used to.'

22

Tom and Betsy arrived in time for the feast of Old Year's Night, very grand in Mistress Emma's trap, borrowed for the occasion. Hannah embraced her friend with warmth.

'I could nae have wished for a more amiable sister.'

Betsy's hands were neatly kept, her skin soft. Her clothes smelt of lavender. Her bonnet was beribboned. 'My,' said Hannah with a touch of longing in her voice, 'what a fine lady ye've become.'

Betsy laughed. 'Nay, Hannah, 'tis ye who've changed. I never thought to see a lady's maid turn into a fishergirl but truly I see that is what ye are now.'

In the rough surroundings of the Lisle home, even Tom seemed to have the airs of a gentleman. His clothes were plain but well-cut and of good stuff. His neckband cleanly white. He took Hannah aside as Betsy helped Meg to lay cold meats and bread upon the table.

'This is no place for thee, little sister.' His face was full of concern. 'Now that I have seen thee, after so long an absence, I am uneasy in my mind. Come back to Buckton with us. I know that Mistress Emma will give thee lodgings for ye were ever her favourite and I can pay for thy keep now that I am manager of the business.'

No more could be said at that moment for the Lisle men trooped in and took their places at table, making small shift for Tom, but Hannah's mind as she served them with supper was on Tom's words.

In truth, she was sorely tempted by his suggestion. Seeing Betsy again made her realise how many of life's comforts she had sacrificed in order to achieve her independence. Later, on the way to chapel at Longhoughton for midnight mass, there was an opportunity for private talk with Betsy and Tom.

It was a cold night with no moon. Blackness rolled up from the sea and a wind like the edge of a knife found every gap in shawl and cloak as they left the harbour behind them and crossed the fields along with all the other inhabitants of Boulmer except the infants and the infirm.

'February fill-dyke.
Either black or white.'

So the old saw went and this year it had been white indeed. Snow had lain till the beginning of March. The thaw had left the fields sodden and sumpy to the ruination of Betsy's smart boots, but Tom had earned good marks from Martha by setting her to ride in the cart with Meg. Betsy's father and older brothers kept at a wary distance from their prospective brother, but Young Wattee, though he would not walk alongside, stayed close enough to hear the conversation. Plainly he found both Hannah and her brother objects of great curiosity.

'Whose child is that?' Betsy, mimicking the tones of Sir George Le Flemont, was relating the news from Budle Hall. Now she changed to the mincing tones of a wench. 'Why, Sir,' says Enid, looking sly, ' 'tis mine,' and she drops him the smallest bob ye ever did see. 'Twas plain that the master saw straightaway the child is a Le Flemont, and a fine, sturdy lad at that. From that day, Enid's kitchen has not wanted for meat or milk nor has her hearth been short of fuel and Nosy Thomas can only marvel at the generosity of such a master!' Their laughter rang out across the bleak fields. 'Enid hath another bun in the oven,' Betsy continued, 'and her husband, thinking all babes are born at six months, will be a mite impatient afore Enid is brought to bed with this one!'

'Poor girl,' Hannah sighed when the laughter died down, 'to have another babe so soon.'

Betsy shrugged. ' 'Tis natural. I expect Tom and me will have a rare flurry of children as soon as we are wed.'

Hannah's quick glance showed her that Tom saw nought wrong in this. He gave a mock groan.

'And I will have to break my back to support ye all.'

The pottery business, Tom told Hannah, was prospering. He paused before continuing. 'There's news frae Daniel. He employs two apprentices himsell now and it seems all Edinburgh is eager to buy his ware.'

'I'm glad,' said Hannah, but there was always that sense of guilt whenever Daniel's name was mentioned, though the incident that fretted her was long since past and no doubt long forgotten by him. She turned the subject to Burnfoot.

'Aye, I must take Betsy haem and yet I dread it,' confessed Tom. 'My father and I are strangers and hard put to find words to pass one hour in each other's company.'

'As to that, never fret,' laughed Hannah, 'for Betsy will find words enough for all of ye. Yet I am no better daughter than ye are a son, Tom. My father and I parted on bad terms because I called him a bully for beating Sarah.'

'I am already terrified at the thought of meeting this tyrant,' said Betsy, feigning fear, 'yet Ma says he was the idol of every serving lass at Chillingham Castle.'

' 'Tis your good fortune that he did not wed thy ma, Betsy,' Hannah assured her, 'and hers, although I do believe that Mistress Lisle would have given him as good as he gave her.'

Betsy looked back over her shoulder at her father and two older brothers, trudging, heads down, insensitive as beasts in the field and Young Wattee, treading on her heels and gawping at her like a loon.

'The father she picked for me is nowt to write haem aboot either.'

The bells of St Peter rang out over the

countryside to bid them make haste and the ancient church was nigh on full when the folk from Boulmer shuffled in. The gentry were already seated in their pews with a brazier of hot coals to keep them warm for it was perishing cold inside. The walls were stout enough. This tower had been a sanctuary against the raiding Scots for centuries but draughts from doors and windows threatened to blow out the candles in their sconces.

Betsy, Tom and Hannah dropped to their knees on the cold stone flags with the Lisle men scuffling and coughing beside them. With his eyes closed in prayer, Tom whispered out of the side of his mouth for Hannah's private ear, 'How in the name of all the saints did my Betsy spring from a bunch like this?'

'Thou hast found the gold,' Hannah whispered back. 'The rest is dross.'

Her thoughts were elsewhere as the priest droned out his long, dull sermon. She was remembering Buckton and her yellow and white bedchamber, Mistress Emma's shining kitchen, Betsy's company on walks by the sea. The impulse to turn away from this hard life that she had chosen and to turn the clock back was strong. But there was a worm in the apple. If she returned to Buckton, she would needs be kept by her brother.

As she knelt with the congregation to intone the liturgy, she knew that she would not go back. She had always known that the road to independence would be hard. How could she contemplate giving up at the first temptation? She would stay. She rose to her feet as the gentry filed out. Spring was on the way and Nell had assured her that life would be easier. She had her answer for Tom.

The traditional feast of Old Year's Night, March 14th, was held each year in Boulmer's largest packing shed. Hannah and Betsy helped the other women with the cooking of pies and potted fish and meat, swept the barn and cleared a space for the dancing. Even Meg was in a friendly mood. Betsy had given her a pretty frock of flowered dimity and persuaded her to wash herself all over for the occasion. Her fresh complexion shone from scrubbing with soda soap and her hair, dressed by Betsy, no longer hung in rats' tails.

Martha was fulsome with her praise. 'Thee's a bonny lass if thee'll but try, Meg. This night will mebbes see another betrothal. Nat Dodds and a few mair will see what they're missing.' She rounded on her scruffy sons. 'And if ye lazy clods smartened theesells up a bit, ye might perchance find a wife! Ye must have blinkers on not to see a good one staring

360

ye in the face.' She jabbed her head meaningly at Hannah.

'Who wants a wife!,' snorted Gregory, the eldest and crudest of the three. 'There's sport enough to be had without a wedding ring.'

Tom, hearing all this, was more disturbed than ever at Hannah's decision to stay. 'These fellows are full of ill-will towards ye,' he warned and Betsy agreed.

'Though they be my ain kin, I tell thee they are an evil bunch of rascals. Come awa with Tom and me.'

But Hannah's mind was made up. 'These oafs do not frighten me,' she said lightly, 'and do not forget that I have a good friend in thy ma, Betsy, and in Nell Murray, the woman I lodge with. I will bide here till I can handle a boat and cure fish as well as the rest of the women or better, then I'll move on and mebbes set up in business mysell. You could say that this is my apprenticeship.'

'But the life is so hard for you,' Tom complained, looking again at her reddened hands and wondering how best to phrase the thought that was in his mind. 'Would'st not think again on Daniel's offer? I know he still thinks fondly of thee.'

Hannah laughed. 'Why, Tom, thou'rt as much a match-maker as Martha and I have no appetite for any of thy schemes. What I seek is not a husband but freedom to do as I please.'

Defeated, Tom squeezed her hand. 'Then mind this, little sister, that Betsy and me are always near to help ye if need be.'

Hinds and serving maids from nearby villages began to arrive in Boulmer by the late afternoon of the next day, excused their duties for the rest of Old Year's Night. This was an opportunity not to be missed for lads and lasses to see what was offering in the marriage market and pursue their inclinations. The girls, wearing their prettiest shawls, clustered round the braziers in the barn, very arch in their manner, very free with their laughter, while the hopeful swains, their hair plastered down with goose grease, rollicked around the brandy kegs with one eye on their fancy.

Meg took no part in these flirtations. She had forgotten that someone had told her she looked attractive and stood by a table with a scowl on her face, slicing up sausages. Hannah was wearing the frock she had worn on her arrival at Burnfoot, her only frock. Made of thin material, it was wonderfully kind to the skin after salt-stiff flannel but the lace frills at the elbow fell over weatherbeaten arms now and the low neckline revealed a white bosom that contrasted strangely with a sunburnt neck.

' 'Tis most unfashionable to be pied,' Betsy teased her. Betsy was freckled pink and white all over.

A familiar voice behind Hannah spoke. 'Ye've put off yer fishergirl breeks for the night, then?' Cousin Will, chin in hand, stood eyeing her dress appreciatively.

'And ye,' she said sharply, 'have put away thy petticoats!'

At this, he threw back his head and roared with laughter, not in the least disconcerted by the allusion to his London folly.

'Come,' said Hannah, 'ye shall make the acquaintance of my brother and his betrothed.'

Tom took a liking to him at once. A lively fellow. What age, he wondered. Twenty? Thirty? It was hard to say. Rapidly changing expressions on Will's mobile features had etched a network of tiny lines. Laughter left its crinkling marks at the corners of his eyes yet the creases between his brows showed that this man could curse as hard as he laughed. When he slapped Tom on the back he almost knocked him off his balance. His handshake was a grip of iron. A handy fellow, this, to have by you in a fight, Tom decided.

Young Billy Wilson drew the bow across

his fiddle. Time to begin the dancing. He had enough spirits inside him now to keep going till he went dry or fell over, whichever happened first. He was always 'Young' Billy though he was forty if he was a day and his old da, who, before him, played the fiddle at every hoppings, had forgotten how old anybody was, including himself. He stayed at home these days by a warm fire and a bottle of brandy for company while Young Billy travelled to Boulmer, Craster and even Alnwick, wheedling fantastic, toe-tapping tunes from his beloved fiddle.

He started the evening with 'Gathering Peascods' and the lasses looked expectantly round for likely partners. Betsy saw the look of excitement pass between her lover and his sister and knew that she would be sitting this dance out. Before either could make a move, however, Will intervened. Bowing low to Hannah, he swept off his beribboned hat in an exaggerated gesture.

'The music calls. Come dance with me,' but the smile on his face froze as she drew back from his extended hand. 'What's this?' he said lightly. 'Canst not dance? Or wilt not dance with me? Which is it?'

Betsy, with complete understanding, made haste to ease the awkward moment. 'Take nae offence, Will, as I must not also. These two, so I've heard tell, are the best dancing pair in the country and will dance with none but each other. I am as spurned as thou art for Tom does not seek to dance with me, his betrothed!' She gave Tom a playful pat on the seat of his breeches. 'Be off with ye and show us what ye can do.'

Miserably, Hannah followed Tom to make up a set for the dance. To rebuff Will had been ill-considered on her part, the recoil from his touch instinctive. As she took her place at Tom's side, Will's angry face was before her eyes.

A few bars of Young Billy's music, however, were enough to dispel all unease. The demanding rhythms played by a half-drunk fiddler who never missed a beat or slurred a note sent all feet tapping. Kicking off her shoes, Hannah flung back her head and laughed in delight. The old magic was at work again. She danced with the grace of a gazelle while Tom, for all his heavy build, picked his way neatly as on pinpoints, with never a move too slow or too hasty.

Betsy clapped her hands. 'There, Will. See for thysell how well they dance!'

But Will's chin was thrust out truculently. ' 'Tis his betrothed he should be dancing with, not his sister.'

'The fault then, if there is one, lies with me,' said Betsy, 'for I canna dance to save

365

mesell. I have a pair of turnips for feet and if Tom spins me roond I get duzzy and fall doon.'

The room grew hot. The ale flowed freely. Will drifted away as the dancers returned to their seats. Elated and out of breath, Hannah flopped on to a barrel while Tom went in search of refreshment for herself and Betsy.

'That fiddler could make a cat dance, Betsy. Why not give him a chance?'

'So,' said Betsy playfully, 'I am to be likened to a cat now, am I? Thou'rt in a rare mood for upsetting folk tonight, Hannah Robson. Thy cousin is mighty sore that ye would not dance with him.'

Hannah bit her lip, remembering.

'He sought nae mair than a dance, Hannah,' Betsy said reprovingly. 'Not a kiss. Not a tumble in the hay. 'Tis time you grew up.' There was an unaccustomed asperity in Betsy's voice and Tom found the girls strangely silent on his return with a jug of cider.

The next tune was intended as a rest for all the dancers. Young Billy was as skilful with the slow rhythms as he was with the gallops. The noise and the chatter ebbed away as the beautiful strains of the old song, 'Waters of Tyne' meandered around the barn, beginning thin and plaintive, swelling in a melody that filled the heart with longing, and soaring to the smoky rafters themselves.

'At least ye canna dance to this,' said Tom, mopping his brow.

'Will can,' said Betsy. 'Look yonder. He's on the floor, alone.'

He was a striking figure in his grey 'slops' and yellow waistcoat. All eyes followed him as, smooth as a snake, he moved to the centre of the floor. Using movements deliberate and measured, he described intricate patterns with the pointed toe of one buckled shoe, lending his body, whippy as willow, to follow the moods of the music.

'He's a canny dancer, an' all,' whispered Tom.

Despite herself, Hannah was spellbound by his grace. As for Young Billy, he could not take his eyes, off the figure who was the very articulation of his music. At the end of the song, when the frustrated maiden cries out in anguish at being parted from her lover by the waters of Tyne, Will leapt high, like a stretched-out cat, then wound down in a spinning spiral until, with the last plaintive notes of Young Billy's fiddle, the dancer was curled within himself like a snail, the very embodiment of melancholy.

The dance was over. There was a roar of approval from the onlookers and Young

Billy himself put down his fiddle to join in the clapping.

Will was on his feet in a trice, all trace of sadness gone. For one brief moment, his eyes sought Hannah who was clapping as enthusiastically as the rest, and Tom, intercepting that glance, was struck by a blinding truth.

'He's in love with my sister.' Following hard came the thought, 'She'll not have him.' This he qualified with, 'She'll not have any man.'

With the next tune, a lively reel, Will appeared before Hannah, perky as a gnat and just as capable of stinging. 'What say ye, cousin? Am I fit to partner thee or must I seek lessons frae thy brother?'

Hannah smiled and held out her hand. ' 'Tis ye must teach us. Any fool can hop a jig but there'll nae be many like thee who can dance to a lament with such grace.'

Briskly, he whirled her round the floor. His touch on her waist, her arm, was the lightest. He held her hand no longer than was necessary for he saw that when she danced with him, she was tense. There was none of the spring that she showed when dancing with her brother. For her part, Hannah was astonished at his lightness. Beside him, Tom seemed ponderous.

He broke into song as the chorus line came round once more:

'Weel may the keel row, the keel row, the
keel row.
Weel may the keel row that my laddie's
in.'

'I'll wager ye've never even seen a keel,
cousin?' He swung her around until the
barrels and rafters and tarry flares, the
laughing, sweating faces and whirling skirts
all merged into one frenzied blur.
'I'll take thee to the Tyne one day and
show thee the Robson keel. A bonny boat.
The *Nellie Bly.*'

23

There were many times during the weeks
that followed the departure of Tom and
Betsy when Hannah regretted her decision
to stay at Boulmer, when her spirit failed
to live up to her bold declaration of
independence. Spring was late in coming
and it seemed that winter would last for
ever with its sleety showers and fog so
thick that the day was still dark at noon.
Occasionally a beleaguered vessel could be
glimpsed ploughing through mountainous
seas, and the next tide would deposit

broken spars and sometimes relics of a more gruesome nature on the shore at Boulmer.

Few fishermen would risk their lives and their cobles in weather like this and, with little fresh fish coming in, the diet for all was crowdie and limpets. Old folk crouched in the chimney corner with their gin and linctus, determined to hang on for one more spring, one more run of the herring, but there were many for whom only one journey remained, the trip across the field to the churchyard at Longhoughton in a wooden box.

Some familiar faces were absent as Hannah went about her daily work. The two old men she and Nell often met when beachcombing, who never lifted their eyes from the tide that brought them fuel and sometimes treasure, were carried away with bronchitis. Dropsy had been the end of the old kelp-burner. A younger woman now made soap from the ashes and the frail girl who worked alongside Nell in the smokehouses went to join the rest of her consumptive family in the churchyard. Babies came. Babies died, not staying long enough to make a lasting impact on the long-suffering women who bore them.

Carriers like Ed Freeman would not risk their waggons on roads that were axle-deep in mud, so even the enlivenment of a visit from him was missing. A melancholy that drained away all purpose settled upon Hannah. Without Nell's cheerful companionship, she would have been lost. Nell, who suffered the same discomforts, who had lost her man and two sons, showed her what true stoicism was.

She was at home every day now spinning her fleece into marketable yarn. The weaver at Longhoughton paid seventeen pence a pound though she'd get as much as two shillings at Alnwick market, could she but get there. Times were hard and it took time to spin a pound of yarn. Hannah was always sure of an adequate supper with Martha, but she knew that Nell sometimes went hungry to bed. She judged the time had come to dip into her reserve of money.

'I have a few crowns, Nell, which I brought with me,' she patted the pouch that lay next to her skin, 'enough to tide us over till better times.'

Nell looked up sharply from her wheel. 'I thank thee, Hannah, for thy kindness, but if what ye say is true, that ye have a store of money, never mention it to another living soul in Boulmer or thy life will not be worth the claes on thy back. There's folk here that'd steal a last crust frae their grandmother.' She saw the doubt in Hannah's eye. 'Withoot a man to protect thee, thee'd nae have a chance,' she insisted.

There was disgust on Hannah's face. 'I have lived here amongst them. Would they act so base towards me?'

Nell sighed. 'When a man's bairns are sick and like to die of hunger he'll do what he wouldna dream of doing in better times.'

Thus warned, Hannah took to concealing her sharp gutting knife in the folds of the heavy flannel skirt which replaced breeches when the women were not working in water. She had reason to be grateful to Nell for her warning, for the necessity of defending herself arose sooner than expected.

In Boulmer, drunkenness amongst the men was condoned, expected even, by the women and looked upon as a symbol of manliness. When normally hard-working fishermen could not put to sea for storms, they passed their time at the cockpit and the alehouse.

'There'll be a crop of babies come December,' Nell forecast drily, 'for the men have nowt else to do.'

Martha, who was not averse to a mug of gin herself, looked leniently and with considerable amusement upon the bawdy antics of her men. As far as Hannah was concerned, however, their lewd remarks and drunken overtures were a continual source of annoyance. She knew well enough that she provoked men of their ilk by her independent nature. They were accustomed to having their way with women. Gregory especially resented her and would like to see her humbled. The threat was there in his evil eye every time he glanced at her. Thus forewarned, she took pains to avoid ever being caught alone with him, yet when the attack came, it was from all the Lisle men, Big Wattee included, and was almost her undoing. Nothing could have prepared her for such a vicious onslaught.

Meg was well aware of her brothers' intentions. She had known that, sooner or later Miss High and Mighty would be laid by one of her brothers and she derived a perverse pleasure at the prospect. Let her grovel. Let her pay for her pride. And so, when she saw her father and brothers steal slyly into the store shed where Hannah was working, she guessed what they were about and made no attempt to interfere. Instead, she walked past the open door, calling no warning to Hannah whose head was bent over her accounts. Hearing Hannah cry out, she paid no heed and walked on.

Under the weight of her attackers, Hannah fell to the ground but not before she had blooded their leader, Big Wattee himself. Her gutting knife flashed as he fumbled with his britches. Bull-drunk and witless, he let out a roar of pain that could have been heard far out at sea and Meg, suddenly shaken out of her complacency, ran yelling for her mother.

'Come quick, Ma! She's murdering wor da!'

Thrashing about like a wild animal beneath Gregory's sweating body, Hannah dug her fingernails into his pockmarked nose, tearing open one nostril, making the blood run free. She found an eye. Her teeth closed on the arm that tore open her bodice. Screaming with fury, he almost stunned her with a blow to her head.

She was struggling for breath beneath the combined weights of Gregory and Dick when Martha came, huffing and puffing, holding up her petticoats. Her sons were grunting like pigs as they tore the clothes from Hannah. Her husband, clutching his genitals with bloody hands, roared and danced with pain while Young Wattee hopped about in agitation, biting his nails and wailing.

'Get off that lass!' she yelled. 'What kind a sport d'ye call this!'

At the sight of their mother, titanic in her fury, the two elder sons broke away from Hannah.

'Four grown men to one poor woman!' Turning to her husband, still rocking and

374

groaning, she hawked up a gob of phlegm. 'Mebbes that'll teach ye not to poke thy pistle where's it's nae wanted. Sarve ye right if she's cut it off. Meg!' she bawled to her daughter who was standing transfixed by the door. 'Fetch a basin of wattor for thy da. Put some bark of oak in't for he's bleeding all over the floor like a stuck pig!'

Ashen-faced, her head reeling from Gregory's savage blow, Hannah raised herself up from the ground, adjusting her torn clothes. There was blood on her chemise but it was not her own.

Martha stooped to pick up the gutting knife and handed it back to her. 'Ye've made them pay for their pleasure.' Her eyes did not condemn.

Hannah thrust up her chin. 'They had no pleasure.' She raised her voice for the benefit of the men who were sloping away, Gregory holding his bleeding nose and snarling like the savage beast he was, Dick binding his arm which would be marked by her teeth for all time. 'Nor will they ever unless it be with my corpse!' Now that the ordeal was over, she found that she was near to tears and could scarce control her shaking limbs.

Martha laid a clumsy hand on her shoulder. 'Divvent break yer heart on't, hinny. 'Tis the way of the world. Men

375

are what they are and women must make the best on't.'

'Thine own husband!' Hannah said accusingly.

Martha laughed harshly. 'He's nae better nor worse than the next man and I care not who he lies with.' She chuckled, 'though he'll nae be lying with anyone for a while, I'm thinking.'

Hannah brushed away a threatening tear. 'I'm sorry, Mistress Lisle. I had to defend mysell.'

The story of Big Wattee's near castration soon reached the alehouse and the back yards where the women met to gossip. The Lisle men were figures of fun, especially Big Wattee who walked bandy for many a day, but Hannah's reputation suffered as a consequence. A toss in the barn was common enough and women were expected to submit. For a maid to damage a man in his private parts was unwomanly and unfair. Even the women shunned her.

The Lisle men, with the exception of Little Wattee, made no attempt to hide their feelings, but they never came near her again. Other men, sniffing a challenge, eyed her speculatively but, upon recalling her finesse with the gutting knife, thought twice before they provoked her.

She was always on her guard. Meg hated her more than ever and without Nell's friendship and the support of Martha, Hannah would have been tempted to pack her bundle. There was little to keep her in Boulmer except her determination not to be driven away. The time to go would be of her own choosing. The herring season was almost upon them and Martha had promised a rise because of the extra clerking she would be doing. She meant to save every penny she could then she would move on. She had no intention of spending the rest of her life in Boulmer.

At the first good break in the weather, the cobles put to sea. Sinister overtones in the introverted life of Boulmer subsided as normal working routines fell into place once more. Spring dusted the neighbouring woods with the first delicate green of pussy willow. Brassy celandine gleamed in the fresh new grass and the herring came swarming down from Scotland, filling the nets with slithering silver. The sea, sublimely complacent now after its turbulent winter, unrolled its curling crystal on Boulmer's sandy bay as if the dark days had never been. The women worked in teams of four, one to carry, two to gut and one to salt and pack. Hannah was now as deft as any of them and, though she was never admitted to their intimate circle, she was content. There by the edge of the sea, with the ravening gulls almost snatching the fish from their hands, the women sang their songs about the sea and the bonnie lads who fished it.

Trading ships came and went, bringing news from other parts of the country. King William, as good as his word, had abolished the hated hearth tax and, in so doing, had earned the gratitude of the poor, short-lived because new taxes soon appeared to pay for the long-drawn-out war against the French king.

Hannah was more interested in the methods of trading by which Boulmer made its living, the import of tar and timber from Sweden and the export of salt fish and kelp. In particular, she observed how unschooled folk were cheated by wily dealers and, as a result of her supervision, the Lisle books began to show a handsome trading profit.

Whenever the Newcastle brig put into harbour for fish and other less legitimate business, Will Robson was quick to check on his cousin's welfare. He saw that she was mighty smart about money, would pass no filed coins nor overlook short change. She was Martha's right hand. Yet, for all that, she was not liked. That was plain to see. The women kept aloof, except for Martha and Nell, and there was open hostility between Hannah and the men. The tale of her defence against assault which would have explained everything, did not reach him till much later. Puzzled and a little disturbed, he returned to the Tyne promising to be back ere long.

For her part, Hannah put the incident behind her but the lesson she had learned was not forgotten. Never again would she walk abroad without a gutting knife. Nevertheless, she meant to enjoy the summer months with Nell.

When their daily work was done, they walked together in the woods and fields that lay beyond the dunes, seeking burnet and cowslip for wine and medicinal herbs for potions and unguents against next winter.

Hannah had already decided she would not see another winter in Boulmer. Come the autumn, she would be off, though where she would go was not yet clear in her mind. The port of Alnmouth further down the coast was a possibility for trading on her own account. She kept these plans to herself for the moment, not wishing to upset Nell. Before the summer was over, however, events outside Hannah's control decided her future for her.

A sudden summer squall sprang up in August. The weather had been oppressively hot and finally crashed in tempestuous storms along the length of the north-east coast, reminding all those who derived their living from the sea that they relaxed their vigilance at their peril. Black clouds and mounting seas merged in an obliterating blanket of rain. Lightning ripped open the heavens.

Will Robson's brig, loaded to the gunwales with barrels of fish, had just set out for the open sea when the storm broke. Like the seasoned sailor he was, Will turned about with all speed and made for safe anchorage. Other vessels were not so lucky. Far out at sea, a ship with most of her rigging gone was fighting a losing battle to hold to her northerly course. Floundering helplessly in the grip of the storm, she was being blown inexorably towards the black rocks of the Farnes. Fishermen on the dunes at Boulmer watched until they could see her no more. No help from land could reach her. She was doomed.

By evening, the storm had blown itself out. A repentant sea gave back its looted trophies and laid them on the beach. Hannah, seeking driftwood, found a seaman's boot amongst broken spars, a carpenter's measure and a crate of bottles. Each subdued wavelet carried its relic of the storm. Further out to sea, a dark object bobbed on the water. A bundle of clothing perhaps? Then a pale hand rose up in unmistakable appeal for help. There was a momentary glimpse of a white face.

Without a moment's hesitation, she dropped her bundle of driftwood and ran into the sea, pushing urgently against the force of the incoming tide till the water rose to her waist, then she lunged out, cleaving the water with scooped arms and thrashing legs.

The man was unconscious when she reached him, perhaps already dead. His face, of a ghastly greenish pallor, floated just beneath the surface of the water; a young face of strangely peaceful expression as though life's cares had already been cast aside. Hannah grabbed a handful of the black hair that wafted silkily over his brow and yanked up his head on to her chest as she turned on her back and kicked out for the shore.

The return to the beach was easier for she was going with the tide, but even so, she was almost spent when at last she felt sand beneath her heels. 'Praise be to God,' she whispered and prayed for the strength to pull her burden ashore. Without the buoyancy of the water to aid her, he lay like a dead weight in her arms as she inched him out of the water and on to the beach.

His face was livid. The eyes closed. Nearness to death transfigured the features yet, even so, Hannah could recognise the

Huguenot artist, Alphonse de Colonnières.

Was she too late? Perhaps her efforts were in vain. She turned him on his side and the sea rushed from his lungs. Taking her cue from this, she turned him full over on to his face and pummelled hard on his back to expel the water.

Unseen by her, a crowd had quietly collected at her back but no one offered help. She was taken by surprise when one of the fishermen spoke.

'He's droonded.'

As if the spell was broken, the others began muttering amongst themselves.

'That's a bonny ring.'

'Search his pockets.'

Horrified, Hannah turned on the speaker, one of the coble crew. 'Stand away! I'll not see thee rob him,' but her words fell on deaf ears. The men were looking at his dress. He wore the clothes of a gentleman. His one remaining shoe bore a silver buckle. The men edged nearer. Fear pricked Hannah's temples. Then a clearly audible gasp from the figure at her feet made her spin round. Colour was returning to his face. The lips puffed out to release a tiny breath.

'There!' she cried in triumph. 'He's not dead. He's breathing.' A sudden spasm contorted the man's body and vomit spewed over the sand. Hannah knelt and wiped his mouth clean with her wet shawl. The men drew closer, an evil look upon their faces.

'He's as good as deed,' one said, and the women at the back of the crowd melted away.

Another pushed forward. 'By the time we've hoyed him back in the sea, he'll be deed as a dab, but we'll see what he can give us first for our pains.' He dropped to his knees on the damp sand. 'Look to his pockets, lads. I'll have that buckle.' The circle of men closed in.

'Ye'll not touch him!' cried Hannah, attempting to shield the wretched man with her own body but the fishermen pushed her roughly aside, their faces alight with greed. They fell upon their victim like carrion crows over a corpse. One tugged at a limp hand. 'I'll have that ring.'

The young man groaned.

'Not so fast, Ned Bailey,' a rat-faced fellow snarled. ' 'Twill be shared amongst the lot of us.'

'Leave him alone!' Hannah's desperate cry was lost in the uproar as the last speaker drew a wickedly sharp knife from his belt and would have cut off the ring, finger and all, had not a cool voice from the back of the crowd interposed.

'Do ye all want to be transported for

thieving then? Or worse still be strung up for murder?'

Hannah looked up in surprise and saw her cousin Will pushing his way to the front of the crowd.

'He's nae deed,' Will went on. 'That I can see with me own eyes. If ye push him back in the sea, he'll nae last five minutes. That's murder and this lassie'll not rescue him a second time, I doubt.'

The men were nonplussed at his intervention. 'Hast taken leave of thy senses, Red Wull? Take a look at this ring. Worth a fortune. Shared among us, fair's fair. Have ye come law-abiding, all of a sudden?'

Another said, 'Who's to find oot, anyway, if we push him back? Only this lassie and we ken weel how to deal with her.'

The expression on Will's face altered. Here was a man that Hannah had not seen before. The jester, the loon who played the fool was not to be seen. His eyes narrowed. His mouth grew cruel and hard. He looked what he was, a dangerous man.

'Ye'll nae touch that lass.' He spat the words out viciously, 'and ye'll nae touch that var nigh droonded bit of man, whoever he is, or by God's blood, I'll see thee hang at the next quarter sessions at Alnwick.'

Reluctantly, muttering oaths, the fishermen drew back as Will stooped and took the dead weight of the man across his back.

'Thee's gone soft in the heed, Wull Robson.' An ugly bully whose broken nose testified to many a fight made to bar Will's way, but he fell back on seeing the look on Will's face. In silence, Will set off across the sands with his burden. Hannah, soaked and shivering though the day was warm, followed.

'Bad cess to Hannah Robson,' the curse rang in her ears. 'There's nee place for the likes of her in this village.'

She hastened to catch up with Will. Without him, she knew that her very life was in danger.

'Ye'll have to leave, cousin.' Will's voice was grim. 'Ye canna bide here.'

'I know,' Hannah said quietly. Boulmer was suddenly a hateful place, full of evil folk. She had no wish to remain.

The inert figure slung over Will's shoulders was bumping about like a sack of chaff but Hannah saw that his eyes were open now, staring fixedly at the sandy lane beneath him. His breath came in short, painful gasps but the blueness had left his lips. 'Where are ye taking him?'

'To Nell,' Will said shortly. 'She'll look after him.'

'I know who he is,' said Hannah. 'He's one of the forrin glassmakers at Howden.'

Will howked and spat. 'Rich men. Think ye they'd have risked their lives for thee?'

Hannah shrugged. 'I'm mighty glad ye turned up on the beach. They'd have hoyed him back, I'm sure of that.'

They wrapped the young gentleman in blankets and put his spoiled clothes to dry by Nell's fire. Warm milk and brandy brought the feeling back to his limbs and colour to his face. His eyes rested gratefully on Hannah as she dried her hair by the fire.

'You saved my life, Mam'selle,' he said in the curious way he had of speaking that she remembered from Budle days. 'I am for ever in thy debt.'

Hannah had changed into dry clothes but still could not control the violent fits of shivering which came over her from time to time. She smiled distractedly. ' 'Twas my cousin Will prevented evil men from killing thee.'

Will was at the ale barrel, drawing himself a measure, his face turned away to hide the conflicting emotions which gripped him. The great ruby ring on the young man's hand winked at him, almost driving him wild. He knew that, but for Hannah's spirited stand by the sea, he would have robbed along with

386

the other men. Aye, and if he were to be truly straight with himsell, mebbes he would have thrown the poor fish back into the water to drown. He spoke roughly, embarrassed by what he considered to be misplaced gratitude.

'What became of thy ship?'

'She broke her back on the Outer Farnes,' Alphonse said sadly. 'I know not if any others are alive. The glassmakers of Howden are my uncles and I was taking a consignment of bottles to Edinburgh along with my beautiful painted window. They are all at the bottom of the sea now.'

'We have met before,' said Hannah, 'when I was lady's maid to Lady Le Flemont at Budle Hall.' She had forgotten how sweet was his smile. It lit up his bedraggled appearance with a gentleness that was almost feminine.

'I do remember, though your dress, like mine at this moment, is different.'

Impatiently, Will broke into these reminiscences and Nell, noting that his face had not relaxed its grimness ever since he carried his dripping bundle into her house, knew that serious matters were afoot. Now he was insisting that both Hannah and the stranger must leave Boulmer before morning.

'I will carry the both of ye on my boat. This is no fit place for thee to linger,

Mounseer, and this maid is like to get a knife in her back for denying the people that great ruby on thy finger.'

In one swift, impetuous gesture, Alphonse wrenched the ring from his finger. It lay in the palm of the hand he extended towards Hannah, winking and sparkling in the firelight.

'Please accept this, Mam'selle, as a token of my sincere gratitude.'

Will's eyes lit up. Here was a gentleman indeed, but Hannah's next words dumbfounded him.

'Put it back on thy finger where it belongs,' she said softly, ' 'tis reward enough for me to see thee sitting here alive.'

She would not take the jewel. Neither Will nor Nell nor the giver himself could prevail upon her to accept it. It went back on the Huguenot's finger.

'We'll make the mouth of the Tyne by one hour after midnight.' Will tore his eyes away from the ring. 'A boatman will take thee ashore at Howden. As for thee, little cousin,' (her hair was drying into wisps and curls in a most distracting manner) 'who art so rich ye can afford to turn away a fortune, I must take thee to my sister who will give thee food and shelter.' Ignoring her immediate anticipated opposition, he said with finality, 'Thou canst not bide

388

here withoot bringing harm to Nell. Get thy bundle together.'

Though she resented the masterful tone, Hannah could not but agree to the wisdom of his words. She had meant to leave Boulmer in the next month or two but seemingly she must go now. She turned to her friend. 'What say thee, Nell?'

Nell ran an affectionate hand through Hannah's tousled hair. 'I say that, for once, Will is talking sense. Ye must go, Hannah, though I am losing a dear friend in your going. And go now afore some mischief is done to ye. Ye have made many enemies tonight.'

'Say rather she hath made a friend for life,' Alphonse interposed gently.

Hannah still hung back. 'What work can I find on the Tyne?' she demanded. 'I still have a living to make.'

'There's work enough on keels or salt pans,' said Will impatiently. 'Get thy things. We must leave on the tide.'

'If 'tis employment ye seek,' interrupted Alphonse, 'I can promise my uncles' help in this matter.'

Will studied the Frenchman. His colour was quite returned to normal and his limbs no longer shook with cold. 'Art well enough for another sea trip, Mounseer?'

'Ready as soon as clothed.' Alphonse stretched out a hand towards the still

389

steaming coat of grosgrain with its heavy embroidered cuffs, the shirt of fine lawn.

'Ye canna put them on,' Nell expostulated. 'They're still sopping wet. I'll find ye some claes of my sons if ye're not too proud to wear them.' She went to a heavy chest and rummaged inside. 'There was no one to rescue them when the boat went doon.'

Without another word, Hannah went to gather her belongings together. Fate had made this decision for her.

24

'Who taught thee to swim?' Will, braced against the wheel, did not relax his scrutiny of the dark waters for a moment.

Hannah sat on the deck at his feet, secured against the rolling of the ship by a rope around her waist, her back against the cabin where the Frenchman lay. They had to shout to make themselves heard above the slap and boom of the lifting keel, the crack of wind-filled sails.

'Tom taught me. When the burn was in flood.'

'There's a deal more water in the ocean than ever was found in Harehope Burn.'

Hannah wriggled further into the tarpaulin Will had provided for her. 'I thought, once or twice, we were done for, the Frenchie and me. Lucky I was wearing breeks. I'd have sunk with felts on.'

The webb of creases around Will's eyes deepened as he strained to penetrate the inky blackness ahead. ' 'Twas bravely done.'

The deep, rolling swell that Will had to contend with was a legacy of the recent storm. Under his hand, however, the brig slipped easily in and out of the troughs without shipping water. Hannah could not fail to be impressed by his seamanship and easy leadership of his crew.

'Are ye nae feeling seasick, cousin?' Will's tone showed no concern, only curiosity.

Hannah would not admit to a certain queasiness. 'But I think your other passenger is ridding himself of the last drop of sea water.' Through the bulkhead at her back she could hear Alphonse groaning and could imagine his wretchedness.

They had been at sea for almost an hour and were nearing the mouth of the Tyne. This stretch of the coastline had an evil reputation and it behoved every sailor to be watchful. A fitful moon appearing from behind the clouds from time to time showed with a glittering of silver where deadly rocks broke the surface.

'Light to starboard, Skipper,' came the call from one of the crew. A flickering light pricked the darkness on a looming cliff.

'Hold hard!' The warning was for Hannah as Will tugged at the wheel. 'we'll take her oot a bit else we'll be on the Black Middens. Cuddy Whitman and his womenfolk keep that flare going in bad weather, may the Lord reward them.' Pluming spray reared up from the foot of the cliff crashing down on the notorious Middens rocks. 'Many a good ship's foundered there and I've nae wish to join them.' The deck lifted as he changed course and smacked down viciously into foam-topped rollers. Through the cabin wall came renewed groans from the Frenchman.

Will was neither very tall nor stockily built. Slim hips were at variance with broad shoulders but in every line of his body there was strength and energy. With bare calves straining against the contrary pull of the sea, splayed toes seeking purchase on the slippery deck, he forced the vessel his way, bringing her in a wide circle to approach the river estuary head-on. They pitched and rolled for a short while longer, which almost undid Hannah, then with slackened sails the brig sidled into Tynemouth harbour, safely home.

Here, in the shelter of a cliff below the ruins of a great castle, were anchored ocean-going ships with many-tiered decks such as Hannah had never seen before. They loomed up out of the darkness, dwarfing the little brig, their ghostly figureheads rocking gently with the tide.

'Who goes there!' called the watch as the brig, with sails furled, slid beneath a schooner's prow into the dancing reflections cast by her bowsprit lantern.

Will, at Hannah's side, called back. 'Trading brig. The *Seabird*. All's well.'

A dusting of stars in a sky swept clean of storm clouds cast a dim radiance over a tranquil scene. On either side of the great river, wooded banks sloped down to the water's edge, their dark masses pricked by the occasional glow of a woodman's fire. The smell of woodsmoke and the warm scents of the land drifted lazily downstream to meet the *Seabird*. Will joined his crew at the oars and brought his ship safely into the Tyne.

The cabin door opened and Alphonse emerged, in crumpled and stained clothes, his pallor visible even in this half-light. 'Are we come safely home then?'

'We'll put thee doon directly,' Will answered. 'Shields is a mite further upriver.' He was peering ahead. 'Whisht!' His sharp command brought the sailors' low shanty to an abrupt end. 'The *Peggy's* in her hole. Not a squeak now!'

Ahead of them the shadowy outline of a frigate was taking shape. 'The press ship. She's at her moorings,' Will muttered to Hannah. 'We'll give her a wide berth.'

Hannah had seen the press gang in operation at Boulmer. Fishermen and the like, men who knew how to handle boats, were exactly the kind of men the navy was looking for and if they could not be enticed by fair means then foul would do as well. At Boulmer, a constant lookout was kept for their vessel and when Captain Boomer's notorious gang leapt ashore they found nought but old men, women and babies.

Were they to board the *Seabird* now, they'd find four stalwart sailors, a rare catch, so Will took the brig in a wide sweep out of sight and sound of any who might be on watch. 'There'll be many a poor soul grieving in her hold this night. May God help them.'

When the danger was past, he turned to Alphonse who had been silently observing Will's command of the situation. 'Yonder lies Shields.' The collection of mean huts scrambling down a steep bank to the water's edge was just discernible in the half-light.

'I'll whistle a boat for thee, Mounseer,

394

to take thee ashore. We will tie up here for the night and make for Newcastle the morn.'

The oars were shipped, the anchor dropped. A light breeze foretelling the coming of the dawn riffled the water. A solitary nightworker at Howden salt pans responded to Will's summons and brought a rowboat alongside.

Alphonse gripped Will's shoulder. 'I thought never to see my parents again. I will find it hard to repay the debt I owe thee and Mam'selle, but believe me, I will try.'

And Will sincerely hoped he would. His last glimpse of his grateful passenger was the mocking wink of a ruby ring on the hand gripping the rope ladder.

Sighing, he touched Hannah's arm lightly. 'Howay to the galley for summat to warm us up.'

The thick, sweet spirit he gave her set up a small fire in her belly. 'Dear Lord!' she gasped, 'that's powerful stuff!' And the crew smiled slyly as they helped themselves to another measure and watched their skipper lead Hannah away.

He took her to a covered portion of the stern deck and handed her a blanket. 'Climb in there, oot the wind. Get some sleep afore we move upriver.'

He had turned to go when Hannah was

assailed by sudden doubt. 'Thy family may not want me. What then?'

'Divvent talk se daft,' he said roughly. 'The Robsons look after their ain kin.'

She was still uneasy. 'Ye never speak of thy mother. Suppose she will not have me?'

'My muther's been deed these last ten years,' Will said briefly. 'Now get yersell in there and divvent fash.' As she clambered inside amongst coils of rope and old sails, he added, 'Thee'll bide with me sister Gracie.' Then he left her.

On his return to the galley, he was greeted with a deal of good-natured ribaldry. 'Where might the skipper be lying the neet then?'

'Alongside ye, ye dirty-minded buggers,' Will grinned, 'and if any of ye goes near that lass, I'll castrate the lot of ye, so help me. Open another flagon and divvent talk se fond.'

Hannah awoke to the sound of a great bell striking six. Stiff and cramped, she crawled out from under the tarpaulin and gasped at the sight that met her eyes. While she slept, the boat had been brought upriver and was now tied up at Newcastle's quay.

An amazing town of turrets and towers and noble buildings rose up before her. Leafy gulleys ran down to the river by

396

the side of high escarpments that gave prominence to churches and dwelling houses. All were encompassed within town walls that climbed in a wandering circuit from the water's edge to the far heights. Dwarfing all else, on its own outstanding prominence, was a massive square keep with a drop of a hundred feet to the river. It made the pele towers back home look like henhouses.

'Well, cousin, what think ye of Newcastle?' Will stood nearby, amused at her astonishment.

'Why, I declare that I never could have imagined such a noble town as this!' Scrambling to her feet, she joined him at the rail. The cobbled quayside was already a hive of activity although the hour was early. Merchants in fine gowns conferred, heads bent close. Tanners in leather aprons hurried by. Old wives with baskets of fish on their heads called, 'Fresh herrin! Ten a penny!' Men with black faces led ponies from the coal pits. Close by, beneath a fine stone bridge of many arches bearing shops and houses upon its back, carpenters were building a ship. Her ribs showed white and clean as if pecked by a horde of scavenging birds.

'And do ye live in this wondrous place, Will?' she asked with awe.

Will smiled, childishly pleased at her

delight and for another reason, too. This was the first time that she had addressed him by name.

'The cabin's been swilled oot,' he said diffidently. 'There's water and a bucket for thee. We'll have wor breakfast with me father when ye're ready.'

There were times, Hannah mused as she took off her soiled blouse and douched herself, when this unpredictable cousin of hers showed a thoughtfulness that was more generally found in a woman. Perhaps, when his mother died, he had taken on her role of caring.

As she combed the tangles out of her hair, she tried to imagine the uncle she was about to meet. A tyrant like her father? She thought not. Will spoke of him as if he were an elder brother. She would soon find out. She picked up her bundle and went in search of her cousin.

The keelman's community that Hannah was about to join was closeknit and fiercely independent. They lived just outside the town walls at Sandgate, so called for its strip of sandy beach. From here they launched their keels, distinctive craft that could carry eight chaldrons of coal, each chaldron weighing fifty-three hundred-weight.

The keelmen earned their living by transporting coal from 'dykes' at the river's edge to the waiting colliers. A man had to be strong to shovel that load from a rocking boat into the side of a ship. The 'keel bullies' as they called themselves, were men to be reckoned with and Hannah's Uncle Samuel was no exception.

At fifty, Sam Robson was as actively engaged as many a younger man. His broad back, stripped to the waist whatever the weather, could be seen any day as he stood up to his knees in coal at a collier's side. His proud boast was that, in a lifetime of keeling, he'd dropped no more than a pailful of coal into the retaining sheet that stretched between keel and collier.

He took one look at his new niece and swung her high above his head. He had the strength of an ox and a laugh that filled the house. Hannah, totally unprepared for this red-haired giant could do nothing but dangle above him until he chose to put her down. She was not pleased to see the grin on her cousin Will's face.

'The very image of Darkie but prettier by far.' He set her on her feet again. 'Ye never said she was se bonny, Will, sly one that y'are!' But Will was busy over a pan of bacon and eggs and Hannah suddenly realised how hungry she was as the appetising smell drifted her way.

'Sit ye doon at the table, hinny.' In more serious vein Samuel drew up a stool for her. ' 'Tis all strange here for ye, I ken that. But thou'rt amongst thy kin and welcome to stay as long as is thy fancy.' He covered her hand with a furry paw. 'Will and me will see thee comes to nae harm and there's space for thee to lie in daughter Gracie's hoose.'

Such was Hannah's introduction to Sandgate. From the very first day, she knew that this was where she belonged. Bewick, Budle, Boulmer faded into times remembered but relinquished. As Samuel's kin, she was accepted without question by the rest of the community which appeared to Hannah wonderfully open and friendly after the intrigues and suspicions of Boulmer. Between Will and her uncle there was an easy relationship that was quite unthinkable between Tom and his father and she wished most heartily that Tom could be here to share her pleasure in making the acquaintance of their new-found kin.

The keelmen's houses were built of stone made available by courtesy of the Earl of Callender who bombarded the town walls during the civil war. Newcastle had held out for King Charles until starved into surrender and there were still ardent Jacobites amongst the keelmen.

Gracie, with her man and little son, lived

400

in the house next door to Samuel and Will. She was only a year or two older than Hannah and welcomed her like a sister. Hannah was to earn her living in the same way as all the other women at Sandgate, 'deeting' the keels, that is, swilling them out after coal had been discharged and, in return, she would be given board and lodgings with Gracie, sharing a garret room with five-year-old Mattie.

To someone like Hannah who had never seen a proper shop before, Newcastle has irresistible attractions. Here was no hotch-potch of stalls but shops grouped together by the merchandise they offered. Thus the clogmakers occupied the stairs that led from Castle Garth to Sandhill; the butchers dwelt in Butchers Bank. A curving street called 'The Side' that lay by St Nicholas's Church, with its marvellously wrought lantern tower, was home to the goldsmiths, milliners and upholsterers. There were leather shops selling shoes, saddlery and gloves and, down on the quay, ships' chandlers selling tar, hemp and nails. There was a market for milk, a market for hay and another for oats and barley. Hannah was amazed by the multitude of trades carried on, all seemingly at considerable profit.

'You would not believe such a place could exist,' she wrote to Betsy and Tom.

'There are hot black puddings sold in the street and excellent pie shops where the gentry dine upstairs and folk like us below. A common council hath arranged much that is for the comfort of the residents. There is no need to carry water over long distances as good water is led through the streets in pipes to pants at several places. We have one at Sandgate and are greatly convenienced. Gracie took me to a place called Sandhill to show me the marvellous Guildhall, with pillars and steps and a balcony overlooking the river. And she showed me where the bronze statue of King James used to stand until the people, maddened by his taxes, tore it up and hoyed it into the Tyne!

'There is a free school but only for boys as yet though there is talk of a small establishment opening for girls ere long. Even if this were so, I am too busy earning my living to better myself as I would have hoped.

There are many benefactors in this town. A hospital has just been built to house fourteen widows of tradesmen for the rest of their lives! Whoever heard tell of such a thing?'

She went on to describe the keelmen and their wives. 'They are proud folk and seek help from no one. There are no paupers amongst them for they look after their own if any fall on bad times. Neither are there any rich men at Sandgate. Nevertheless, though our fare is simple, we do not go hungry. The children, to my mind, would benefit by drinking more milk for they are small compared with our fat Benjie, yet wiry for all that. There is much trade and commerce here. Fortunes are to be made and, can I but discover the secret, I may yet make mine here. Please give my best love to Mistress Emma and tell her she is ever in my thoughts.'

Saturday night, Hannah was to discover, was the night of the week when everyone young enough to enjoy himself went into the town. The week's work was done. The fires under the salt pans were allowed to die out. The ropemakers closed their sheds. Every Tom, Dick and Harry repaired to the cockpits, the bowling green or the bearpit at nearby Jesmond, calling at many an alehouse on the way and finishing up with a jig in the Hay Market square if they could still stand up.

Hannah went with the other young women into town, but first, considerable preparations were necessary. Standing guard for each other in the boathouse, the girls sluiced coal dust from their white bodies and put their thick breeches to steep. Then, dressed very properly in blue skirts bordered with rows of tucking and just short enough to show an inch or two of ankle, they set off arm-in-arm to flirt with the apprentices and tease the black-faced pit-boys. They might buy a tuppeny poke of whelks and maybe have a fling at a reel if the piper didn't get himself too drunk too soon, but they would all come home together, arm-in-arm, as they had set out. This outing was for display purposes only. The more serious business of courtship came later.

These women were as merry companions as Hannah could hope to find, with a quick wit and outrageously bawdy sense of humour. Though their songs were about their Billy-Boys and Bobby Shaftoes, love did not appear to play an important role in their lives. It was a subject for lewd speculation and ribald jokes, as if the women were ashamed of their own sentimentality and needed the anonymity of someone else's song. They were tough, undemonstrative and fiercely protective of their men and bairns against any critical outsider. They were also of unfailing support to each other in times of stress and Hannah grew to respect them all once she had mastered the unfamiliar nuances of their speech. Tyneside folk have a harsher edge to their words than the men of the countryside and some words, brought across the sea by ancient Viking raiders, were quite unknown to Hannah.

Only Molly, of all the girls, was shy with Hannah. Plumply serene, the prettiest of them all with her chestnut hair and wide grey eyes, she kept a certain reserve between them.

'Will's girl,' said Gracie, then laughed indulgently. 'One of them, I should say. The scamp.'

But when Will came looking for a partner for 'Strip the Willow' on Hannah's first Saturday night, it was not Molly he sought out from the gaggle of girls at the chestnut brazier but his cousin.

'Why do ye nae dance with thy girl?' Hannah asked and instantly regretted her boldness.

Will's face darkened. 'Naebody tells me who I shall dance with. Are ye coming or no? I mind we made a good pair once.'

Hannah, laughing at his cross face, grabbed him by the hand and tugged him into the centre of the market place where partners were forming their lines. 'Tis only a dance, she told herself, and put Molly's hurt face out of her mind.

Gracie, tapping her feet in time with the music, drew the attention of her little son to the antics of his lively uncle. 'Look at thy Uncle Will, Mattie. When ye grow up, ye'll mebbes dance like him.'

'And look at Hannah,' she might have
added. The pair seemed oblivious of all
other dancers as they swung and tripped,
flung apart, came together. Gracie looked
curiously from the flushed face of one to
the other and it seemed to her that there
was more than a dance going on between
them. Gracie knew her brother well. He
took his love lightly wherever he could find
it. 'Twould be a pity if he were to add his
young cousin to the list of broken hearts.
Perhaps a word in Hannah's ear might not
come amiss.

25

Hannah had been at her new home for
almost a month and was scrubbing out a
keel with two other women when a familiar
voice called over the water. 'Mam'selle
Hannah!'

Alphonse de Colonnières, in elegant
braided coat and velvet hat, stood waving
excitedly from the wherry that was bringing
him ashore. As soon as the boat touched
bottom, he leapt out on to the sand and, to
the amazement of Hannah's companions,
swept off his hat and bent his neatly
peruked head over her hand.

'Mam'selle, it gives me great joy to see you again.'

Hannah laughed. ' 'Tis a new Alphonse that I see, not a half-drowned, seasick scarecrow! I am much pleased to see thee restored to health.'

'I have lain abed with a fever since last we met,' Alphonse followed Hannah to a nearby bench out of earshot of the other deeters, 'else ye would have seen me here afore now to enquire after thy well-being. Didst suffer after our terrible ordeal, Mam'selle Hannah?'

Hannah shook her head, 'I am more used to a dowsing in the sea than thee.'

'What of Will? Where is he?'

'Will is as he always is, never in one place long enough to wear out the seat of his pants. He's away with the brig just now. The keelmen leave him to do their trading while they shift coal. He returns tonight.'

Alphonse looked about him, children playing in the sand in the late September sunshine, women possing clothes outside the sturdy stone cottages, carrying water from the Sandgate and, in the background the busy hum of the town, all the bustle of industry. 'Art content here, Hannah?'

She nodded. 'Never more so.' She nodded in the direction of the deeters who had resumed their scrubbing. 'I am among friends.'

'I have come to ask you and Will to honour my parents and my uncles with a visit at your convenience. They are most anxious to meet you and to express their thanks for saving my life.' His smile was self-deprecating. 'I am their only son. As such, they are inclined to make too much of me. If I might tear thee away from your coalie-boats, would tomorrow afternoon be suitable?'

What she liked about this young man, Hannah decided, was his easy manner which lacked any hint of condescension. She might just as well be a fine lady dressed in silks and satins sitting alongside him, so courteous was he. She had no hesitation in accepting.

'I will endeavour to show thy parents a cleaner face than this.'

Will's reaction upon his return later that night was one of pleasant surprise. Because of his sometimes precarious mode of living, he was never sure when he might need influential friends. The glassmakers of Howden were rich and well-respected in the district, giving employment to many. In addition, his discerning nose caught the whiff of a possible reward for his part in Alphonse's escapade. Dressed in his Sunday best, he was ready and waiting with Hannah on the following afternoon when the hired boatman from Howden appeared at Sandgate.

Hannah was prepared for the grand house, the panelled rooms, the furniture upholstered in damask and all the ornaments that are to be found in the houses of the rich. What she had not anticipated was the warmth, affection even, with which she and Will were received.

Candles were already lit in the room against the encroaching darkness of an autumn afternoon and a bright fire crackled on the hearth. Alphonse's two bachelor uncles, splendidly stout in full-skirted coats of olive-green velvet, rose to their feet as the visitors were ushered in. A woman smiled at them over a small table set with silver teapot and kettle. Alphonse's mother, whom Hannah remembered vaguely as a sick and weary traveller when she stayed overnight at Bewick Grange, was beautiful, bejewelled and most elegantly dressed. She held out her hand to them and bade them welcome.

Alphonse's father took Hannah's hands within his own. 'So young a maid,' he marvelled, 'to risk her life for our son.' He turned to Will. 'And you, Monsieur, had the courage to spirit him away from those who meant to harm him. You have our deepest gratitude.'

In the shadows another figure stirred as Hannah and Will took their seats and

Hannah was surprised to see the genial face of Sir Walter Heslop.

'I add my commendations on your bravery, Hannah, in rescuing this young man. Apart from being a most amiable fellow, he is the last of the original line of glassmakers who settled here a hundred years ago and therefore,' he winked at Alphonse, 'a very precious asset.'

The uncles, Hubert and Ernest, standing by the hearth, their silver buttons twinkling in the firelight, nodded portentously and let their fond glance embrace their nephew. 'The hope of the family rests with him.'

Hannah's eyes met those of Alphonse. ' 'Twas an adventure, to be sure,' she said lightly, sipping from a small painted cup. This was her first taste of tea and she thought little of it. A glass of good gooseberry wine, in her opinion, was infinitely superior. The little sugary cakes, however, each one stuck with an almond, had her full approval.

'Thou'rt a wonderful cook, Madame de Colonnières,' she ventured.

Alphonse's mother responded with a silvery laugh. 'Thank you, Mam'selle, for such a charming compliment but I cannot claim the credit. Those dainties come from France, not without some difficulties as our two nations are still at war.'

Sir Walter smiled broadly. 'Will, here,

and his marrer, the carter of Eglingham, have a marvellous facility for carrying on trade nevertheless.'

Eyes turned to Will, balanced on the edge of his chair, teacup in hand, as if poised for instant flight, contrasting strangely with the languid Alphonse.

'I trade under any conditions, be there profit in't, for 'tis my livelihood.'

The words were lightly spoken but Hannah could sense his wariness.

Hubert, the elder of the Gustave brothers, leaned forward, a smile about his lips. 'I know that, without your good offices, my wine closet would be in a parlous state, though I would not wish that truth to be known outside these four walls. Master Will, I wish you success in all your ventures and indeed, hope to interest you in some business of a more legitimate nature.'

Brother Ernest weighed in. 'After our grievous loss of a whole consignment of glass when the unfortunate *Sally Logan* went down, we will not comfortably entrust our shipments to any unproven captain again. My brother and I greatly respect your intimate knowledge of these coasts and would feel more confident in our trading if we might engage your services as skipper on our Scottish route. What say you, Master Robson?'

411

Will put down his cup. This was the sort of talk he understood.

'Another threat to our trading,' Hubert added, 'and one that is just as alarming as coastal rocks, is the French navy, These brigands are sending some twenty English ships a week to the bottom of the sea. How do you rate this danger, Master Robson? You may speak freely.'

Will helped himself to another sugared dainty and popped it into his mouth before replying. 'Why, sirs, if I am given the right ship, I'll see the Frenchman afore he sees me. Once I've seen him, he will never catch me. If he should follow too closely on my tail, I'll lead him round the Farnes and watch him founder.'

Ernest clapped his hands. 'Capital! Upon my word, I like your spirit.'

'State your terms and preferences,' said Hubert. 'I see we can do good business together.'

Sir Walter leaned towards Hannah. 'While they are at their bargaining, let me take this opportunity to redress a wrong done to you, Hannah. I ask you, please, to try to understand that grief at the untimely death of our dear daughter clouded our good sense at that time. Unforgivably, my lady and myself laid the blame for that tragic event upon one whom we should rather have commended for her devotion

412

to a mistress who was out of her mind. When passion cooled, we saw the rights of it, how you had been most grievously misjudged. I am asking you now to find it in your heart to forgive us both.'

Hannah frowned. Painful memories, so long undisturbed, rushed to the surface once more. She saw, not the kindly face of Sir Walter, but the hard accusing stare of his wife.

' 'Tis all in the past, my lord.' She spoke quietly, not wishing this private matter to be made public. 'I understood my lady's anger though I did not merit it.'

'Lady Heslop has been sorely troubled in her mind since the day you left our employ. Indeed, she went to your home to express her regret but you were gone. Now we have your sister Sarah working as stillroom maid and Mistress Joan is kept busy with orders for her weaving. In this way, my lady hopes to redress the wrong done to your family.'

The concern in her old master's eyes touched Hannah deeply. 'My lady must upset herself no further. I bear no grievance only sadness at the unhappy fate of thy sweet daughter.' This, Hannah found, was true. Those tragic events were as remote as if they had involved someone other than herself, long ago and far away.

'Should you ever wish to return to

413

our house,' Sir Walter, hopeful now, was feeling his way carefully, 'naturally in a superior position of some authority...'

Hannah cut in firmly. 'I am sensible of thy kind intention, Sir Walter, but I make my own living now and am beholden to no one.'

'As a keel deeter?' His smile held a touch of mockery.

'I will not always muck out boats,' she answered shortly.

When the time came for the visitors to leave, Will was in high spirits, all wariness dispelled now that he and the merchants had outlined their business interests. His step was jaunty, full of swagger as he walked with Hannah to the quay.

The gentlemen insisted upon accompanying them thus far and the reason became obvious when they arrived at the river's edge. A new rowing boat, painted blue and silver and secured to the jetty by a rope, swung gently on the tide. Her lines were sharp and clean, her width braced by sturdy thwarts, her rowlocks were of gleaming brass. Her name, *Spirit of the North,* was painted on her prow.

Hubert turned to Will. 'Well, Skipper. Do you like your new boat?'

Uncomprehending, anxious lest he jump to a wrong conclusion, Will looked, speechless, from one brother to the other.

Alphonse laughed. ' 'Tis your own rowboat now, Will, to use as you wish. It is my uncles' pleasure.'

The disbelief on Will's face changed to delight. 'This bonny boat is mine?' He flung his hat in the air and with one leap landed fair and square in the middle of his prize.

'We called it *Spirit of the North*,' said Hubert, 'for that is what it embodies. 'Tis your just reward for the great service you did the house of Gustave when you saved the life of its heir.' He turned to Hannah, standing at his side, watching Will's antics with delight. 'As for you, brave maid that you are, you make it hard for two old gentlemen adequately to thank you. A lady who will turn away a priceless ruby is not easily pleased.'

Hannah looked uncomfortable. 'I have thy thanks, sir. That is enough for me.' She took Will's extended hand and stepped into his boat.

'Nevertheless,' called Ernest as Will untied the painter, 'we will find a way.'

As the *Spirit of the North* pulled away into the surge of the tide, with Hannah sitting at her ease like a lady while Will rowed his 'bonny boat', the gentlemen returned to the house, much pleased with their afternoon's work. Over a glass of

415

brandy, they discussed possible rewards for Hannah.

'Mam'selle is as full of pride as a goose is of fat,' Alphonse warned. 'You will need to be discreet in your gift or we will never see her more.'

His father looked up. 'You know Mam'selle well, mon fils?' It was more than a passing enquiry. Any serious liaison with a Northumbrian fishergirl, however valiant, was out of the question. There were plenty of well-born Huguenot girls in England when the time came for Alphonse to select a bride.

Sir Walter stepped in with advice. 'I know this maid well, from the time she was in my employ. She is something of a scholar, reads and writes well. In the matter of accounting, she has been known to trip up my lady herself.' He smiled wryly at the merchants. 'It takes a smart monkey to catch another. I suggest you will not please her better than by giving her a position where she can use these skills. Let her help old Standwell on the quay. She will look after your interests well. At the same time, she will gain the advancement she craves.'

The uncles were delighted with the idea. 'Isaac grows old. Although no one understands better than he the workings of the vend, yet his hearing and his sight are beginning to fail. A young pair of legs to run his errands, a quick mind to help him with figures should please him mightily.'

In this, the uncles were mistaken.

The offices of Messrs Gustave and de Colonnières occupied the ground floor of a house on the quayside which had once belonged to a noble lord and was now tenanted by exporters of all descriptions. Squeezed between coffee houses and warehouses it looked directly on to the wide quay where goods were bought and sold, ships chartered, crews engaged. Here were beggars and pickpockets a-plenty as well as traders with big purses.

From his perch on a high stool by the window, Isaac Standwell kept a close watch on who did business with whom in this busy trading port of the north. Not a ship was loaded or unloaded without his knowledge. No piece of information that might benefit his masters was overlooked by this most trusty servant. He saw which skippers were open to bribery, which merchants conspired together and against whom. He had worked like this with the complete confidence of his masters for over fifty years and saw no reason now why he should take on some unknown wench as an assistant.

Hannah, knowing nothing of Master

Standwell's feelings, could scarcely believe her good fortune. She was to exchange work on the keels for the occupation she liked best and in which she knew herself to be fully competent; the keeping of accounts, assessing profits, tracking losses. After putting Martha Lisle's books in order, she was confident that clerking for the glassmakers would not be beyond her capabilities.

Keel-deeting, never an attractive occupation even in summer, was less so now in November, when a dank fog hung perpetually over the river, penetrating flannel and wool, chilling the women to the very bone. Yet there was no envy, only amazement, in their reaction to Hannah's news. Few of them could do more than sign their names.

Will and her Uncle Samuel were plainly delighted that she should have this chance to better herself and more so when they learned that she had no intention of leaving Sandgate to seek lodging elsewhere. Hannah made it plain that clerk or deeter, Sandgate was where she belonged.

On the first morning of her new employment, while it was still dark, Will walked with her past the milk market and over the Pandon Burn bridge. The great bell of St Nicholas, the one they call the 'Major', began its preliminary clanking and, as they crossed the quayside, tolled the hour of six. There was no need for a bellman in this town, nor excuse for any lazy lie-abed. Will halted outside a door much worn by wind and weather and rapped sharply with his knuckles. Without awaiting a summons from within, he opened the door and pushed Hannah inside, taking himself off with the speed of a weasel.

Isaac Standwell pushed back his spectacles and squinted up from the ledgers that lay open in front of him. Picking up one of the candles ranged along his desk, he held it high and peered, scowling, at Hannah. His head sat like a polished egg between hunched shoulders, though he did aspire to a wig, a frayed affair, Hannah noted, lying amongst the pots of ink and pens. There were no teeth left in his gums to add a little distance between hooked nose and chin and Hannah decided he resembled nothing so much as a bad-tempered troll as she waited politely for him to speak.

In no way reassured by what he saw, he wrenched off his spectacles. Black as a Spaniard, she was. Silent. Wilful by the looks of her. What could she know about the keeping of confidential ledgers? No woman he had ever known could keep a secret. But he must do as he was bid.

There was talk that this chit of a girl had saved young Master Alphonse from drowning. A likely tale! Some trick played by the wench, no doubt. Well, he would put her through her paces and make no bones about it if he found her wanting in any way.

When he slid down from his high stool, he reached no higher than Hannah's shoulder which infuriated him the more. 'Come.' He directed her curtly to an open book with quill pen alongside. 'Write thy name and date of birth, if ye know it, so I can see what manner of hand ye have.'

He could find no fault in the neat, flowing signature. 'Hannah Robson, born November 1st, 1670', and Hannah was careful to incite no criticism in the days that followed. She understood how jealously he guarded his position of trust with the glassmakers. She carried out his instructions to the letter without query, never doing more than she was asked although she longed to relieve him of the tedium of complicated sums, longed to put his desk in order so that bills would not go astray with such frustrating regularity. The opportunity provided for her by the brothers Gustave was too precious to be jeopardised by ill-conceived disagreement.

Covertly, she acquainted herself with

every facet of the business so that, on occasion, she surprised the old man with her grasp of trading regulations. He would not acknowledge her abilities, however, lest she got above herself and was always ready with a sharp word of criticism. Nevertheless, honesty compelled him to report at the end of one month's trial that his new assistant would do well enough providing she kept to her place. She was quick with figures and, thankfully, was no chatterbox. She could stay.

It was an odd partnership, the crusty old man and the young woman whose dark beauty brought merchants and seafarers gawping into the dusty little office on the quay upon any pretext whatsoever. Hannah moved into a world of commerce that she found exciting and stimulating. She observed closely the tactics of the old man when he was chartering a vessel, commissioning a skipper or haggling over the price of raw materials that were needed for the production of glass. She especially admired his diplomacy when dealing with the Common Town Council who kept the ranks of the Newcastle vend, the great trading pool, firmly closed against all outsiders. This concession was not without its price. All Newcastle traders were required to pay hefty river dues, regularly contested by Master Standwell.

Hannah had the good sense to realise that she was being favoured with a most valuable apprenticeship, one which might ensure for herself an independent future. Already she was earning more than she had ever done in her life and, with six shillings in her pocket every Saturday night, she was able to pay Gracie adequately for her lodgings and put something by for a certain purchase she was resolved upon, a pair of shoes for Mattie. Like most of the bairns at Sandgate, he went barefoot, but his frailty, when compared with other five-year-olds was obvious to Hannah if not to his mother. He was never without a cough and frequently ran a high fever. There was no one in the town so skilled in medicine as Widow Dodds from whom Hannah might seek advice. Only the very rich could afford a physician's fee.

Gracie and Nathan her husband loved their little son dearly, the only survivor of seven aborted pregnancies, but they were at a loss to understand Hannah's anxiety over him. When she brought home for him a pair of leather boots, they were touchingly grateful, if a little mystified.

'Thou'rt a kind lass,' Gracie hugged her. 'Thy parents must be sore grieved without thee.'

Hannah thought otherwise.

From time to time, Will picked up

snippets of news about Burnfoot, usually from Ed the carter. In this way she heard about the stack fire which brought everyone out with pails of water, including Benjie, lest the cow byre caught alight for a second time. There was news also that Widow Dodds had fallen on the ice. Sister Joan had taken over her role of nurse as far as she was able.

The master of Budle Hall, Will reported, had found another young heiress to marry and Nell at Boulmer had taken a child to foster.

'Whose child?' Hannah asked.

'Ye mind Dorothy Lee that took over the kelp-burning when Goody Newman died?'

A poor thing. Always ailing. Hannah remembered her.

'She was hanged at Belford last Martinmas for the cutting of purses. But 'tis an ill wind that blows naebody good for now Nell has company and earns four pounds a year from the parish besides.'

'I mind Dorothy Lee fine,' Hannah said slowly. 'She would be stealing to feed her bairn.'

26

Hannah became a familiar figure on the quayside in her dark blue felts and plaid shawl as she went about Master Standwell's business. The chandler, ropemaker and cooper became accustomed to dealing with the glassmakers through her. The officers of Trinity House on Broad Chare were ready with advice on competent mariners when she called. Neither was she averse to entering the coffee houses and taverns if the merchant she sought was likely to be found there. A certain aloofness in her manner and her neat dress refuted any thought that she might be other than a very proper young woman.

Moreover, a tale was circulating that she had once castrated an overbold lover. Though men might eye her speculatively and lay a bet or two when drunk, one discouraging look from Hannah was usually enough to make them hold their tongues. Besides, everyone knew that she was a Robson and no one in his right mind would take on both Sam and Will, so she went about unmolested upon the glassmakers' business.

She was usually the first to hear the latest news and rumours circulating in the town, which she conveyed without delay to Master Standwell's ever receptive ear. Whose ships had been pirated by the French, what losses and where. What fresh taxes were in the offing. A different head wore the crown but taxation was just as harsh under William as it had been under James, though the monarch was no longer the tax-maker.

The menacing figure of Louis XIV over the water still had to be fought and his most recent action in support of the ex-king, James, gave William and his government no peace. James was in Ireland now, trying to stir up support against his son-in-law.

There were those with hoary heads who could remember when taxes were needed to help the French king fight the Dutch. Now it was the other way about.

'Damn all wars I say,' cursed the skippers of the great trading ships which voyaged to the East Indies. French pirates robbed them on the high seas. At home, their best seamen were pressed into the very navy that should be protecting them.

Though French men o' war rarely ventured into northern waters, Will was ever wary on his trading trips to Scotland, ever on the lookout for an enemy standard flying from a topmast. He had the full confidence of the glassmakers and would not betray their trust.

Alphonse's uncles were still greatly exercised in their minds as to how they might suitably reward Hannah for her heroism. Less generous men might have considered that sufficient recompense had already been made in finding agreeable work for her. Indeed Alphonse's father, who should have been more grateful than any for the rescue of his son, was the least enthusiastic of the family in their search for further reward and thought his cousins' generosity a little excessive when they made it known that they intended to buy a small house for Hannah.

'She is a simple spinster,' he objected. 'How will she manage the affairs of a householder?'

'Very well,' said Ernest, 'if her achievements on the quay are any indication.'

His brother Hubert was in complete agreement. 'The only question is in what locality would she choose to live? With her friends at Sandgate or within the town walls, perhaps near her place of work?'

' 'Tis my opinion,' said Alphonse, 'she will not wish to leave Sandgate and the keelmen's community. She is content to be with her own kin.'

Following upon this conversation, Samuel

426

Robson had a visit from the glassmakers. He knew the two brothers well enough as esteemed benefactors to the town but had not entertained them in his humble home before. Their richly clad posteriors, however, settled as comfortably on his oak bench as on any damask upholstery. They took a measure of good French brandy, no questions asked, and told him of their plan.

Samuel was delighted and promised his full co-operation in the purchase of a suitable piece of land and the hiring of reliable masons, carpenters and plumbers. Hannah was not to be informed until the house was ready to hand over to her.

All through that winter, Hannah followed the progress of the new house and was glad when its roof was laid to keep out the rain and the snow. It stood, like its neighbours, facing the river with rising fields at its back where the cows grazed in summer. Her questions regarding the owner were met with a strange lack of interest. Her uncle said he believed it was for a keelman's relation. Her cousin Will said it was for an old hag with six black cats and a cross-eyed pig.

One sleety morning in late February as she battled her way against the wind on her way to work, she saw that the workmen had gone. The little house stood complete, waiting for its new owner. Doubtless, it was for some overcrowded family.

Later that morning, an errand took her to Mother Gifford's coffee house to deliver a note to a certain merchant. She found the room crowded as was usual on a wintry day such as this for the proprietress kept a good fire. Several gentlemen drying off their sodden hose greeted her with a courteous 'Good morning, ma'am'.

She found her man, delivered her note and was about to leave when a familiar voice called her name. Alphonse, who was frequently to be found here with his artist friends, was making his way towards her. Ever the dandy, he was dressed today in a coat of rich, claret-coloured stuff over wide, lace-edged breeches and carried an elegant, silver-topped cane. A bunch of fancies was knotted at his shoulder.

'How canst sit in this smoke, Alphonse!' she coughed. 'At Boulmer we hung the herrings in this.'

'I was on my way to visit thee, Hannah.' He removed his cloak from its peg and offered her his arm.

'But were waylaid by good company in the coffee house,' she smiled. They had become good friends over the last months, often working together over the shipping arrangements for Alphonse's much sought-after windows.

The master of the *Spirit of the North*
was securing his boat to a bollard and
was about to jump on to the quay when
he caught sight of Hannah, on Alphonse's
arm, leaving the coffee house. He drew
back instantly and one of his cronies,
marking the look on his face, grinned.

'Aye, she's a bonny lass, that cousin
o' yours and there's mair than one man
after her.'

'Shut yer gob,' snapped Will, bending
out of sight.

'Boatman!' a merchant hailed him. 'How
much to take me to Wylam?'

Pulling upriver against the tide worked
wonders in cooling off a rage while,
unaware of the incident, Alphonse and
Hannah continued on their way to the
office.

'What was thy business with me,
Alphonse?' Gently, on the pretext of
rearranging her shawl, Hannah disengaged
her arm. 'Another window to be shipped?'

' 'Tis in the nature of a surprise,'
Alphonse teased, 'and you are not to
make guesses for I will not tell.'

Hannah smiled. A greater misfit in the
harsh world of business than this guileless
and creative creature would be hard to
find. 'A pleasant surprise, I hope?'

'Most certainly, and you are to be
apprised of it this afternoon. My uncles

429

wish to meet you at three o'clock at this address.' He handed her a slip of paper.

Hannah noted, with some surprise, that the meeting place was at the Sandgate. 'And what will Master Standwell say to my absenting myself, pray?'

'I will remind you,' Alphonse said impishly, 'that my uncles pay the living of Master Standwell and therefore he is not likely to complain.'

The Major was striking the first stroke of three when Hannah excused herself from work. Expecting a scolding, she was instead treated to an enigmatic, toothless smile by the old clerk as he nodded her on her way. As she approached the meeting place, she saw the glassmakers' carriage already drawn up there, with the uncles, Alphonse and his father seated within, all looking mightily pleased with themselves. At sight of her, they stepped down and, without explanation, insisted upon accompanying her to the keelmen's cottages. The uncles, especially, were in the gayest of spirits and broke into gales of laughter at Hannah's puzzled face when they eventually halted in front of the newly built house. Hubert produced a key from his pocket at which both uncles straightened their faces.

'We hope we have found a fitting recompense for a maid who spurns rubies. Pray take the key to this little house, Mistress Hannah, which is your own for evermore, and little enough for what is owed to you.'

Hannah was dumbfounded. In a dream she took the key and then, to the consternation of the glassmakers and of the curious women who had gathered around, she wept.

'Nay,' she reassured them, dabbing her eyes with her shawl and smiling through her tears, 'pay no heed. 'Tis pure joy that makes me bubble like a babby, to think I have a house of my own.'

The word spread through Sandgate. 'Yon new hoose is for Hannah!' and 'Hannah's Hoose' it was called from that time onwards.

After her Uncle Samuel, whose complicity was quickly uncovered, Hannah sought out her cousin Will to tell him her good news. She found his reaction strangely offhand. He, whom she had expected would share her happiness, was distinctly churlish in his manner which disturbed her greatly.

'Oh aye,' he said, with curling lip, 'and I daresay Mounseer Alphonse in his fine carriage will have liberty to come and go as he pleases.'

Hannah scowled back at him, as thoroughly out of temper as he. 'All my friends will be welcome. Thee as well when thou'rt in a better frame of mind.'

Gracie, however, was as delighted as Hannah herself and inspected the new house without trace of envy though it was a great deal more commodious than her own. There was a stone range in the kitchen with an iron basket for fire in the centre, an oven at one side and boiler for hot water at the other. A swinging iron arm held the kettle hook and a spit big enough to turn a sucking pig or a brace of rabbits. The oak dresser was already equipped with earthenware platters and porringers.

'There's space for a pig in the yard,' Gracie nodded approvingly.

'And chickens,' said Hannah, remembering Burnfoot.

'Ye've a netty all to yersell.' Gracie looked with longing at the small hut that housed an earth closet.

'A keelman caught short will not care whose netty it is,' Hannah laughed. 'I've nae doubt I'll be sharing it with many.'

There was a neat little parlour with its own hearth and a shelf above bearing a wonderfully decorated German clock. An extravagance, said Gracie, when there was a good clockface on St Nicholas's for all to see.

Hannah, standing by the window, murmured in wonder, 'Bairns playing on the sand, keels and traders coming and going on the river. I couldna wish a bonnier view. Am I not the luckiest of women, Gracie?'

'Ye'll have all the bachelors after ye, hinny.' Gracie was thinking of her brother. If he had any sense at all he'd make a move now before someone else snapped her up, but Will had made himself unaccountably scarce of late and when Hannah invited all her neighbours to a proper housewarming, he did not come.

'He's away at Boulmer,' her uncle said with a wink. 'The moon's on the wane,' but, sitting on the settle by Hannah's kitchen fire, he wondered what his son could be thinking of to pass up such a woman as this. She was as much at home here as if she'd been bred a keelman's daughter. His eye travelled over his niece's slim waist and pert backside as she went about with jugs of ale. Begod, he spat expertly on to the hot coals, if he thought he had a chance, he'd show his laggard son a trick or two. But then, as he watched her deftly turn away the too-bold approach of one far gone in drink, he saw more clearly that this lass neither wanted nor needed a man. Not yet. 'Twould need someone quite out of the ordinary to capture this maid's fancy.

Will was back home for Pancake Tuesday. No resident of Newcastle would willingly absent himself for this last holiday before Lent. When the Pancake Bell, silent for the rest of the year, rang out from St Nicholas's, tradesmen closed their shutters, apprentices hung up their aprons and the men and women of Sandgate left their keels to join the crowd going to Sandhill for the start of the annual game of football.

To inflict a holiday upon a man like Isaac Standwell, whose work was his total pleasure in life, was no benevolence. The Town Council, however, had decreed that all clerks and apprentices be given leave from noon of this day and so, with a token show of grousing, he dispatched Hannah to join her friends.

'Stay clear of rowdies and drunken brawls,' was his final admonishment, 'and see ye bring nae disrespect upon the name of our employers.'

Hannah sought out Gracie and little Mattie on the now deserted quay. Shutters were up at the cooper's and chandler's establishments and half-finished ships lay untended in their dry docks. Without the clatter of tools and the sawing of wood the riverside was strangely quiet.

Mattie ran to meet her. 'Howay, Auntie Hannah,' he tugged her impatiently by

434

the hand, 'or we'll be ower late for the kick-off.'

The level concourse of Sandhill was already crowded when they arrived. The mayor, Sir Nicholas Ridley, stood on the steps of the Guild Hall, waiting to give the signal to start. Fashionable ladies and their escorts looked on from the balconies of elegant houses in the Close nearby while common folk thronged the sidewalks and clung from any vantage point to see the kick-off for the 1690 football game.

By tradition, the contest, between a team of smiths, goldsmiths, potters and pewterers and an opposing team of fullers, clothiers, weavers and coopers, always began here in Sandhill and finished on Cowhill, the highest point on Newcastle Town Moor. There were few rules and no limit to the numbers who might take part in the game. Anyone in the crowd who had a mind to, could join in.

The mayor's flag dipped. A roar went up from the crowd and the leather ball was sent soaring into the air. Hannah held hard to Mattie as the crowd surged forward. Those who managed to get a foot near the ball at this moment were bound by only one consideration; to keep the ball 'oot the wattor'! The Tyne was icy cold and full of flood water. Whoever kicked the ball in, fished it out.

435

The smiths and their supporters were away with the ball, everyone following in hot pursuit through the closed markets and up Pilgrim Street. There were clarts everywhere after recent heavy rain and players and spectators alike were soon covered in mud. Past the Trade Meeting Halls they surged, all of them unoccupied today. Even the Grammar School bowed to custom and allowed its scholars to lay aside their slates for today. Spectators perched on the Weavers' Tower had an excellent view as the leading players streamed through the Pilgrim Gate and on to the Town Moor on the final sprint.

'Watch oot for the pits!' they yelled, too late for some who emerged from shallow coal diggings looking like dripping black devils.

It was a triumphant goldsmith apprentice who brought victory to his side with a kick that sent the ball rocketing high over the winning post and the weavers' team would have to wait another year before taking up the challenge.

Barrels of ale awaited winners and losers alike by the mill on Cow Hill. Faws had already set up their stalls and were selling crispy pancakes soused in treacle and spice. Glowing braziers were there to dry off wet clothing and keep the cool airs at bay. Then, as dusk fell, flares were lit and the faw fiddler struck up. The piper squeezed his bag and the hoppings began.

Gracie, standing with Hannah and Mattie, caught sight of her brother in the midst of the dancers. But who was his partner? Surely he could not know that Hannah was here or he would be over to claim her. These two were regular dancing partners. For a moment, the whirl of dancers parted and Will was plainly seen, in a state of high elation that Gracie put down to too much ale, dancing with Molly.

Gracie cursed the fickle nature of her brother that he should reject Hannah in this way, but Hannah's next words showed that there was no call to waste pity on her.

'Why there's Will! Dancing with Molly.' If Hannah felt a twinge of jealousy, she did not show it. 'See how happy Molly looks. I think she loves thy brother dearly, Gracie.'

Thereafter, Gracie resolved to mind her own business and lose no more sleep over either of them.

Will left Molly after that dance and joined the men at the cockfight. By midnight, he was so full of ale that he could scarcely stand upright and spent the rest of the night on a heap of sawdust. The next morning, as he trundled home, holding his thumping head, he swore that he'd never get drunk again.

The glassmakers' business kept him away from home for the next two weeks, taking bottles to Scotland and bringing back oysters. He was in a rare good humour on his return as he swaggered in rolling sailor's gait through the Sandgate, his bundle over his shoulder. To be well paid for doing the job he liked best, skippering a good boat, seemed to him like taking candy from a babby.

Then, glancing over to Hannah's house, his good humour evaporated. Alphonse's carriage was drawn up outside her door, confirming his own unvoiced fears. Now the generosity of the glassmakers was made plain. His proud cousin was not above selling her favours.

The afternoon was late and the light fading. A lamp glowing behind closed curtains in her parlour carried implications of intimacy that set his imagination aflame. Anger rose inside him that she should stoop so low and in such a place, in Sandgate, the home of her kin. Dropping his gear, he vaulted the low wall that enclosed Hannah's herb patch, threw open her door and strode purposefully into her parlour.

The scene that greeted him denied the accusation before it left his lips. Hannah, teapot in hand, presided over a table laid with a fancy cloth and set with cups. With her were Alphonse and two ladies, one of whom Will recognised as Alphonse's mother. The other was a younger and very elegantly dressed woman of striking dark looks who was quite unknown to Will. They looked up, startled at his rude entry but Hannah seemed not a whit perturbed.

'Will,' she exclaimed, 'this is a happy time for thee to call. Alphonse has brought his betrothed to meet us.' She turned to the dark stranger. 'Mademoiselle Éloïse, may I present my cousin Will who rescued your beloved from the wicked men who would have robbed and killed him.'

Completely undone, Will tore off his bonnet and bowed low over the lady's hand to hide his reddening cheeks. Who could have imagined such an unlikely situation!

'Villy!' Madame de Colonnières sang out. 'Come and sit by me. Tell me, how goes your new boat?'

Hannah handed him a dainty cup as he took his place gingerly on the settle.

Alphonse himself seemed unaware of any drama. In his view, the keelmen were all slightly *fou* and Will the maddest and most endearing of them all. His eye rested lovingly upon his fiancée, sitting with such dignity in these humble surroundings. He was very much in love with Éloïse whose family, like his own, had fled from Alsace. Once he had decided that his bachelor days were over, he lost no time in bringing his betrothed to meet Hannah whose approval, he discovered, was important to him.

Hannah, serenely wielding her new teapot, looked with content on her company. Alphonse and Éloïse were splendidly matched. Madame seemed perfectly at ease on the sofa, which was understandable since she herself had chosen it for Hannah's comfort. Will, after his rather stormy entrance, was behaving admirably. For some inexplicable reason, he had declined to visit her in her new house until now.

Sensing some misunderstanding on his part, she detained him after the others had left. 'Were not the glassmakers wonderfully kind to give me this house?'

Will's emotions were still in something of a turmoil. ' 'Tis nae mair than ye deserve. Ye risked thy life for Alphonse. Naebody can do mair than that.'

She took him to see her kitchen. 'Wilt stay and sup with me? I have a piece of bacon boiling in the pot and a drop of rum to fry the carlings in.'

The kitchen was warm and cosy. Hannah set candles on the table, a loaf of bread

440

and Alphonse's gift of a bottle of French wine. Realising that he had been behaving incredibly foolishly, Will smiled across at Hannah. Her black hair gleamed. Her eyes, so vividly blue in daylight, slumbered deepest violet by candlelight. His heart leapt in a wildly disturbing way every time she looked at him. Sheepishly he made his confession. 'I thought Alphonse sought ye for a mistress, Hannah, and that was the reason they set ye up in this house.'

She let out a peal of laughter. 'Oh Will! Me—a kept woman! Ye should know me better than that.'

Indeed he should and was to have a further reminder when, a little later, she slipped out of his tentative arm, firmly emphasising the fact that a brotherly role was the only acceptable one. But there was affection in her dismissal. 'Ye must be off now, for since I am become a housewife, I rise early.'

Will's mood, therefore, was not despondent as he collected his gear and made for home. If this was the form their friendship was to take, so be it. That suited him. Was he not the canny one, the one to shy away from the marriage noose? He should be glad she was not one of the husband hunters.

The hour was late. All the keelmen's houses were in darkness but for his own

441

where a dim light showed. His father, then, was not yet abed. He quickened his step. The great bell of St Nicholas rang out the hour of midnight as he picked a careful way through ruts and puddles.

Silence fell as the last stroke died away. Only the small sounds of the river accompanied the crunch of his clogs, the lap of the incoming tide, the irregular bumping of flotsam against the jetty and then a different sound, one that brought him to a standstill, ear turned to the wind. A hen disturbed by a rat? A seabird? Or the call of a man in trouble?

It came again, an unmistakable cry for help as quickly muffled as uttered. He distinctly heard the splash of oars now. Out there on the dark water, a boat moved, but the glim at her prow was no more than a pinprick so that, try as he might, he could make out neither size nor shape as she slid away down river. Towards Shields, he reminded himself. Towards the *Peggy's* hole. The sounds grew fainter but Will continued to stand, persuading himself that this was none of his business. When all was quiet on the water once more, he went on his way.

His father, dozing by the fire with stockinged feet stretched to the dying embers, his sea boots standing legless beside him, started awake at his entry.

Relief at the sight of his son was written plainly on his face.

'Boomer and his gang are abroad the neet,' he said. 'I was afeared they'd got ye.'

The boat on the river. The cry of a frightened man. Prickles ran down Will's spine to think what an easy catch he would have made, walking alone at midnight by the river. 'I was supping with Hannah,' he told his father. 'But I heard them go by. They got somebody.'

'They could have taken thee an' all,' his father said grimly. 'Didst carry owt to defend thysell with?'

'Nowt but me fists,' grinned Will. 'But they'd have to catch me first.'

His father rose stiffly from his chair and made for his pallet in the alcove. 'Carry a cudgel, man, as long as the *Peggy's* tied up at Shields.'

The rest of the keelmen were alerted next morning.

'King William has but to put the navy to rights and men would join of their own accord,' said Nathan, Gracie's man. 'There'd be nae call for pressing then. Many a bully-boy would go to sea if the terms were right.'

But everyone in the kingdom knew that conditions for the common sailor were vile though the officers lived in comfort.

443

A Tynemouth man, having once been impressed, was known to have cut off his right hand rather than risk being caught again. It was the dread of every wife that her man might be taken. Pay, if it came at all, was always in arrears and she would be left with her bairns to starve.

27

In his position as skipper, Will was allowed to hire out any unused cargo space in the glassmakers' chartered vessel, retaining for himself a percentage of the fee charged. Such complicated accounting was quite outside his talents, especially since river dues to the Newcastle vend were involved. He was in the habit of seeking advice from Master Standwell on such transactions and appeared one morning at the office on the quay with just such a problem.

'Now, Master Standwell, what thinkst would be a reasonable charge for carrying clay? A cheap enough commodity on land but one which will take more space and weigh more heavily than a cargo of bottles.'

'Who wants clay?' asked Hannah with sudden interest.

'A potter in Edinburgh. Seemingly there

is little good clay to be found in Scotland.'

'There is little good of any sort in Scotland at present times,' grunted Isaac. 'The news I have is that the country is all at sixes and sevens. Some still hanker for the Stuarts. No good business was ever done in a rebellion.'

As Isaac and Will deliberated over the proposition, Hannah picked up the letter from Edinburgh. The signature was that of Daniel Fergusson. A picture of the reserved, soft-spoken Daniel came into her mind, bringing with it a warm flush of pleasure.

'I know this potter,' she said. 'Daniel Fergusson and my brother Tom were apprenticed to the same master potter some years ago. I would swear to his trustworthiness.'

A few weeks later, the bell on the office door tinkled and Daniel appeared in the entrance. At the sight of Hannah, on a high stool dressed in scrivener's smock, he was temporarily bereft of speech.

Hannah laughed. 'Good day to thee, Daniel. Be so good as to shut the door or Master Standwell and I will be blown clean away.'

Three years had elapsed since last they met. His once spare frame had thickened somewhat. The well-tailored coat of black grosgrain enhanced a depth of chest that

Hannah did not recall. His fashionably long waistcoat embraced the beginnings of a manly paunch, He saw a young woman of striking beauty and neat figure with an air about her of calm assurance that had been missing in the young Hannah he remembered. She was laughing at him now, enjoying his confusion.

Collecting himself, he whipped off his hat and bowed. He wore no wig but his thickly curling hair was fashionably dressed. 'Mistress Hannah,' he stammered, 'I never thought to find thee in a shipping office on the Tyne. Ye have quite disarranged me so that I know not what to say.'

Hannah slid down from her stool with a hand extended in welcome. 'I have the advantage over thee, Daniel, for this visit is not a total surprise. Your letter advised us of your interest.' She turned to Master Standwell who was scrutinising the new arrival through lop-sided spectacles. 'This is Master Fergusson the potter from Edinburgh who seeks bulk lading with us for his clay.'

'Ah!' Master Standwell laid aside his pen. 'What news frae Scotland? Will our ship be safe?'

Daniel made a despairing gesture with his hands. 'Who can answer for Scotland? Clan fights clan. William's men against the Jacobites and the Covenanters against

446

them all. But Edinburgh, where I work, is quiet now and, by the grace of God, I am able to conduct my business peaceably without involvement in politics.'

'And in thine own heart?' Isaac asked shrewdly. 'Where dost stand in the question of a ruler?'

'I give nae allegiance to a papist king,' said Daniel shortly, 'though he be a Stuart at that.'

Isaac rubbed his hands. 'Well said. Well said. We will get on very well I see. My masters, the glassmakers, are Huguenots and will have no truck with papist sympathisers. With others of their inclination, they have gone to the expense of mounting and equipping a company of cavalry for Ireland to put James down.'

'I had heard as much.' Daniel's eyes kept straying to Hannah who took no part in this conversation but busied herself with drawing up a contract. Politely, he heard the old man out.

'Pray God the Dutchman's cause will prevail there as well as in Scotland,' Isaac returned to his ledgers once more, 'else we will have a great reversal of our fortunes here. For this reason,' he peeped over the top of his spectacles to make sure that Daniel was still giving him his full attention, 'I must keep myself informed and am much obliged for thy opinions.

My assistant though she be a no-good, rubbishy sort of girl, can draw up the charges for thy commission.' Hannah's broad smile reassured Daniel that her master was no ogre.

His business completed, Daniel was disposed to linger, but Hannah summarily dismissed him by resuming her work. 'Join me in the pie shop at the foot of Bent Chare at two of the clock.' She nodded him off. 'I take my dinner there.'

Still bemused at finding her in such a place, he took his leave and went for a turn about the quay to clear his head of the conflicting emotions raging there. To be sure, on learning that the skipper he had engaged was a Robson, he had wondered if he could be kin to a girl he once knew.

Once knew? Once loved.

Once loved? He forced himself to look squarely at reality though the exposure was deeply disturbing. What he discovered was that, despite the passage of time and the changes it had wrought, he still loved her, with every breath of his body, and would do so for as long as he lived. No other woman, and he had met several who were well-disposed towards him, no other woman would do for him.

It remained to be seen whether Hannah's feelings were any warmer towards him and he would not risk damaging his chances by a too hasty declaration of his feelings. If, in the end, her answer was unchanged, he would remain a bachelor for the rest of his life as he had already resolved to do before this chance reunion came about.

At two strokes of the Major, he was seated at a bench in the corner of the noisy, smoky little shop that was famed far beyond the limits of the town for its excellent mutton pies. Apprentices, sailors, fishwives and washerwomen filled the place with their bawdy laughter, their shouts for more ale, more pies.

Hannah saw him at once and cut through the crowd with a word to this one and that, a smart retort to one with a lewd tongue, a penny for the lavender seller. Watching her, Daniel reflected that she was as much at home here as if she had been born on the Tyne. Heads turned when she flopped down to share a dish of pies with the stranger.

'Now, Daniel, your news.' She was all sweet amiability as she bit into a steaming pie. Her eyes travelled fondly over the contours of his face, marking the changes that three years had wrought. He wore a beard now which gave him an air of sedateness at variance with his present inner turmoil.

'My news is small bait compared with whatever adventure carried thee from Budle

Hall to Newcastle quay. Mayhap one day I'll hear it. For my part, my story goes like this.

'After leaving Buckton in Tom's capable hands, I set myself up in a small way in Edinburgh which I was able to enlarge when my father died leaving me a small legacy. There are few potters in Scotland, ye know, Hannah, so I could scarcely fail to prosper.'

'Thy fault is thy too humble modesty,' Hannah berated him. 'I know that our beloved Master Joshua held thy work in high esteem. A potter of great quality, he named thee.'

'Tom is the truly creative potter.' Ever generous, Daniel deflected the compliment. 'I hear nought but praise for the way he hath restored the former fortunes of the Buckton pottery.'

'Aye,' Hannah agreed. 'Mistress Emma is well pleased, I believe. Ye know that my brother is now married?'

'I did hear so,' said Daniel.

'To my dear friend Betsy who was a servant with me at Budle Hall.' Her eyes met his in a look devoid of subtlety. 'What of thee, Daniel? Art a husband too?'

Daniel felt himself colouring like an idiot schoolboy. His answer came clipped and short. 'Nay, I share a home with my aged mother.' The next question was hard to

450

deliver lightly, as if it were of little import to anyone. 'What of thyself, Hannah? Does some fortunate man claim thee for a wife?' But she only laughed at him.

'Now, Daniel, ye know me better than that.'

A new arrival caught her eye. She sprang to her feet and waved her kerchief to attract his attention.

'My skipper,' said Daniel.

'My cousin Will,' said Hannah and made room for him on the bench.

There was no reason for Daniel to prolong his stay on the Tyne. He had visited the local claypits and found a good yellow clay that suited his purpose admirably and had arranged with Will for its transportation to Edinburgh. Now, on the morning of his departure, he sat by the window of the public room of the Fox and Lamb and ate his breakfast of bread and bacon.

This was a popular inn with pilgrims bound for the sacred shrine of Our Lady of Jesmond, being the last overnight stop before reaching their destination. They were all about him now, adjusting their bundles. Some were already outside, staves in hand, in the street to which they had given their name.

Despite the crowded rooms, the inn was comfortable, the beds clean and the food wholesome. Daniel marked it down for future visits and slipped an extra piece of silver to the landlord so that he might be well remembered and his comfort catered for. Of a surety, there would be other visits. Now that he had found Hannah, he had no intention of losing her again.

A sudden disturbance amongst the pilgrims in the street outside arrested Daniel's attention. One amongst them shouted the news brought by an exhausted messenger, but the excited uproar drowned his voice and Daniel had to seek out the innkeeper for an explanation.

'We are fair mazed with rumours,' grumbled the landlord, 'but if this be true then there is cause for rejoicing. They say that King James has been soundly beaten in Ireland and has set sail for France.'

'May he rest there for evermore,' Daniel said fervently. 'I know not how war affects a landlord but 'tis bad news for enterprise and industry—'

'Why it affects a landlord ill, sir. Dead men carry no purses. Soldiers never pay. I was for Charlie and his father before him but I'm done with the Stuarts now they've gone papist and I'm glad to see the back of James.'

Daniel had half a mind to visit the office on the quay once more. The news would cheer Master Standwell and his Huguenot masters but he resisted the temptation to see Hannah again. Master Standwell would learn the tidings soon enough. When the 'Chevy Chase' stopped outside the Lamb and Fox, to change horses, he was content to climb aboard and drive away with much to occupy his mind.

At the glassmakers' house, there was great rejoicing at the news of James's defeat in Ireland and of his subsequent flight to France. The possibility of King Louis supporting any further attempts on James's part to regain the throne of Britain was extremely small.

'Had the Battle of the Boyne gone against William,' Hubert pointed out, 'your wedding, Alphonse, would of necessity be a meagre affair indeed.'

In the event, it was an occasion for lavish display and sumptuous feasting. Hannah and Will were included and joined in the festivities as welcome as any of the honoured guests. Lady Heslop was there. No more than a polite little bob was required from Hannah these days as she was a young woman of some standing in the community and looked as elegant as any of the ladies in a dress of sprigged muslin with satin ribands at the elbows and lace falling at her bosom. From Lady Heslop, however, she received, to her considerable surprise, a warm embrace.

There was news of her family. Her sister Sarah was the bonniest lass in Bewick and had all the stable lads at the hall in a fever. Her mother's health was not good but sister Joan was running the household and helping Widow Dodds into the bargain very adequately despite her disability. There was no mention made of her father and Hannah did not ask after him but she resolved, at the first opportunity, to send what money she could spare to her mother. Deep down, despite the repeated rejections, there was still that desire to please.

When Alphonse and his bride opened the dancing with a quick and lively galliard, Will appeared before her with hands outstretched. As they spun and whirled, their toes scarcely touching the highly polished ballroom floor, other more sedate dancers fell back to give them space.

'Bravo! Bravo!' The clapping began.

Alphonse turned to his bride. 'We have the two best dancers in the country to dance at our wedding, my love.'

' 'Tis fortunate for you that she can swim as well as dance,' was Éloïse's sober reminder.

On Daniel's next visit, Hannah took him to see her house. He could scarcely contain

454

his surprise. 'A change in fortunes indeed, Hannah!'

'I'll wager she has not told thee how she came to own such a house,' said Will. He had been cleaning out his boat when he saw Daniel follow Hannah into her house and promptly found a pretext to join them. Wiping his hands on his breeches, he took a seat on the kitchen bench.

Very much at home, this cousin, thought Daniel.

As Hannah sought ale from Gracie who brewed regularly, he ventured, 'Unless she hath a husband, and I believe that is not so?'

Will snorted. 'There is no husband.' Then he proceeded to tell the story of the shipwreck and its consequences.

'I knew her brother well,' Daniel nodded. 'They can both swim like fishes.'

Will held up a finger at the sound of Hannah's returning footsteps. 'Not a word. I'll get wrong for making ower much of the affair.' He continued, 'I trust thy clay reached Edinburgh in good condition?' He was wondering if some complaint brought Daniel back to the Tyne.

'Prime,' said Daniel. 'I am here to employ thy services once more.'

Hannah brought cakes and ale to the table at that moment. 'More clay so soon, Daniel?'

The query was innocent enough but it seemed to Will that Daniel's reply was unnecessarily defensive. He covered the moment of unease with, ' 'Tis good for our business. We'll not find cause to grumble nae matter how much clay he needs.'

Hannah made no answer. The friendliness of her expression did not change but to someone like Will who had learned to read her every mood, the sudden wariness in her eyes did not pass unnoticed.

Whenever Daniel appeared in Newcastle, which was often, Hannah made him welcome, as did Will. In truth, he experienced some difficulty in ever finding Hannah alone. Will always put in an appearance whether he was walking Hannah home from the quay or paying a visit to her house.

Patiently he waited for some sign that their relationship might be deepening but she gave him no indication that he was anything more than a good friend. He had to confess that he shared her affections with Will. She treated them both like elder brothers, brothers who needed from time to time a sharp word of criticism as well as tender caring for their comfort. Daniel was unwilling to risk losing this undoubted affection and so the weeks and the months went by without him speaking his heart.

The folk of Sandgate grew accustomed to

456

seeing the big Scotchman about and spent some time in surmise and speculation as to what he was about. Gracie was almost speechless with exasperation at Hannah's attitude.

'Thee's var nigh twenty-and-one year old. There's two good men who'd have ye if ye but crook thy little finger at them. Wilt not step doon from thy high horse and put one at least oot of his misery?'

But Hannah would not face the truth of Gracie's words. 'You read the signs awry, Gracie. To be sure, Daniel once asked for me long ago when he was not old enough to know what he wanted. Now he, like thy brother, knows that I am not for marrying anyone and so we are all of one mind.'

Gracie refused to be convinced. 'I never yet heard of a lass who was not the marrying kind. Do you not want bairns of thine own? Or are they to be bastards like Silly Milly's brood on Butchers Bank?'

'I can make do with other folks' bairns who are less trouble to produce.'

The thought flashed across Gracie's mind that Hannah perhaps feared the ordeal of childbirth but she rejected it at once. How could a maid with Hannah's proven courage fear such a natural function?

Hannah went on, 'Thy little Mattie is as dear to me as any child of my own.'

457

This was true, Gracie reflected. There was a strong bond of affection between Hannah and her own little boy. The boy's poor health was a constant worry to Hannah. She would make him potions to clear the phlegm from his congested lungs and would sit up all night by his bedside when he had a fever. When the child was well, there was nothing she liked doing better than teaching him his letters. Though he had not yet reached his seventh birthday, he could write his name and do simple sums and could read the stories that she wrote for him.

'He is a clever child,' she insisted to Mattie's confused parents, 'and ye must seek a place for him at the Royal Grammar School before he is much older. We'll make a scholar of this one, you'll see.'

All the deep wells of love in Hannah were touched when, with his tufty golden head resting against her bosom and her arm about him, she read him stories. Her little brother Benjamin, who would for ever be associated in her mind with the nightmare of his birth, had never aroused such tenderness within her.

When she allowed herself to indulge in introspection, she was disturbed by what she saw. There was a worm at the core of her existence. She knew that she was not as other women. She saw with envy the happiness that might be brought about by the love of a man yet whenever such bliss was within her own reach, she retreated angrily, causing pain to others. Some poison working within her transformed even the gentlest touch upon her into a potentially bestial act, the prelude to rape, and the man himself into an evil lecher. The very thought of physical love clamped her head and heart in bands of steel which she had no power to release.

Gracie's words concerning Daniel went deep. She had hurt and humiliated him once before and must not invite him into such a position again. All would be well were he content to remain a dear friend, like Will, but Daniel was not like Will.

28

During the two years that Hannah had worked in the glassmakers' employ, her responsibilities had grown as Isaac Standwell's frailties increased. Though still of sharp perception and acute financial awareness, his failing eyesight made Hannah's assistance invaluable. It was a situation he was loth to accept. Impatience with his own shortcomings made him increasingly irritable but this did not lessen Hannah's admiration for his grasp of business affairs and she lost no opportunity to learn from him. Always, at the back of their combined endeavours, was total loyalty to the glassmakers.

Alphonse was a frequent caller, his errands usually relating to the packing and shipment of the painted glass windows which were bringing him fame. He was there one day when Will burst into the office, straight off the ship, still in his tarry clothes.

'Where's the militia that's supposed to protect honest citizens!' Will demanded. 'I saw with me ain eyes French pirates coming ashore at Druridge Bay. They sacked Widdrington and got clean away without a musket challenging them.'

Will had been homeward bound from Scotland, some ten leagues north of the Tyne, when he sighted the enemy ships making off, leaving behind them a smoking countryside. 'Half a dozen light frigates, some privateers and a fire ship,' he reported. ' 'Twould have been an ill-matched encounter for our little ship.'

'Lie low, Keelman Willy,' warned Isaac, 'the *Peggy* will be back in the Tyne ere long. There'll be mair impressing after this outrage.'

'Thank God the press gang has no use for artists,' Alphonse said humbly, 'though I'd be happy to avenge Widdrington. I made a beautiful window for that church. Destroyed by now, I do not doubt. Come Will,' he turned to slap Will heartily on the back, 'to the Baltic. A dish of lambs' tongues and a glass of sack will settle your spleen.'

After they had gone, Hannah looked across at Isaac.

' 'Tis your belief this raid by the French will bring Captain Boomer trawling the Tyne for men again, Master Standwell?'

'As sure as night follows day. The keelmen will need to look over their shoulders at all times.'

'For the first time, I see an advantage in being a woman,' said Hannah. 'The navy hath no use for me.'

The old man grinned. 'Nor for me, praise the Lord.'

The pie shop was buzzing with the news of the French raid when Hannah joined Gracie and Mattie there. The keelmen were voluble in their feelings. 'The buggers'll get mair than they bargain for if they set foot on the Tyne.'

But the women were troubled. 'We want nae Frenchmen at Sandgate,' said Gracie. 'Wor dwellings by the river's edge would be easy pickings.'

Gracie was pregnant again, as she had been on many occasions since Hannah came to live at Sandgate. She had miscarried every time so that Mattie was still an only child. Finally, Hannah's concern for Gracie had prompted her to approach her husband, a man of few words and not given to open discussion of family matters, so she was prepared for a rebuff.

'If ye want her to carry thy child full term,' she said with some asperity, 'do not expect her to do such heavy work.'

'Other women get on with their work just the same,' he objected. 'What's wrang wi' her?'

'Other women are more robust than Gracie,' Hannah persisted. 'She's not a cow that can turn aside from pulling the waggon, drop its calf and then carry on working. She's a woman and a frail woman at that.' He had grudgingly followed her advice and Gracie's term was nearly completed without mishap. Hannah had declined to be present at the birth and Gracie did not press her. She would look after Mattie and cook the food.

Daniel chose to make his next visit to Newcastle on horseback since he intended to break his journey at Buckton. Mistress Emma's reply to his letter had assured him of a warm welcome and a comfortable bed for the night. Though he had passed this way frequently by coach during the last twelve months, he had seen no more of the pottery where he had served his apprenticeship than the tops of the kilns. Now he was to see Mistress Emma once more, his friend Tom and his wife.

The blustery wind blowing straight from the sea threatened to tug off his tightly wedged beaver as he turned away from the Great North Road and made for Buckton. The old smells assailed him as he drew near, taking him back in memory; of the rich, damp earth by the spring that fed the horse trough, the pine needle path through the dark resinous copse, a whiff of Mistress Emma's hencoops and the drenching fragrance of phlox, her favourite flower.

His heart lightened with pleasurable anticipation as he turned into the yard and there they were, waiting to greet him—Mistress Emma, greyer, smaller, with tears of happiness filling her eyes, Tom, a great bruiser of a fellow now, and his comely wife.

He was back at the long oak table with a mug of ale in front of him, fresh-baked bread, cold meat and pickles, just as though he had never been away.

There was much to talk about—the state of the pottery market, the price of coal and the rising cost of importing cobalt, an essential mineral for the production of the popular blue and white ware that both houses depended on. There were cherished glaze recipes to be exchanged, successes and failures to be related.

'Now, what of Hannah?' Betsy broke in. 'She writes to say that ye meet from time to time. How fares my fiery friend?'

'Hannah is much respected among the merchants of Newcastle,' he said, 'and has not demonstrated her fire of late though I do not doubt but that she can still blaze away if provoked.' The note of tenderness that had crept into his voice did not escape Mistress Emma's keen attention.

Tom wagged his head in disbelief. ' 'Tis hard to imagine Hannah making her mark in such a great town as Newcastle.'

'Not hard at all,' his wife retorted, and now Daniel perceived that she was some way advanced in pregnancy. 'She was born to the keeping of accounts and clerking. The only time my father's fishing thrived was when Hannah managed his books though 'tis a mercy she shifted away from Boulmer and my clod-pate brothers.'

With a sudden gesture of despair, Daniel thrust both hands through his hair, unable to conceal his anxiety any longer. 'Scholar, lady's maid or fishwife. No matter. I would love her dearly were she no more than a common cut-purse.'

Ah, thought Emma, this is why he came.

His outburst, so foreign to his usual reticence, silenced them all. 'I seek advice,' he went on. 'And yet I do admit to a certain deviousness for, if I do not like thy counsel, I have nae doubt but that I will not take it. My unhappy state is that I am driven almost beyond endurance to keep silent over my feelings for Hannah lest, if I speak my heart too soon, I should lose the affection which I presently enjoy.'

He looked despairingly at his hearers. 'If Hannah should reject me, as well she might, she has done so once already long ago, then our present felicity of friendship will be sundered. I could not bear to remain in her company knowing that she would never wed me.' He made an effort to regain his self-control. 'I think I am resolved yet even now, I dither, wax and wane as my spirit goads or fails me. My friends, what say ye? Do I go boldly? Cast the die? Win or lose? Or grow old in friendship never knowing whether or not I might have claimed more.'

The clock on the mantelshelf ticked away the seconds. A distant cow moaned a reminder that it was milking time. Daniel's poignant plea hung in the air, as though no one would take it up. Tom's brow was

465

knitted in perplexity. Such complications over a straightforward issue were beyond his understanding.

Emma broke the silence. She leaned across the table to take Daniel's hands in hers, strong brown hands made sinewy with working clay, in her pale, birdy fingers. 'Hast given her no hint of thy feelings, Daniel?'

'Not intentionally, Mistress Emma, lest I frightened her off. Yet she may have some inkling.'

'Then that is what ye must do,' Emma said firmly, 'in the gentlest way possible so that she may lead thee on if she so desires and silence thee if not. Whichever way she chooses, thy mind will be put at rest.'

'She is no longer a young harum-scarum,' put in Tom, greatly upset to see a respected senior colleague so undone. 'Nae doubt she regrets her too hasty refusal in times gone by and only awaits an opportunity to put matters right.'

'I wouldna be so sure,' said Betsy slowly. 'She once telled me she never meant to wed.'

'Pooh!' said Tom. 'A girlish fancy, nae mair than that. Ask her again, Daniel, and I'll eat my hat if thou'rt not soon to become my brother!'

Smiling now, Daniel gripped Tom's shoulder affectionately.

'I have it in mind to buy a fine new house presently being built in Edinburgh's most sought-after square, I'll buy it tomorrow if she'll have me.'

'Do you know our cousin Will?' asked Betsy.

Daniel was startled. He had almost forgotten this other thread to his anxiety. 'I do, indeed. He is my friend.'

'We wondered, Tom and me, once or twice,' Betsy spoke haltingly, 'if he were something more than a friend to Hannah?'

Daniel shrugged helplessly, beset anew with doubts. 'Who can tell?'

'Find out,' urged Tom.

'Ask him. Straight oot,' instructed Betsy.

'And then,' Emma brought her warm motherliness to comfort him, 'tell her you love her and see what next befalls.'

Daniel ran Will to earth in the boatshed, not cleaning, painting or scraping his beloved boat which was his usual occupation when not at sea but posed heroically on a tub, dressed in his Sunday slops and jacket while Alphonse sat in front of him, busy with drawing board and charcoal.

'I am to be a window,' he greeted Daniel. 'What thinkst of that!'

'What I think is that likely thee'll be too thick to see through, Master Will.' Daniel picked his way over coils of rope and lobster pots to stand behind Alphonse.

'What say you, Daniel? Is it like?' Alphonse drew back from his work to examine it critically.

The drawing truly had caught the very character of Will, standing, legs apart, hand on hip. There was pride and stubbornness in the out-thrust chin, a touch of mockery in the smile.

'What dost think, Daniel?' Will called out. 'Howay, man. Speak thy mind.'

Daniel shook his head in wonderment. 'I'm altogether mazed,' he said. 'The very spit.'

'Imagine it with the sun behind,' said Alphonse. 'Jacket of heavenly blue. Waistcoat gold and a boat behind on the waters of Tyne.'

'Where will it hang?'

'In the new church being built at Bycar. A rich patron hopes, by this benevolence, to ensure a place for himself in the world hereafter.'

'Will, in all his glory, will distract poor maidens at their prayers,' Daniel suggested.

'And if I be stuck in the winder, I canna do much aboot it,' Will objected. 'How much longer, Alphonse? Me leg has gone to sleep.'

Alphonse put away his charcoal. 'I have done enough.'

Flexing his muscles, Will stepped down from the tub to look at his portrait. 'I had thought my nose to be more pronounced,' he objected, running a finger down his not insignificant nose. 'Dost not think I have a noble nose, Daniel?'

'Certainly a powerful one,' Daniel agreed, 'and I have a mind to lead it to the tavern for a pot of ale.'

The note of urgency in his voice did not go unmarked by Will. 'With all my heart,' he said. 'Standing stiff makes a man uncommon dry.' He paused to take note of Daniel's smart appearance. 'Thou'rt a proper gallant the day, Daniel, with thy clean bands and silver buckles. Art going a-wooing?' he teased, and in that split second, he experienced a sickening convulsion of the stomach though he kept the smile on his face. He saw, with blinding clarity, that his jest had scored a bull's eye and he knew without Daniel saying another word, who was the maid in question.

Courteously declining the invitation to join them, Alphonse sought the services of a boatman to take him downstream to Howden. 'Daniel has business with you and I must return to my workshop.'

The Baltic Tavern, as always, was full of noisy, roistering sailors, whores and beggars. Daniel waited until he and Will

469

were both seated with a pot of ale in front of them before he brought up the subject that was on his mind.

'I'll not put myself in the wrong with thee, Will, for thou'rt a good friend. Tell me that ye have hopes of marrying her thyself and I will return to Scotland without ever saying a word, to the lassie.'

Will's bluster was very convincing. Only when Daniel had gone off to seek Hannah, with light step and in good heart, did he allow dejection to overcome him. Daniel, sober, prosperous and reliable was an ideal husband for any maid. What chance had a knockabout keelman who couldn't keep a penny in his pocket, alongside a man like Daniel?

When Daniel came seeking him later in the day, he was in the boathouse, snoring drunk, and Daniel went away without waking him.

Gracie's time had come. 'Go to thy Auntie Hannah,' Gracie patted her little boy's head. 'Mebbes, when ye come back, there'll be a little sister or brother waiting for ye.'

Hannah gave Mattie his tea and watched him absently as he played with her kitten. The anxiety of Gracie's labour was added to a day already hateful with trauma. Daniel's declaration showed clearly that

470

she had failed to indicate the nature of her feelings for him. Now, for a second time, she had crushed and humiliated an upright and sensitive man whose friendship she clearly cherished.

Such a relationship was unthinkable now. Though her words had been carefully chosen, they were words of rejection. He was wounded too deeply for any lighthearted reconciliation to be envisaged. He had turned away from her with stricken face and walked off into the shadows, leaving her by the riverside, alone and full of remorse.

Darkness had fallen and the inside of the boathouse was pitch black when Will was rudely shaken awake by one of the keelmen. 'Rouse thysell, man! Thy friend's been taken by the gang!'

The clouds cleared instantly from Will's brain.

'Aye, the Scotchman. Wor Mary saw him by the river at Close Side. Boomer's gang jumped on him from behind and afore she had time to shout, they had him over the side and on his way to Shields.'

Will was on his feet, tightening his belt, checking his knife. 'Get the lads. Two more men. Thee and me.' There had been one brief moment of indecision. The ignoble thought had flashed through

Will's mind that Providence had shown the way to dispose of Hannah's suitor. Angrily he soused his head with a scoop of cold water. Such thoughts were not to be entertained. Daniel was his friend. And Hannah's friend. Dear to both and must be rescued.

'The *Peggy* will be sailing on the night tide for sure.' He was racing over the sand. 'I'll see to the boat.'

Cottage doors were flung open. Chunks of yellow lamplight chequered the darkness. The sound of running footsteps brought Hannah to the water's edge where willing hands were launching the *Spirit of the North.*

'What's amiss, Will?' she cried. A fearful sense of impending disaster was tugging at her heart.

' 'Tis Daniel,' Will hollered. 'Taken by the press gang. Never fret! We'll get him.'

When the last swish of oars had died away, the women who had elected to sit up with Gracie resumed their vigil and Hannah, with Mattie's hand trustingly in hers, walked wearily back to her house.

'We must get down on our knees and say our prayers, Mattie, that God will protect thy mother and Uncle Daniel this night for both will need His help.'

She put Mattie to bed in the parlour but

there would be no sleep for her until the night's work was done. She could picture the *Peggy* now, that evil black hulk, crewed by ruffians and led by a captain whose savagery was notorious. Once on board, Daniel, sweet, gentle Daniel, would surely be lost for ever; maybe Will and his companions too. As the hours went by, Hannah's tortured mind led her again and again to that last meeting with Daniel.

'I will wait,' he had begged, and she, growing weary with his persistence, had turned him away with brusque finality. Thus destroyed, he had walked unwarily into danger.

She wanted Daniel as a dear friend. She had failed to make him understand that she would never take a husband.

29

By the movement of the waters, the four men in the boat could tell that the tide was approaching its peak. Urgency sharpened their wits and lent strength to their arms for certain it was that the *Peggy* would sail on the turn. There would be more than one poor soul taken during the gang's foray ashore and Captain Boomer would want to make away with them and collect his bounty without delay. Once the *Peggy* sailed with Daniel on board, rescue would be impossible.

The task in front of them, if the men pulling at the oars stopped to consider it, was well nigh impossible anyhow. No one had ever been known to escape from the *Peggy*, but Will was resolute and unafraid, allowing no doubts.

There was no moon, not even the glimmer of stars, but Will needed neither to help him guide the Spirit unerringly downriver to that darker shape swinging gently on its anchor cable. At a sign from him, the rowers lifted their oars from the water, letting the boat drift silently. With only the lightest touch they steered her away from the pool of light cast by the lantern on the *Peggy's* bowsprit and brought her round to the stern, alongside the frigate's own rowboat.

'Wait on,' Will whispered as one of his companions made to cut the *Peggy's* rowboat adrift. 'Only cast away her oars for now.'

He got to his feet, grabbing a hawser to steady himself as his eyes raked the side of the ship for some means of boarding her. Never in his worst nightmare had he imagined himself wanting to do such a thing. A man would be a fool to try, but at that moment Daniel's voice floated down, instantly stiffening his resolve. Daniel was on the top deck, at the stern end.

'I tell thee, I am a potter. What use am I to thee?'

'Ye can haul and scrape and scree up a mast as well as the rest of us,' a rough voice answered. 'King Willie's not over nice about his sailors as long as his ships can put to sea.'

The canvas shoes of the guard flapped across the deck as he made his way to his post on the fo'c's'le. Daniel was unattended. The time for action had come.

Will alone would go aboard. The others would wait at the oars ready to make a quick getaway once the rescue was accomplished. That would be the time to cut loose the *Peggy's* rowboat and not before lest it attract unwelcome attention.

With practised aim, Will sent a coil of rope snaking up the side of the prison ship to lie across the outrigged channel which secured her shrouds. A quick tug to tauten the line and he was up the side like a monkey. Cautiously, he raised his head above the bulwarks. The guard had taken up a position in the bows facing the river with his lantern by his side, his back against a strut and his musket slung carelessly across his shoulder. The rest of the deck was empty though sounds of drunken revelry and the strains of a mouth organ issued from the crew's quarters in the fo'c's'le. Let them make as much noise as they like, thought Will grimly as he gingerly mounted the bulwark. The better it will be for us. He looked aft, searching the shadows for a sight of Daniel.

The noise of a passing vessel on the other side of the river stayed him for a moment but the light at its prow passed quickly by. No one willingly interfered with Captain Boomer. Daniel, however, had heard the passing ship and, in a last desperate attempt to attract attention, began shouting at the top of his voice. Roundly cursing his friend, Will hastily shrank back amongst the shrouds as the watch, roused from his lethargy, came to investigate, passing less than a foot from Will's hiding place.

The captain had heard the commotion. From his cabin amidships, a voice of authority rang out. 'Let him yell. If he brings his friends, we'll have more fish for the net.'

Silently Will acknowledged the unpalatable truth.

' 'Tis no use ye gettin' in a rage, Scotch laddie.' The watch was addressing the dark recess beneath the poop deck. This, then, was where Daniel was confined. 'If ye keep up this din, ye'll go below with the other bonnie lads and, I'm telling ye, the air is a mite fresher up here, so ye'll save yer breath if ye've any sense. Thee's been ketched. Thee'll serve time and that's the end on't. But ye'll have no need of that fine pin, I reckon.'

Daniel cursed softly as his jewelled cravat pin was removed and Will unsheathed his knife. He must get rid of the watch, and quickly. Precious time was being wasted. One blow should do it. Silent as a cat he crept forward, knife raised, until he was but a pace away when the guard turned and made off by the portside without confronting him. Breathing a prayer, Will put his knife away. Swiftly, noiselessly, he crossed to the poop.

A white face stared at him in astonishment from a pile of tarpaulins. Not a word was spoken. Two quick slashes of the knife cut through the leather thongs binding Daniel's wrists and ankles. There was not a moment to lose. The music had died away and there was movement for'ard. Will deduced that the *Peggy* would soon be making sail. Even as they raced together for the ship's side, the bosun's call came loud and dear on the midnight air, 'All hands ahoy,' and Will's heart sank. In a moment the crew would be streaming out over the deck, shinning the masts, heaving the anchor. No time for finesse now. He and Daniel dropped with a clatter into the boat beneath and shoved off from the side of the *Peggy*. The men at the oars pulled away with all their might and the *Spirit* leapt upstream.

Shouts and running steps on the deck above declared they had been discovered, but with the *Peggy's* rowboat now drifting loose, pursuit would be difficult. Will allowed himself a small measure of congratulation. The hardest part was over.

Above the uproar, came the voice of Captain Boomer, beside himself with anger, 'Prime your muskets! Shoot to kill. I want every man-jack of them, dead or alive.'

'Keep yer heeds doon, lads.' Will's voice croaked with tension as little waterspouts spattered the water around them. 'They canna see us. They're aiming wild.'

Wild maybe, but many shots were coming uncomfortably close, one or two slamming against the side of the boat and Will blessed her sturdy construction.

Daniel at the rudder, chafing life back into cramped limbs, prayed aloud for the lives of these men who had risked all to save him. Everything depended on the oarmen being able to get out of range as swiftly as possible. Already the turning tide was dragging against them.

Minutes passed that seemed like hours

before the cries and shouts behind them began to fade. The fusillade of shots was thinning out, the water flattening. The men dared to exchange glances. The impossible had happened. They had rescued a pressed man from the *Peggy*. What a tale to tell their children.

There was triumph in Will's cheeky grin as he glanced at Daniel, then all the power was struck from his body in one shattering blow as a musket ball carried off his kneecap. The last musket to find the range sent the gallant leader of the exploit into a bloody huddle at the bottom of the boat.

Hannah had been standing at the water's edge with the rest of the women for some time, listening fearfully to the commotion downriver. Her relief was overwhelming when the *Spirit* came into view. Soon she was able to make out the faces of the men. Daniel! Daniel was safe. Three crewmen—three?

The premonition of disaster which had gripped her all night long prepared her to face now the sight of Will, carried ashore by his marrers, grey as a corpse, his leg in a bloody mess. For certain she had known it would be either Will or Daniel—or both.

She took charge at once with an authority that went unquestioned. 'Take him to my house. I will tend him.'

As the bedraggled party passed by the lamplit window of Gracie's cottage, the stillness of the night was broken by the cry of a new-born babe.

30

Little Mattie was lifted, still sleeping, from the pallet in Hannah's parlour and carried upstairs. The men laid Will in his place. His eyes were closed for nature had intervened to rob him of consciousness when the pain grew too great to bear. The bluish pallor of his skin, the dark bruised-looking lips frightened Hannah.

'Fetch Samuel.' The men in their distress were glad of action. She turned to half-awake women gathering at the door. 'Fetch clean clouts. Tear up thy petticoats and do it quickly for see how he bleeds.'

With shaking fingers, Daniel tore the linen into strips while Hannah made firm pads to tie against the deadly red fountain of Will's lifeblood. Samuel came and, with bent head, held his son's limp hand.

'Jesu Lord, I pray thee, work Thy miracle now. If I never ask another boon as lang as I live, divvent let my canny lad die.'

At last, the deep red stain ceased to

spread through the clouts. The last layer of bandages stayed unmarked and Hannah sank back on trembling knees. 'I believe thy prayer be answered, Uncle Samuel. The blood has ceased to flow.'

Hannah stayed by Will's bedside for what remained of the night, while Samuel dozed in his chair. With Daniel at her side, she watched each fluttering breath that escaped from his blanched lips, praying that the feeble rhythms would not falter. At one point, Will opened his eyes for a brief, unfocused moment then sank back into the shadowy streams where he was fighting for his life.

Daniel was almost out of his mind with grief. 'He did it for me,' he endlessly repeated. Though Hannah's heart was full of fear, she did her best to comfort him.

The new day broke with a shower of hailstones rattling against the window panes. Men on their way to the keels pulled their oilskins close, glancing soberly at Hannah's Hoose as they passed. Everyone in Sandgate now had heard the news that Nathan's Gracie had a live infant at last and Will Robson was in a bad way with a musket wound of his leg.

Hannah and Daniel, struggling against the overpowering need for sleep, were startled awake by a fearful rigor that suddenly gripped the injured man, setting the whole bed in a turmoil. Terrified that the bleeding might be started again by Will's frenzy of shaking, Hannah wrapped her arms around him, and held him close.

The action had been instinctive but it released within her a tumult of emotions. In her arms she held a man's body. His shaking torso was pressed against her bosom yet she did not fling it from her. She laid her cheek against the clammy face and surrendered to a feeling of exaltation that was at the same time of such refined pain that a low moan escaped her lips. She was a cold candle touched by a lighted taper and her body blazed. There was an unaccustomed looseness in the taut recesses of her being. Tears of inexplicable relief started to her eyes as she rocked poor Will to and fro. She was a mother with a child and, though she did not yet know it, a woman with her lover.

'He's cold, Daniel! Do ye mend the fire with all speed.'

When, at last, the shaking subsided, when Will's chattering teeth were stilled, he opened his eyes. With sudden clarity he looked about him; at his father's anxious, tearstained face, at Daniel standing with the bellows still in his hand, at Hannah, holding his own sweat-drenched body close. With consciousness, the pain returned and a groan escaped his lips.

482

Hannah turned to Daniel. 'Get the laudanum from my medicine chest. In the dresser cupboard.'

'My leg,' muttered Will, searching his father's face.

'A ball through the knee, son,' said his father. 'Bide still. Thee's lost a pailful of blood.'

A little while later, little Mattie crept downstairs in his nightshirt seeking breakfast. He was astonished to find his Uncle Will, with blood all over him, asleep in the parlour and Uncle Daniel and Auntie Hannah dozing by the fire. He grabbed his boots from behind the door where he had put them the night before and, holding his shirt close to his little bare bottom, ran home to his mother. She showed him his new sister, red and wrinkled, not like a proper girl, and she gave him his breakfast.

A beam of wintry sunshine entering Hannah's window settled on her cheek, prodding her awake to the reality of what she had hoped was merely a bad dream. Her hands were sticky. Sticky with Will's blood. Recollections of the fearful night came flooding back.

Daniel appeared with a steaming cup. 'Take some milk, Hannah. I will cook eggs for our breakfast.'

Gratefully, she took the cup. Daniel

had aged ten years overnight. Was it only yesterday, Hannah marvelled as she studied his haggard face, that, upright, neatly groomed, he had asked her to marry him? If she had accepted him, none of these terrible events would have come about.

She laid a hand on his arm and spoke with infinite tenderness. 'Let there always be friendship between us, Daniel.' But he, exhausted, could only nod.

As she drank the warm, restoring milk Hannah reflected on the date. November 1st in the year 1691. It was her twenty-first birthday, a birthday she would never forget as long as she lived.

She did her best to make Will comfortable. She bathed the wound with witch hazel and anointed it with balsam made from the leaves of Solomon's Seal, but dealing with the splintered bone and shredded muscle was outside her experience. She sent a lassie with a note for Isaac Standwell to the quayside office and he, in turn, lost no time in informing the glassmakers that their skipper was grievously indisposed. Before an hour had passed, Alphonse appeared at the door of Hannah's house with a surgeon of the highest repute in attendance.

He was a man acquainted with all the latest practices in medicine and surgery and his fee was correspondingly high. His present attendance on this common keelman, however, was guaranteed by two of his most wealthy patients, Messrs Hubert and Ernest Gustave. He was generous, therefore, with time spent at Will's bedside.

The leg was a mess. There would be fever, without doubt, but he decided against further bleeding as the man had already suffered considerable loss of blood. The glassmakers, who appeared to be under some sort of obligation to this common fellow, had specifically asked him to save the leg if possible, whereas his first intention had been to have it off. And, indeed, it might come to that.

For the moment, therefore, he restricted his services to ordering a purge. The brothers Gustave had suggested that the patient be moved to their own house at Howden but he was well enough where he was. The doctor had never been inside a keelman's cottage before and was pleasantly surprised by its clean and wholesome state. In addition, there was a very able young woman to nurse him.

When he called a few days later, however, he saw what he had at first predicted. Fever raged. The leg was swollen, discoloured and showing signs of mortification. It must come off.

Daniel was thrown into despair at the news but Samuel, who had seen wounds like this before, was glad that the limb was to be removed before the poison spread to the rest of Will's body. The lad had babbled in delirium these past three days and Samuel was sick to the heart with the fear that his only son was going to die.

Hannah, who had faced every task up till now with unwavering resolution, had to turn aside from this act of irrevocable defilement. She sat with Gracie and her new baby, waiting for the doctor to emerge from her own front door. Neither woman could find words to express the grief that weighed down their spirits.

At four o'clock on this bleak November afternoon, the day was already dark. Thick fog rolling up the river from the sea obliterated all the small sounds of Sandgate but the keening of the birds. The door to Hannah's cottage opened. The link boy standing by the waiting chair jumped forward to relieve the surgeon of his bag of instruments. Well might the mourning seagulls screech and moan. For the bonniest dancer in all Tyneside would never dance again.

Gracie reached out a hand to Hannah. 'Now we must watch and pray. Certain it is that he would have died of the poison had the leg remained.'

There was no visible improvement after the operation, Will's life hung by a thread. He raved. He struggled and fought with those who would restrain him. He cursed such curses as Hannah had never heard before. He reviled his dearest friends who were trying to help him. Hannah could scarcely recognise her cheerful cousin of other days in this wild-eyed madman. His skin flamed to the touch. Vessels at neck and temple throbbed as if they would burst. No medicine but laudanum could give him peace. And then, when it seemed that the inner heat must surely consume him, he broke into a drenching sweat that mercifully cooled his poor tortured body. The madness subsided leaving Will enfeebled and weak.

There was no question of Daniel returning to Scotland at this stage. He moved in with Samuel, taking Will's place there. The two men supported Hannah in every way, carrying a daily supply of water from the pant at Sandgate, keeping the coal box filled, taking over her vigil to allow her to sleep.

Alphonse, who was a frequent visitor, brought wine and fruit. His mother sent supplies of clean bed linen. Other keelmen's wives helped in any way they could but were happy to leave Will in Hannah's care for there was an authority about her that commanded respect.

No one with a festering wound was allowed anywhere near her patient though how a wicklow could jump from a sore thumb to poor Will was beyond anyone's understanding. Neither would she permit Gracie to bring her baby into the sickroom. Will could see his new niece through the window, for a sickroom was no place for an infant. On these things, she would brook no argument. She informed Master Standwell that she would return to the office as soon as her charge was out of danger and he had to be content with that.

No mother ever cared for a sick child more devotedly than Hannah tended Will. Daniel, watching her feed him with sips of warm milk and honey, understood that Will occupied a place in her affections that he could never hope to fill. Yet he had not sought to marry her? She kept him clean and his bed wholesome. To prevent sores forming where he lay, she anointed his body with an unguent made from pigs' lard and rue made fragrant with lavender. She removed unsightly brown crusts from his teeth with sage leaves and refreshed his mouth with peppermint water. He marvelled at her skills.

'How came ye to have such knowledge of nursing the sick, Hannah?'

'I had a teacher once,' Hannah often thought of Widow Dodds, 'who took me amongst wounded soldiers. I have never forgotten her instructions.'

Hannah's reward came one day when Will's clouded mind suddenly cleared. He looked at Hannah and smiled. 'What, you still here? Have ye nowt better to do?' Then he ate a whole porringer of boiley.

She had to fight hard to control the sudden rush of tears. 'And where else would I be,' she demanded, 'since it's my house thou'rt lying in and my bed thou'rt occupying!'

As he began to rebuild his strength, she would allow him no repining over the lost leg. When she judged the time was right, she had him out of bed. 'Ye've lain abed long enough, Will Robson. Daniel will take one arm and thy father the other and we'll teach that one leg to do the work of two.'

'Like a cock-eyed chicken,' he quipped, then almost swooned with the pain as the blood rushed to the place where he once had a leg. The next time he stood up, however, the sensation was not so painful. Soon he was hopping about Hannah's house using her broomstick as a crutch.

'Ye'll be back at sea soon,' Hannah prophesied, a thought which he, himself, had not yet dared to entertain.

By tradition, the Company of Carpenters and Wheelwrights held their weekly meetings in the Wall Knoll Tower of the Sally Port, a short walk from Sandgate. At the close of business one winter's night they found a young woman awaiting them. They knew who she was all right, this wench standing beneath the flare in the wall with her shawl wrapped tight about her. She was Samuel Robson's niece that worked in Isaac Standwell's office on the quay. When she gave an order to the carpenters to make a peg leg, they knew whom it was for. All the town knew that Will Robson had scaped a pressed man from the *Peggy* and paid for it with a leg.

It was to be of sound wood, she instructed them, with cushioned cup to accommodate the stump and strong leather straps guaranteed not to break. 'He is a sea-going skipper,' she said, 'and must be steady, even in a gale.' Master Craftsman Jonathan Jamieson presented himself at Hannah's cottage the very next day with his slate and his measuring tape and, within a fortnight, Will had his wooden leg.

Daniel, seeing that he was no longer needed, made plans to leave. The parting between Will and himself was charged with emotion. He gripped Will's hand, grown

490

soft and white. 'For as long as I live, I am thy man, yet nothing I can do will repay the debt I owe.'

And Daniel did not forget that there were others who had put their lives at risk for a stranger and he intended to show his gratitude in a way acceptable to all.

Accidents like Will's were not rare on the riverside but, of all the guilds and clubs in Newcastle, only the keelmen looked after those amongst them who were unable to work through sickness or injury. By a generous contribution to the Keelmen's Friendly Society, Daniel paid his debt of gratitude to the community.

He was careful to take his leave when Hannah was engaged at the office. He could not trust himself to conduct that farewell in a manly fashion and avoided the quayside as he made for the Fox and Lamb where his horse was still stabled. From now on, he must shut her image out of his mind. His thoughts must be directed towards getting on with his own life, his work in Edinburgh. Daniel sought out the landlord and paid his dues.

He left the town by Gallows Gate taking the road across the Town Moor recalling, as he passed familiar landmarks, in what lightness of spirit he had passed this way in October. Today, the condemned creatures being carted from the town prison to their

491

place of execution on the Moor were not more wretched than he. But he must come to terms with life. The pottery, temporarily in the charge of his sister's husband, who was a competent advocate, and worked by two young apprentices, required his presence. His mother waited anxiously for news. He took the road for Morpeth and headed north. There was snow in the wind and he had a mind to make Berwick for a bed that night. He would not think of Hannah.

Although Hannah was deeply grateful for Daniel's support in the early days following Will's accident, she had to admit to a feeling of relief when she heard that he had returned to Scotland. His avowed love for her which she could never return created an awkwardness between them. She looked forward to having Will to herself and was dismayed when he moved out, back to his father's house. He went one day when she was out, took all his gear, tidied up the parlour and left.

Gracie could not understand why she should be so upset. 'Ye must know he wouldna bide with thee once he could look to himsell. I'd ha thought ye'd be glad to see the back of him, after all this time.'

But she was not glad. She was bereft.

She was sitting by the window in Gracie's cottage watching Will trying to launch the *Spirit of the North* with the help of his father. 'Look at him!' She jumped to her feet in alarm as Will's peg leg sank deep into the sand causing him to stumble. 'He'll break the other one if he's not careful.'

'Sit doon,' snapped Gracie with unaccustomed sharpness, 'Let him be. He has to fend for himsell.'

Chastened, Hannah sank back.

'Will could nae have had a better nurse than ye, Hannah, and all of us are grateful.' Gracie spoke more kindly. 'But he's got to stand alone now or he'll be good for nothing for evermore.'

His father understood that well and kept at a distance as Will pushed out the boat, threw in his crutch and hauled himself awkwardly over the side. 'Hoy-oop!' his cry was of sheer delight.

'Get yer hands aroond them oars and stop rocking the boat,' ordered his father. 'Now, how dost feel?'

'Grand, man. Grand.'

Hannah could hear the note of pride in his voice and knew she must relinquish her place in his life. 'Ye're right, Gracie,' she acknowledged. 'It's nae my business any more.'

'Give us a spell to get me balance,' Will

493

was shouting to his father, 'and I'll be off shrimping the morn!'

Hannah tried to resume life as it had been before the night of the rescue but her mind kept returning to those days when she had despaired of Will's life, to those bouts of delirium, to the first miraculous signs of recovery.

Her parlour was empty without his bed and the things that a man keeps about him. On more than one occasion, little Mattie caught her daydreaming in the middle of reading him a story. With John Bunyan's *Book for Boys and Girls* open in front of them, he often had to prompt her.

'Behold this post-boy' she would begin, 'with what haste and speed—' and then she would stop and gaze out of the window, leaving him to finish the verse with—

'He travels on the board, and there is need,
That he does, his business calls for haste.'

Then she would laugh out loud, ruffle his hair with her hand and hug him tight. At eight years old, he was much too old for such cosseting but he was fond of his auntie and tolerated the cuddling.

'Why divvent ye have some bairns yersell, Auntie Hannah?' he asked innocently and, for the first time, the suggestion seemed not unreasonable.

31

The war against the French had been going on for so long now that it was accepted as a fact of life, to be tolerated as a necessary evil. People in Britain were aware, with a certain amount of pride, that the only force to oppose Louis in his bid for domination in Europe was led by their own King William. Contact with the enemy was remote, however, except for battles at sea and of little concern to the common man. No French troops had set foot on British soil since the foray at Druridge Bay. Queen Mary, ruling in William's absence, was well-loved. All her subjects desired was to be left in peace after the disturbances of James's short reign.

All this changed when, in the spring of 1692, Huguenot spies in Europe brought news that Louis was planning a massive invasion of Britain. Alarm spread throughout the nation. Laggard administrators of the armed services were catapulted into action. The navy, which was now called upon to defend Britain's shores, was revealed to be undermanned, undershipped, underarmed and underpaid, while Louis, according to the latest reports, was amassing a fleet of forty-four men o' war at Brest, a further thirty-five at Toulon and enough transports to carry ten thousand French troops as well as James's Irish regiments across the Channel. Louis was about to give James one more chance to regain the throne of England; all this while King William himself was out of the country, campaigning in Europe.

In a wave of loyalty to the queen, all the noble families of England hastened to put themselves at her service. The most urgent need was for ships and men to sail in them and forests throughout the land were denuded of their timber. Country gentlemen were persuaded to cut down trees on their estates long before they were ready for the axe. Soon, every shipyard throughout the length and breadth of England echoed to the sound of hammer and chisel.

Privileged sons of noblemen, gripped by this fever of patriotism, left their universities to take commissions at sea under such famous sea dogs as Sir Ralph Delaval, Sir Cloudesley Shovel, Admiral Carter and Sir George Rooke.

Fresh taxes were necessary to pay for the new navy. The price of bread doubled then trebled and, as always, it was the poor who suffered most. Taxes on salt, sugar, malt, paper and hops put these commodities out of the reach of the poor so that more were forced to seek relief from the already overburdened parishes.

In such desperate times the king's shilling, paid on joining the fighting forces, was sometimes the only alternative to starvation. As the recruiting officer travelled the country with his drum and paradiddle many a poor peasant, who in happier times would have stayed on the land, joined the colours. Meanwhile, press gangs, with rougher persuasion, were busy on every waterfront. By fair means or foul, the new fleet of ships must be manned.

Sir Walter Heslop of Bewick, like all landowners, was hard hit by the new land tax of four shillings in the pound, yet could still afford to chuckle over the plight of his old enemy, Sir George Le Flemont of Budle, who was now doubly taxed. By Parliament's latest decree, there was to be a tax on dividends. Since Sir George derived most of his considerable fortune from the prosperous East India Company, he would be called upon to make a handsome contribution to the war funds.

With every fresh report from the Continent, the fear of invasion grew. Men on the heights of Dover kept a watch, day and night, for the first sighting of French masts on the horizon. For Louis, so the spies reported, awaited only a fair wind before he sent his massive fleet to sea.

At this time of national peril, Daniel, in his place of work in Edinburgh, came to a decision that was to change his life for ever. Since his return from Newcastle, his existence had seemed futile and pointless. His work no longer interested him and the thought of spending the rest of his life making pots appalled him, although he had been well content before he came to know Hannah. He was weighed down by the feeling of rejection and, rightly or wrongly, believed that he was of no value to anyone, except perhaps to his queen. In these dangerous times, when every available man was needed to keep the French at bay, he decided to join the colours. He wrote to tell Tom of his decision and to seek his help.

His letter, read out over breakfast at Buckton, caused considerable astonishment.

'I mind that thy senior apprentice completed his indentures this year on Lady Day and know him to be an honest and capable fellow. I would take it most kindly if ye would allow him to carry on my business here in Edinburgh during my absence abroad. He will find a good assistant here and my advocate brother will oversee all financial matters including his wages. I can well be spared and will seek a rendezvous with the recruiting officer as soon as I receive thy reply.

Ever thy faithful and sincere friend,

Daniel Fergusson.'

'Hannah has turned him down,' Betsy nodded. 'I thought she would.'

With affairs settled to his satisfaction, his mother accommodated with his sister and the pottery under good management, Daniel tied a change of clothes, his Bible and a clasp knife into a bundle and boarded the coach for Newcastle once more.

There was a great deal of activity in the town, people thronging the streets and cheering the militiamen as they prepared for their long march to Portsmouth. Posted by the Guild Hall was a bill announcing that a rendezvous for recruits was to be held the following day outside the Black Boar in the Bigg Market. Daniel intended to keep that appointment but first had business with the mayor.

As he pushed past the merchants counting out their silver pieces he felt curiously detached from their world of commerce. Their faces, he noticed now with sharpened awareness, showed no contentment, only greed. He had stepped outside this daily round. The old women selling pies, the fancy gentlemen in their sedan chairs, these things belonged to another time and place. All self-doubt left him as he climbed the steps of the Guildhall and requested an interview with the mayor.

'A most unusual request' was how Sir Nicholas Ridley greeted Daniel's application, but when he took into consideration the spread of the young man's shoulders, the depth of his chest, his upright bearing and the strong character that marked his face, he agreed to play his part. 'Thou'rt a good bargain for any recruiting officer,' he affirmed. 'No doubt but that he will sign thy bond and ye may count on me to see it is kept.'

Some days later, the keelmen of Sandgate heard with astonishment and some anger that Daniel the Scotchman had gone for a sailor; not pressed this time but of his own free will.

'If that is what he wanted,' muttered Will, 'we should have left him on the *Peggy*. It seems I gave a leg for nowt!'

When Mayor Nicholas Ridley visited Sandgate, he had a different story to tell. 'That's a true friend to every keelman,' he assured them, 'for the condition of his signing was this bond.' He waved a parchment, stamped with the seal of Newcastle's great office. 'That no keelman be pressed for the navy for three years from this date. Your friend tried hard for five years exemption but that was more than the recruiting officer was prepared to accept. Ye have three years free from pressing and that I'll guarantee. Ye have my word on't and Captain Boomer will be informed.' He looked quizzically at the group standing silently before him, at old Sam Robson and his peg-leg son with a queer look on their faces. 'Ye'll know better than me why a Scotchman has done you this favour.'

The grateful wives would have sought out Daniel there and then to thank him but he was already on board the *Queen May*, now standing off Tynemouth. In St Ann's, the keelmen's chapel, the men and women of Sandgate got down on their knees and offered a heartfelt prayer for his safety.

The *Queen May* was a clean and lively frigate of ordered appearance, vastly different from the ill-kept *Peggy*. Daniel marked her well-scrubbed decks and comfortable officer accommodation before he was hustled below to join other recruits in the hold and the hatch was closed against him.

Slivers of spring sunshine finding their way through cracks in the bulkheads provided the only light for the fifty or so men collected here. Most sat quietly on their bundles, alert and apprehensive. There was little talk except from those who'd spent the king's shilling at the nearest tavern.

Some had served before, men with hard, weatherbeaten faces who had tried other ways of making a living and failed and there were others, evil-looking men hoping to escape the penalties of crime by running away to sea. There was a hammock for every man and a shelf for his belongings. Daniel sat on his bundle and, with his Bible in his hands, offered up a silent prayer. He was better dressed than most and his bearing proclaimed him to be a man of some consequence, but all differences would be levelled when, dressed in sailors' slops and tunics, the new recruits were mustered for work.

Shouted commands and the sound of chains straining over a winch, told the confined men that the *Queen May's* anchor was raised and she was under way. With a lurch that threw them in sprawling heaps, she sought the wind. Her sails cracked wide and open and she made for the open sea and for Portsmouth where the fleet that would challenge the Sun King was already assembling.

The hatchcover was lifted off, blinding the men in the hold with bright sea light. A red bewhiskered face showed against racing, billowing clouds. 'Show a leg, me hearties! Let's see what ye're made of.'

On deck, the wind blew fresh and clean after the dank odours of the hold. The frigate was bowling along at a spanking rate and had already left the cliffs of Tynemouth far behind. Daniel was given a bucket and brush and sent to scrub out the bilges as his first lesson in seamanship.

He had never been to sea in his life but faced the future without apprehension. As a volunteer, he expected better treatment than a pressed man but whatever the future held, the die was cast. As a snake is shriven of its old skin, so he had left his former concerns behind him on the land. He meant to do his loyal best for queen and country and if he were to be embroiled in battle, he hoped he would not show a craven face.

The glassmakers were delighted when Will announced his intention of resuming charge of their sea-going cargo. With an extra rail near the wheel for safety and a sail

503

laced over the gap in the bulwarks, he felt confident that he could carry out all his old duties as well as ever.

The traumatic experiences of the last year had left their mark on him. He was leaner, older-looking and, as far as Hannah was concerned, unapproachable. He still called to see her from time to time but was at pains to maintain a distance between them which Hannah found inexplicable and hurtful. The merest hint of closeness between them seemed to alarm him. He would twist away from a hand laid affectionately upon his shoulder and draw back from her nearness.

' 'Tis as though my person now offends him,' she complained to Gracie.

The memory of how she cared for him when he lay helpless was for ever in her mind. For a while, he had been her child. There was no part of his body that was not known to her, the sweating hollow under his arm, the lean buttock, the jutting hip bone, smooth as ivory, the concave, wasted abdomen and all the soft, white places untouched by wind and weather. Even these private male parts had lost their threat.

'He no longer needs me.'

Gracie looked at her curiously. 'Art in love with him, hinny?'

The instant flood of colour in Hannah's

face was answer enough. 'Love!' The hot denial got no further. She spread her hands helplessly. 'I don't know, Gracie? What is love? I love little Mattie, but not like this. When I wake in the morning, when I close my eyes in sleep, he is in my thoughts. I never had such feelings before and know not how I shall govern them.'

Gracie laughed at her rueful face. 'Haddaway, woman! 'Tis not the end of the world. Most lassies have been in and out of love a score of times afore they are your age. Thou'rt almost an old maid, Hannah, and thee'd better do summat about it afore ye blow up with passion.'

'What is to be done?' Hannah implored. 'Tell me, for I am sure I know not.'

Seeing Hannah, the cool one, in this state, Gracie decided that she must be taken seriously. 'Wouldst marry him? Him with only one leg?'

'Marry!' Hannah was aghast. 'Who said ought about marrying, though that he has one leg is neither here nor there. 'Tis Will, though,' she reflected, 'who calls the tune. We who were once close friends are now kept apart by his coolness.'

'If ye hae nae thought of marriage or of persuading him to lie with ye, then ye have nae call to go touching and fondling him. 'Twill only serve to tease him to distraction,' Gracie said severely. 'The remedy lies with yersell, Hannah. I know my brother. He reckons he is spoilt now for any woman. If ye want him, ye must tell him so for he'll not be the one to set the pace.'

Will brought Hannah a bag of oysters after his next trip to Scotland. 'Not a Frenchman to be seen,' he told her. ' 'Twould seem that even the brigs and privateers are being called in for Louis's invasion. I tell thee, Hannah, had I but two good legs I'd follow Daniel and take my place on an English man o' war. Such a battle is coming that will need every man to stand up and fight for England.'

'I take comfort in whatever keeps thee here,' Hannah said softly, and at once the guarded look returned to Will's eyes. He got up and made to go.

'Wilt not stay and sup with me?' she coaxed. 'Alphonse has brought a bottle of good canary wine that will make good company for oysters and steak pie.' She had asked him before. Always, like tonight, he found an excuse.

'My father awaits me.'

Hannah could contain her emotions no longer. The time, she judged, had come to speak openly to Will as Gracie advised.

'Have I done ought to displease thee, Will? Our old friendship seems no longer to give thee pleasure.'

He backed from her too-searching gaze. 'How could ye ever doubt our friendship, Hannah? Thee, to whom I owe so much.'

' 'Tis more than gratitude I seek.' Hannah was astonished at her own boldness but, once embarked upon this road, there was no turning back. Will was already reaching for his crutch but she would have her say before he left her. 'I love thee, Will.' Spoken in less than a minute, the simple statement released all tension within her. Happiness made her pulse race and her heart beat faster. Her eyes sought Will's, shining with a light he had never seen before.

The effect on him was dramatic. He collapsed into a chair with head bowed in his hands, in an attitude of utter despair.

'Such a blow, dear coz?' she laughed at him. 'Say something, be it no more than a benediction afore ye spurn me for my boldness.'

He did not share her gaiety. 'Do not speak of love, Hannah. At least spare me that.'

Mortified to the core, she shrank back, like an overbold crab retreating into its shell. ' 'Tis said now,' her voice was small, 'and cannot be unsaid. I did not mean to cause thee embarrassment so pray forget all that thy silly cousin hath said.' She wanted only for him to go now, to leave her alone with her shame.

He looked beyond her, out of the window at the bobbing masts and tossing gulls. ' 'Tis not thee that makes this a poor tale with a wretched ending, Hannah, but the loss of a man's leg which fits him but ill for a husband. Had ye said those sweet words to me this day twelvemonth, I would have sped like a bullet from the gun to fetch the minister from St Ann's to wed us on the spot. Now, I have put away all such thoughts. I pray to God for strength whenever I see thee walking by the quay or seeking out the shipwrights, hanging out thy washing, teaching Mattie his lessons. Each sight of thee is harder to bear than the last. I beg of thee, make my task easier. Never speak of love again between us for it cannot be. The Will Robson that might have been fit for thee is only to be found in a stained-glass window in Bycar chapel.'

'Thou'rt no less a man for being short of a leg.' The way was suddenly clear to Hannah. 'And since ye'll nae ask me then I must play the man, for in this matter, I will not be put down. Will Robson, thou'rt the only man I have ever loved and I am asking thee to take me as thy wife. For the love of God, for my heart's desire, I beg thee.'

32

When, in later life, Sir Daniel Fergusson looked back on his distinguished career at sea, the month of May in the year 1692 would for ever stand out. It brought to mind his first ship, the *Steadfast*, a three-tiered man o' war; his first engagement with the enemy and his first encounter with the truly great men of his time who put service to their country before any thought of personal safety.

Bad weather, frequently the ally of a beleaguered island nation, intervened to delay Louis's planned invasion of that year. His two great fleets primed and ready to sail were holed up, one in the port of Brest, the other in Toulon in the Mediterranean. After two of his first-rate ships were wrecked on the Rocks of Ceuta in an attempt to pass through the Pillars of Hercules, the rest of the Toulon fleet had no option but to stay in harbour until the storms subsided.

The breathing space thus offered to Britain was providential. William used it to whip up support in the Low Countries and persuaded the Dutch to send four squadrons of stout ships to join the English fleet under Admiral Russell. When Daniel and the rest of the so-called 'shacko-me-filthies' disembarked from the recruiting ship in Portsmouth at the beginning of May, their astonished eyes looked upon a vast array of fighting ships. More than ninety splendid, three-tiered ships of the line, all with pennants flying, lay in Portsmouth harbour. Behind them, on the Downs, the militia and trained bands from all parts of the country were assembled. A beacon on every hill stood ready for lighting. It was a sight to make the heart of every Briton beat faster. Never before had the French king been faced with such a consolidated force at sea and if, despite all efforts of the gallant seamen, the Frenchmen succeeded in making a landing, they would have to contest every yard of ground with the waiting regiments of foot soldiers. Daniel, the humdrum, unadventurous potter was filled with an exhilaration he had never known before.

For the first four days he was set to pull a pair of oars from sunrise to sunset, ferrying the fighting men and their supplies to the waiting ships. Then, with pride, he took his place as a member of the crew on the good ship *Steadfast* in Sir Ralph Delaval's squadron.

On the morning of May 15th, the alarm

was raised. From the Dover Heights, the masts of the great French fleet could be seen pricking the skyline, and the allied ships made ready to sail at once. The crowd on the quayside multiplied as if by magic as the word spread that Louis was on his way. Loud huzzahs greeted the raising of anchors. The martial roll of drums that accompanied the running up of sheets stirred the blood so that every man watching from the quay at that moment would have changed places willingly with any of the common sailors or soldiers now engaged in such a noble enterprise.

With sails filling in the breeze, the men o' war took up their allotted positions. Sedately, and full of purpose, they rode out to sea.

Daniel was halfway up the foremast when the French opened fire. Within five minutes of the first salvo the deck beneath him was transformed into a scene of frantic activity—gun nozzles spouting flame, spars crashing down from above, men running with firebuckets. It was Daniel's baptism of fire and it lasted four long hours.

He would be up the mast one moment securing torn sheets, then down in the hold fetching powder for the gunners or swilling slippery pools of blood from the deck. He saw a red hot gun explode and a young powder monkey of barely sixteen years blown into fragments. He saw his own captain fall to the deck, his sword still in his hand, ready to repel all boarders.

'Fight the ship,' the dying man whispered, betrayed by his spouting jugular. 'Fight her as long as she swims.'

When at last the French retired, not an allied ship had given way. The invasion had been turned aside and Louis's great fleet was in disarray.

A hero's welcome awaited the triumphant allied fleet on its return to Portsmouth, but while the crowd huzzahed and banged their drums, Daniel, blackened by smoke but otherwise unscathed, was helping to carry off the wounded.

Fifty surgeons sent by a grateful queen waited on the harbourside to relieve the sufferings of the wounded and a chest of gold to be divided amongst all who had fought so loyally to save England from invasion. Church bells rang. There were bonfires in the streets. The nation rejoiced but there was little provision for all the maimed and blinded men who would never sail again.

Appalled by their plight, Queen Mary vowed there and then that a suitable place of retirement must be found for them. Retired soldiers were accommodated in the fine new hospital at Chelsea. Her sailors must be cared for with equal concern. A mansion at Greenwich, begun but never completed by her uncle, King Charles II, was selected and work began at once.

So ended Daniel's first engagement at sea. Thereafter, the *Steadfast* was his home and her motley crew his close companions, some friends, some enemies. He had acquired a taste for the sea which he would never lose and a new love to replace the old.

The Chelsea hospital so admired by Queen Mary had been a long time in the building but now, in 1692, its first pensioners were being admitted.

Many times during the years of its construction, Polly Watson had come by boat upriver from Billingsgate to check its progress. Such a mansion it would be and her Rob had been promised a place there. He would be able to sit at his ease in the fine gardens and watch the river. Mebbes she would be able to find employment in the kitchens or laundry as one kind commissioner had suggested.

As the weeks and months dragged by with the hospital no nearer completion, Polly's dream began to fade and, in the end, Rob never saw what was to have been his new home. He died, where he had lived, in Mother Susan's garret and much trouble there was in getting him down those narrow stairs. Rob's body, though incomplete, was a great weight.

Polly was now on the streets for, though Mother Susan was not overparticular about the pox, she would not employ a woman with chancres. 'For it do put the men off,' she said.

So Polly sold firewood in the streets, trundling it behind her in Rob's little cart. Some of the time she was cheerful but most of the time she was wretched. The cheerful times were when she had enough money to buy gin. The wretched times were when she hung over the side of London Bridge, watching the dark, swirling waters and praying for the courage to jump in. One day, she knew, this is how she would end all the misery, the stink, the hunger, the cold and the dirt. She would join Rob in some lovely place like those Scottish glens she remembered from way back, before Rob had his legs blown off with a cannon ball.

After refitting at Portsmouth, the *Steadfast* was off to sea once more. Some of Daniel's more disillusioned companions were all for deserting but they would have been unlikely to get further than the waterfront and punishment for this crime was severe.

Discipline at sea was strict and not always just. By the time Daniel had completed another voyage, he had seen a man keelhauled for insubordination. Another who had fallen asleep on watch had been hung from the bowsprit in a basket with a can of beer, a loaf of bread and a sharp knife and left to choose his manner of dying, starvation or drowning. Flogging was the usual punishment for most offences and Daniel, like the others, had weals to show which were not always merited. He endured the flagellation without rancour as a way of hardening his body in the same way as he disciplined his mind against nostalgia by cutting out all thoughts of England. Daniel the potter was a pale shadow beside this new, leaner man. Already an able seaman, he had the next rank of leading seaman in his sights. He would never throw another pot and had already decided to approach Tom with the suggestion that he might like to buy the Edinburgh business.

The life he had chosen was hard but he wanted none other. Victuals were inadequate and, for the most part, bad. Dishonest merchants took advantage of the fact that stores for seamen were not inspected and, as a result, all manner of maggoty, rotten food was shipped before the vessel left port. The biscuits were weevily and the beer sour. Lack of fresh fruit and vegetables brought on the scurvy. After five or six weeks at sea, telltale pimples began to appear on the gums. Teeth would loosen and fall out. Old sores on the body reopened and would not heal. Lethargy associated with the disease caused many a fatal accident. None of these hardships affected Daniel. Man of iron. Cold as charity, some said.

To Daniel's way of thinking, however, the compensations of a life at sea by far outweighed the hard times. His heart soared when he stood at the fo'c's'le in faraway southern seas while the prow beneath him ploughed a white defile through water of the deepest blue. He watched flying fish leaping in a shower of diamonds and dolphins smiling up at him from the side of the ship. He saw a great whale spouting and endured the terror of a hurricane. On the other side of the world where the night sky was in reverse, he caught a fever that almost had him tied up in a sail and dumped overboard. The scar across his face was the result of a lively encounter with a French pirate. Such were his experiences.

His ability did not go unnoticed. He attained the rank of midshipman and, after a further three years, was successfully examined for a lieutenant.

33

Daniel had been at sea for ten long years when his ship was laid up in Portsmouth for repairs. There was shore leave for the crew but the Admiralty Office was, as usual, in arrears and only half of the wages due to the seamen was distributed.

Lacking the money for the long coach trip from London to Edinburgh, Daniel sought to go by sea instead. A collier bound for the Tyne was about to sail and, though he had no wish to visit Newcastle again, he paid his dues and went aboard. After one night at the Lamb and Fox, he would take the morning coach to Edinburgh.

Compared with the *Steadfast*, the collier wallowed in the troughs of the North Sea like a cockleshell and Daniel was not sorry when it turned for Tynemouth and moved into the quieter waters of the Tyne.

The skipper cast a curious glance at his uncommunicative passenger; never a word or smile or pass-the-time-of-day, not since he boarded at Tilbury. A rum-looking character though he wore the uniform of an officer of the king's navy, with a face burnt by foreign suns and scarred with a livid line from cheekbone to jaw. Not a man you'd want to meddle with. Standing up forrard. Stiff as a statue, like a figurehead. Taking a sudden interest in the land, now. And look at the scowl on him when he turns round.

'Shields, sir,' volunteered the skipper. Daniel nodded and turned again to the river. He was remembering the *Peggy*. Some memories were banished for ever, never to return, but he could not forget that night of horror on the *Peggy* and Will's brave, tragic rescue. Every detail was engraved on his mind. Here was where the *Peggy* had been berthed.

'Ye'll need to take a rowboat now, sir,' the skipper interrupted his thoughts. 'I canna go further with this keel. Newcastle's up beyond Sandgate that ye can see from here.'

Daniel dragged his mind back to the present. The scene today was one of peaceful trading. Small boats plied to and fro on a sunlit river. The *Peggy* would have been broken up long since. He hailed a passing rowboat.

A keel laden with coal passed by bound for a waiting collier but his furtive glance revealed no familiar face. This was not the time for emotional reunions. There was to be no taking up of old friendships. All that was gone for ever. He must make all speed for the Lamb and Fox, a good dinner with a bottle of rum, for he had turned to the sailor's drink, a night's sleep and off in the morning coach to Edinburgh.

Women were deeting the keels on the beach at Sandgate but they were nothing to him. Their lives, their friends, their children concerned him not at all. His eye could pick out Hannah's roof without impact on his heart. It was just another house with a small herb garden in front and washing behind.

And now he acknowledged that the hurt was healed. He had at last freed himself from the chains of a devotion which had caused him so much pain as a youth. He wondered how he could have been so infinitely weak, so unmanly. He should have gone to sea much earlier. There is no place for such lovesickness in a life at sea.

The turrets and walls of Newcastle town now appeared. There was more smoke about than he remembered. It hung in a sooty pall over clustering chimneys. Coal was king here, right enough. The quay was as busy as ever; merchants coming and going, bales of merchandise awaiting shipment, gentlemen in sedan chairs, whistling messenger boys. Involuntarily, he glanced at old Standwell's office as he stepped ashore. The old man would likely be dead by now, and, with barely suppressed astonishment he read the name now painted above the door:

Hannah Robson:
Stevedore and Cargo Contractor:
Export Agent.

She's achieved all this! He found himself laughing out loud. Little Hannah Robson! Stevedore and Cargo Contractor! He warmed with pride for her.

'Hi mister, mind yer great feet. Ye nearly smashed wor hitchie dabber.'

A little girl bent to rescue a pretty glass disc. 'An' it's wor special one an' all.'

Daniel fished in his pocket for a coin which was quickly accepted as due recompense. ' 'Twould indeed have been a pity to break such a pretty toy.'

'From the Howden glassmakers and there's nane like it in Sandgate.' She was not in the least overawed by Daniel and steadily returned his stare.

Daniel was looking at her carrot-coloured hair. There was a certain keelman with hair like that. How old would the child be? Nine? Ten? Eleven? Hard to say. He hazarded a guess. 'Art Will Robson's child?'

'Don't be daft,' the girl said witheringly. 'He's me uncle.' She turned and pointed to a younger child who waited patiently for the game of hopscotch to be resumed, making no move to come nearer. 'Red Wull's her da.'

This one was small-boned, neat as a doll. She wore a blue frock that matched the colour of her eyes. Her hair was raven black. There was a tilt to her firm little chin and Daniel knew with certainty he was looking at Hannah's daughter.

'What's your name?' he asked her softly, but the redhead interposed sharply.

'Don't tell him, Mary. We're not supposed to speak to forriners.'

He laughed. 'I'm no foreigner. I'm an old friend of your ma and your da.' In spite of himself, he found his heart warming at this unexpected encounter. That fateful union, which had been the cause of so much grief to him in the distant past, had been blessed with a child who already carried the stamp of her mother's character upon her. He had only to look at the way she stood! Legs firmly planted, a little apart, sturdily independent. The other child must be Gracie's.

He smiled as he stood there in the sunshine feeling strangely lighthearted despite the hostile scrutiny of the two little girls. His eyes strayed to the figure dimly

521

glimpsed at the window of the shipping office.

'Is that your ma in there?' he asked the younger child.

Again it was the redhead who answered. 'Aye and that's my brother Mattie with her, Mr Nosy Parker.'

Ignoring her impertinence, Daniel reconsidered his position. There was no real reason why he should not now make his presence known to Hannah. The past was finished and done with and there was no longer anything to fear from meeting her again. He would not linger. A brief word or two would suffice then he would plead urgent business and hurry away. He would tell her what a charming daughter she had. (That little one still had not spoken but stood regarding him sternly, dabber in hand, waiting to resume the game.) He seemed to be moving towards a resolution when his thoughts were briskly interrupted.

'Mary! Isobel! Who are you talking to?' The voice of the woman who had been the only love of his life rang out loud and clear and it shot him through the heart. Bullseye first time. He turned quickly on his heel and walked away, lost from sight in a moment behind the bales of wool; nor did he slacken pace until he reached the Lamb and Fox.

There was a new landlord. 'He's had a nasty shock, I'd say,' he told the inquisitive pot boy. 'See his hand shaking when I gave him his rum?'

Hannah took the children by the hand and led them away. After a few steps, she halted. There was a puzzled expression on her face when she turned and looked in the direction the stranger had taken.

'Some sort of sailor, you say?'

Glossary

boiley, invalid's dish of bread and warm milk, sometimes with honey added

ca'canny, go carefully

canny (adj.), endearing, likeable

varry canny, as answer to the enquiry, 'What fettle?' (how are you?) Constitutes a cautious claim to well-being

clarts, a mess of mud

court leet, place of assembly for trying local offences

crack, chat, gossip

divvent, don't

duroy, coarse woollen fabric

faw, gypsy

fettle, mood, condition

gannin', going

gey, extremely, very

ha'd on, hold on, wait a bit

hinny, term of endearment, dear

hitchie dabber, small disc used in game of hopscotch

howay!, come on

hoy (v.), to throw

marrer, mate

neet, night

netty, lavatory

pele towers, forts built during the border raids

ploat (v.), pluck

plodge (v.), walk about in water deeper than that associated with paddling

sark, shirt

smit, infectious habit

snitch, nose

soapwort, plant with property of softening water and producing lather

wor, our

This Large Print Book for the Partially sighted, who cannot read normal print, is published under the auspices of

THE ULVERSCROFT FOUNDATION